THE PEASANTS
SPRING

THE
PEASANTS

A TALE OF
OUR OWN TIMES

IN
FOUR VOLUMES

AUTUMN
WINTER
SPRING
SUMMER †

† To be published July, 1925

THE PEASANTS

SPRING

Reymont. Spring.
    The third volume in a drama of peasant
life. As a result of their uprising the men
of the village have been cast into prison,
leaving their families to suffer cruelly in
their absence. Every household feels the
heavy touch of sorrow. Spring returns to the
land, but not to the hearts of the peasants.
With Antek in prison and out of the way of
Yagna's wiles, Hanka's problem grows easier,
though she waits for her husband's return with
smouldering jealousy and resentment.

ALFRED · A · KNOPF

NEW YORK   MCMXXV

PUBLISHED APRIL, 1925, BY ALFRED A. KNOPF, INC.

MANUFACTURED IN THE UNITED STATES OF AMERICA

PUBLISHER'S NOTE

The Peasants has been translated from the
original Polish by Michael H. Dziewicki,
Reader of English Literature at the University
of Cracow. I wish to make special acknowl-
edgment to Dr. A. M. Nawench of Columbia
University for his invaluable assistance in seeing the work through the press.

A. A. K.

THE PEASANTS
SPRING

CHAPTER I

S PRING had come.

Like a toiler who, having slept the sleep of exhaustion, is forced to rise ere dawn after a too short rest, and go out and plough without delay, the April morning was rising lazily.

It was grey dawn.

Silence reigned everywhere, save for the copious dews that dropped and dripped from the trees, wrapped in dense mists and slumbering.

Over the black earth, plunged in stillness and deep darkness, the sky was beginning to glimmer palely, and look like a sheet of wringing wet bluish canvas.

All the low-lying meadows were whitish with mantling haze, which resembled the frothy head of milk in a pail.

Cocks presently vied with one another, crowing in the yet invisible hamlets.

The last stars went out, closing their tired and sleepy eyes.

And now a glow was kindled in the East, as when they blow on embers half quenched in the ashes.

The floating mists rolled heavily hither and thither, surged about the dusky fields as floods in the spring thaw, or went up the sky in thin blue spirals, like incense smoke.

The day was at odds with the paling night, which crouched and clung close to the earth, covering it with its thick wet cloak.

The light was slowly spreading all over the sky, and coming down nearer and nearer to the ground, and struggling with the entangling fog. In places, along the uplands, there were seen drab dew-soaked expanses, peering out of the night,

and plashes of water that shimmered with lack-lustre sur-
faces, and brooks that poured their streaming contents along,
between the dissolving mists and the brightening dawn.

And as it grew lighter, the flush in the East changed from
livid violet to the blood-red tints of a huge conflagration.
Things grew visible: the black circle of forest at the sky-line,
the long row of poplars on the ascending road, drooping
forward, as though tired by the weary climb, sprang into
sight; and the hamlets sprinkled over the country-side, and
hitherto buried in shadows, now peeped forth here and
there in the morning light, like dark rocks in a swirl of foaming water, and some of the nearer trees were silvered all
over with morning dews.

The sun had not risen yet, but it was clearly on the
point of bursting out of the crimson glory round it, upon
the world now just opening its bleared eyes, and stirring a
little, but still resting and drowsily enjoying its rest. Now
the stillness seemed to ring yet more loudly in the ears, for
the earth was, as it were, holding its breath: only a feeble
breeze, faint as the breathing of an infant, blew from the
woods and shook the dew-drops from the trees.

Out of the greyness of the early morn, above those fields
still deep in slumber and in shadow, like a church filled
with silent worshippers, suddenly rose the ditty of a lark.

Up from the ground it soared, and, rising, flapped its
wings, twittering with silvery sounds—the tinkling of a
Mass-bell, as it were—or like a fragrant column of springtide
perfumes, rising, rising upward; and from the hallowed
heights and silences of the eastern sky it called aloud to all
the country-side.

And in a little others joined its song, soaring to heaven,
and, as they beat their wings, proclaimed the approach of
day to every creature!

The sun was coming, it was close at hand.

At last it peered above the far-off forest, as if it rose from
an abyss; as if divine invisible hands were holding up its
huge and glittering paten over the drowsy lands, and blessing with the blessing of its light all things that in them were

—living or dead, coming to life or dying out of it—beginning thus the holy offering of the day, while all things fell and worshipped in the dust, mutely closing their unworthy eyes before its sacred majesty.

Now day had dawned.

Like odoriferous smoke, the haze was wafted upwards from the meadows to the gold-splashed sky; and birds and living things of every kind burst out into a chant . . . a cry, a thankful prayer, a prayer rising from the heart!

Then did the sun appear above the dark woods and countless villages, high, mighty, shedding warmth below—the eye of God's own mercy—and commence its reign, its peaceful gentle mastery over all the land.

It was just then that Agata, the Klembas' aged kinswoman, made her appearance upon a sandhill near the forest, where several stacks belonging to the Manor stood by a roadway full of deep ruts.

In early autumn she had started on her pilgrimage of beggary, and eaten "bread of our Lord's giving" ever since.

And now she had come back, just like those homing birds that always find their nests again in spring.

Old, feeble, very short of breath, and something like a roadside willow, rooted in the sand, decrepit, phosphorescent, tottering to its fall—she walked all in rags, staff in hand, wallet on back, and a rosary dangling at her side.

The sun was rising when she passed the Manor stacks with quick short steps, raising her weatherbeaten shrivelled face to the sun, while her grey eyes, though bloodshot, sparkled bright with joy.

Ah! Back again in her native village, after the long hard winter!—The thought gave wings to her feet; her wallet jogged upon her shoulders, and her beads tinkled at her side: but soon her breath grew short, her labouring lungs failed her, and she had perforce to stop and then go on more slowly and painfully. But her hungry eyes scoured the country round; she smiled on those grey fields, now greenish with a haze of growing corn; on the villages, coming little by little out of the enveloping fog; on those trees, as yet bare of foliage, that stood as guardians of the road, and on those others, scattered solitary about the plain.

By this time the sun was pretty high, and cast its beams over the farthest fields of all. The whole country gleamed with rosy dew; the black ploughed lands shone in light, the waters glittered, streaming by in the ditches, the voices of the larks rang loud through the cool air. Farther, beneath some outjutting crags, the last patches of vanishing snow still glistened. On a few trees there hung clusters of yellow catkins that dangled in air like amber beads. In certain nooks, and from the beds of pools drying in the sun, young grass with golden blades was springing up amongst last year's dry rust-coloured leaves, or wild flowers were opening their yellow eyes. A light breeze had caught up the rich dank odours of the plain that basked idly in the sunlight; and everything around was so bright, so vast, and full of such delicious sweetness that Agata would fain have had wings, to soar upwards with a great cry of joy and rapture.

"O good Lord! O dear Jesus!" she gasped, sitting down to take the whole view, as it were, into her tender heart that throbbed with gladness.

Oh, how the springtide was rolling on over the broad plains, while the lark's anthems announced its coming to all! . . . And that sacred sun! . . . And oh, the soft warm caresses of the wind, like the kisses of a mother! . . . and the still, mysterious yearnings of the land, awaiting the plough and the sower! . . . Oh, and the seething of life everywhere coming forth, and the breezes pregnant with that which was soon to be the blade—the flower—the full corn in the ear!

Oh, how the spring was coming forth, like a bright lady clad in sunbeams, with a face like the rosy dawn, and tresses like streaming waters! Here she was, floating down from the sun, and hovering over the cornfields this bright April morning; and from her outspread hands fluttered many a lark, set free to sing her praises blithely! In her wake flew rows of cranes, with joyful clangorous notes, and wild geese, in wedge-shaped formation athwart the pale-blue sky. Storks went forth along the marshy levels, swallows twittered by the huts, and all the winged tribes came singing merrily. And as often as that sunny mantle of hers touched the earth, grasses sprang up, quivering to the breeze; swollen buds glistened under their coating of viscid gum, and leaflets whispered low; for a new strong lush life was rising everywhere.

And oh, how she caressed and fondled all those poor lowly tumble-down cottages! With what eyes of mercy did she glance beneath the thatches, and awake to life the chilled and palsy-stricken hearts of men, who now—in this hour of longed-for consolation—put aside their griefs and sombre broodings, and dreamed that a happier lot might yet be theirs!

The land resounded with life, as a bell long silent, when given a new tongue. It was the sun's gift, and the magnificent peal rang out and boomed with clamorous joy, waking timid hearts and singing of things most marvellous, until it found an echo in every soul. Tears started to every eye: the immortal spirit of man, rising up in its strength, knelt in raptures to embrace the land—that world of its own—aye, every swollen and pregnant clod of it!—every tree and stone and exhalation—all that he cherished and held dear!

Thus felt Agata, as she dragged herself slowly along, greedily gloating over that Holy Land of her dreams, and reeling at times as if from strong drink.

The Mass-bell, tinkling in the steeple, recalled her to her senses at last, and she fell upon her knees.

". . . Thy holy will, O Lord, has brought me home.

". . . Thou hast shown mercy to the friendless one!"

She could hardly get the words out. A great torrent of tears welled up from her heart and poured down her withered cheeks. So moved was she that she could no longer find her beads, nor any but incoherent utterances, struck out from her soul like burning sparks. At last, with a mighty effort, she rose and went forward, her eyes on the country-side around her.

It was now broad day. All Lipka was spread out before and beneath her, in a circle round the mill-pond, now dark-blue and glittering like a mirror through the thin veil of whitish haze over it. Along its shores the cottages were crouching on the ground, and seated like goodwives amongst their yet leafless orchard-trees. A little smoke rose above some of the thatches, panes gleamed in the sunshine, and freshly whitewashed walls contrasted strongly with the dark trunks that partly hid them.

And now she could make out each of the huts apart. The mill, with its noisy clutter more distinct as she advanced, stood at one end of the village, close to the road she was following, and at the opposite end the church raised its high white front amongst huge trees, its windows and the golden cross on the steeple shining afar, and the red-tiled roof of the priest's house visible close by. And beyond, to the very sky-line, extended the bluish-grey ring of forest, the wide expanse of cornland, villages at a distance, nestling in their orchards; outjutting crags, winding roadways, lines of slanting trees, sandhills scantily clad with juniper-bushes, and the thin thread of the stream, sparkling as it ran on to the mill-pond, in and out among the huts.

Nearer to her lay the ground belonging to Lipka—as it were, long strips of canvas or cloth that variegated the sloping uplands. They ran in sinuous bands, one close to the other, separated only by the winding footpaths between them, thickly planted with spreading pear-trees, and overrun with briers and brambles; or by drab fallows, clear-cut and sharp in the yellow morning light. Patches of land sown in autumn, now beginning to turn green, dark-hued potato-fields of last year's crop, bits of newly ploughed soil, and waters on the low levels, with a greyish glimmer as of molten glass, completed the picture. Beyond the mill stretched peaty-coloured meadows, on which storks were seen to wade and heard to "klek"; and farther, cabbage plantations, so flooded as yet that only the tops of the furrows emerged from the water like stranded fishes: over these, white-bellied lapwings flew about. At the crossways there stood crucifixes or statues of saints. And above this little world, the hollow wherein the village nestled, hung the hot bright sun, and the lark trilled out its song: a plaintive lowing was heard from the cow-byres; geese screamed; human voices called one to another; while the wind, bearing all these sounds upon its wings, blew with so warm and so gentle a breath that the land seemed plunged in that quiet ecstasy in which new life is conceived.

Yet there were not many workers to be seen in the fields. Only a few women, close to the village, were scattering dung about, and stray whiffs of its sharp pungent smell came to her nostrils.

"The lazy fellows! What can they be about on such a day as this, when the land is simply begging to be tilled? . . . Why are so few at work?" she muttered, in no good humour.

To approach the fields yet nearer, she left the road for a narrow path that crossed a ditch where the grass grew lush, and plenty of daisies already opened their pink eyelashes to the sun. She well remembered how, in former years, the fields were at that season all dotted over with red petticoats, and echoing to the lasses' songs and cries; and she knew well that in such weather it was just the time to manure and till and sow the land. What, then, could the matter be? Why, she saw only one single peasant, standing somewhere in the fields and walking along, throwing grain broadcast in a semicircular sweep.

"He must be sowing peas, so early in spring. . . . One of Dominikova's lads, no doubt," she said, and added, with all her heart: "May God in His mercy grant you a bountiful harvest, O dear sower!"

The path was rugged and uneven, full of fresh molehills and many a puddle. But, absorbed as she was in every bit of land she saw, she paid no heed to these.

"This is the priest's rye-field. How well it grows! I remember, when I started on my wanderings, the farm-servant was ploughing here, and his Reverence sat close by."

Again she crawled on painfully, breathing hard and looking round with tearful eyes.

"This is Ploshka's rye . . . but it must have come up late, or rotted somewhat in the ground."

She bent down—no easy task for her!—to stroke the moist blades lovingly, as she would have stroked a child's head, with tremulous withered fingers.

"Ah, here is Boryna's wheat! A magnificent piece of ground. Of course: is he not the first farmer in Lipka?— A little frostbitten, though; the winter has been very severe," she thought, looking out over the flat expanse of fields ploughed last autumn, and the blades sunk deep in the earth and soiled with mire, testifying to the heavy winter snows and floods.

"Oh," she sighed, "the folk here have suffered not a little." And she shaded her eyes to look at a couple of lads who were coming by from the village.

"The organist's pupil, and one of his sons. . . . What large baskets! Ah, no doubt they are going to Vola with their annual list for confession. Yes, that is what they are about."

She greeted them as they went by, and would have chatted with them willingly; but they only mumbled a reply, and hurried on, deep in conversation with each other.

"And I have known them ever since they could walk!" she said, disappointed and out of sorts. "Ah, well! how should they know a beggar like me?—But Michael has grown up finely, and will surely now be playing the organ for his Reverence."

She was presently close to Klemba's property. "Lord! there is not one man to be seen!" she cried.—She was now so near the village that she could smell the smoke of the chimneys, and see the beds and cushions laid out to air in the orchard. Her heart was brimming over with thankfulness for having been spared till now, and allowed to come back to her people. In this hope she had been able to live through the winter: it had upheld and strengthened her against cold and want and death itself.

She sat down under some bushes, to arrange her dress a little, but could not. Joy made her limbs quiver and her heart flutter like a strangled bird.

"There are still some good kind people here," she whispered, looking hard at her wallet. She had put by, she knew, quite enough for her burial.

For many a year she had set her heart upon one thing: to die (when our Lord should call her) in her own village, lying in a cottage, on a feather-bed, and beneath a row of holy images upon the wall: as all goodwives die. And for many a year she had been saving against that last, that sacred hour!

Now at the Klembas', up in the loft, she had a chest, and within that chest a great feather-bed, with sheets and pillows, and new pillow-covers: all clean, and none of them ever used, in order to be always in readiness. There was no other place to put that bedding, for she never had a room or a bedstead to herself, but was used to sleep in some corner, on a litter of straw, or in the cow-house, according to circumstances, and as the people of the house allowed her. For she would never assert herself, nor make any complaints, being well aware that things take place in this world according to God's will, and are not to be changed by sinful man.

And yet—in secret, silently, and asking to be forgiven for her pride—she had dreamed of this one thing: to be buried like a village goodwife. For this she had long prayed in fear and trembling.

Naturally, therefore, on arriving in the village, and aware that her last hour was not far off, she set about considering whether there was anything that she had forgotten.

No. She had got all that was required. With her she carried a Candlemas taper that she had begged after a night-watch over a dead body; a bottle of holy water; a new sprinkling-brush, a consecrated picture of Our Lady of Chenstohova, which she should hold when dying, and a few score *złoty* for her burial, which might possibly also suffice for a Mass to be said, before the body, with candles and the rite of sprinkling performed at the church-door. For she never dreamed that the priest would accompany the body to the grave.

That was out of the question. Not every landowner had the luck of being honoured thus; besides, the fee for that alone would swallow up all her savings!

She sighed heavily and rose to her feet, feeling much weaker than usual. Her lungs hurt her greatly, and she was so racked with coughing that she could hardly crawl along.

"If," she mused, "I was able to hold out till hay-making, or till the harvest begins! Oh, then I could willingly lie down and die, dear Jesus! lie down and die!"

She thought her hopes sinful, and wanted to excuse them.

But now arose the disquieting thought: who would take her in and let her die in his hut?

"I shall," she said, "look for some good kind-hearted people: and they may be more willing if I promise them a little money. Indeed, no one cares to have trouble and annoyance in his own cottage on account of a stranger."

As to dying at her relations', the Klembas, she durst not even think of that.

"So many children!—No room in the cabin; and the fowls are laying now, and place must be made for them.—And then, it were a disgrace for such landowners to have a beggar, their kinswoman, die under their roof."

All this she was pondering without any bitterness, as she plodded her way on the road along the dike raised to protect the meadows and cabbage-plantations from a flood.

The mill-pond shone bright on her left, reflecting the sun's golden locks in its deep-blue waters. On its banks, overgrown with drooping alders, flocks of geese screamed and flapped their wings; on the still miry roads, troops of merry children ran about and shouted.

And Lipka stood on this side and on that of the pond, as it had stood no doubt ever since the world began, buried in its wide-spreading orchards, and in the undergrowths of its enclosures.

Slowly Agata trudged on, but with swift glances that took everything in at once. The miller's wife was sitting on the threshold of her house, amongst a boisterous troop of goslings, yellow as wax, that she was taking care of. Agata greeted her, and went quickly past, well pleased that the dogs which lay basking along the walls had not taken note of her.

She crossed the bridge, where the waters began their rush to the mill-wheels, and the road forked out into two branches that embraced the whole village.

After an instant's hesitation, her desire to see everything mastered her, and she turned to the left, making her way a little longer.

The forge, which she passed first, was silent and lifeless; against the sooty walls stood the fore part of a cart and several rusty ploughs: but the smith himself was away, and his wife, in smock and petticoat, busy digging in the orchard.

Agata went around, stopping before every hut, leaning over the low stone fences, and gazing curiously at all she saw within. Dogs came up and sniffed at her, but seemed to recognize one of the inhabitants, and went back to lie in the sun.

Wherever she went, she found a strange stillness and emptiness.

"All the men are away . . . attending either at some law court or a meeting somewhere," she finally said to herself, as she entered the church.

Mass was over; his Reverence sat in the confessional; some dozen or so of people from distant hamlets were in the pews, at intervals heaving deep sighs, or uttering some words of their prayers aloud.

From a lamp suspended in front of the high altar, a ripple as of bluish smoke ascended tremulously through the sunlight that poured down from the windows high above. Without, sparrows chirruped, and now and then ventured into the aisles with straws in their beaks; from time to time a swallow came twittering in by the great doorway, swept round, skirting the cold silent walls, and speedily flew back to the bright world outside.

Agata said a few short prayers and hurried out, eager to get to the Klembas'. Just in front of the church, Yagustynka met her.

"What, you here, Agata!" she exclaimed in astonishment.

"Yes, here I am, and still alive, good dame"; and she bent to kiss her hand.

"Why, they said ye had turned up your toes somewhere far away. But I see that 'our Lord's bread,' though easily earned, has not done you much good. There's a churchyard look about you," the old hag said, eyeing her mockingly.

"Ye say true, good dame; I have scarce been able to drag my old bones hither."

"Off to the Klembas', eh?"

"Surely. Are they not my kith and kin?"

"Your wallet is pretty well filled: they will receive you kindly. Also ye have there, I dare say, a few coins knotted in a clout. Aye, aye! they will certainly admit your kinship."

"Are they all well?" Agata interrupted, pained at her jeers.

"They are. Except Thomas, who is in poor health, but getting better in prison."

"Thomas! In prison?—Pray make no such jokes; they do not amuse me."

"What I said I repeat. But let me add that he is in good company; the whole village is there too along with him. When the law comes in, with its trap-doors and gratings, it takes no account if a man has land or not."

Agata stood bewildered. "Jesus, Mary, Joseph!" she moaned.

"Now hurry along to Klemba's wife: you will soon be fed up with news. . . . Aha! the men are taking a holiday, with a vengeance!" she said, and laughed maliciously.

Agata crept away: she could not believe the news. On

her way, she saw several women whom she knew, and who greeted her kindly; but she made as though she had not heard them, and of set purpose went as slowly as she could, putting off the dread confirmation of what the old woman had told her. She lingered long, gazing here and there, unwilling to know the worst.

At last, however, she made bold to enter Klemba's hut, which was at hand; but she trembled all over, and looked with frightened eyes at the orchard and the cottage in the background. Close to the windows, the cows were drinking noisily out of a large tub; and on the other end of the long open passage through the hut, she could see a sow with her little ones wallowing in the mud, and fowls looking eagerly for food on the dunghill. The tub was empty now. Taking it up (for she somehow felt more courage, coming in thus with something in her hand), she entered the large dusky room, and "praised God."

"Who is that?" answered a plaintive voice from the inner chamber.

" 'Tis I—Agata." With what a catch in her voice did she utter the words!

"Agata! Well, I never . . . !" said Dame Klemba, appearing suddenly on the threshold, with her apron full of little goslings, while their mothers came hissing and gaggling round her.

"Ah! God be thanked! And folk said ye had died so long ago as last Yule-tide; only no one knew where, and my goodman even went to the police office to find out.—Take a seat: ye must be tired.—You see, our geese have been hatching."

"A goodly brood! What a number, too!"

"Yes: threescore less five.—Come out in front of the house; I must feed them and take care lest the old ones trample them down."

She let them escape from her apron, and they began to run about, fluffy like yellow catkins; while the mother birds came up, gaggling with pleasure, and stretching out their long necks over them.

Dame Klemba brought them a mixture of minced eggs, nettle-leaves, and groats, set out on a board, and squatted down to protect them; for the parents, with loud indignant screams, tried hard to get at the food, and tread the little ones down and peck at them.

Agata sat down in front of the house. "They are all marked with grey between the wings," she said.

" 'Tis the mark of their breed: very large-sized. I got the eggs from the organist's wife: one in exchange for every three of mine.—Ah, 'tis well you have come; there's so much work, one does not know what to do first."

"I will bestir myself at once—at once!"

She made an effort to rise, meaning to set about doing something or other; but her strength failed her, and she reeled against the wall.

"Evidently," the other said, noting her livid face, and her strangely swollen and discomposed appearance, "evidently ye are too much used up to be of service any more."

She was vexed to see her like this; it was clear to her that the woman would not only be useless, but cause no little trouble besides.

Agata must have guessed what she felt, and said in a timid apologetic tone:

"Do not fear: I will not cumber you, nor intrude on your meals. I shall but rest awhile, and then go away. I merely wanted to see you all, and ask about you." Her eyes brimmed with tears.

"Well, but I am not turning you out.—Sit down; you will only leave us if you choose."

"Where are the lads?" she asked presently. "In the fields with Thomas, I suppose?"

"Have ye not heard, then, that they are all in jail?"

Agata joined her hands in silent agony.

"Yagustynka had told me as much, but I could not believe it."

"Ah! she told you the truth—gospel truth!"

She drew herself up stiffly and wept, as she remembered what had happened.

"Aye, it was as a very Doomsday for Lipka. They were taken away to town, all of them—all!—How I outlived it, I cannot tell. . . . 'Twas three weeks ago now, and it is as fresh in my mind as a thing of yesterday. Only Maciek, and the girls who are in the fields spreading dung, and I, poor wretched creature, have been left!

"Get away!" she suddenly cried to the geese. "Would ye then kill your own children as swine do? Would ye?"

And she called together the goslings, which were all going off into the enclosure after the mother birds.

"Nay, let them run about," said Agata; "no hawk is in sight, and I will look after them."

"Ye can scarce drag your limbs: how should you run after geese?"

"Ever since I crossed your threshold, I have felt better."

"Then try.—I will get you some food. Shall I boil milk for you?"

"Thanks, mistress, but on Saturdays in Lent I never take milk. Give me a pot of boiling water. I have bread with me, and shall crumble it in and eat."

In a little, Dame Klemba brought her a dish of hot water, seasoned with salt, and Agata took her meal of crumbled bread. Meanwhile the former told her all about the battle, its causes, and its end. How Boryna's skull had been cracked by the keeper, whom Antek slew in his turn to avenge his father; how the old man had been lying insensible ever since; how others too had been badly hurt in the fight, and how little they cared for that, because they won the victory.

"But," she went on to say, "on the following Sunday, not four days after, when wet snow was falling thick, and one could hardly step out of doors, we were preparing to go to church, when the Gulbas lads came round, shouting: 'The gendarmes are here!'

"So indeed they were—thirty of them, besides officials and justices . . . a whole court!—and they quartered them-selves upon the priest. Then they set about putting questions and taking notes, and bringing everybody to them under guard for examination. No one resisted; they all spoke out bravely, telling the truth as frankly as at Holy Confession.—This ended about eventide. The court was for carrying the whole village away, even the women! But there was such a crying and wailing of children that the men began to look about them for staves, and would have fought to the uttermost. . . . Then his Reverence must have spoken to the justices, for they left us here. Not even Kozlova did they take, though she used most evil speech to them: only the men were put in jail. And as to Antek, son of Boryna, they ordered him to be conveyed thither in bonds."

"In bonds! O Lord!"

"They bound him, but he snapped the ropes asunder like tow. And all were afraid of him, who seemed as though mad with fever, or possessed with a devil. And he stood up before them, and looked them in the face, saying:

" 'Make my hands and feet fast with manacles and fetters, and watch over me well.—Else I slay you all, and do to myself an evil thing!'

"He was so amazed for his father's loss that he himself offered his hands and feet to the gyves. And thus did they carry him away.

"Never shall I forget how they took him: never, till I die. And my goodman did they take likewise, and my sons, and the other men: about threescore of them.

"But what fell out here at that hour—what lamentations, what awful curses were heard—I could in no wise tell you!

"And now spring is here; the snows have melted away, the fields are dry and crying out to be tilled, and the time for ploughing and sowing has come: but we have no one to work here!

"Only the Voyt, the smith, and a few decrepit old men have been left; of the young men, only the fool, Yasyek Topsy-turvy!

"Yet 'tis now the season for yeaning and calving; and of our women, many are brought to bed in these days; and we must think of our lads over there, and take food to them.

with a little money and a clean shirt or two; meanwhile, we
are over head and ears in work, and there is no hiring
labour elsewhere, every peasant having first of all to shift
for himself."

"Will they not be soon set free?"

"The Lord knows! Our priest went to the police; so did
the Voyt: and they say that, the inquiry over, sentence will
be given. But three weeks have gone by, and not one man
is back home. Roch, too, went to make inquiries last
Thursday."

"Does Boryna live still?"

"He does, but even as one dead; he lies like a log, insensible. Hanka sent for the best doctors, but they did
naught."

"What could they do? Physicians are in vain when the
ailment is mortal."

Klembova then told her visitor all that had taken place in
winter; for Agata had not heard anything.

She let her arms drop in sheer amazement and horror at
what she now learned: the news made her heart ache.

"O my God! I was all the time thinking of Lipka, but
never, never dreamed . . . All my life I have heard nothing
like it.—Is Satan come to abide with us?"

"Belike he is."

"It must be so. Our Lord is punishing us for the grievous
sin of Antek with his stepmother. But there are other sins
besides, that now spring forth and are seen by all."

Agata feared to ask what these were; she raised a shaking
hand and, crossing herself, mumbled some devout prayer.

"Yes, all the people have to suffer for them. While
Boryna is lying there for dead"—here she lowered her voice
—"they say that Yagna is making up in real earnest to the
Voyt. Antek is away, Matthew also: she has no young
fellow by, so she takes the first willing man she meets!
What a world we live in, my God!" she ejaculated, wringing
her hands.

Agata had nothing to reply. The news she had heard
depressed her so, that her former fatigue now came upon her

with increased power, and she crept to the byre to get some rest.

About sunset she was seen again, going the round of her acquaintances; and when she came back to the Klembas', these were at supper.

A spoon had been set and a place reserved for her; not a first place, of course. But she had little appetite, and preferred telling them what she had seen in the towns she had visited as a pilgrim.

Then night fell and they lit a candle in the room previous to retiring for the night, she brought out her wallet, and, while they surrounded her with breathless curiosity, slowly took forth the various things she had bought for them: for each one, a holy picture; for the girls, a necklace (ah, how they, one after another, went peeping into the looking-glass, to see how theirs became them, drawing up their necks, like so many turkeys!); good strong knives for the lads; for Thomas, a large packet of tobacco, and for his good dame, a great frill, deeply scolloped and adorned with many-coloured embroidery, all so beautiful that the housewife herself clapped her hands to see it!

All were extremely pleased, all feasted their eyes upon the gifts; while Agata, enjoying their pleasure, told them in detail how much each article had cost and where it had been bought.

They sat up long, talking of the absent ones.

"The village is so deadly still, it makes me feel a lump in the throat!" Agata said at last, when all had done talking, and there was a deep dull silence around her. "How different it was this time last year! The whole village shook with shouts and laughter."

"Yes, and now it looks like a vast grave," Klembova chimed in mournfully; "only fit to be covered with a tomb-stone, and have a cross raised above."

"So 'tis.—Mistress, may I go and rest upstairs?" Agata asked meekly. "My bones ache with journeying, and my eyes begin to draw straws."

"Sleep wheresoever ye choose: there is no lack of room now!"

But as she was going up the ladder to the loft, Klembova spoke to her through the open door:

"Oh, I had all but forgotten to tell you. . . . We have taken your feather-bed out of your chest. . . . During the Carnival, Marcyha was down with the smallpox . . . and it was very cold . . . and we had nothing to keep her warm with.—So we borrowed it of you. . . . It has been aired by now, and shall be taken upstairs to-morrow."

"My feather-bed?—Well, 'twas your wish. . . . All right, since ye wanted it."

She broke off, unable to say more, and groped her way up to the chest. Raising the lid, she ran her hands feverishly over her funeral outfit.

Yes, the feather-bed that she had left completely new had been taken! New, not even once used! . . . How she had picked up the stuffing, feather by feather, gleaning them upon the goose-pastures, to have her last bed ready for her! She burst out crying: the blow was too cruel.

And she prayed for a long time, seasoning her prayers with bitter tears, and lovingly complaining to her dear Jesus of the wrong done to her.

V

CHAPTER II

THE next day was Palm Sunday.

Bright and early, Hanka rose, putting on only her petticoat, and throwing a shawl on her shoulders, for the cold.

Round she looked everywhere, even to the boundaries of the enclosure and over on to the road. It was quite empty and void of life: only the dry light of dawn clad the leafless tree-tops along its line.

Returning to the porch, and kneeling down with difficulty (for she expected to be confined in a week or so), she began her morning prayer, with drowsy eyes wandering over the landscape.

The day, laden with white fire, was coming apace, and the ruddy glow of dawn melting away into a golden expanse in the East, like the rich silk canopy over the Monstrance, when the Monstrance is not yet in sight.

There had been a slight frost overnight; hedges, roofs, cottages shone with white radiance, and the trees had the air of so many fleecy clouds.

The village was still sleeping in the haze that crept along the ground; but a few cabins nearer the road now began to show their snowy walls. The mill went on uninterruptedly; the river babbled and bubbled low, audible but unseen.

Cocks were noisy and many birds chirped in the orchards, as if saying their morning prayers together, when Hanka went out again to look over all the place and wake the sleepers.

She first opened the half-door to the sty. A large porker struggled to get up, but was so fat, it rolled back upon its substantial hind quarters, and only turned its snout towards

22

her, grunting, as she inspected the trough and put in some fresh food.

"Its hams are so clad with fat, it can hardly rise. Truly, the fat is at least four inches thick!" And she felt its sides with delight.

Entering the poultry-house, she then, to attract the fowls, threw some of the pig's food she had brought with her. Down they came in a hurry from their roosting-place, with the cocks crowing lustily.

She drove away the ganders, which attacked them, and carefully examined the eggs, one by one, holding them up to the light.

"They will be hatched out in an hour!" she said, for she could just make out a faint pecking sound within.

Just then Lapa, indifferent to the ganders hissing round him, came out of his kennel, drowsily and yawning audibly.

At her sight, with a bark and a wag of his tail, he came to her through the crowd of hens; the feathers flew about. He leaped up at her, put his paws on her breast, and licked her hands, she patting his head the while.

"Ah, this dumb creature has more feeling than many a man! . . . Now, Pete! Time to rise!" she cried, beating on the stable-door, until she heard a grumbling and the sound of a bolt shot back; thereupon she opened the cowbyre door, where the kine were lying in a row before their mangers.

"What, Vitek! Sleeping so hard, and so late? Up, young imp!"

The boy awoke, rose from his straw bed, and began to draw his breeches on, though murmuring; for he was afraid of her.

"Give the kine some hay to eat, before I milk them; and then come at once and peel potatoes. But not a handful to Lysula, look you!" she added sternly: Lysula was Yagna's property. "Let her mistress feed her!"

"Oh, she does; and so well that the poor beast is bellowing for food, and eats the straw that's under her!"

"She may starve, for aught I care: 'tis no loss of mine!" she said, with fierce animosity.

Vitek muttered some words and, when she had gone, fell back on his pallet, to doze for a few seconds more.

In the barn, upon the straw-strewn threshing-floor, lay the potatoes chosen for planting. She looked in there, and also into the shed close by, where all their farming-implements were stored. Then, having seen, as she did regularly each day, that nothing was missing or had been damaged during the night, she went out into the wheat-fields, where she continued her interrupted morning prayers.

Now that the sun had risen, there was as a blast of flame rushing through the orchard. The dews were dropping from the trees, the wind rustled softly in the boughs, the larks trilled forth their carols louder and louder. Folk began to move about, the waters of the mill-pond beat upon the banks, gates opened with a rusty creak, geese screamed, dogs yelped, and now and then a human voice was heard.

Folk were rising later than their wont. It was Sunday, and they were glad to rest their tired limbs a little longer.

Hanka prayed only with her lips: her thoughts were elsewhere. . . .

She gazed over those broad lands, bounded afar by the thick veil of the forest, which the flames of the eastern sky were flooding, making the young fir-trees stand out like amber amidst the bluish underwood; over those other fields, shimmering tremulously in the quivering yellow glare, and growing their moist greenish fleece of sprouting corn; over the thin watery streaks—threads of silver—that ran here and there in the deep furrows along the damp cornlands, under the cool wafts of the breezes, and in the sacred hush in which all life manifests itself on earth.

And yet she noted none of all these things.

They rose up before her, those past days of hunger and want and injustice, with the memory of Antek's faithlessness, and of her manifold sorrows and afflictions—so great that she wondered how she could ever have found strength to bear them, and to await this happier lot now granted her by our Lord.

For behold, there she was, once more upon the farm-lands of Boryna!

And who would now have the power to oust her thence?

During the past six months, she had undergone more than many go through in all their lives: now she could suffer what the Lord should choose her to suffer, until Antek returned to himself, and the land was theirs for ever.

She recalled now how and when the young men had started for the forest expedition.

She had been forced to stay behind; to join them would, in her state, have been a difficult and dangerous attempt.

Antek, she had been told, was not with the others; and this made her uneasy. It was, she thought, no doubt out of spite against the old man his father . . . or possibly to spend the time with Yagna!

The thought had gnawed at her heart: but as to going and spying after him—never!

And then, just before noon, the Gulbas boy had run in, crying: "Victory! the Manor-folk are beaten!" and went past.

She arranged to go with Klembova and meet the men as they were coming home.

And then Paches had come, shouting from afar: "Boryna is slain, Antek slain, and Matthew, and many more!" and, clapping his hands, dropped down with an unintelligible mutter; and his teeth were set so fast (for he was quite senseless) that they must needs prize them open with a knife to give him water.

Happily, others came pouring in along the road from the forest, ere the lad was brought to. These related all that had taken place; and, a little after, Antek arrived, alive and walking by his father's cart; but covered with blood, livid as a corpse, and beside himself.

Deep as was her sorrow, and near as she felt to weeping, she mastered herself nevertheless; and old Bylitsa, her father, took her on one side, and said:

"Look to it: Boryna will presently be no more, Antek

is out of his wits, and there is none to see after Boryna's cabin. The smith will establish himself therein, and who will drive him out then?"

Instantly she had hurried back to her hut and, taking quickly with her her children and all she could lay hands on, returned to her former lodgings on the side of the cabin opposite to where Boryna lived.

So while Ambrose was still bandaging the old man's head, and the folk were out of doors, and the whole village seething with the excitement of victory, and resounding with the groans of the wounded—Hanka slipped quietly into the cabin, and settled there, not to be turned out again.

She watched and guarded the place with great vigilance; for the land was Antek's, and his father was near his last gasp, and might expire at any moment. She knew well how important it was to be first in possession; for he that first fell upon a heritage and took possession of it could scarcely be driven away, and was sure to have the law on his side.

The smith, furious that she had stolen a march on him, now threatened and abused her dreadfully; but she did not mind.

Was she to ask his leave . . . or anyone's? She had taken over all the property, and was guarding it with the fidelity of a dog: who else had the right? She knew that the old man must soon die, and that (as Roch had warned her) Antek would be put in prison.

To whose protection, then, should she fly? Let her help herself, and Heaven might help her.

When Antek was arrested, she took it quietly enough: she had nothing else to do.

And, moreover, with all the house and farm-work upon her shoulders, when could she find time for lamentation?

She neither shirked labour nor (though alone and single-handed) quailed before her enemies: Yagna, and the smith and his wife, all bitterly hostile; the Voyt, whose inclination for Yagna made him favour her strongly; and even his Reverence, whom Dominikova had set against her.

But they all were powerless; she yielded not one jot.

Day by day, her grip upon the homestead grew firmer, and ere a fortnight had gone by, the whole farm was under her control and obeyed her commands.

True, she had to grudge herself food and sleep and rest of any kind, toiling incessantly from early dawn till late into the night.

For one so timid by nature, continually in the past snubbed and brow-beaten by Antek, and accustomed neither to such work nor to such responsibilities, this position was at times especially hard and intolerable: but the dread of being turned out of the place, together with her hatred for Yagna, gave her the strength to pull through.

Whencesoever her energy had come, she remained steadfast at her post; and shortly everyone began to regard her with wonder and respect.

"Dear, dear!" would the best housewives of Lipka say to one another; "once we thought she could not say 'Boo!' to a goose; and lo, she is as good as an able husbandman!" Ploshkova and others even went the length of asking her advice at times, and willingly gave her their own counsel and help.

This she accepted with gratitude, but did not seek society at all, remembering too well how she had been dealt with so short a time ago.

Besides, she cared little for gossip, and had no liking for neighbourly chats and bits of scandal bandied round over the fences.

No. She had enough with her own troubles, and her neighbours' shortcomings did not interest her.

At this stage of her thoughts, Yagna recurred forcibly to her mind—Yagna, with whom she was waging silent but desperate and stubborn warfare. The thought was like a stab in her breast; it made her start up and hurriedly end her prayer, crossing herself and beating her breast.

Returning in no pleasant mood, she was all the more vexed to find everybody asleep in the cottage, and in the outhouses as well.

She rated Vitek soundly, routed Pete out of his litter of

straw, and scolded Yuzka too, for "lying abed when the sun
was a span high!"

"If I but take my eyes off them to pray for a moment, I
find them all snoozing, each in his corner!" she grumbled,
as she lit the fire.

Afterwards, taking the children outside, and cutting some
bread for each of them, she called Lapa to play with them,
while she went in to see after Boryna.

On that side of the cottage, all was as still as death; and
she slammed the door angrily. Yet she did not wake Yagna;
and the old man still lay as she had left him the night
before, his ashen face, overgrown with a stubbly beard,
showing above the red-striped coverlet; worn, gaunt, im-
passive as the wood-carven image of a saint. His eyes,
wide open and motionless, stared right before him; his head
was wrapped up in cloths, and his arms hung limp and
lifeless, like broken boughs of a tree.

She set his bed in order, shook up the covering about his
legs (for the room was close), and gave him some fresh
water, which he drank slowly, but made no other motion,
lying as still as a felled trunk. Only in his eyes there was
a faint glimmer, as that of a river which, between night and
dawn, is shadowed forth feebly for the twinkling of an eye.

She heaved a mournful sigh over him, and then, darting
a glance of hate at the sleeping Yagna, struck a pail with her
foot.

The noise did not wake the latter. She lay, her face
turned towards the room, the coverlet thrown back from her
bosom on account of the heat, so that her shoulders and
throat were bare. Her parted lips, cherry-red, showed a row
of shining teeth, like beads of the purest white; her dishevelled hair, fair as the finest sun-dried flax, was streaming
over her coverlet and down to the floor.

"Oh! I could dig my nails into that pretty face of yours
so deep that it would never be pretty any more!" she hissed
with fierce aversion, a sharp pang stabbing at her heart.
She mechanically smoothed her hair and looked into the
glass that hung by the window, but shrank back on behold-

ing her own faded discoloured features and red-fringed eye-lids.

"She! . . . she has naught to try her; feeds abundantly, sleeps in a warm bed, brings forth no children: what should mar *her* beauty?"

And she slammed the door violently as she went out.

This noise woke Yagna; but old Boryna lay as he had lain, staring straight before him.

He had been thus ever since they had brought him home from the fight. At times only did he seem to rouse himself and, taking Yagna's hand, strive to speak; but he always relapsed into insensibility, and could never utter a word.

Roch had brought a doctor from the town, who had examined the man, written a recipe on a scrap of paper, and taken ten roubles. The medicine, too, was costly, and did no more nor less good than Dominikova's incantations, recited gratis.

It soon was clear to all that he would never mend, and so they let him be.

All they now did was to change the wet bandages on his head, and give him a little water or milk to drink; solid food he could not take.

Folk said, and Ambrose, who had experience in such matters, said too, that should Boryna not come to his senses again, he would die shortly, though of course without pain. This end, then, they were daily expecting, but it did not come, and the delay was irksome.

It was Yagna's right and duty to take care of the patient and stay by him; but how could she—she who was unable to remain there an hour? She had more than enough of him as it was; and she was, moreover, weary of the continual struggle with Hanka, who had usurped her place and set her completely aside. She therefore kept out of doors by preference, rejoicing to bask in the warm morning light, and to go out free into the village. She abandoned the care of her husband to Yuzka, and used to wander about, no one knew where, often returning only in the evening.

Yuzka then looked after him; but this was only when

others were by, she being as yet but a little girl, silly and a gadabout, so that Hanka was obliged to watch over the dying man alone. The smith and his wife, indeed, were popping in to look round any number of times a day; but it was she that they came to watch, and to see whether she had taken nothing out of the cottage, eagerly anticipating the possibility of Boryna's recovering his senses enough to bequeath his property.

They snarled round him like dogs quarrelling round a dying sheep, each impatient to get his fangs first into the poor beast's entrails, and carry off the best piece of the carcass. Meanwhile, the blacksmith clutched at everything he could see and lay his hands on; it had to be snatched from him by force and the strictest watch kept; and no day passed by without brawling and furious invectives.

The proverb says that "God gives to everyone who rises with the sun." Yes, but the blacksmith would rise even before, even at midnight, and go galloping ten villages away, if he were but sure of making a good profit.

And now Yagna had scarcely risen and donned her petticoat, when the door creaked, and in he walked with stealthy steps, straight to the bed where old Boryna lay, and peered into his eyes.

"Not a word yet?"

"As he was, so he is!" Yagna said bluntly, putting her hair up under her kerchief.

She was barefoot and scantily attired, still rather drowsy, and overflowing with the strange charm that came forth from her like rays of heat; he could not help eyeing her through his half-closed lids with a greedy stare.

"Do you know," he said, coming close to her, "the old fellow must have a goodly lot of money here? The organist told me that, even before last Yule-tide, Boryna was ready to lend a cool hundred roubles to a man in Debitsa, and the loan only failed because he wanted too high a rate of interest. He must have it somewhere here, hidden away in the cabin.—So keep an eye on Hanka! . . . And ye might take a quiet look round at your leisure. . . ."

"Why not?" she said, throwing her apron over her bare arms, for she felt his glances upon her.

He walked about the room, peeping absently behind the pictures that hung on the walls.

"Have you the key of the store-room?" he asked, with a sly look at the small closed door just by.

"It hangs by the cross near the window."

"About a month since, I lent him a chisel which I want now, but can find it nowhere about. I think it is in there, thrown somewhere amongst odds and ends."

"Look for it yourself. I am not going to seek it for you."

Suddenly, hearing Hanka's voice in the passage, he drew back from the larder-door and hung the key up again.

"Then I shall look in to-morrow," he said, taking his cap. "Has Roch been here?"

"How should I know? Ask Hanka."

He lingered on a little, scratching his fell of red hair, while his eyes darted to and fro with a furtive expression; then, smiling to himself, he walked out.

Yagna, throwing off her apron, then set about making the bed, now and then glancing at her husband, but taking good care never to meet his open ever-staring eyes.

She loathed and feared and hated him indeed for all the ill he had done to her, and when he called her and stretched out his clammy hands to hers, she felt an agony of repugnance and dread: such a waft of death and the grave emanated from the man! And yet, in spite of all, it was perhaps she who most sincerely wished him to live on.

For she only now realized what she had to lose by his death. With him she had felt herself the mistress; all obeyed her; and the other women, willing or not, had to give her the first place. Why? Only because she was Boryna's wife. And Matthias, though choleric and hard upon her at home, paid her every attention in the presence of others, and made them all respect her.

This she had never seen clearly until Hanka had swooped down on the hut and got the upper hand there; then, at last, she felt herself helpless and ill-treated.

For the land she cared not one whit: what was the land to her? Nothing at all. And though she had been used to give orders, and plume herself on her importance and pride herself on her riches, still she was well enough off at home not to grieve much over their loss. What stung her to the quick was that she must give way to Hanka—to Antek's wife; that it was which she felt intolerable, and which roused all her malice and antagonism.

Her mother, too, together with the blacksmith, was continually egging her on. Else perhaps she might soon have given up the fight; for all those petty bickerings wearied her so, that she would gladly have thrown up everything and gone back to her mother.

But Dominikova had replied sternly: "Never, while he is alive! You must see after your husband; your place is there!"

So she had stayed on, though with dissatisfaction inexpressible: no one to speak to, to smile at, or to call upon!

At home she had that ghastly man by her; and Hanka ever ready for strife; and war—war—war beyond all bearing!

She would sometimes take her distaff the round of the cabins—but that too was an unbearable ordeal. There were only women in the village, dull, heavy, lachrymose, or stormy and boisterous like a day in March: nothing but complaints everywhere, and not one farm-lad in sight!

And now her thoughts began to go back to Antek.

True, she had, in the last days preceding the catastrophe, felt greatly estranged towards him, had never met him but with pain and terror, and been in the end so treated that the very memory was gall and wormwood. But then, she had always had him waiting behind the hayrick in the evening, if she cared to see anyone. . . . In spite, then, of the fear of discovery and his frequent reproaches for her delay, she had gone willingly, forgetful of all the world, when he would seize her in his arms—no permission asked—the fiery monster that he was!

And now she was alone: quite, quite alone! The patient

follower, the persistent watcher, the masterful lover, was there no more. The Voyt indeed caressed her, dallied with her among the hedgerows, or went with her for drinks to the tavern, and would fain have taken Antek's place. But she only allowed him such liberties because they flattered her senses, and there was no one else at hand: who could compare him with Antek?

Besides, she had another motive in this: to flout the village —and Antek not less!

Ah! in the last three days after the fight, how shamefully he had slighted her! Had he not sat all day, all night, at the old man's bedside, nay, even slept upon her own bed, scarce ever leaving the hut; and yet seemed not to see her, though she was always by his side, looking like a dog with wistful eyes for any sign of love?

Never had he once looked upon her: he had eyes only for his father, for Hanka, for the children—and for the dog!

It was that, possibly, which had quenched all her love for him. And so, when he was taken away in irons, he had appeared to her as someone else—as a stranger. She could not find it in her heart to grieve for him; and she eyed with grim pleasure Hanka, tearing her hair, beating her head against the wall, and howling like a dog when her puppies are drowned.

She spitefully enjoyed her agonies, while turning away in disgust from the dreadful madness in Antek's face.

The man he was now she could not so much as remember distinctly, any more than the face of some person she had seen but once: so great was the estrangement between them!

But she recollected all the more clearly the Antek of old— of those loving days—days of trysts and embraces, of kisses and raptures—him for whom her whole being yearned again and again when she woke at night, and her heart, bursting with passionate grief, cried out aloud to him, wildly moaning and longing.

To him of those past days of bliss did her soul cry out; though, indeed, was he anywhere now in the wide world?

Just then he was present—living in her mind—a most sweet vision, when suddenly Hanka's shrill voice drove him from her.

"That woman makes a din like a dog flayed alive!" was her mental comment as the vision faded.

The sun's rays were peeping in obliquely, reddening the murky room; birds warbled; and as the warmth increased, the night's white frost fell in crystal drops from the roof, while she could hear the geese screaming and splashing in the pond.

She set the room in order, for it was Sunday, and she would presently have to get ready for church, and prepare the palm-boughs for the ceremony. She had the red osier shoots, cut the day before, and covered with silvery buds, standing there in a water-jug; and she was about to bind and adorn them carefully, when Vitek shouted through the door:

"Mistress says your cow is lowing for want of food, and you are to feed her."

"Tell her my cow is no business of hers!" she returned, at the top of her voice, and listened to what the other would scream in reply.

"Oh," she thought, "you may yell till you're hoarse: ye will not put me out of humour to-day!"

And thereupon she began to choose at leisure the dress she was to wear to church. But a sudden dreary thought came to cloud her bright sky and make the whole world sombre for her.—Why should she attire herself at all?—for whom?

For those hateful women, whose eyes would count the cost of every ribbon, whose tongues would cover her with foul aspersions?

This painful reflection made her turn away from her dresses, and she set about combing her abundant locks, as she gazed mournfully out of the window at the village, bathed in sunshine and agleam with dew; at the white cabins, visible behind their orchards, with plumes of blue smoke crowning their roofs; at the red wavy shadows of many a woman's petticoat, glancing through the green of the trees on the shore, both reflected in the waters; at the geese, which seemed to swim in long lines athwart the azure image of the sky and form dark semicircles, uncoiling themselves like snakes; and at the white-bellied gleaming swallows, sweeping down and up again along and above its surface.

Then she looked away from all these, and up to the dark-blue sky, wherein the clouds moved like a flock of woolly sheep on a pasture-ground; and, far above, birds were flying unseen, so high that only their long plaintive thrilling cry was to be heard—a sound that filled her heart with such sadness that her eyes grew dim, as she cast them down and gazed on the world around her, on the rolling water and the waving trees. Only she now saw nothing in them but the echo of her own dejection, that caused the tears to start on her pale cheeks, dropping down one after another, like the beads of a broken rosary, that fell out of the innermost core of her heart!

What was it that now came over her?—She had no idea herself.

Something, she felt, was seizing her, lifting her up, carrying her away—an invincible longing; and whithersoever it should take her, thither she would go without fail. So she wept on involuntarily and almost painlessly: thus a tree, laden with blossoms, warmed by the sun and waving in the breezes of a springtide morning, drips with abundant dew, draws life-giving sap from the soil, and lifts its boughs and blossoming sprays.

"Vitek!" the shrill voice of Hanka was crying again. "Ask the lady there if she will kindly come round to breakfast."

Yagna woke up from her trance, wiped her tears, finished combing her hair, and hastened in.

They were all sitting at breakfast in Hanka's room. The potatoes smoked in a huge dish, over which Yuzka had just poured a quantity of cream, fried and seasoned with onions; they had set to lustily, and all the spoons were hard at work.

Hanka had taken the first place, in the middle; Pete sat at one end, Vitek squatting on the floor beside him; and

Yuzka took her meal standing and seeing to the service. The children were enjoying a well-filled platter by the fire, and at the same time using their spoons to keep off Lapa, that wanted to eat from their dish.

Yagna's place was near the door, opposite to Pete.

The meal was a dull one, taken with downcast eyes most of the time.

Yuzka tried in vain to rattle away after her fashion; Pete came in now and then with a word, and even Hanka, touched by the wistful look in Yagna's eyes, strove to make conversation. But her guest said not one single word.

"Who gave you that bruise, Vitek?" Hanka inquired.

"Oh, I struck my head against the manger!" But he turned as red as a crayfish and rubbed the place, with a meaning glance towards Yuzka.

"Have you brought any palm-boughs yet?"

"As soon as I have done breakfast, I shall go for them," he replied, eating at a great rate.

Here Yagna put down her spoon and went out.

"What has come to her?" Yuzka whispered to Pete, as she helped him to some more *barszcz*.

"Some folk have not your gift of continual babbling.— Has she milked her cow?"

"I saw her take a pail to the byre."

"By the by, Yuzka, we must get some oil-cake for the 'Grey One.' "

"Yes, I saw this morning that her milk was turned to beestings."

"If so, she will calve in a day or two."

"Will you come to church for the palm-bough blessing?" Yuzka asked her.

"Go along with Vitek. And Pete may go likewise, when the horses have been seen to. I must stay and take care of Father. And perhaps Roch may be coming in, with news of Antek."

"Shall I tell Yagustynka to come to-morrow for the potato-planting?"

"Surely: we alone should be too few for the work, and the choice has to be quickly made."

"And about the dung?"

"Pete will have done carting it to the field by to-morrow at noon, and will set about spreading it along with Vitek after dinner; you too must help them as soon as you have time."

A loud cackling of geese outside—and in burst Vitek, gasping for breath.

"What! can you not even let the geese be?"

"They wanted to bite me: I was only keeping them off!"

And he threw down a large bundle of osier rods, sprinkled all over with catkins, and still wet with dew; which Yuzka instantly made into smaller bundles, tied them with red woollen thread, and asked him in a whisper:

"Was it the stork that gave you such a blow on the forehead?"

"It was; but tell no one." He cast a look at his mistress, busy taking the Sunday clothes out of the chest. "I'll tell you all. . . . I had noticed that it used to spend the night in the porch; so I slipped in there, when everyone was asleep. . . . Though it pecked at me, I had it fast, and was about to wrap it in my spencer and carry it off . . . but the dogs got scent of me, and I had to run for it. . . . One of my trouser-legs is torn.—But I'll have the bird still."

"What if the priest gets to know that you have his stork?"

"His? It is mine! . . . And who will tell him?"

"Where can you put it, that it may not be found?"

"I know of a hiding-place, safe from the gendarmes themselves. After a time I shall take it back to the cabin, and let them believe I have caught and tamed another stork. Who will find out that it is the same one?—Only say naught, and I'll get you some birds—or a leveret."

"Am I a boy, to play with birds? You silly thing!—Off and dress: we shall go to church together."

"Yuzka, let me carry the palm-boughs, will ye?"

"A pretty saying! Ye know that only women may take them to be blessed."

"I mean, through the village: ye shall have them back before we are in the church."

He begged her so earnestly that she consented, and turned to Nastka, who had just come in, clad in her best, and with a palm-bough in her hand.

"Any news of Matthew?" Hanka asked her at once.

"Only what the Voyt said yesterday: he's better."

"The Voyt knows naught, and makes up tales to please us."

"But he told his Reverence just the same."

"Then why said he nothing about Antek?"

"No doubt because Matthew is with the others, and Antek in a separate cell."

"He's but a babbler that wants to talk."

"Did he say aught to you?"

"He comes daily, but only to see Yagna. With her he has some private business, so they meet and speak of it. Apart. In the enclosure."

She had lowered her tone, and laid stress on every word, looking out of the window the while. Just then, Yagna appeared outside the porch, very well apparelled, a palm-bough in one hand, a prayer-book in the other. Hanka's eyes followed her out.

"The folk are on their way to church."

"Why, the bells have not sounded yet!"

But, just as she spoke, they rang out with a clash and a roar, booming and thundering their call to church.

In a few minutes, all the people had gone.

Hanka, left alone, put the pots on the fire to boil, and then took the children out of doors to comb them thoroughly —a thing she had never time to do properly on work-days.

She then went with them to the straw with which the potato-pits were strewn, and left them there to play. After which, having gone into the hut, and looked into every pot and pan, she said her rosary; for she had too much difficulty with her prayer-book.

It was now hard upon noontide, and Lipka was plunged deep in Sunday rest, with no sounds but the chirping of sparrows, or the twittering of the nest-building swallows under the eaves, in the warm early spring weather. Over everything hung the strangely resplendent canopy of a bright blue sky; and the fruit-trees stretched out their branches, covered with big buds, and the alders fringing the pond waved their yellow catkins silently, and the rust-coloured poplar shoots swelled with viscid aromatic sprouts opening to the light, like the gaping beaks of nestlings that want food.

On the warm cabin walls, flies had already begun to cluster, and from time to time a bee hummed about the daisies, or over the bushes, bursting out into little tongues of green flame.

Only a damp wind still continued to blow from the outlying fields and woodlands.

It was about the middle of Mass; for the sounds of far-off chants mingled with the notes of the organ, and at times with the faint tinkling of tiny bells, which could just be heard in the quiet spring air.

Time went by slowly, till—when the sun was highest—all was most silent, and only a stork clattered along, skimming the ground in its low flight, or crows on the watch to steal away a gosling would fly over the pond, arousing the ganders' angry screams.

Hanka went on with her prayers, watching meantime over the little ones, or going in to see her father-in-law, who lay motionless and staring glassily as ever; little by little ripening for death, like an ear of corn in the sun, awaiting the reaper's sickle. . . . He could recognize no one. Even when calling for Yagna and taking her hand, his eyes were looking far away. But Hanka fancied that the sound of her own voice made him move his lips, while his eyes expressed the wish to say something.

It was a pitiful sight indeed, she thought, when she came thus to visit him.

"Lord! who would have expected it? Such an able farmer, so clever, so wealthy a man! and now lying here like a tree smitten by a thunderbolt, with branches still leafy, but already inevitably given over to death!—not dead, yet no longer living.

"And indeed, though the God of mercy is the Almighty One, still the doom of man is hard, and not to be escaped. . . ."

But it was now past noon, and the cows had to be milked; so she heaved a sigh, and ended her prayers. Sighs were but sighs: work was duty, and must come first.

On her return with brimming pails, she found everybody back home again. Yuzka told her about the sermon, and the folk that were at church; and presently the room became very noisy; for she had brought with her several girls of her own age, who set about swallowing the buds from the consecrated palm-boughs, which were believed to be a preservative against sore throats. They laughed a good deal, more than one of them finding the downy catkins impossible to get down (they made them cough so) unless with the aid of drinks of water, or thumps upon the back: which latter remedy Vitek was very willing to administer.

Yagna did not come in for dinner; she had been seen walking out with her mother and the blacksmith.—They had scarce got through the meal, when Roch come in. All welcomed him warmly, feeling that closer ties than those of blood united him to them. He had for each a kind word, and a kiss on the crown of the head; but he would take no food. He was exceedingly tired, and glanced uneasily about the room, Hanka following his glances, but not venturing to ask questions.

Without looking at her, he said in a whisper: "I have seen Antek."

She started up from the chest she was sitting on, and the strong emotion which gripped her heart prevented her from saying a word.

"He's quite well, and in good spirits. A warder was present; but I had speech with him for at least an hour."

"Is he—is he in irons?" she asked, in a strangled voice.

"The idea! No more than the others. . . . He is not ill-used; do not frighten yourself."

"But Koziol says they are flogged there, and chained to the walls."

"It may be so in other cases; but Antek told me no one had touched him."

She clasped her hands with joy, and her face lit up.

"On my departure, he said that ye had without fail to kill the pig before Easter: he too would like to taste the Hallow-fare." [1]

"Alas! the poor man is starving there, no doubt," she remarked, plaintively.

"But," Yuzka ventured to put in, "Father told us that, when fat, it was to be sold."

"He did; only," Hanka said inflexibly, "now that Antek orders it to be killed, his will takes the place of his father's."

"He also sends you word," Roch continued, "that you are to do the needful as concerns all the field-work.—I had told him what a good beginning ye had made."

"And what did he say to that?" asked Hanka, radiant.

"He said that ye were able to do whatever ye chose to do."

"Yes, I shall be able—I shall!" she cried, her eyes bright with intense resolve.

"But will they set him free soon?" she inquired anxiously.

"Directly after Easter, it may be, but perhaps somewhat later. At any rate, as soon as the inquiry is over. It drags on so," he added, with partial truth, avoiding her eyes, "because the accused are so numerous—the whole village, in fact."

"Did he ask about the house . . . or the children . . . or me?"

She longed also to add: "or Yagna?" But she durst not put the question so openly; nor had she the art of drawing him on to tell her what she wanted. Moreover, it was now

---

[1] *Hallow-fare*—in Polish, *swiecone*—consists of various meats and pastry solemnly blessed in each house by a priest on Holy Saturday, and eaten at Eastertide, together with the consecrated Easter eggs; probably a Christianized survival of some spring festival among the heathen Slavs.—*Translator's Note.*

too late: the news of Roch's coming had spread throughout
the village, and the bells had not yet tolled for Evensong,
when the women came crowding in to hear the news about
their absent ones.

Sitting down near the entrance outside the cabin, he told
them all he knew about each one in particular. He had
nothing distressing to relate; but the women who heard him
began presently to whimper, and even to weep aloud.

He afterwards went out into the village, entering pretty
nearly every hut. With his saint-like figure and his long
white beard, and the words of consolation which he uttered,
he filled every cabin with light and comfort and hope.
Yet their tears flowed still more abundantly, and their feelings of sorrow revived, and they were depressed by the
memory of past sufferings.

The day before, Klembova had told Agata that Lipka
now resembled an open grave. She had spoken the truth.
The place looked as in the days of old, when the plague had
passed over it, and most of the inhabitants had gone to their
graves, or as when the lands had been devastated by war:
so that the cottages were desolate and filled only with
women's laments, the wailing of children, complaints, mourn-
ing, and that sharp torture which is the reminiscence of
agonies gone by.

What they were suffering now baffles description.

Three weeks had passed; and Lipka, instead of calming
down, felt the injury and wrong done increasing every day,
nay, every morning and noon and nightfall: whether within
the huts or without, cries of indignation resounded, and a
craving for revenge, like a hellish weed sown by Satan, sprang
up and flourished in every heart. And many a fist was
clenched, many a reckless word said, and many an imprecation thundered forth.

So that Roch's words to soothe them—just as a stick
thoughtlessly thrust into a heap of dying embers may make
them burst into flame again—had only the effect of rousing
the smouldering bitterness and the memory of injustice
committed.—That afternoon, but few went to Vespers.

They gathered in groups filling the enclosures, or out upon the roads, and even in the tavern, full of grief and uttering fierce curses.

Hanka alone felt a little comforted. Her husband's praises had filled her with strength and glad expectation, and she was eager to work and show him that she was equal to the emergency—eager beyond all expression.

The other women had left the place; the smith's wife had gone to sit at Boryna's bedside; and Hanka went to the sty with Yuzka. They let the pig out: it was so fat that it fell wallowing in the dirt, and refused to stir any more.

"Give it nothing else to eat to-day, so that its bowels may be cleansed."

" 'Twas well, then, that I forgot to feed it this afternoon."

"Good: if so, we shall kill it to-morrow. Have you told Yagustynka to come?"

"I have. She says she will be here in the evening."

"Dress yourself and run to Ambrose. He must come here to-morrow after Mass at the latest, and bring with him all things needful."

"But will he be able?—His Reverence has said two priests will come hither to-morrow to hear confessions."

"He knows well I'll give him vodka in plenty: he'll find time, be sure.—No one can kill a pig, and cut it up, and season it in such good style as he. . . . And Yagustynka likewise will be of use."

"Then may I go to town early in the morning for the salt and other seasonings?"

"Say for an airing, you little gadabout.—No, we can get all we want at Yankel's: I shall go there directly.—And, Yuzka!" she called after her; "where are Pete and Vitek?"

"Out in the meadows, I dare say. I saw Pete take his violin with him."

"If you find them, send them hither. They must bring round the trough that stands in the outhouse, and place it here in front of the cabin: in the morning, we shall scald and scour it."

Glad to get out of doors, Yuzka ran straight to Nastka, with whom she went to seek old Ambrose.

Hanka, however, did not go to the tavern then, her father having crawled round to see her.

She gave him something to eat, and had the pleasure of telling him what Roch had said about Antek.—Suddenly Magda burst in, crying:

"Something is the matter with Father: come this instant!"

Boryna was sitting up, his legs out of bed, and looking round the room. Hanka ran to prevent him from falling. He eyed her well, and then looked fixedly on the blacksmith, who had just run in unexpectedly.

"Hanka!"

He spoke aloud, distinctly, in a voice that startled her.

"Here I am," she answered, trembling.

"How is it out of doors?"

It was a strange voice—strange and broken.

"Spring is here, and the weather warm," she faltered.

"Are they not up yet? Afield, they should be!"

Bewildered, they sought words in vain: Magda burst out crying.

"Defend what's yours, boys! No giving way!"

His voice had risen to a shout. Suddenly he stopped, and rocked to and fro so violently in Hanka's arms that the smith and his wife tried to take her place. But though her arms and back were aching, she held him nevertheless. All three gazed on him, awaiting his next words.

"The barley must be sown first.—To the rescue, boys! Rally round me!" he shrieked all at once in an awful voice, and fell stiffly back, while his eyes closed, and something gurgled in his throat.

"O Lord! he is dying—dying!" Hanka screamed, and shook him with all her might, unconscious of what she did.

Magda put a consecrated taper in his hand, and lit it.

"Michael! The priest!—At once!"

But ere her husband could go out, Boryna opened his eyes; and the taper fell from his hand and broke.

"It has passed. . . . Look, he seeks something," Michael

whispered, bending over him. But the old man, now quite himself again, pushed him aside unhesitatingly, and called:

"Hanka! Send these folk away!"

Magda, in tears, fell down before him; but he seemed not to know her.

"None of that. . . . No use. . . . Send them out," he repeated obstinately.

"Do pray go—into the passage at least; do not vex him," she said imploringly.

"Magda, you go: I will not budge hence," the blacksmith hissed, guessing that Boryna had something to tell Hanka.

But the old man heard and, raising himself up in bed, gave him so terrible a glance as he pointed to the door, that Michael shrank back with a curse and rejoined Magda, who was weeping outside. But, quickly recovering his self-possession, he slipped round as close as he could to the window that was just by the head of Boryna's bed, and did all he could to make out what was said within.

After the smith had gone, "Sit down here, by my side," Boryna commanded Hanka. Greatly moved, she obeyed him.

"You will find some money in the larder: hide it, lest it be snatched from you."

"Where is it?" she asked, trembling with excitement.

"In amongst the corn."

He spoke distinctly, stopping at every word. Mastering her fear, she looked into his eyes, which glistened strangely.

"Defend Antek . . . rather sell half the property. . . . He must not be forsaken . . ."

He said no more, but fell back on to the pillow, trying to stammer a word or two and lift himself up, but uselessly; and now his eyes were quenched and dim.

Hanka, terrified, cried out; and both the others rushed in, ministering to the sick man, and gave him some water to drink. But he did not come to himself, and lay, as he had lain, stiff and motionless, with staring eyes that seemed to note nothing around him.

They sat long with him, both women silent, but in tears.

Dusk fell, the room grew dark, and they went out. Only so much remained of day as empurpled the mill-pond from the last glow in the West.

Turning round upon Hanka, the smith asked her: "What has he told you?"

"What ye both have heard."

"But what said he when alone with you?"

"Nothing else."

"Do not enrage me, Hanka, or you'll rue it!"

"What do I care for threats of yours?"

"The old man put something in your hand," the smith added, throwing out a feeler.

"Ye may go seek it in the dunghill, then."

He rushed at her and might have done her some injury, but that Yagustynka, who came up just then, said after her sour fashion:

"Oho! you both get on so lovingly that the whole village is talking about you two!"

With an imprecation, he went his way.

The night had come—starless, with a wind that rustled soft and sad through the trees, presaging a change of weather.

There was light and noise in Hanka's room, supper preparing at the crackling fire, elderly women holding forth with Yagustynka upon various matters, and Yuzka sitting outside with Nastka and with Yasyek Topsy-turvy; while Pete was drawing out of his violin such wailing notes as made their hearts feel sorrowful. Hanka alone was unable to stay seated, and, continually pondering over Boryna's words, looked again and again round into the room where he lay.

"Pete, have done!" she cried. "Why, it will presently be Holy Monday, and still you fiddle and fiddle!—'Tis a sin!"

She scolded the man, simply because she was so upset, and fell nigh weeping. He gave over, and they all went into the big room.

Several times that evening she heard the dogs barking loud within the enclosure, and set them on:

"At him, Lapa!—At him, Burek!—At him!"

But each time the dogs ceased suddenly, and came back, wagging their tails with satisfaction.

This took place so often that a fearful suspicion arose in her mind.

"Pete, take heed to lock and bolt everything well. Someone is prowling nigh, and no stranger either; for the dogs know him!"

At last all went to bed and to sleep—all but Hanka. She made sure that all the doors were locked; then she stood lending an attentive ear for a long time.

"Among the corn!—In one of the barrels, I dare say. . . . Ah, what if someone has forestalled me?"

The very thought made her heart throb, and brought a cold sweat to her brow. That night she hardly slept at all.

CHAPTER III

"YUZKA, kindle the fire; fill all our pots with water, and put them on to boil. I am off to Yankel's to get the seasonings."

"Then hurry; Ambrose will be here straightway."

"No fear; he cannot come so early. He has his duties to perform in church."

"Only to ring the bell for Mass. Roch is going to take his place for all the rest."

"Well, I shall be in time. Meanwhile, you hurry the lads, make them scour the trough quickly, and bring it outside the cabin.—Yagustynka will be here presently: let her wash the tubs.—Also the empty barrels must be taken out of the larder and rolled into the pond, to get the staves properly soaked and swollen out.—Do not wake the little ones; so long as they sleep, they'll be less in the way."—And, having given her orders and tied her apron over her head, she hastened out into the air of an early and very muggy and rainy morning.

The day was dismal, wet, and most unpleasantly cold; grey mists dripped and drizzled, the slippery roads were sodden and dank, the drab-coloured huts loomed faintly through the rain that fell; the trees, drooping gloomily over the pond, were seen like tremulous shrinking swaying shadows, as dim as if they had been made of mist; in this foul weather, there was scarce any landscape visible, and no one was out as yet. It was only when the Mass-bell began to tinkle that a few red petticoats were seen picking their way through the mire to church.

Hanka tripped on swiftly, thinking she might perhaps meet Ambrose at the turning of the road; but he was nowhere

48

in sight. Only the priest's old blind horse, as usual at that hour of the day, was going down to the pond with a large barrel, drawn on sledge-runners, stopping and stumbling at every rut, yet finding its way to the place by scent: the farm-lad waiting for it having sheltered himself from the rain in the bushes, and begun smoking a cigarette.

Just in front of the priest's house, a britzka drawn by a couple of well-fed chestnut horses, had pulled up and the ruddy-faced incumbent of Laznov stepped out of it.

"Come to hear confessions, along with his Reverence of Slupia," she thought, as she looked in vain for Ambrose. She went on round the church by the poplar road, where the mire was yet more abundant, and the trees, plunged in the vapoury mizzle, looked like shadows seen through a steam-clouded pane. Passing the tavern, she struck off in the squashy pathway that led to her sister's.

She would, she reckoned, have time enough for a call on her father, and a talk with her sister, with whom, now that she had removed to Boryna's, she was on very friendly terms.

"Yuzka told me yesterday that Father was not well!" she exclaimed on entering.

"Ah, what's to be done? He is lying in bed under his sheep-skin, and moaning, and talking about being ill," Veronka moodily replied.

"How cold it is here! I feel it creeping up the calves of my legs!"

"And have I any fuel at all? Who will go and fetch me a few dry faggots? How can I trudge to the forest and come home with a load of brushwood when there's so much other work to do? You see, I must manage all by myself."

They then both fell to lamenting over their sad fate.

"When Staho was here, I thought nothing of all he did at home. When the husband is gone, ah! then one knows what a help he is!—Are you going to town?"

"Certainly; I should have gone before, but Roch told me that visits would not be allowed until Eastertide. Therefore shall I go on Sunday, and take my poor husband a few morsels of our Hallow-fare."

"I fain would do the same for mine; but what have I to take to him? A mouthful of bread?"

"Be easy; I will prepare enough for them both; and we shall take it together."

"God reward you for your kindness; I will work for you in return."

"Do not speak of work in return: 'tis a gift I make you from my heart." She lowered her voice. "Well do I know poverty: it is a dog whose teeth bite deep."

"And that is so faithful and attached that it never will leave us till we die!—I thought I had a little money laid by, and hoped to purchase a pig in spring, and fatten it up, with no small profit when autumn came. Well, I had to give all to Staho, and my savings have run out like water: I have naught now. That is what comes of his standing up for the rights of our folk!"

"Nay, say not so. He went freely to protect them, and an acre or so of the wood will be yours."

"*Will be!* Aye, but 'while the grass grows, the steed starves!' And 'To him that can pay, the musicians play.' But 'Poor man, coin to money your sweat, and be glad that ye ever have eat!' "

"Are ye greatly in want?" she inquired, hesitatingly.

"I have naught in the world," she cried, flinging out her hands in despair, "but what the Jew or the miller will give me on credit!"

"Would I could help you! But the homestead where I dwell is not mine. I am baited as with dogs around me, and must take such heed lest they drive me from the cabin that I am at times clean out of my wits."

The previous night's experience came back to her forcibly.

"Meantime," her sister put in, "Yagna takes no care. She is a shrewd one, she, and enjoys herself to the full!"

"How so?"

She had risen from her seat, and was looking at her sister with alarm. Had Yagna found and taken the money?

"Oh, she only takes what pleasure she can get out of life:

dresses well, calls on her good friends, and has seven holidays
a week. She was seen sitting with the Voyt in the tavern
parlour yesterday, and the Jew could not fetch them drinks
fast enough!"

"Everything must come to an end," Hanka muttered sullenly, tying her apron over her head to go.

"True: but then 'Pleasure, once taken, cannot be snatched
from you'—and she knows it."

" 'Tis easy to be wise in that way, if one has naught to
care about!—But, Veronka, we are to kill the pig to-day:
come you this evening to help." And, cutting short her sister's everlasting complaints, she made her way out.

Her father, who was now in the room she had once
occupied, lay moaning and almost hidden under a heap
of straw.

"What ails ye, Father?"

She sat down by his side.

"Nothing, my dear daughter, nothing: only the ague
shakes me sorely, and my inwards are wrung and twisted."

"Because 'tis here as wet and as cold as out of doors.
Rise and come over to us; ye can tend the children. And
then—we shall kill the pig . . . if so be as ye have a mind to
eat of it?"

"To eat? Aye, a little. They forgot to give me any food
yesterday.—I shall come, Hanka, I shall come!" And he
sighed, but with pleasure, as he crept out of the straw bed.

Hanka, her mind full of the thought of Yagna, walked
over to the tavern as fast as she could.

The Jew no longer exacted payment in advance, but with
the most obsequious eagerness weighed and measured out
all she wanted, setting out many another article besides, to
tempt her.

She was very short with him. "Yankel!" she said haught-
ily; "give what I ask, and no more. I am no child, and
know what I wish to have."

But the Jew only smiled. She had bought things for between ten and twenty *zloty*, and also enough vodka to suf-

fice for the coming festival of Easter besides; and rolls in scores, and loaves of fine bread, and eight salt herrings . . . and even, to crown all, a small bottle of rum. Hardly could she carry the parcel, when made up.

"What! That Yagna enjoys herself: and I, who work so hard, am I to be worse off than a dog?"

But, though such was her thought on setting out, it was speedily followed by remorse. The expense was unnecessary. —But for shame, she would have made the Jew take the rum back again.

She found everybody in the cabin busy preparing things. Ambrose sat by the fire, exchanging verbal thrusts with Yagustynka, who was engaged in scalding the various vessels to be used; and the room was full of steam.

"We were waiting for you, to knock your little pig on the head!"

"Ye have arrived very early!"

"I made Roch take my place in the sacristy; the priest's manservant is to blow the organ-bellows, and Magda will sweep out the church. I have arranged everything, so that you may not be disappointed. The priests will not begin hearing confessions till they have finished breakfast.—But how cold it is to-day!" he cried out querulously; "I feel it to the very marrow."

"Broiling at the fire, can you talk of the cold?" Yuzka cried out in amazement.

"You are silly: I feel so cold within, that even my wooden leg's quite numb!"

"Ye shall soon have something to warm you.—Yuzka, soak a herring directly."

"Give it me salt as it is; nothing takes the salt out like vodka—when there's enough of it."

"Ye're always the same," Yagustynka observed snappishly. "Should ye hear glasses jingle even at midnight, ye'd rise on the spot for a drink."

"Right, my good woman. But your tongue is very dry, is it not? you too would like to wet it in vodka, eh?" He laughed and rubbed his hands.

"My ancient! I'll drink glass for glass with you any day!"

Here Hanka interrupted them; their continual hints and innuendoes about vodka were teasing her.

"Very few people are going to church as yet," she remarked, to change the subject.

" 'Tis early. They will presently come with a rush to get rid of their sins."

"Aye," said Yagustynka, "to spend the time, hear something new, and prepare to sin again!"

Here Yuzka's shrill voice piped: "The girls were already preparing confessions yesternight."

"Because," Yagustynka said, "they are ashamed to confess to their own priest."

"Better, old crone, ye sat in the church-porch and said your beads and did penance, than backbite your neighbours so!"

"I will, Wooden Leg! when ye sit by my side there!"

"Oh, I am in no hurry. I intend first to toll for you and put you to bed with a shovel!"

The words enraged her. "Bait me not, or you'll rue it!" she snarled.

"My stick will ward off your bites; and 'twere pity to lose your last teeth!"

She made no answer. Just then Hanka filled a glass, and drank to them both, and Yuzka brought a herring to Ambrose, who slapped it against his wooden leg, skinned it, broiled it over the coals, and ate it with relish.

"To work! We have been dawdling too long!" he cried, taking off his coat, tucking up his shirt-sleeves, and giving his knife a last edge on his whetstone. Then, seizing a large club, used to mash potatoes, for the pig, he hastened out, everybody following him.

Pete aided him, and the beast, though resisting with all its might, was dragged out into the yard.

"Quick! the dish for the blood!"

All stood round, eyeing its plump creamy sides and trailing belly, which the drizzle from the mists that filled the orchard was wetting fast. A few women stood outside the yard, and several children, eager to look on, had climbed the palings.

Ambrose crossed himself, and came forward slantwise towards the pig, his club held back at an angle on one side. Then, coming to a standstill, he suddenly lifted his arm, and, twisting his body round with so forcible a writhe that his neck shirt-button flew off, brought his weapon down right between the ears. The animal's forelegs gave way, and it went down squealing. He redoubled the blow, this time with both hands. The pig rolled on to one side, kicking convulsively: Ambrose then, astride on its belly, thrust the whole of his knife's gleaming blade into its heart.

A dish was at hand: the blood, streaming like warm water, spirted out in rhythmical squirts, with a bubbling sound.

"Away, Lapa!—Look at that wicked dog!—Wants to lap some, and Lent not over yet!" he cried, breathless with exertion, as he drove the dog from the dish: for a centenarian, the effort had been considerable.

"Shall we do the scalding in the passage?"

"Rather take the trough into the room where the carcass is to hang till we quarter it."

"Will there not be too little space in the room?"

"Not in the larger room—your father-in-law's. He will suffer nothing. Only let's hurry: the bristles come out more readily while the carcass is yet warm."

As he gave his directions, he was busy pulling out the long bristles down the back.

In a short time the carcass was scalded, unhaired, thoroughly cleansed, hung up in Boryna's room, and stretched out wide open with a lath tied to a rafter.

Yagna was out, having gone to church early in the morning, and never dreaming that such a liberty would be taken. Her husband lay as usual, staring with lack-lustre eyes.

They worked noiselessly at first, often looking round at him; but soon they forgot his presence, interested as they were in the pig, whose thick layer of fat far exceeded their expectations.

"We have lulled him to sleep, we have brought him in here: 'tis time that some vodka should flow in his honour!" cried Ambrose, washing his hands over the trough.

"Come to breakfast, and you'll have some drink."

Indeed, before he sat down to the potatoes and *barszcz* which formed the meal, he had tossed off a copious draught of vodka. He ate little, though, being in a hurry to go on with the work, and urged the others to make haste, especially Yagustynka, who was by no means his inferior in the salting and seasoning line, and knew as much as ever he did.

Hanka, too, did her best to give aid, and so did Yuzka, eager to stay in the hut beside the newly killed porker, and not at all willing to go out.

But Hanka cried out to her: "Be off at once, and order them to cart the dung away, and lend them a hand yourself, while they are spreading it! The sluggards! I fear the work will not be over by this evening."

So Yuzka, much against her will, ran out into the yard, where she was heard for a long while, venting all her ill humour on the two farm-lads, and scolding them violently.

The cabin became noisier, little by little, as gossip after gossip dropped in to chat in neighbourly wise, and clasp their hands, and admire the porker.

"So fine! so laden with fat! Far finer a one than either the miller's or the organist's!"

Hanka felt much pleased, and was puffed up with these praises of the fatted beast; and though indeed she grudged the vodka, she could not help inviting them, according to the custom among the peasants to offer drinks, and bread and salt, on such an occasion. And she became very talkative to all the folk who crossed the threshold one after another and came in, as one comes into church for a short visit on the feast of the patron saint.—Children, too, were plentiful all round the house, and peeping in at every window.

All through Lipka, besides, there now began to be a good

deal of unusual movement: folk splashing along in the mud, and carts clattering in from other villages, all crowding to church for their Easter confession, in spite of the detestable roads and the dismal weather, so wretchedly changeable! Every now and then there came a flaw of rain, and then a warm breeze would blow athwart the orchards, or frozen snow pour down like groats, or the sun look smiling out of the clouds and scatter its gold over all the world. But the weather is usually so in the first days of spring—like a young lass that laughs and cries, and is blithe or sullen, just as it occurs to her, and she herself cannot tell why.

But no one in Hanka's surroundings had any care for the weather just now: work and talk went on with equal noise. Ambrose bustled about, and kept the others lively with his merry jests. He was obliged, however, to pay frequent visits to the church and see that everything there was going on well: on his return, he would complain of the cold and want something to warm him up.

"I have so well beset the priests with penitents, that neither will stir till noon," he said.

"Of the priest from Slupia they say," Yagustynka observed, after a gibe at the incumbent of Laznov which nettled Ambrose not a little, "that he always bears a scent-bottle with him, for that he dislikes the scent of common folk, and fans himself with his handkerchief after every confession."

"You hold your peace, and let priests alone!" Ambrose cried out in a rage.

"Is Roch in church?" Hanka hastened to inquire; she too disliked the old woman's waspish tongue.

"He has been there all the morning, serving Masses, and putting things in order."

"And where is Michael, then?"

"Gone to Rzepki with the organist's son, to make out the confession-list."

"'Plough with a goose-quill, sow paper with sand: ye will get much more pelf than by tilling the land!'" muttered Yagustynka.

"Truly it is so. He gets an egg at least for each name he puts down."

"And the confession-tickets come to a kopek and a half! No wonder his wallets are crammed with good things. Last week the organist's wife sold near upon fifteen hundred eggs."

"Folk say they came on foot, carrying only one small bundle with them: now they could fill over four of the biggest wagons."

Ambrose tried to defend him. "Well, but he has lived and worked here for a score of years and more; and the parish is a big one; and he is hard-working, shrewd and thrifty: of course he has put money by."

"Put money by! Money wrung from the people, and as much as he possibly could! Ere the man will do a service to anyone, he must know what he's to get thereby. Why, he is paid thirty roubles at a funeral: for what?—for thumping on the organ and bleating Latin chants!"

"At any rate, he's a skilled craftsman in his own line, and takes great pains to do his best."

"Aye, aye, he is skilled: knows when to sing shrill and when gruff—and especially how to diddle folk out of their money."

"Another would have drunk away all his earnings; and he is breeding up his son to become a priest."

"To his own exceeding glory and profit," the rancorous beldame rejoined.

At this most interesting point they broke off. Yagna had come in, and stood petrified on the threshold.

"Is it our pig's size that amazes you?" Yagustynka asked, with a laugh.

"Could ye not have done this work on the other side?" she stammered, red as a peony. "My room is all befouled with it."

"Wash and scour it, then! Ye are not short of time," Hanka replied coolly, with a stress on the last words.

Yagna made an angry gesture, but said no more. She walked about the room, took up her "Rosary of the Passion," threw a shawl over her yet unmade bed, and left the hut in silence, her lips twitching with the fury she sought to hide.

Yuzka, who met her in the passage, said: "Ye might well help us, we have so much to do!"

She only stormed at her in reply, and rushed away in a frenzy. Vitek, who had remarked which way she had gone, said she had stepped over straight to the blacksmith's.

"Why should she not? It will relieve her to talk of her grievance."

"But," Yagustynka said, lowering her voice, "ye will have him here speedily . . . and it will be war!"

"Good woman, what's my whole life but warfare?" Hanka answered quietly, but she felt that her words were true, and that a savage quarrel was at hand.

"He will come in a trice," Yagustynka declared, not without compassion.

"Fear not—I shall stand the brunt of the battle," she replied, smiling.

Yagustynka, nodding her admiration, looked significantly at Ambrose, who had just laid his work aside.

"I must look in at church and ring the Angelus," he said. "I shall be back for dinner directly."

And so he was, and told them that the clergymen were dining, and the miller had brought them a netful of fish as a present, and they were to go on hearing confessions in the afternoon, as so many people were waiting.

The dinner, though short and hurried, was well provided with liquor, Ambrose complaining bitterly that, for such herrings— salt as Lot's wife—the vodka was far too weak. Then they set to work again, and he quartered the beast, cutting off the parts fit for sausages; while Yagustynka, having unhinged a door and made it do duty for a table, placed the sides upon it, and was busy cutting them into flitches and salting them carefully. Just at that moment the smith came in; his face showed that he was fighting for self-control.

"I was not aware," he began, sarcastically, "that ye had bought so large a porker."

"Well, I have—and killed it too."

She felt somewhat frightened.

"A fine beast. It must have cost you some thirty roubles."
He eyed it over scrutinizingly.

" 'Twere hard to find a pig so thickly lined with fat," the
old woman remarked, laughing and offering him the bacon to
examine.

" 'Tis Boryna's pig!" he suddenly burst out, unable any
more to contain his rage.

"A shrewd guess!" Yagustynka jeered; "why, to know
whose it is, you need only to see the tail!"

"And by what right have ye dared to slaughter it?" he
cried indignantly.

"No shouting, please. This is not a tavern.—By what
right? Because Antek sent me word by Roch to kill it."

"And who is Antek to give orders here? Is the beast his?"

"Most surely," she replied: her fear had gone from her
now.

"No, it is ours!—For what ye have done, ye shall pay
dear."

"In this matter I am not answerable to you!"

"No?—To whom then?"

"Peace! and hold your tongue. Here lies the sick man to
whom it belongs."

"Which you, not he, will eat!"

"But you, at any rate, shall not so much as smell it!"

"Give me," he said, changing his tone, "one-half of the
carcass. Ye would not have me raise the devil, would ye?"

"Not one trotter of it shall you have on compulsion!"

"Then let me have a quarter—and a flitch thrown in—of
your own free will."

"I will, if Antek orders me. Else you shall not get one
bone."

"Antek! Antek!" he cried, again roused to fury. "Is it
Antek's, then? Are you raving?"

"It is Father's," she said firmly, "but Antek is now in his
place and disposes of all. Later, it shall be whose our Lord
may will it to be."

"Let him dispose in jail of what he has! If he likes husbandry, he may play the husbandman down in Siberia, where he is to go!" he shrieked, foaming at the mouth.

"He may go thither," she retorted fiercely, though fear for Antek was stabbing at her heart; "but were you yet a greater Judas than you are, you would not gain one inch of land thereby."

The smith's feet were shuffling on the floor with excitement, and his hands closing on his capote convulsively, so strong a craving he felt to clutch her by the throat. But he still mastered himself: he was not alone. She had no longer any fear at all: wielding the knife she used to cut the strips of flesh, she looked on the man with quiet scorn. After a time he sat down, lit a cigarette, and gazed about the room with red-rimmed eyes, revolving something in his mind. Presently he got up, and spoke to her calmly.

"Come round to the other side of the hut; we may yet find something to agree upon."

Wiping her hands, she went out of the room, but left the door ajar.

"I wish not only not to go to law, but not even to quarrel," he began, puffing at his cigarette.

"Because it will not serve," she retorted.

"Did Father-in-law say aught to you yesternight?"

The smith was by now quite friendly and smiling.

"Oh, no; he lay as still as he lies now." Full of suspicion, she was on her guard to divulge nothing.

"That pig is but a small matter; let us trouble no longer about it. Cut it up . . . eat it up by yourselves, just as you please: no very great loss for me.—One often says things of which one repents afterwards.—Pray forget what I said.— I want to speak of something more important. You ought to know that they talk in the village of cash—large sums— concealed within this hut. . . ." He paused and fixed his piercing eyes upon her face. "Now 'twere well worth while to seek for it, lest, should he die (which God forbid!), it might be mislaid, or fall into some stranger's hand."

"But will he say where he has hidden it?"

"To you he might, would you but draw him out with cunning words."

"Well, I will do my best; but he must first come to his wits again."

"And if ye keep it secret, and we find the money, then we might share and share alike. Nay, if the sum were large enough, a part might serve to set Antek free. Let no one else know of it: why should any know? Yagna's deed of gift makes her quite rich enough; we might even go to law, and have it annulled.—As to Gregory, think how much he has received during his service in the army!" He approached her more closely.

"You are right . . . quite, quite right," she stammered, struggling hard to give him no inkling of the secret she knew.

"I think he must have concealed it somewhere about the cabin; what think ye?"

"How should I know? He never spoke a word to me about that."

"But he said something yesternight . . . something about corn, I think?" the smith suggested.

"Aye. He said it was to be sown."

"About barrels too, did he not?" he persisted, looking her intently in the face.

"Of course. The seed-corn that's in the barrels," she made answer, apparently not making out to what those questions were tending.

He cursed silently, with bitter disappointment. And yet he felt more and more that she must be privy to the secret. Her face was so stiffly set, her eyes so carefully deprived of expression.

"Tell no one this thing I confide to you."

"Am I such a tale-bearer and everlasting gossip?"

"Well, well, I only caution you.—Now give good heed. The old man has had a glimmer already: his wits may quite come back to him any day."

"God grant it be soon!"

His glance lingered over her. At length, pulling at his moustache, he left her to herself and went out, she following him the while with a contemptuous look.

"A Judas, a traitor, and a thief!"

Exploding with hate, she took a few steps after him.—It was not for the first time that he had flourished before her eyes the awful possibility of Siberia's mines and Antek working in them, fettered to a wheelbarrow!

Not that she believed implicitly all he said; she knew that he spoke out of spite and to make her afraid, so as to get the most he could out of her by bullying.

Nevertheless, she was in great dread, and had carefully sought to be informed what Antek's punishment might be: she had no hope that he would be acquitted.

True, he had acted in defence of his father; but there must be some punishment for the death of the forester. There must!

Such was the opinion of all the more intelligent folk. She had been to consult a lawyer in the town, with a letter from his Reverence to introduce her. He had explained that the penalty might be either very heavy or very light; that patience and money spent without grudging were absolutely requisite here. But she was most terrified by the village people, who shared the blacksmith's view of things.

The words he had now spoken had therefore oppressed her most cruelly. She went on with her work, but felt almost unable to stand; and conversation was impossible. Moreover, when the smith had gone away, his wife came to tend the sick man, drive away the flies (there were none!), and certainly spy over all she did.

Magda, however, was soon tired of the task, and offered to help her in the work. But Hanka replied:

"Do not trouble, we can do all by ourselves: have you not work enough in your house?"

Her tone was so decided that Magda gave up the attempt, and only tried at times to join timidly in the talk, being by nature a shy and reticent woman.

But that same evening, who should make her appearance once more but Yagna, in her mother's company!

They greeted her as if on excellent terms, and in so friendly and flattering a way that Hanka, touched by their kindness, answered them in like manner, sparing neither pleasant speeches nor vodka, though she kept on the watch nevertheless. But Dominikova put the glass away from her.

"What! in the Holy Week? How could I drink vodka at such a time?"

Hanka maintained that it was no sin to drink even then, on such an occasion and in one's own house.

"Ah!" groaned Dominikova, "one is always but too ready to find an excuse to let oneself go, and enjoy pleasure!"

"Mistress, drink to me," Ambrose exclaimed; "I have not an organist's scruples."

"To you the very sound of glasses when they clink is a temptation," Dominikova grumbled, as she set to work at the sick man's bandages.

"Poor creature!" she cried in pity; "lying there insensible, with all God's world lost to him!"

"And not to taste sausage or vodka again for ever!" Yagustynka chimed in, turning the pity into a gibe.

Dominikova rebuked her tartly: "You laugh at everything, you!"

"Shall weeping lessen my pain? My laughter is all my fortune."

Ambrose remarked: "Let those only that have sown evil garner in sorrow, and atone for it by penance!" This was a shrewd hit at Dominikova, who retorted, glaring on him sternly:

"They say truly that Ambrose, though he serves in church, curries favour with sin in order to enjoy the good things of this life!" And she added, lowering her tone threateningly: "But he alone will turn away from the good and befriend the wicked, who considereth not the punishment which he shall receive hereafter!"

Silence fell upon all. Ambrose worked on, though surly.

He had a sharp retort ready, but kept it back, knowing well that anything he said would be reported to his Reverence the next day, and after Mass at latest: it was to some purpose that the old dame was such a church-goer. Everyone, besides, shrank from the fixed gaze of those owlish eyes of hers; even Yagustynka, the defiant, was overawed and quailed before her.

Yes, and so did all the village. More than one had experienced the power of those evil eyes; more than one, on whom she had laid a spell, now groaned with twisted limbs, or in the clutch of some dire disease!

They worked on then, with bowed heads: only her face, rugged, withered, and white as bleached wax, was seen towering amongst them in the room. She too remained silent, along with Yagna; but they were both so active and diligent that Hanka had not the heart to refuse the aid they were giving.

But after Ambrose had left, called away to church by the priest's servant, they remained alone, diligently packing flitches and pork into the tubs and barrels.

"The meat will be cooler in the larder that's on this side, for the fire here is much smaller," the old dame decided, rolling the vessels in there at once, with the help of Yagna.

All this was done so quickly that they were put in the larder before Hanka had time even to protest. She was extremely mortified, and, immediately calling Pete and Yuzka to her aid, carried over to her own side all that remained.

At dusk and by lamplight they set to making sausages, blood-puddings, and brawn. Hanka, whose annoyance had not passed away, sat mincing the materials with a sort of dark rage.

"Leave the things here, for her to eat or steal? Not I!— . . . But oh, the cunning hag!" she hissed through her clenched teeth.

"To-morrow morning, when she has gone to church, you can carry everything out into your own larder without noise or fuss. Surely she will not break in and take it back by

force!" Such was the advice of Yagustynka, as she pressed
the ingredients of the sausages into the long dried guts,
writhing upon the table like serpents, and every now and
then hung them up to be smoked in the chimney.

"Ah! the stroke was planned between them, and they came
on purpose for that!"

She was exasperated.

"The sausages will all be made ere Ambrose be back here,"
the old woman observed.

Hanka would speak no more, absorbed in work, and in
planning how to get the hams and flitches into her possession
again.

The fire crackled on the hearth with a lively flame; the
whole room was in a glow, and the various ingredients of
the blood-puddings were bubbling in several cauldrons.

"O Lord! my mouth waters at the very smell!" sighed
Vitek, sniffing greedily.

"Do not stand sniffing here, or I will know why!" cried
Hanka. "Give the kine to drink, fill the mangers with hay,
and put straw under them. 'Tis late already . . . when
will you have done it all?"

"Pete is coming; I cannot do all by myself."

"And whither has he gone?"

"What, know ye not? He is helping them to put things in
order on the other side."

"Oho!—Hey, you, Pete!" she cried, calling out into the
passage. "See to the cattle for the night—at once!"

Her tone, as she gave that order, had been such that the
man came out instantly into the yard.

"Let her stir herself and clean her own room at least!
Look at her, that grand lady—will not soil her hands—must
needs employ a manservant!" So said Hanka, in a towering passion, whilst pouring out a steaming potful of liver and
chitterlings. The sound of a bell and a cart clattering by
outside gave another turn to her thoughts.

It was the priest, carrying the Holy Viaticum to someone,
as her father, old Bylitsa, who then came in, told her.

"But who can it be? No one was ill, so far as I know."

"He has passed the Voyt's cabin!" Vitek, out of breath, came shouting outside the window.

"To one of the *Komorniki?* I think not."

"Perhaps to your people, the Prycheks, Yagustynka; they live that way."

"Ah, nothing ever was the matter with them, the miscreants; no evil ever comes nigh them!" she said, in a faltering voice: though constantly at odds with her children, she felt a quiver of anxiety.

"I'll see how matters stand and return at once." And she hurried out.

But the evening dragged on, and yet she was not back.— Ambrose, who had returned, said the priest had been called in to Agata, a kinswoman of the Klembas: she had come back from begging only the Saturday before.

"But how is that? Is she not at the Klembas'?"

"No; she has removed to die: either at Koziol's or at the Prycheks'."

There was no more talk then, for there was much work to get through, especially as both Yuzka and Hanka were often obliged to leave it for the byre or the stable.

It was dark outside, and irksome within.

A chilly rain was pelting, and the wind lashed the walls, whistled through the orchards, made the trees rustle and murmur, and sometimes blew down the chimneys, scattering fire-brands about.

It was hard upon midnight when all the work was over— and Yagustynka had not yet returned.

"In such foul weather, she must have been loath to grope her way back!" Hanka thought, while she patrolled the premises before going to bed.

Truly, it had been a pity to turn a dog out of doors on such a night! The roof creaked with the wild blasts; all over the sky, brown masses of rain-clouds were pouring down their heavy burden of water; and nowhere on high was there the least twinkle of starlight. Everybody else had long ago gone to sleep; the wind danced and revelled in the fields, and swept great sheets of water from off the pond.

So they waited no longer for her, but went to bed.

She appeared the next morning, but as louring and sullen as the swampy miry day itself. She just warmed her hands at the cabin fire, and then made for the granary, to pick out seed-potatoes from the heap which had been dumped down on the threshing-floor.

She was mostly alone at that work, Yuzka having to go and scatter the dung which Pete had been carting since day-break. Having been soundly rated by Hanka for sloth on the day before, he now, to make amends, stormed at Vitek, flogged the horses furiously, and made them splash through the mud at full speed.

"The rascal!" muttered the old woman. "To punish the horses because he himself was lazy!"

When Yuzka spoke to her, she gave her no answer, but sat gloomily, hiding her eyes red with tears under the apron she had thrown over her head.

Hanka looked in, but only once. She was waiting for Yagna to come out, that she might have an opportunity both to take the meat over to her own side, and to examine the corn-barrels. But, as if of set purpose, Yagna never left the hut.

Impatient, Hanka at last went in to see Boryna, and then—apparently seeking for something—she entered the larder.

"Whatever ye want I can find for you!" Yagna exclaimed, and, seeing her go in, followed before she had done more than plunge her hand into the corn.—Fruitlessly; but the money might be lying quite at the bottom. She left the place; and, certain that Yagna was on the watch, resolved to put off the attempt to a more convenient season.

"And now for the gifts we must make," she thought, look-ing sorrowfully at the sausages that dangled in a row from a horizontal pole. Boryna and all the foremost husbandmen were in the habit, whenever they killed a pig, to send their next relations and best friends a sausage, or some other dainty bit.

" 'Tis hard, in truth; but you can do no otherwise, or they

would say you grudge them," Bylitsa advised her, guessing aright what was in her thoughts.

In spite, then, of the temptation to shirk that duty, she put the intended presents on a number of plates and dishes, now substituting a larger for a smaller piece, now the reverse, now adding, now taking away a blood-pudding . . . and so on: until she had done, and, dejected and weary, called for Yuzka.

"Put on your best garments, and take these things round."

"O Lord! what a quantity of meat is here!"

"What can I do? I must give it away. We have to live with folk.—'Jack his flail can whisk alone, but not dance and frisk alone.'—This big piece take to Uncle's wife. She hates and rates me; but there's no help for it.—This to the Voyt: a rascal, but on good terms with Matthias, and (it may be) serviceable one day.—For Magda and her smith, a whole blood-pudding, a sausage, and a piece of bacon. They shall not say we have eaten Father's pig by ourselves. Talk against us they will, of course, but less.—This sausage is for Prychkova. She's saucy, bitter of tongue, but one of our best friends.—And this last piece for Klembova."

"Shall Dominikova get naught?"

"Later in the afternoon. Of course she shall. She's to be dealt with as filth: with care and from afar. . . . Now take these things round separately, and waste no time in talk with other girls, for there is work at home for you."

"Do give Nastka something: they are all so poor!" Yuzka said beseechingly. "They have scarce wherewith to buy salt!"

"Let her come: she shall get something.—Father, take this to Veronka; she was to have looked in yesterday."

"She had to clean the miller's cabin in the afternoon; they are expecting visitors."

Hanka, having sent Yuzka off, and put on a warmer dress, ran out to see that the lads worked properly, and to assist Yagustynka.

To the old woman, now so strangely reticent, she said: "We hoped you would come back for supper."

"What I saw was supper enough for me—and it lies on my stomach yet."

"It was Agata, I believe?"

"Yes, poor thing! Passing away . . . and in Koziol's hut!"

"Why is she not at the Klembas'?"

"Because those folk, as long as a kinsman asks for naught, or comes full-handed, allow him to claim kindred; but would set their dogs on any other, how near soever!"

"What say you? Surely they have not driven her out?"

"Well, she came to them on Saturday, and was taken with a sickness that same night. . . . They say that Klembova took away her feather-bed, and turned her out almost naked."

"Klembova? Can it be? So good a woman!—Nay, it must be a slander."

"I invent naught, and tell you only what mine ears have heard."

"At Koziol's too! Who would have thought the woman so merciful?"

" 'For ready money—'tis strange, but true—even a priest will be kind to you!'—Koziol's wife has got a score of *zloty* out of Agata in cash. For that sum she will keep her till she drops off—which she expects to do any day. . . . Funeral extra, of course.—She will give up the ghost one of these days: there will be no long waiting, oh, no!"

She broke down, unable to choke down a sob.

"What ails you, my dear?" Hanka asked, in a kindly tone.

"I have supped full of human woes, and have eaten over measure! One's heart is not a stone; one tries to harden it by churlishness towards everyone; but it will not do. And there comes a time when it can bear no more, and crumbles away to sand with the pain of it!"

She burst into a tempest of tears, shaking all over; but, after a time, went on speaking, but with such heat and bitterness that the words burned into Hanka's tender heart.

"And to this desolation there is no end—none! When the priest left Agata, I stayed by her side. Then there came

one from over the water—Philip's wife—crying out that her
eldest daughter was a-dying. . . . Away I hurried to her.—
Lord, what a hut! as cold as ice itself! Window-panes gone,
wisps of straw instead. Only one bed: the others sleep on
litter, like kennelled dogs.—Aye, the girl is dying, but of
what? Of hunger! Their last potato is eaten, their feather-
bed sold: every litre of groats is got from the miller by begging, for no one will lend aught to tide things over till harvest. Who could pay? Philip is in jail with the rest of
them.—Scarcely had I left these, when Gregory's wife told
me that Florka Prychkova had been brought to bed and was
in want of aid. . . . Vile wretches they are, and have de-
frauded me: but I went notwithstanding. In their hut, too,
misery shows her teeth! Lots of children—Florka abed—
not a kopek of savings—and no help from anywhither.
True, the land is theirs: but can they eat it?—No one to
cook for them. . . . And their land is untilled, for Adam,
her goodman, is in prison likewise.—A son has been born to
her—a strong lusty little fellow—but will he get food to live?
Florka is thin as a lath—not one drop of milk can she
give him; and their cow has but just calved. All is for the
worst everywhere. No one to work, and no work to be got;
and neither money nor help from any quarter. . . . Oh,
would that our Lord might send all these poorest folk a
merciful death! They would not then suffer so!"

"Has anyone in the village aught to spare?" said Hanka.
"All are poor, and the cry of misery is heard everywhere."

"'Who has no goodwill shirks his duty still.'—I do not
say this to you; the farm is not yours, and I know well what
ye have to undergo. But there be those who might do
something: the miller—the priest—the organist—and many
others."

"Perhaps they would, if they were but told of all," Hanka
said, taking their part.

"He that has a kindly heart needs no telling, and finds
it out by himself. My dear, they are well aware of what the
poor have to endure: it is on their very poverty that they
thrive and grow fat. Why, 'tis now the miller's harvest-

home, when folk are crowding round him for flour and
groats, giving up their last mite to him, or taking loans at
high interest, to be paid in future work: money for food
must be found, even should one be forced to sell one's bed
to the Jew!"

"Indeed, no one is willing to give things gratis," Hanka
said with a heavy sigh, as the memory of her recent past
surged up.

"I sat with Florka for a long time," Yagustynka went on to
say; "and many women came in, telling us what was going
on in Lipka. They said——"

"Mercy on us!" Hanka suddenly exclaimed, starting to
her feet. A gust had just blown the door in, so violently as
almost to wrench it off its hinges. And she had closed it
with such care, and placed stakes to prop it up against the
wind!

"With such a gale as this, I fear there will soon be more
rain."

"As it is, the carts afield already sink axle-deep in mire!"

"But with a few days of warm sun, the ground will soon
be dry again: 'tis spring."

"Ah, if we could but begin to plant potatoes ere Eastertide!"

So they went on talking, busy with their work, and the potatoes drummed upon the floor continuously: those too small
thrown on to one heap, and the damaged ones on to another.

"These will fatten your sow, and the kine will drink the
boiled water."

But Hanka was scarcely listening, pondering how to get at
her father-in-law's money. At times she looked out through
the open door at the trees, waving and wrestling with the
blasts, that were cold and damp, and pungent with the smell
of the dunghill close by. The farm-yard was empty, save
for a few fowls running about with ruffled feathers. The
geese all sat in a corner close to the hedge, and gathered their
chuckling little ones under their wings. Now and again Pete
came in, driving his empty wagon, and slapping his arms
against his sides; then, giving the horses a bundle of hay,

and (Vitek aiding) filling the cart with dung, he pushed
it on over the ruts and holes, and drove away into the
fields once more.

Many a time, too, did Yuzka hurry in, loud-voiced,
blowzed, breathless, on her way to somebody's cabin with
presents, and chattering all the way as she came and went.

Unquestioned, she talked and talked, and was presently
seen starting again, bearing a dish carefully wrapped up in
a napkin.

"A chatterbox that girl is, but no fool," Yagustynka observed.

"No fool, indeed; only she has naught in her head but mischief and games."

"What would you have?   Such a tiny thing!"

"Vitek!" Hanka cried on a sudden.   "Someone has entered
the cabin.   See who it is."

" 'Tis the blacksmith, just come in."

A misgiving took hold of her, and she went straightway to
her father's side, where he was lying—on his back, as usual—
while Yagna sewed at the window.   No one else was there.

"What has become of Michael?"

"Somewhere about, seeking a key he lent to Matthias not
long ago," she explained, without looking Hanka in the face.

The latter went into the passage, into her own room, where
Bylitsa was sitting with the children by the fire, and making
them little toy windmills—even into the farm-yard buildings: he was nowhere in sight.   Then back she darted
straight to the larder on her father's side, though the door
was shut.

And there she saw the blacksmith, standing beside a corn-
barrel, with his arms buried in the corn up to the elbows,
and seeking something there with might and main!

"What!" she cried with a gasp; "your key is hidden in the
corn, is it?"   And she placed herself in front of him with
a threatening air.

"No . . . I am seeing . . . whether it is not mildewed
. . . and whether it will do for seed-corn," he said, stutter-
ing, taken quite by surprise.

"What business of yours is that? Say, what brings you in here?" she cried.

Unwillingly, he drew his arms out, and muttered with ill-concealed anger:

"Ye spy upon me as if I were a thief!"

"How should I know what business brings you in here? Here's a fellow who enters other people's premises: why? I find him groping in the corn-barrels: why should he not also wrench the padlocks off, or break open the chests?" Her voice was rising to a scream.

"Did I not tell you yesterday what we have to look for?" he answered, striving to be calm.

"What ye said was all a blind. You sought to throw dust in my eyes, while you were after something else. But I saw through your plotting, you traitor, you!"

"Hanka!" he shrieked, to terrify her; "stop that talk, or I will stop your mouth!"

"Would ye? Lay but a finger on me, and I'll raise such an outcry that half the village will be here in a trice, to learn what sort of a jail-bird you are!"

As she uttered the threat, he cast one more glance around; then, with a blasphemous oath, he left the room; exchanging with her, as he did so, looks that—had it been possible—would have stabbed to the very heart.

Hanka's outbreak had completely upset her, but a cup of water presently brought her round again.

"It must be found!—And also concealed in a safe place: for what money soever that man finds, he will make off with," was her mental comment, going back to the granary. But, half-way there, she stopped and went back to the cottage. Opening the door, she apostrophized Yagna thus:

"You who sit here in the cabin to watch over it, how do you let a stranger enter the inmost room?"

Yagna answered scornfully: "Michael is not a stranger: he has as much right in there as you have."

"A dog barks, and you lie! Ye two are in league together; but mark well what I say.—If aught disappear from the cottage, then, as sure as there's a God in heaven, I'll bring ac-

tion and denounce you as his accomplice. Remember that!"
she screamed, infuriated.

Yagna, snatching the first weapon at hand, leaped from her
seat.

"Would you fight me? Do but try: I'll tear the beauty
off your dainty face, and paint it such a scarlet that your
own mother shall not know you!"

And she went on upbraiding and vilifying her to the full-
est powers of her voice and of her enmity.

How this might have ended cannot be guessed. They were
about to close with each other, when Roch happened to come
in. This brought Hanka to her senses in so far that she
spoke no more. But she rushed from the room, and the door
slammed like thunder behind her.

Yagna remained still for some time, her bosom palpi-
tating, her lips trembling like one with the ague. At length,
flinging into a corner the small hand-mangle she had
clutched, she threw herself upon the bed, and gave way to
an uncontrollable burst of pitiful wailing.

Meanwhile, Hanka, on her side of the house, was telling
Roch what had taken place. He listened patiently to her
tale; but it was so incoherent and broken with sobs that he
could scarcely make out a word, and rebuked her very
severely. Putting aside the food she had set before him, he
reached out for his cap, in great indignation.

"I am going away, never to set eyes on Lipka again, since
ye behave thus! Oh, how all this must rejoice the Evil
One, aye, and those Jews who make a mock at us Christians,
calling us brawling idiots! O merciful Jesus! was there too
little of distress and sickness and starvation, that, to crown
all, women must also fly at one another!"

He stood panting after this appeal; and Hanka, seized
with contrition and dread lest he should leave them in anger,
kissed his hand and earnestly begged for pardon.

"Ah!" she added, "if ye but knew how hard it is to dwell
with her! She does everything to spite and injure me. . . .
Her very being here is a wrong done to us all! . . . So many
an acre of land made over to her! . . . And then—know ye

not what manner of woman she is? and what she does with
young men?" (No, it was beyond her power to bring in
Antek's name.) "And now," she added with bated breath,
"they say that she is sinning with the Voyt!—Therefore,
when I behold her, all within me seethes with hatred, even to
slaying!"

"Vengeance is mine, saith the Lord! She too is human,
and she feels it, if any do her wrong. And for her sins she
must some day suffer heavy chastisement. I tell you, then,
do no wrong to her."

"What! have I wronged her in aught?"

She stood amazed, unable to conceive in what way Yagna
could have suffered wrong at her hands.

Roch ate a morsel of bread, looking out into vacancy meanwhile, and thinking deeply. At last he departed, after having patted the heads of the little ones that came to his knees.

"One of these days, I shall look in again at eventide.
But now I say to you only this: Let her alone, do your duty
and our Lord will see to all the rest."

CHAPTER IV ✓

R OCH, grieving bitterly over all the evil in the village, walked slowly on along the shores of the pond. Yes, things were so bad in Lipka that they could not possibly be worse.

That diseases prevailed; that some died of starvation; that quarrels and fighting were rife amongst them; and that death was now taking a heavier toll than in preceding years: all that was not the very worst. To such things the people were accustomed, and bowed to them as to the inevitable. The worst of all was this: that the fields lay untilled, there being no one to till them.

The spring had come, with all her train of birds, now returning to their last year's nests; the fields were drying on the uplands, the waters draining away everywhere; and the land simply cried out to be ploughed, and manured, and blessed with the sacred blessing which the sower gives.

But who could go afield? All had gone to prison. Only women remained, with neither vigour of arm nor of brain to do things aright.

Moreover, for some of them the time of childbirth had arrived, as is usual in spring; and cows were calving, fowls hatching, swine farrowing. Then it was the season to sow and plant the gardens. Potatoes awaited selection, dung had to be carted, water drawn off from the fields. Without men to help, they could never do all that, even should they wear their arms to stumps. And besides, feeding and watering cattle, cutting straw for fodder, chopping up fuel or bringing it in from the forest, and a thousand other duties (such, for instance, as caring for the innumerable children running about everywhere)—ah, well! it was wearing toil, O Lord! and in the evening one's bones and loins ached grievously, and not half the work done! V

And the land lay there, expectant. Warmed by the sun, dried by the breezes, drinking in the soft fertilizing rains and the sweet influence of those spring nights, it began to teem with green blades of thick grass, and wheat swiftly sprouting. Larks trilled over the plains, and storks wandered in the wet meadows, and many a flower in the marshes now raised its head towards the shining sky; that sky which daily, like a beautiful tent spread out above them, seemed to rise higher and farther from the earth. And now their longing eyes could distinguish far away the sharp outlines of woods and hamlets, never visible in the dusky days of winter; and the whole country-side, awaking as out of a death-trance, arrayed itself joyfully like a bride for her wedding-day.

Everywhere around Lipka, as far as the eye could see, men were hard at work. Whether in fair or in rainy weather, the air thrilled with merry songs, ploughs glittered athwart the fields, men were trudging, horses neighing, wagons rumbling blithely. Only the fields of Lipka lay waste and silent, like a vast mournful burial-ground.

Over and above all this, anxiety for the dear ones in prison tortured them.

Hardly a day passed by without several people trudging to town, bearing bundles of food on their backs for the captives, and vain requests that they, being innocent, should be set free.

In short, the state of the village was deplorable; and the men of the vicinity now began to see that the injury done to their neighbours was also done to the whole peasant class. "Only apes are foes to apes," they said; "we, who are men, ought to stand up for our brethren, lest the same fate befall us likewise."

So it came to pass that the other villagers, who had formerly quarrelled with the men of Lipka over territorial limits and matters of like nature, or out of envy, because these had set themselves above their neighbours and claimed superiority over them—now set aside all such bickerings, and often came to Lipka in secret to ascertain the truth of the matter: some from Rudki, others from Volka or Debitsa, or even men who were of the "nobility" of Rzepki.

The day before, when they came for their Easter confession, they had inquired diligently about the prisoners, and their faces had set fiercely, while they heard; and they broke out into curses on the injustice done, and pitied the people that had suffered so much.

Roch was thinking of this event, and pondering over a certain important step to take, frequently stopping to shelter himself against the wind, with a far-off look in his eyes.

It was brighter and warmer now, but the wind increased steadily, and roared all over the country. It made some of the slenderer saplings bow deeply, sighing and lashing the pond with their whip-like boughs; it tore off fragments of thatch from the roofs, snapped the brittle boughs, and swept overhead with such violence that everything seemed in motion and tossing about: orchards, palings, cabins, solitary trees—all, as it were, moved along with it; nay, even the pallid sun itself, emerging now and then from the scudding clouds, appeared fleeing precipitately through the sky. And over the church a flock of wild birds, with outspread wings, sailed down the wind, unable to make head against its might.

Yet, notwithstanding the harm it did, it did also great service in drying the lands, which ever since morning were taking a lighter tinge, while it swept the roads clear of water.

Roch was roused from the thoughts which absorbed him so deeply, by the sound of quarrelling voices. He hastily drew near.

One quick glance showed him a large crowd of women, in red petticoats, surrounding a group of men on the farther side of the pond, in front of the hut where the Soltys lived and in all the enclosures thereabouts.

He went forward quickly, eager to know what was the matter; but, recognizing the men for a company of gendarmes along with the Voyt, he turned off into the nearest enclosures, whence he drew nigh the throng, creeping cautiously from orchard to orchard; for somehow he objected to meeting the eyes of the police.

The tumult increased. Women were in the majority; children, too, had flocked there from every side, edging in amongst their elders, pushing and elbowing one another, overflowing the enclosures and pouring out into the roads, with little heed either of the deep mud or of the lashing boughs. All were babbling together; sometimes one voice rose above another, but there was no making out what was said; the gale was too high. Looking through the trees, Roch could perceive only that Ploshkova headed them all: a big fat crimson-faced woman, who cried out louder than anyone else and, shaking her fist furiously under the Voyt's very nose, made him shrink back, while the others screamed their approval, like a flock of offended turkeys. The wife of Kobus also was there, on the skirts of the crowd, vainly striving to get at the gendarmes, against whom many a fist was shaken, and here and there a stick or dirty broom.

The Voyt, sorely embarrassed, was trying to appease them and scratching his head, while drawing the women's onslaught on to himself, so that the gendarmes cunningly managed to extricate themselves from the throng, and retired in the direction of the mill. The Voyt, following in the rear, continued to answer them back and threaten the boys who had begun to pelt him with mud.

"What do they want?" Roch asked of the assembled women.

"They would have our village supply them with twenty wagons, horses and men, for road-mending in the forest!" Ploshkova told him.

"Some big official is to pass this way, and they want to get the holes in the road filled up."

"Neither wagons nor horses nor men! we have said."

"Who is here that can drive?"

"Let them set our lads free first: then we shall think about the roads!"

"The Squire! let them put him to a wagon!"

"Or set to work themselves, and keep their snouts out of our cabins."

"Ah! the hounds, the carrions, the scurvy knaves!" many voices shouted at once, in a rising chorus.

"All the morning they have been with the Voyt, laying their heads together in the tavern."

"Aye, aye, drinking vodka, and then going round to every hut for labourers!"

"But the Voyt knows the state of affairs perfectly well," said Roch, vainly attempting to make himself heard in the tumult. "He ought to have explained matters at the Bureau."

"He! He is the best friend of our enemies!"

"He only cares to get money!" they all shouted again.

"Yes, he advised us to give them a score of eggs, or a fowl per hut: then they would let us alone, and press men to work from the other villages."

"A score of stones for him rather!"

"Peace, good woman; ye might smart for contempt of an official."

"I don't care. Let them take me to jail. I'll stand up to the very biggest official and tell him what injustice we have to bear."

"Afraid of the Voyt? What, I?" Ploshkova cried. "The tainted wretch! I fear a scarecrow as much as him! He forgets that 'tis we that have made him Voyt, and what we have made we can unmake."

"He would punish us, would he? Do we not pay taxes, send our boys to the army, do whatever they tell us? Is it too little for them that they have taken our men from our midst?"

"Whenever they show their faces, some evil attends them."

"They shot my dog in the fields last harvest-time!"

"They had me before the court, because my chimney took fire!"

"And what a flogging they gave young Gulbas for flinging a stone at them!"

All were crowding around Roch and shouting together. He cried out:

"Can screaming serve your turn? Be quiet!"

"Then go ye to the Voyt and lay the matter before him!"
Kobusova the fiery suggested.

"Else we go thither—and our brooms with us!"

"Go I will; but only after you have dispersed. Now,
pray, off with you: each has so much to do at home!—I
shall lay the matter before him fitly." He spoke very earnestly, fearing lest the gendarmes might return.

The noonday Angelus was sounding from the belfry.
They slowly left the place to talk things over in eager excitement, standing in knots outside their cabins.

Roch went hurriedly to the Soltys, at whose house he was
then dwelling, as he taught the children in the empty cabin
of the Sikoras, down beyond the tavern, at the other end of
the village. But the Soltys was not at home, having driven
over to the district town with tax-payments.

Soha's wife told him of all that had happened, but in a
quiet subdued manner, and wound up by saying:

"God grant that no harm may come of these disturb-
ances!"

"'Tis the Voyt's fault. The gendarmes only do as they
are bid. But he is well aware that there are, so to say, only
women left in the village, and that they have no one to work
on their own fields, let alone working for the government. I
shall go and get him to arrange matters, so that no fines be
imposed."

"It looks very much like revenge taken for the forest business," she remarked.

"Taken by whom?—by the Squire? My good dame, what
has he to do with the Administration?"

"Gentlefolk always agree better with gentlefolk, and are
hand in glove with each other. Besides, he said he would
be even with the Lipka folk."

"Good God! not a single day of peace—always some
fresh affliction coming upon us!"

"May nothing worse than this befall us, I pray God!"
she answered, clasping her hands in supplication.

"They were all screaming together like a flock of magpies,
and, Lord protect us! how they gabbled!"

"He that itches will scratch!"

"But it can do no good, and may bring still greater harm!"

He was sorely agitated and apprehensive of some yet greater impending evil.

"Are ye," she asked, "returning to the little ones?"

He had risen from his seat.

"I have sent them home. Easter holidays have come, and besides, they will be wanted in the house, where so much is to be done."

"I went this morning to hire labourers in Vola, offering three *złoty* a day and their board, but could get no one. Everyone wants to plough his own fields first. They promised to come, but only in a week or two."

"My God!" he said, heaving a sigh; "one man has only a couple of arms: what can he do?"

"Ah, but ye are of use to the folk, and of no little use. Were it not for your wise head and kind heart, I cannot tell what would become of us."

"Could I do all I long to do, there would be an end of suffering on earth!"

He threw out his arms with a gesture of pained helplessness, and hastened away to the Voyt's dwelling. But it was long before he got there; cottage after cottage attracted him.

The village had somewhat quieted down. Some of the more excitable women were still loud in talk outside their cabins, but the greater part had gone to cook the dinner. Only the wind howled along the roads and swept through the trees as heretofore.

But presently, dinner over, and the gale notwithstanding, the whole place was swarming with folk, and an increasing clatter of women's tongues resounded about the gardens, in every part of the farm-yards, before the huts, in the passages and in the rooms they led to. For only women and lasses were toiling there; of males, there were only little boys.

They were all the more feverishly earnest in their work because the day before had been a sort of half-holiday, with

the confessions to the priests who had come; and the morning
had been lost because of the gendarmes.

Easter was near, Holy Tuesday had come already, and so
much still to be done! A spring cleaning was necessary,
clothes had to be made for the children, and in some cases
for the grown-ups too; and corn required to be ground, and
the Hallow-fare to be got ready! In every cottage the goodwives' brains were whirling to find out how all this was to
be accomplished. Most carefully did they look through
their store-rooms for anything to be either sold to the tavern-
keeper or taken over to town to get the needful funds. Several women even drove off at once after dinner, with saleables
under the litter in their carts.

"I hope no tree may fall on you by the way!" Roch said
warningly to Gulbas' wife, who had such a wretched jade
to her cart that it scarcely made any headway against the
wind.

And with that he entered her farm-yard, where the girls,
who had been trying to plaster up the chinks, could reach
no higher than the tops of the windows. In that work he
helped them, made some slaked lime in a tub for the white-
wash, and a sort of straw brush to lay it on.

Then he walked on to Vahnik's, where the lasses were carting dung, but so clumsily that half of it fell out into the road,
while they pulled the unruly horse along by the bridle.
Up came Roch, shovelled the dung into the cart, set all to
rights there, and whipped the horse into obedience.

Farther, at Balcerek's, there was Mary, held to be (bar-
ring Yagna Borynova) the comeliest girl in the village, sowing peas in black and highly manured soil close to the hedgerow. But she wriggled about like a fly caught in resin, her
kerchief twisted round her head, and her father's capote put
on over her petticoat to protect it, and trailing on the ground.

"No need to hasten so; you have plenty of time!" he said,
smiling, as he drew near.

"Why, know ye not, 'If peas be on Holy Tuesday sown,
each gallon will give you a bushel when grown'?" she cried
in response.

"Ere your sowing be ended, those first sown will be out. But, Mary! ye cast the seed too thick; when they come up, they will lie in a tangle on the ground."

And he taught her how to sow as the wind blew; the silly girl had never thought of making the peas drop equally everywhere.

"Vavrek Soha had told me you were a handy lass," he remarked casually, as it were, while retracing his steps along the miry furrow.

"Have ye spoken with him?" she asked, stopping in her work, and suddenly out of breath.

She had flushed a dark crimson, but was ashamed to repeat her question.

Roch's only answer was a smile; but, as he left her, he said: "At Eastertide I shall tell him with what a will you work."

Again, on the lands of the Ploshka, a couple of little boys were at work on a potato-field hard by the road. One drove, the other meant to plough. But as each of them hardly reached to the mare's tail, and had next to no strength at all, the plough zigzagged like a tipsy man, and the mare was ever and anon for going back to the stable. At which they both used the whip on her, and also bad language.

"We can manage, Roch, we can manage; 'tis only these nasty stones twist the plough awry, and the mare would fain go to the manger," the elder one blubbered, to excuse himself, when Roch took the handles and traced a straight furrow, teaching him meanwhile how to deal with the mare.

"But now," the boy cried boldly, "we shall have ploughed the whole field ere nightfall!" He peered round suspiciously, to see whether anyone had been witness to Roch's assistance; and when the old man had gone, he seated himself on the plough, turned away from the wind (as he had seen his father do), and lit a cigarette.

Roch went on, looking about him to help where help was required.

Silencing brawls, settling disputes, giving good advice, he also came in aid, however hard the work, whenever aid was wanted. Klemba's wife could not chop up a hard knotty stump—he did it for her; Dominikova required water from the pond—he brought it; and, farther on, children were wayward, and he awed them into obedience.

A wise and pious man, and one who knew people as few did, he knew at one glance what to say and how to say it; how to drive away sadness with a merry tale; how to laugh with one, pray with another, and reprove a third with words of grave wisdom or stern warning.

So kind-hearted was he, so full of sympathy for all, that he would often and unasked spend many a night by a sickbed: and to the sick he did so much good that they set him even above his Reverence.

In time, folk had begun to look upon him as one of God's saints, who always brought mercy and consolation to their lowly huts.

Alas! could he ward off all misery? Could he prevent all misfortune, feed all the hungry, heal all the sick, and alone supply the many hands they stood in need of?

For, indeed, the village was a large one. Of dwelling-houses alone there were hard on threescore, and a great expanse of cornland stretched round them; there was also much cattle, plenty of other live stock, and many a mouth to feed besides.

All this, since the men had been taken away, now lived mostly by God's providence alone; and so, as a matter of course, their troubles and needs, their complaints and murmurs, multiplied very much indeed.

This Roch had long known and realized; but it was only that day, when going from door to door through the village, that he saw how fearfully all had gone to rack and ruin.

That the fields now lay fallow, no one ploughing or sowing (for the little that they did was mere child's play), was but a lesser evil. Wherever you went, you could see the spread of gradual decay: fences knocked down, beams and rafters peeping through the torn thatches, gates wrenched from their hinges, hanging like broken wings, and flapping against the walls; and many a cabin, too, leaning much out of the perpendicular, and sorely in need of beams to buttress it.

All about the huts were pools of stagnant water, or mud and filth up to the knees around the walls: which made walking no easy matter. At every step the desolation and downfall of the village was so evident that it made the heart bleed. In many a homestead, too, the kine would often low in vain for their fodder, and the horses, with no one to curry them, were caked and plastered with dung.

So it was everywhere. The very calves, with mud all over them, would wander alone about the roads; household utensils rotted in the rain, ploughs rusted away, sows farrowed in the wagon-baskets. When anything was warped or torn or broken, it remained as it was: who was there to set things to rights?

The women?—Why, they, poor things! had scarce time and strength to do what was most urgent. Ah! but if the men came back, then things would change in the twinkle of an eye!

And they therefore awaited their return as a great mercy of God, and, trusting in Him from day to day, possessed their souls—as well as they could—in patience.

Yet neither did the men return, nor was it possible to know when they would be set free.

Twilight was scattering greyness over the land, when Roch left the last hut beyond the church (that of the Golabs) and plodded over to meet the Voyt.

The gale had by no means abated, and fought with the trees so fiercely that walking was perilous: every now and then the broken limb of a tree would be hurled to the ground.

Stooping forward, the old man glided along by the fences, hardly visible through the eerie grey twilight, opaque as powdered glass.

"Are ye seeking the Voyt? He is not at home, but at the miller's," said Yagustynka, appearing unexpectedly.

He turned suddenly, and made for the mill; he could not bear that old mischief-maker.

She, however, following and walking fast at his side, said in a low whisper:

"Pray look in at the Prycheks'—and at Philip's too—I beg you."

"If I can be of any use . . ."

"They begged me so to ask you.—Pray visit them!"

"Good, but I must see the Voyt first."

"Thanks, and God bless you!"

He felt her lips tremble as she kissed his hand. He was amazed: she had usually been on skirmishing terms with him.

"To everyone," she said further, "there comes a time when, like a stray dog, driven away by all folk, one is glad to be caressed by some kindly hand." And ere he could find a word to reply, she hurried away.

He was told that the Voyt was no longer at the miller's, but had driven over to town with the gendarmes. And Franek ushered him into his own little room, where several people from Lipka and the neighbouring villages were sitting to have their corn ground. Roch would have waited there, but Tereska, the soldier's wife, who sat with the others, came to him timidly and in secret, to get news of Matthew Golab.

"Ye were with the prisoners, and must know, surely. Is he in good health and spirits? . . . When will they let him out?" She put these questions, however, with downcast eyes.

He looked at her with stern sorrow. "And your goodman in the army, how is he? Is he well? and like to come home soon?"

She blushed deeply and fled away into the mill.

He shook his head. "Poor blind creature!" he thought, and went after her. But the lamps were burning dimly in a dusky air, full of meal-dust, and he could not find where she had hidden herself from him. The mill went clattering on; the waters hurled themselves upon the wheels with such incessant din; the wind roared round the roof and walls, so like wheat pouring out of some enormous sack, that all was in a quiver, and, it seemed, about to fly to pieces. Roch then gave up the search, and went to see those poor people according to his promise.

Now the night had fallen; here and there lamps twinkled
amongst the tossing trees like wolves' bright eyes. But, all
around, it was strangely luminous; the huts were seen clear-
cut in the distance; the sky hung aloft, bluish-black and
cloudless, save for a few flying scuds like scattered snow-
flakes; and the stars oversprinkled it in ever denser multitudes, while the gale waxed mightier and mightier, and
reigned over all the land.

So, all night long, it continued blowing. Few could
close their eyes. It made such a terrible draught in the
huts, and smote the boughs against the walls, and broke the
window-panes, and tore and beat on the huts like butting
rams, till they feared it might carry Lipka away bodily
into space!

It subsided a little before dawn; but hardly had the
crowing cocks sung daybreak, and the weary inhabitants
fallen asleep, when the thunders uttered their roars, the
lightnings blazed across the sky with blood-red streaks, and
a torrent of rain poured down. It was said afterwards that
a thunderbolt had then fallen somewhere in the forest.

But when morning had fully come, it cleared up glori-
ously; the rain ceased, warmth came steaming up from the
fields, the small birds chirruped cheerily; and though the
sun was hidden still, the white low-sailing clouds fell asunder and the azure sky appeared. And folk predicted fine
weather.

All through the village now arose lamentations and outcries. Very much harm had been done by the gale; the
roads were so strewn with rows of fallen trees across them,
and fences blown over the ways, with portions of torn-off
roofs, that they were impassable.

At the Ploshkas', the sties had fallen, crushing all their
geese to death! There was no hut but had suffered in the
storm: so the enclosures were filled with women as full of
tears as a showery day.

Hanka had just sallied forth to inspect the farm-buildings
and see what damage had been done, when she met Sikora's
wife, who came rushing into the yard.

"What! have ye not heard? Staho's hut has fallen! By a miracle, they have escaped being crushed," she cried from afar.

"Jesu Maria!"

The news petrified her.

"I have come for you.—Those folk are clean out of their wits!"

Throwing an apron over her head, Hanka ran to the spot.

It was quite true. Nothing of Staho's cabin remained but the walls. All the roof had gone, except a few broken rafters, still hanging above. The chimney, too, had fallen: only a ruined fragment of it stood there, like the snag of a decayed tooth. The floor was covered with splinters and bits of thatch.

Veronka, sitting outside the wall on a heap of fallen rubbish, was embracing her little ones, who wept aloud with her.

Hanka rushed to comfort her through the crowd she was surrounded with; but she saw nothing, heard nothing, and her sobs continued, violent and convulsive.

"O my poor, my miserable children!" she moaned, and several other women shed tears of compassion, to hear her.

"Whither shall we wretched creatures go? where lay our heads?" she cried frantically, clasping her children in her arms.

Old Bylitsa, meanwhile, shrunken, haggard, livid as a corpse, went about the ruins, now driving the fowls together, now giving a few wisps of hay to the cow, tethered to a cherry-tree, now crouching close to the wall, whistling to the dog, and staring at the people like a man demented.

They thought, indeed, that he was out of his mind.

With a sudden movement, they all made way, bowing to the very ground: it was the parish priest, come upon them unexpectedly.

"Ambrose has just informed me of this calamity. Where is Stahova?"

They drew aside for him to see her; but she, blinded by her tears, took no notice.

"Veronka," Hanka said to her in a whisper, "here is his Reverence himself, come to see you!"

She started at the words, and, seeing the priest, fell at his feet in a tempest of tears.

"Peace, be still; do not weep.—What is to be done? It is—aye, it *is*—God's will!" he said twice, brushing a tear away, and deeply moved.

"We must go hence, and beg our bread through the world!"

"No, no; do not give way so. There are kindly folk, and they will not suffer you to perish. Moreover, the Lord will help you in His own way. Has any one of you been hurt? No?"

"In that, God has been merciful"

"Truly, a marvellous escape!"

"They might well have all been crushed to death, like Ploshka's geese," someone said.

"Yes," another remarked, "all without exception."

"Any cattle or live stock lost, eh?"

"God ordered things so that all was then in the enclosure and nothing lost."

The priest, taking a pinch of snuff, looked round at the heap of rubbish, all that remained of their cabin; and his eyes again brimmed with tears.

"Really, it is a very great mercy. Ye might have been all crushed flat."

"But had that been, I should not be looking on these ruins now, nor live to see our home destroyed. O my Jesus, my Jesus! Here am I with my little ones, homeless! What shall I do, and whither shall I go?" she cried once more, and tore her hair in despair.

The priest shifted uneasily, and spread his hands out with a gesture of indecision. Someone slipped a plank under his feet, saying: "Lest your feet be wetted!" And, indeed, the mud was ankle-deep. He moved on to the plank, and took another pinch of snuff, considering what he should say to comfort her.

Hanka was busily engaged with her sister and father,

while the other women pressed round the priest, and feasted their eyes on him.

More women and children were arriving every instant, and their clogs splashed through the mud, and the gathering crowd made comments in hushed voices, amongst which the sobs, now less violent, of Veronka and her children were heard. On all the faces around, so far as they were visible, with their aprons pulled down over their brows, there were seen much sorrow and deep concern, dark as the cloudy sky overhead: hot tears rolled down many a cheek.

But, in their concern and sorrow, they were calm, and resigned to this visitation of God on their poor neighbour. "What then! should everyone take the affairs of others too much to heart, what room would be left for his own?"

After a pause, the priest turned to Veronka, and said: "Above all things, ye ought to thank the Lord God that your lives have been spared."

"Surely, and if I have to sell my pig for it, I will get the wherewithal for a Mass."

"No need for that. Keep your money for your most urgent wants: I shall say Mass for you as soon after Easter as the Rubric allows."

She kissed his hands gratefully, and clasped his feet, peasant-fashion, whilst he gave her his blessing with the sign of the cross, and, like the best of fathers, caressed the little ones who came crowding round him.

"Now, tell me the manner of it."

"The manner of it?—Why, we went to bed early, having no oil in our lamp, and no wood to make a fire. It blew hard, and the cabin shook, but I had no fear, because it had resisted fiercer gales. The draughts in the room kept me awake for some time, but I must have fallen into a doze at last. All at once, there was a crashing banging sound, and the noise of the walls splitting. O Lord! I thought, the world is falling to pieces!—Out of bed I leapt, but had hardly taken my little ones in my arms, when everything overhead began to crack and break down. I just got to the porch outside, while the roof was thundering down upon me. Ere I got my wits back, the chimney too fell with an awful noise. In the yard it was blowing fearfully: we could scarce stand, and the thatch went piecemeal down the wind. I had a good way to go to the village in the night; all were sleeping sound there, and I could make no one hear me. So I returned and took shelter with the children in the potato-pit till morning."

"God was watching over you.—That cow, tethered to the cherry-tree, whose is she?"

"Ours. She feeds us: we owe our lives to her alone."

"A good milker, no doubt: loins as straight as a beam.—With calf, I see?"

"She will calve in a few days."

"Take her over to my cow-house; there is room, and she may stay till the grass is grown.—Now, where will you dwell? Tell me where."

At that moment a dog fell a-barking and made a fierce onset upon the people there. Driven off, it sat down on the threshold, and howled dismally.

The priest had shrunk back at its attack. "Is that dog mad?" he asked. "Whose is it?"

"'Tis Kruchek, our dog. Aye, the misfortune has made it daft. A good watch-dog," stammered Bylitsa, hastening to silence it.

The priest then took his leave, beckoning to Sikora's wife to follow him. Holding out both hands to the goodwives who pressed forward to kiss them, he walked away slowly, but was seen for some time talking with the women upon the road.

The womenfolk, having duly pitied their unfortunate neighbour, now departed hastily, all at once remembering breakfast and the work before them.

No one remained about the ruins except the family; and they were thinking how to rescue something more out of the wrecked hut, when Sikora's wife came up, breathless.

"Your abode must be with me, on that side of the cabin where Roch has been teaching. There's no chimney, to be sure, but you can arrange a makeshift fire-place that will do for the nonce," she said hastily.

"But, good dame, how am I to pay the rent?"

"Take no thought as to that. If ye get money, pay what ye choose; if not, then aid us in our work, or simply say, Thanks; 'twill do. Why, the room stands empty! Most heartily do I invite you; and the priest sends you this bit of paper for present necessities."

She unfolded a three-rouble note.

"May the Lord grant him health!" Veronka exclaimed, kissing the gift.

"There's not another man on earth so kind as he!" Hanka said; and old Bylitsa added:

"In the priest's byre, our cow will not be so very badly off!"

The removal took place at once.

The Sikoras' cabin was by the roadside, not far off; and they carried there such articles as they had managed to get out of the ruins on so short a notice. Hanka ordered Pete to lend a hand, and Roch came a little later, helping them at such a rate that Veronka was settled in her new lodgings before the midday Angelus had rung.

"Now I am next door to a beggar-woman!" she complained bitterly, with a glance round her. "Four corners and a hearth: not one image! not one unbroken dish!"

"I shall fetch you a holy image," Hanka said, soothingly. "Also, any vessels that I shall be able to spare.—And soon Staho will be back, and get men to restore the cabin with him.—Where is Father?"

She wanted him to go to Boryna's with her. But the old man had stayed at the ruined hut, sitting on the threshold binding up a wound in the dog's side.

"Come ye with me," she said; "Veronka's lodgings are not large, and we shall find a corner for you at our place."

"Nay, nay, Hanka; I remain here: here was I born, and here will I die."

No arguments, no entreaties, could shake his determination.

"I shall make myself a straw bed in the passage . . . and if you will have it so, I'll tend the little ones and eat my meals at your home in payment. . . . But take the dog with you: it is wounded. . . . It will take care of the house.—A good watch-dog."

"But," she pointed out, "the passage walls may fall upon you!"

"No, no; they will stand longer than many a man shall live. . . . Do take the dog."

She yielded at last. There was really but little room at Boryna's, and the old man would have been hard to lodge.

She told Pete to slip a string through Kruchek's collar, and take it to the cabin.

"Burek has fled somewhither: Kruchek will fill its place well.—O you good-for-nothing fellow!" she cried, seeing that Pete could not manage the dog.

Old Bylitsa helped to drag it away, chiding it severely. "You foolish Kruchek! Here, there's naught to eat; there, you'll get plenty, and a warm place to lie in!"

But she went before them, in order to look in at her sister's new abode, before going home.

To her surprise, she found Veronka again in tears, and several women with her.

"How have I ever deserved such kindness from you?" she sobbed.

" 'Tis but little we can give; we too are poor: but take what we bring you, it is given with goodwill." So said Klembova, putting a large parcel in her hands.

The others chimed in:

"Such a mishap!"

"We know what it means to you, and our hearts are not of stone."

"And your goodman is away too, as ours are."

"And that makes it so much harder for you!"

"Our Lord has sent a far heavier trial to you than to us."

They had put their heads together to bring her what they could: pease, pearl barley, flour . . . and so forth.

"O kind goodwives, dear to me as ever my own mother

was!" And she embraced them fondly, with many a sob, whilst they wept with her.

But Hanka had no time to stay; so, glad that there were still good people in the world, she hurried back to her cabin.

Though there was no direct sunlight, it was a pretty fine day, and plenty of sun filtered through the clouds. The sky rose above, like a great sheet of bluish canvas, with white ragged kerchiefs of cloud laid out upon it. Beneath, the fields expanded unendingly, distinctly seen, verdant in places, and in others tawny with stubble or with bits of fallow land, or bright with streams, glittering like window-panes.

Larks sang loud. From the plain was wafted the fresh odour of springtime, redolent with moist warmth, and the honey-sweet aromas of poplar-buds.

There was a breeze, but so soft that the down of the first verdure on the boughs was all but motionless.

About the church were congregated sparrows in such countless multitudes that the wide-spreading branches of the maples and lindens were black with them as with soot, and the deafening din of their chirping was heard throughout the village.

On the smooth lustrous pond, the ganders screamed, watching their goslings, while the sharp squattering of the washerwomen's beaters told that a good deal of linen was being bucked.

Rooms and passages stood wide open from one end of the huts to the other, the wash was drying on the hedges, bedding was being aired in the orchards, and in some places they were whitewashing the walls. Swine, much vexed by dogs, sniffed about in the ditches; and here and there a few cows, lifting their horned heads from behind the fences, would utter a plaintive bellow.

Many a wagon, too, was rolling along to town to make purchases for Eastertide; but, immediately after noonday, there came the old pedlar Yudka in his long cart, with his wife and a young olive-branch.

With a following of unfriendly dogs, they were driving

from hut to hut, and seldom did old Yudka leave with empty hands. For he was no cheat, such as the tavern-keeper and many another: he gave good prices, and, if anyone needed a loan till harvest-time, would grant one on easy terms: a shrewd man, who knew all the folk in the village, and how to deal with them. Often enough he had a calf trotting after his wagon, or half a bushel of good corn inside of it. His Jewess did business, but on her own account, mostly by way of barter; getting eggs, cocks, or moulting hens, for which she would give (at a scandalous profit) the frills and ribbons, the braid and pins, and other articles of finery, so much coveted by the female sex.

As they passed Boryna's, Yuzka rushed in with a shrill cry:

"O Hanka, do buy some red tape! . . . And we want log-wood to colour the Easter eggs! . . . And we need thread also!"

Her voice had sunk to tones of whining entreaty.

"But you shall go to town to-morrow, and buy whatsoever is needed."

"Yes, yes, in town it will be cheaper, for they cheat less!" she exclaimed, delighted at the thought of the morrow's drive; and ran at once, without prompting, to inform the pedlars that they needed none of their wares, and had nothing for sale.

Hanka, peeping outside the door, shouted after her: "Keep the fowls together, lest one should stray into that wagon of theirs!"

Tereska, the soldier's wife, now came running into the premises, away (it seemed) from the Jewess, who was shouting something to her.

She rushed into the cabin, stammering, exceedingly red, and very indignant. A tear or two glistened in her long lashes.

"O Tereska! what is the matter?" Hanka inquired with curiosity.

"Why, that swindling woman will give me no more than

fifteen *zloty* for this woollen skirt. Quite new! And I am in such terrible want of money just now!"

"Let me see it. . . . Is—is it dear?" She would have liked to buy the skirt herself.

"Worth at least thirty *zloty*! Quite new; seven cubits and half a span of stuff! I put more than four pounds of pure wool into it, and paid, moreover, for the dyeing."

She spread it out on the table, where its vivid rainbow tints blazed in the light.

" 'Tis more beautiful than any skirt I ever saw! Oh, what a pity I cannot buy it now! . . . I too am short of money for Easter. If ye could but wait till Low Sunday?"

"But, alas! I want the money instantly!"

She rolled the skirt up swiftly, averting her head with a sense of shame.

"The Voyt's wife may purchase it: she generally has money in her purse."

Hanka took it once more, measured its length, and unwillingly returned it.

"You want to send something to your goodman in the army, no doubt?"

"Yes! . . . he wrote . . . complaining . . . in great want. —Farewell!"

She left the hut in a great hurry. Yagustynka, who was busy mashing potatoes in a tub, burst into a roar of laughter.

"You made her run so fast, 'tis a wonder she did not lose her petticoat as she fled!—It is for Matthew she wants the money, not for her husband!"

"What, are they intimate, then?" Hanka asked, much surprised.

"Where do you live? In the forest?"

"But how was I to know about such a thing?"

"Well, 'tis a fact; Tereska runs over to Matthew every week, and wanders about outside the jail all day like a dog, and sends him all she can get."

"My God! what, has she not a goodman of her own?"

"True, but he is far away in the army, and none knows

when he will return . . . and the woman felt lonely all by herself . . . and there was Matthew at hand—a strapping young buck. Wherefore, then, should she deny herself?"

Hanka thought of Antek and Yagna, and fell into a brown study.

"So, when they took Matthew, she made friends with Nastka, his sister; they fadge together very well, and each goes to the town along with the other: Nastka on the pretext of going to her brother, but in reality for Simon, son of Dominikova."

"Upon my word! ye know of all that happens!"

" 'Tis not hard to guess; those fools cannot conceal aught. Think of it!" she added sarcastically; "this creature selling her last skirt that Matthew may get something good to eat!"

"In faith, folk will do strange things.—I shall visit Antek."

"The way is far . . . and in your present state? . . . It might do you harm.—Could not Yuzka go? Or . . . or someone else?" Yagna's name was on the tip of her tongue, but she did not utter it.

"God helping, I shall take no harm. Roch said they permit visitors at Easter, and I shall go.—Ah! but we ought to have brought those flitches of bacon over to our own side ere now!"

"Aye, they have lain in brine these three days: that will do.—I'll go at once."

Yagustynka went, but was back directly, much agitated, and with the news that half the meat had been taken away!

Hanka ran to the store-room, and Yuzka after her. Both stood presently before the tub, dismayed, and wondering how the meat had disappeared.

"No dog has done this!" Hanka exclaimed; "I can see the cuts of a knife quite plainly.—And a stranger, had he stolen aught, would have taken all.—It's Yagna's work!" she said at last, rushing like a whirlwind into her room. But she found it empty, save for old Boryna, staring as ever into vacancy.

Thereupon Yuzka remembered that, on leaving the hut that morning, Yagna was carrying something under her apron, which she had then thought to be the dress she was, in company with Balcerek's daughter, making up for Eastertide.

"She has taken the meat to her mother's. He that is greedy for a thing cares little whose it is," said Yagustynka. The words put Hanka in a passion.

"Yuzka! call Pete. What remains must be taken over to my store-room now!"

This was done directly. She would have wished to take the corn-barrels too at the same time, in order to overhaul them at her ease; but she decided that there were too many of them, and the smith might come to hear of the matter.

But she looked out doggedly for Yagna all the afternoon, and, when she came in at dusk, swooped down upon her and accused her on the spot.

"Aye, I have eaten it!" she coolly replied; "I have as much right to it as you have!" Almost all the evening, Hanka continued to upbraid her; but, as if to exasperate her of set purpose, she answered not one word more. She even came in to supper as if nothing had happened, and looked her rival in the face with a smile. Hanka could not get the better of her, and raged with impotent hate.

Everything therefore made her angry that evening; she flew out on the slightest provocation, and finally sent everyone to bed earlier than usual. The morrow was Maundy Thursday, and they would have to begin preparations for Easter.

She too went to bed earlier than her wont, but it was long before she could sleep. Hearing the dogs bark furiously, she looked outside.

Yagna had not yet extinguished her lamp.

"It is late," she called out crossly to her from the passage. "Ye waste oil: think ye it costs nothing?"

"Ye may burn oil the whole night long, for all I care!" was the retort; which put her into such a state that she had not yet fallen asleep when the first cock crew.

Early in the morning, Yuzka, though she was a great lie-abed, jumped out first, her mind full of her journey to town;

she speedily woke the farm-lads, told them to get the horses ready, and went back in a temper to quarrel with Hanka, who had told Pete that the bay mare alone was to be put to.

"I will not go in the worst wagon of all, and drawn by a blind mare!" she cried, bursting into tears. "Am I a beggar, to travel in the dung-cart? They know me in the town for Boryna's daughter!—Father would never have allowed me to go in such wise."

By dint of wrangling she got her own way, and started off in the large britzka, with a couple of good horses, and the driver on the seat in front, after the fashion of a farmer's goodwife.

"Get some gilt paper, some red, and of all the other colours!" Vitek screamed to her from within the garden, where he had been digging away ever since dawn, Hanka intending to plant cabbages there that very day. Time passed, however, and she did not come; so he ran out into the road, and went off with the other boys twirling rattles along the hedgerows. (No bells, as is the custom on Maundy Thursday, were to be heard any more.)

The weather was rather quieter, but less cheerful, than on the preceding day. The night had been cold; the morning was dewy, hazy and cool till late in the forenoon: the swallows twittered shivering under the eaves, and the geese, driven to the pond, uttered louder and harsher notes. But, notwithstanding, the whole village had been up and busy ere sunrise.

Long before breakfast-time, there had been the noisy hum of strenuous work; and the children, sent out of the cabins, where they would have been in the way, filled the lanes with the din of their whirring rattles.

At Mass, celebrated on that day without bells or organ, there were but few present.

No one had any time to go to church. All necessary preparations for the great feast had to be made now. Chief of these was the baking of loaves and cakes; and, in wellnigh every hut, both doors and windows were now fast closed, lest the dough might fail to rise. The fires burned bright, and the smoke of the chimneys went up to the cloudy sky.

This, too, was the reason why not infrequently the cattle lowed beside their empty mangers, and the swine rooted in the gardens, and the poultry wandered about the roads, and the children were left to do as they pleased—fight each other, or climb trees for birds' nests. All the women were so absorbed in the kneading and rolling out of the dough for loaves and cakes, and all that pertained thereto, that they had forgotten nearly everything else besides.

And in every home this bustle and stir was the same: whether at the miller's, the organist's, or the priest's; whether amongst the farmers or the *Komorniki*. However poor, they had—were it by a loan or even by selling their last half-bushel of wheat—to prepare the banquet of the Hallow-fare, in order to get, at least once a year, meat and other dainties in abundance.

As there were not baking-ovens in every hut, makeshifts were built up in the orchards, and girls ran about, feeding them with dry faggots and logs. And from time to time there were seen women uncouthly attired and white with flour, carefully carrying dressers and kneading-troughs, full of cakes as yet unbaked and hidden from the air, as the statues of the saints are seen carried in a holy procession.

There was work, too, to be done in the church. The priest-man had fetched a number of young fir-trees from the woods; and the organist, together with Roch and Ambrose, were adorning Our Lord's Sepulchre.

When Good Friday came, the work was still more absorbing, so that but few noticed the arrival of Yanek, the organist's son, who had come over for the holidays, and was going about the village, now and then taking a peep into the cottage windows.

Entering anywhere was out of the question: the passages, nay, even the orchard paths were blocked up with presses and bedsteads and all sorts of furniture; for on that day they whitewashed the cabins in all haste, scrubbed the floors, and cleaned the holy images that had been taken outside.

A great hurry-scurry and confusion prevailed everywhere:

people were running about, urging the others to make haste and thereby increasing the turmoil. Even the children were now employed to clear the premises of mud, and sprinkle yellow sand everywhere.

It being an ancient custom to eat nothing warm from Good Friday till Easter Sunday, the people chose to suffer a little hunger in our Lord's honour, eating only dry bread and potatoes that had been roasted.

The hurry and bustle were just the same at Boryna's, with the difference that there were more hands to work and less trouble about money, so that all was ready sooner.

On Friday, at the first glimmer of dawn, Hanka had, together with Pete, finished whitewashing the cabin and out-houses, after which, and a hasty toilet, she had gone to church, where the other women were already assembled to be present at the carrying of the Lord's Body to the Sepulchre.

In the cabin, a big fire was blazing up the chimney; and on it, in a vast cauldron that a couple of men could hardly lift, an entire ham was simmering, while sausages bobbed up and down in a smaller pot; from these the room was penetrated with so strong and delicious a scent that Vitek, busy whittling toys for the little ones, would again and again lift up his nose, and sniff and draw a deep breath of longing.

Before the fire-place, and in the brightest light of the flames, sat Yagna and Yuzka, amicably engaged in colouring the Easter eggs, though each vied with the other and kept her methods secret. Yagna washed hers first in tepid water, dried them, and then overlaid them with dots and patches of melted wax, and plunged them successively into the seething contents of three small pots. It was tedious work; the wax scaled off sometimes, or the eggs broke under her hands, or burst in the boiling; but she succeeded with about thirty. And then, oh, what things of beauty they were!

The idea of Yuzka as Yagna's rival! Hers had been boiled with ears of rye and onion-skins that stained them a

pretty reddish-brown, which she had embellished with
variegated white and yellow patterns, uncommonly pleasing
to the eye. . . . But, when she saw Yagna's work, she remained open-mouthed with amazement, presently followed
by vexation and annoyance.—Why, they dazzled the eyes
with their red and yellow and violet tints, and colours like
fields of blue flax-flowers! And upon those backgrounds
there were painted such wonders that she could not believe
her eyes: on one, cocks perched upon a fence and crowing
open-beaked; on another, a lot of geese hissing at a sow
that wallowed in the mud: here you saw a flock of doves
flying over a crimson field, and there fantastic traceries of
a bewildering type, and like the frost-patterns on the panes
in winter.

Wondering, she gazed upon them again and again.
Hanka, too, looked at them when she got back from church
with Yagustynka, but said not one word. Only the old
woman, after a glance at them all, gave vent to her surprise:

"How in the world have ye come by such fancies? Dear,
dear!"

"How? Why, they just flowed from my head to my
fingers."

She was pleased with herself.

"Ye might take a few to his Reverence."

"I shall offer him some; it may be that he will accept
them."

"His Reverence, indeed! Never saw such marvels! Will
be thunderstruck with them!" Hanka muttered ironically,
when Yagna had gone from the room.

That evening many villagers sat up late.

It was a black night, overcast, though still. The mill
clattered on steadily, and the lamps gleamed in the hut-
windows till close on midnight, throwing many streaks of
light out into the lanes and over the trembling surface of
the pond.

Saturday came, quite warm and a little hazy, but brighter
than the previous day; so that the people, notwithstanding

the hard work done already, rose blithely to encounter what was coming.

Outside the church, there was a great noise and tumult: for, according to immemorial custom, on that day (which brought Lent to its close) they had come together in the early morning to give a funeral to the *ʒur* [1] and herrings on which they had been feeding all Lent through. There were no grown-up men in Lipka now; so the youngsters arranged the funeral, with Yasyek Topsy-turvy at their head. They had got, somewhere or other, a big pot of *ʒur*, to which they had added certain filthy matters besides.

Vitek let himself be enticed into carrying the pot, which dangled from his shoulder in a net, whilst another little fellow, at his side, dragged along the ground a herring cut out of wood and attached to a string. They went foremost, the others trooping behind with a deafening noise of rattles and shouts.

Yasyek directed the procession: though somewhat idiotic in life, he had quite enough brains for such tomfoolery. They went in procession round the pond and church, and turned off to the poplar road where the funeral was to take place . . . when suddenly Yasyek struck at the pot with a spade and shivered it to pieces! And the *ʒur*, with all its filth, poured over Vitek's clothes!

This practical joke made everybody laugh very heartily, except Vitek, who flew at Yasyek and fought with him and with the other boys until, overpowered by numbers, he was forced to flee roaring home.

There he got a beating besides from Hanka, for having ruined his coat; and then she sent him to the woods to get sprays of pine-boughs for decorations.

Pete laughed at him into the bargain; nor did even Yuzka show him sympathy. She was busily engaged in strewing all the premises as far as the road with sand brought from

[1] *Zur* is a sort of soup made of flour and water, mixed with bran and left to ferment till it is sour. It is then boiled with various seasonings.—*Translator's Note.*

the churchyard; its yellow was deepest there. She scattered it over the whole drive up to the porch, and all round the eaves, encircling the cabin with a saffron-coloured girdle.

And now, in Boryna's cabin, they began to set forth the victuals that were to be blessed by the priest.

The great room had been well scoured and sanded, the windows cleaned, and all traces of cobwebs brushed away from the images on the walls. Yagna's bed, too, had been covered with a beautiful shawl.

Hanka, Yagna and Dominikova, working together, though in all but absolute silence, had dragged a large table near the corner window, parallel to the bed where Boryna lay, and covered it with a white linen table-cloth, the edges of which Yagna had embellished with a border of red paper fantastically cut out. In the centre, and opposite the window, they then set up a big crucifix, adorned with paper flowers, and in front of this, upon a dish turned bottom upwards, a lamb moulded out of butter by Yagna so cleverly that it seemed alive. Its eyes were rosary beads; its tail, ears, hoofs and the banner over it were made of crisp red wool! After this, there came a first row of great loaves and wheaten cakes large and small, white or tawny; some stuck all over with raisins (certain of these being specially made for Yuzka and the little ones); others, again, were very dainty ones all of curds, or frosted with sugar and sprinkled with poppy-seed. And, quite at the end, there stood, on one side, an enormous dish full of great snaky coils of sausages, and hard-boiled eggs (white, for they had been shelled) within the coils to adorn them; on the other, a pan containing an entire ham, and a huge piece of so-called "head-cheese," all these gay with coloured eggs strewn about. But the whole affair still awaited the coming of Vitek with the sprays and sprigs of pine-needles to give it the finishing touch.

As they brought this work to an end, several neighbours came in with dishes and baskets containing their own Easter victuals, which they put near the table on a side-bench.

There was not time enough for the priest to go round to all the cabins, so he had told them to bring their Easter feast to a few of the largest cottages.

Lipka being his own dwelling-place, he used to give the blessing there last of all, and very often only near nightfall. The people, consequently, prepared everything early, that they might be in church in time for the "blessing of the fire and of the water," having previously extinguished their own fires at home, which were subsequently to be again lighted at the newly consecrated flame.

Yuzka ran to church for that purpose; but she had to wait very long, and it was nearly midday when she returned, carefully protecting the light of a taper just kindled in church. Along with the fire, she brought a bottle of holy water. Hanka immediately lit the fire-wood set ready for kindling, and first of all drank a gulp of holy water, piously believed to preserve folk from ailments of the throat; she then gave some to each of the others in turn, and lastly sprinkled with it the live stock and the fruit-trees of the orchard, that the cattle might bring forth their young without trouble, and the trees abound with fruit.

Later, seeing that neither Yagna nor the smith's wife had taken any care at all of Boryna, she washed his body with tepid water, combed his matted hair, and changed his linen and bedding; he meanwhile lying as usual with blankly staring eyes.

After noontide, it was a sort of half-holiday. Although some people had still a little of the more tiresome work to finish, the most part were getting themselves ready for the coming feast, combing and washing and scrubbing the children, till many a hut resounded to their cries and screams.

It was only just before nightfall that the priest came in from the outlying villages. He wore his surplice; Michael, the organist's pupil, went after him, bearing a holy-water pot and sprinkling-brush. Hanka came to meet him at the gate.

He came in quickly, being in a hurry, said the prayers,

sprinkled "God's gifts," and cast a glance on Boryna's livid hairy face.

"No change? eh?"

"None. The wound is all but healed, yet he is no better."

"The boy who sold me the stork—where is he?"

Vitek turned very red, and Yuzka pushed him forward.

"Ye have trained it well: it keeps the fowls out of the garden, and none dare venture in.—Here are five kopeks for you.—Are any of you going to see your husbands to-morrow?"

"Half the village at least."

"Good; but behave yourselves, and do not brawl.—And come to the Resurrection Service now: it is at ten.—At ten, mind! And," he added sharply, as he went out, "should anyone fall asleep, Ambrose has orders to put him out of the church."

Several people followed him as far as the miller's.

But Vitek, showing the copper coin to Yuzka, said crossly: "My stork will not drive his fowls out for long. Oh, no!"

The darkness fell slowly. Dusk came down over the earth, drowning cottages, orchards and fields in a bluish semi-transparent murk. The low cabin-walls alone were here and there dimly visible. Athwart the orchards flashed a few flickering lights, and a pale half-moon gleamed in the sky.

It was the calm of Easter eve that enveloped the village; through the darkness, the church-windows, high above the cottages, were seen shedding floods of light afar, and out of the great wide-open door poured streams of splendour.

Then the first carts came rumbling in, stopping in front of the churchyard; and the people arrived on foot from the farthest hamlets. Many also came from the cottages of Lipka; not infrequently the doors would open and a streak of light flash forth, plunging into the jet-black pond; and the patter of footsteps and half-hushed murmurs came multitudinous through the warm and misty air. Greeting one another on the way, the crowd, like a river that rises slowly but unceasingly, pressed onwards to the "Resurrection Service."

In Boryna's cabin and the surrounding outhouses, no one remained on guard but the dogs, old Bylitsa and Vitek, who was hard at work with Maciek, Klemba's son, making a cock that was to perform wonderful feats a few days later.

Hanka first sent Yuzka to church, along with the little ones and Pete; she herself, she said, would follow presently.

Yet, when dressed, she lingered on, awaiting something, it seemed; for she continually went out and watched the road from the passage. When she had seen Yagna set out with Magda, and heard the smith in talk with the Voyt on their way to church, she returned to the hut, and showed something in silence to the old man. He thereupon went outside to watch, while she walked on tiptoe to her father-in-law's store-room. . . . A good half-hour elapsed before she came out, carefully buttoning something in her bodice. Her eyes sparkled; her hands were shaking.

Murmuring incoherent words, she went on to the "Resurrection Service."

CHAPTER V

IT was pitch-dark in the lanes; in every cottage all the lights were out; the laggards were now dropping in to church. Outside stood a number of carts, with horses unharnessed, whose pawing and snorting made their presence heard in the gloom. Close to the belfry, several Manor-house coaches loomed apart.

Hanka, on entering the porch, set something straight in her bodice, loosened her shawl that wrapped her too closely, and vigorously elbowed her way to the first pews.

The church was very full indeed. The close-pressed congregation was massed in the aisles; and, with mingled prayers, ejaculations and coughs, they swayed and swung from wall to wall, till the banners stuck in the pews, and the fir saplings which adorned the church, began to wave also.

Scarcely had she pushed through to her place, when the priest began the service.

They fell on their knees devoutly, and the press became still greater, till all knelt close together, like a field of heads —a cluster of human plants—but with eyes swiftly darting and flying up to the high altar, whereon stood the figure of Jesus, risen from the dead, with bare limbs, draped only in a crimson mantle, holding His banner in His hand, and showing His five wounds to them all!

By degrees their prayers grew intensely fervent; words uttered low, and presently sighs, came welling up to their lips, like the sounds of raindrops falling on leaves; and then their heads bent lower still, their arms were stretched forth towards the altar beseechingly, and stifled weeping was heard. Under the shadow of the dark naves with their lofty pillars, the crowd seemed as clumps of brushwood amongst the great trees of some immemorial forest; for, though the altar was ablaze with tapers, the church itself was shrouded in gloom, and the black night crept in through the windows and the wide-open portal.

But Hanka could not compose herself to pray; she trembled all over, not less upset than when in her father-in-law's store-room a while before.

Once more, and shudderingly, she felt her hands plunging in the cool grains of corn; and she pressed her shoulders forward, to make sure that the bundle was still nestling between her breasts.

Joy and terror alternately held her in their grip. The rosary slipped from her fingers; she could not remember her prayers; looking round with eyes aflame, she recognized no one, though Yuzka and Yagna with her mother sat close by.

In the pews which stood on either side of the sanctuary, the ladies from the manors of Rudka, Modlitsa and Volka were reading out of prayer-books; at the sacristy-door several squires stood talking to each other; gaudily arrayed, the miller's wife and the organist's were standing close to the high altar on either side. But, just outside the Communion railings, once the place for the first amongst the Lipka farmers—who were the overseers at every service, who carried the canopy over his Reverence and supported his steps in the processions—there now knelt a dense multitude of peasants from other villages, and scarce any to represent Lipka but the Voyt, the Soltys and the carroty-headed blacksmith.

Besides Hanka's, other eyes too wandered in that direction, sorrowful, and remembering the absent dear ones. Those men, once the foremost in the parish, were alone not to be seen there now! The thought depressed them, and bore many a head down to the pavement, with painful memories of their present bereavement.

Alas! it was the greatest festival in the whole year—Easter! So many other faces were there, from other parts of the parish, full of gladness, though a little emaciated by the long fast of Lent. Folk had come, splendidly clad, to swagger in the church like Manor-folk, and occupy all the best places; and the poor men of Lipka—where were they? In dungeons, suffering cold and hunger, and longing for home!

For all but them it was the great day of joy. The others would presently return home and enjoy life and rest and food, the sunny springtime, and friendly talk: but not the poor Lipka folk!

They would crawl back to their desolate homesteads, lonely, drooping, miserable; would eat their Easter meal in tears, and go to their couches full of unrest and vain desires.

"O Lord! O Lord!" were the dreary half-stifled ejaculations that went up around Hanka's pew, and made her at last come to herself again and look upon the well-known faces and eyes dimmed with tears. Even Yagna hung her head over her book, crying bitterly, till her mother nudged her to bring her back to reality. But the source of her misery was far different, and nothing could allay it. Was it not at Christmas, in this very pew, that she had heard *his* burning whisper and felt *his* head droop down upon her knee? The thought tore her breast with a sudden excruciating yearning.

It was then that his Reverence began to preach, and they all rose from their knees, thronging round the pulpit as close as might be—every face turned to hear him. First he spoke of our Lord's Passion, and of those vile Jews who crucified Him for coming to save the world, deal justice to the oppressed, and uphold the cause of the needy. And he set the sufferings of Jesus so vividly before their eyes that many a one grew hot with indignation, and more than one peasant, eager to avenge Christ, clenched his fist; and all the womenfolk sobbed aloud in chorus.

And then he turned upon the people themselves; bending forward over the pulpit, he shook his fists, crying out that every day, every hour, everywhere, Jesus was crucified by our sins, slain by our wickedness, our ungodliness, our contempt for God's law; that we all crucified Him within ourselves anew, forgetful of His sacred wounds and of the blood He shed for our salvation!

At the words, the whole congregation burst into a tempest of wailing and sobbing; and such a storm of lamentation swept through aisles and nave that he had to pause awhile. Then he went on to speak, but more cheerful and with words of comfort, of the Resurrection of Christ. Of that springtide which the Lord in His bounty sends—and will always send—to sinful men, until such time as He shall come to judge the living and the dead, and abase the proud, and hurl the wicked into the fires of hell, and place the good on His right hand in everlasting glory. Yea! the time should come when all injustice should have an end, all wrong receive its punishment, all tears be wiped away, all evil enchained for ever!

He spoke so earnestly and with such kindness of heart that every word of his sank into their minds with sweet mastery, and brought sunshine into every soul; and everyone felt consoled and radiant—except his hearers of Lipka. These quivered with anguish, with the remembrance of the wrongs done them racking their minds. They burst out crying and groaning, and threw themselves down upon the pavement with outstretched arms, asking from the bottom of their hearts for mercy and relief in their woes.

Throughout the church the emotion was profound. A universal cry arose; but soon they remembered where they were, raised up the prostrate women of Lipka, and comforted them with kind words. His Reverence, too, deeply moved, wiped away his tears with his surplice sleeve; and then he reminded them how our Lord chastiseth them that He loveth; and said that though they had not done aright, their punishment would very shortly be ended. "Let them but trust in the Lord, and they would very shortly see the return of their husbands."

Thus he quieted and relieved them, and they once more began to take confidence.

Presently the priest, from the high altar, intoned the

grand "Resurrection chant"; the organ took it up with a
roar and boomed sonorously; all the bells rang out and
pealed aloud. And then his Reverence, bearing the Most
Holy Sacrament, surrounded with a thin blue cloud of
incense smoke and the tumultuous din in the belfry, came
down towards the people. The chant was continued, bursting forth from every throat; the waves of the crowd tossed
and rolled, a fiery blast of enthusiasm dried every tear and
lifted every soul to Heaven. So all together, like a living
and moving human grove, swaying hither and thither as
they sang the hymn in grand unison, went forward in procession, following the priest holding the Monstrance aloft
in front of him, as a golden sun that burned above their
heads, with chants sounding on all sides and bright tapers
all around, scarce visible through the smoke shot forth
from the censers: the object of the gaze of every eye, of
the love of every heart!

With slow and measured steps did the procession wend
along the nave and thread the aisles, in a close-packed,
surging, vociferously sonorous crowd.

Hallelujah! Hallelujah! Hallelujah! The noise was
deafening; the very pillars and arches thrilled to the chant.
Hearts and throats burst forth with one accord; and those
glowing voices, instinct with mystic fire, flew up to the
vault like flame-birds, and sailed out afar into the night,
seeking the sun away in those regions to which at such
times the soul of man mounts upon the wings of rapture.

It was close on midnight when the service ended and the
congregation began to break up. Hanka lingered behind.
She had been praying ecstatically; for the priest's words
had filled her with confidence, and the service itself, together with the memory of what she had that very day
achieved, gave her such intense joy that she desired to lay
it all at the feet of Jesus Risen. But Ambrose at last came
jingling his keys and signifying to her that she must now
leave the church.

As she went out, even that passion of fear for Antek
which lived within her heart and was wont to start up on the

slightest occasion, had as she thought suddenly died out
of her.

She saw at a distance the rest of her household plodding
home. The carts were rolling along in an unbroken procession, and the foot-passengers had to go in groups by the
side of the road, almost invisible now that the moon had
set and darkness reigned.

In the warm quiet night, damp with abundant dew, the
breeze blowing athwart the fields was laden with the raw
moist odour of the earth; and from the roads there came
the honey-sweet fragrance of budding poplars and birches.
Folk swarmed along through the shadows; where the gloom
was less pitch-black, a few heads appeared, dimly visible.
Steps and voices resounded on every side; angry dogs
barked, rushing along behind the palings; and in hut and
cabin, lights began to gleam.

Hanka, after taking a look into the byre and stable as she
entered, went in and laid herself down at once.

"Let him but return and be master here: I shall never
say a word to him of what has been," was her resolution
while she was undressing.—"Ah, but," she thought once
more, hearing Yagna opening the door on the other side,
"what if he should fall and go to her again?"

Listening, thinking, she lay still for some time. All was
growing silent, with the hum of voices fading into the
distance, and the faint clatter of the last wagons going
away.

"——Then there would be no God, no justice in this
world!" she ejaculated fiercely.—But a deep sleep came
over her, and she gave up thinking of this.

.   .   .   .

The village awoke very late the next day.

Morning was already opening his pale-blue slumberous
eyes, and as yet those of the Lipka folk were all fast closed.

The sun rose directly in the East, making the ponds and
the dewy meadows glitter: its beams floated down from
the pallid sky above, singing to the world its Hallelujah—
its song of warmth and light.

Merry and sparkling, that song was echoed among the ground-mists: birds twittered gladly, the waters tinkled and bubbled with mirth, the great woods murmured, the breeze blew, the young leaves quivered, the very clods were a-tremble; and from the undulating fleeces on the corn-lands, bright dew-drops fell like tears upon the earth.

"Ah! the grand day of joy for us is dawning:
Conqueror of death, Christ rose on Easter morning!
Hallelujah!"

Yes, Christ had risen—He, tortured and slain by the wickedness of men. Again He had returned to life, He, the Well-beloved, as light rising up in darkness; had opened the cruel grip of death; for the welfare of man He had vanquished the invincible. And behold Him now, in that spring season, hiding mysteriously in His sacred sun, to sow happiness throughout the world—to rouse the faint—to quicken the dead—to raise the fallen ones, and make fertile the fallows!

One cry echoed over all the land: Hallelujah! for the great day that the Lord had made!

In Lipka alone were the folk less uproariously joyful than in former years.

They slept most soundly. Only when the sun had risen above the orchards did the people begin to move, and the doors to creak, and unkempt tousled heads to peep outside the cabins at the country-side steeped in light, ringing with the songs of larks, and overspread with delicate verdure.

So at Boryna's, too, the folk were sleeping. Hanka alone, anxious that Pete should get the horses and britzka ready, rose a little earlier, and then set to making out the portions of the Hallow-fare for each.

Yuzka, fussy and chattering, was presently engaged in tidying the children, and putting on their best clothes; and at the well in the court-yard Pete and Vitek were washing themselves thoroughly, while old Bylitsa amused himself with the dog in the porch, and from time to time sniffed inquiringly. Had Hanka yet begun slicing the sausages?

According to custom immemorial, they lit no fire that day, but ate the Hallow-fare cold. Hanka had just fetched it out of old Boryna's apartments, and was setting it out on plates, for everyone to get an equal portion of sausage, ham, cheese, bread, and eggs, and sweet cake.

Then, having first completed her own toilet, she called everyone in . . . even Yagna, who at once made her appearance, beautifully arrayed, and looking fair as the dawning sun, her eyes of turquoise-blue shining beneath her glossy flaxen hair.—All were in the very best apparel. Vitek, indeed, was bare-footed; but he wore a new spencer with bright buttons; the latter begged from Pete, who made his appearance clean-shaven, his hair freshly cut straight over his forehead, wearing a completely new suit—a black-blue *zupan* with green and yellow-striped trousers, and a shirt tied with a red ribbon. When he came in, everyone was amazed at his transformation, and Yuzka clapped her hands with delight.

"O Pete! your own mother would not know you!"

And Bylitsa observed: "Once he has thrown off that dog's skin of a uniform, he's as fine a peasant as any!"

Greatly flattered, Pete smiled, rolled his eyes at Yagna, and drew himself up stiffly.

Hanka, crossing herself, drank to each in turn and made them sit down at table, on the benches. Even Vitek took a seat timidly at one end.

They ate with the utmost deliberation, taking into themselves with religious silence all the savour of the food they had gone without for so many weeks. The sausages had a strong flavour of the garlic with which they had been abundantly supplied; the room reeked with it, and the dogs pressed in to enjoy its pungent scent.

No one said a word until the first pangs of hunger had been appeased.

Pete was first to speak. "Are we to start directly?"

"Yes, as soon as breakfast is over."

"Yagustynka," Yuzka reminded her, "wished to go to town with you."

"If she come in time, she shall: but I do not wait for her."

"Any provender?"

"Enough for one feed only: we return in the evening."

They continued to eat till their faces were flushed with delight, and they felt their garments tight about them, and some had eyes starting from their sockets. This slowness in eating was intentional, that they might stow away as much as possible and enjoy their meal to the full; and when Hanka rose from table, there was nothing empty about them; Pete and Vitek even carried away to the stable all the remains of their portions, to finish them later.

"Now," Hanka's command rang out, "put the horses to, this instant!"—And, having made up for her husband such a parcel as she scarce could lift, she dressed for the journey.

Yagustynka came in quite out of breath, and just as the horses were pawing the ground outside the cabin.

"We were about to start without you!"

"Alas! and the Hallow-fare is over?" She sniffed ruefully and drew a long breath.

"There is yet a morsel or two: sit down and take what's left."

The poor hungry creature needed no pressing. Ravenous as a wolf, she set to, and swept the platter clean.

"When the Lord Jesus created the pig, He knew well what He was doing!" she exclaimed, after a few mouthfuls; adding, as a gentle hint in the form of a joke: "Strange, though, that men let it wallow in the mud during life, and are afterwards so willing to wash it in vodka!"

"Well, here is some: drink our healths and be quick: there is no time!"

In about the space of a Pater, they were off. From the britzka, Hanka reminded Yuzka not to forget her father. She immediately went to him with a plateful of various meats, and tried to speak with him. Though he did not reply, he swallowed all she put in his mouth, staring vacantly as ever. Possibly he might have taken some more; but Yuzka soon tired of feeding him, and ran out to the gate to look at the many women, either driving (there were upwards of a score of wagons) or else trudging to town with great packs on their shoulders.

Soon, however, the clatter ceased, and melancholy reigned throughout the village.

Yes, melancholy! notwithstanding the bright sun on high, and that pond as of glass mingled with fire, and the trees all bathed in aromatic perfumes and brilliantly fresh green tints, and the quiet loveliness of spring now spreading over the world—the blue haze on the vast rolling plain, the larks that sang, the far-off villages tremulous under the blaze of day, and resounding with loud pistol-shots and merry-making!

Lipka, Lipka alone, was sad, abandoned, forsaken; and the hours there crept drearily and wearily by.

Noon was at hand, when Roch went over to Boryna's, to see after the sick man, and have a talk with the children, and sit in the sun. He read for a while, often lifting his eyes to the road, and presently saw the smith's wife come in with her little ones. She sat down outside the hut, after having looked in at her father's.

"Is your goodman at home?" Roch asked her after a pause.

"Oh, no! Gone to town with the Voyt."

"All Lipka is there to-day."

"Aye, and the poor sufferers will have some morsels of the Hallow-fare to comfort them."

Yagna was just going out.

"What!" he exclaimed. "Have ye not gone to town with your mother?"

"And what business have I there?" she returned, stepping out of the enclosure, and looking wistfully along the road.

Magda sighed. "She has a new skirt on to-day!"

"'Twas Mother's!" Yuzka told her sullenly. "Did ye not see that? All those coral and amber beads on her bosom were Mother's as well. The kerchief on her head is her own—nothing else!"

"True. So many a thing have his dead wives left him!

He never would let us touch any; and now all are hers, to strut about in!"

"Yet she railed at them the other day—told Nastka the garments were mouldy and noisome!"

"Oh, may they smell of devil's dirt to her!"

"Let Father but be healed! . . . I shall tell him instantly about the corals. . . . Five strings of them there were, every one as long as a whip, and each bead as big as the largest pea!"—And Magda, having said her say, heaved a deep sigh, and spoke no more.—Yuzka slipped away; Vitek, outside the stable, was busily constructing a toy something like a cock; while the children played in the porch with the dogs, under the eyes of old Bylitsa, who watched over them as a hen over her chickens.

"Is the field-work here finished?" Roch inquired of him.

"Aye, as far as pea-sowing and potato-planting go: no more."

"Few folk here can say as much."

"All will be well, we are told: the men are to be set free on Low Sunday."

"Who, then, knew so much . . . and said it?"

" 'Twas a whisper that went about the congregation.— And Kozlova is to go and beseech the Squire!"

"The more fool she! Was it the Squire who cast them into prison?"

"His intercession might set them free."

"Once he did speak, but naught came of it."

"Had he but a little goodwill! But my goodman says he hates Lipka, and will do naught for us. . . ." Here Magda broke off abruptly, and became more interested in her children, and Roch listened in vain for any more information from her.

"And when," he asked with interest, "when is Kozlova going to him?"

"At once, as soon as noon is past."

"Well, then, all she will get of it will be a walk and some fresh air."

She did not reply. Just then, the Squire's brother, Mr.

Yacek, commonly held to be somewhat feeble-minded, came in from the road into the enclosure, with his long yellow beard and wandering eyes, bowed down, pipe in mouth and violin under his arm as usual. Roch went out to meet him. They surely must have been well acquainted; for they went and sat together on the stones by the shore of the mill-pond, and talked so long that it was well into the afternoon when they separated. But Roch came back to the porch, out of sorts and gloomy.

"That gentleman," Bylitsa remarked, "has grown so thin, I scarcely knew him."

"Did ye know him of old, then?" said Roch, dropping his voice as he glanced at the blacksmith's wife.

"To be sure, I did. . . . He was a gay youngster once upon a time. . . . Aye, and a sad fellow with the wenches. . . . In Vola, they said, not one of them slipped through his fingers.—Ah, and I remember what splendid horses he used to ride—and what a rake he was.—Aye, aye, I remember well," the old man said maunderingly.

"For that he is now doing a sore penance. A sore penance, I say.—Are ye not the oldest man in the village?"

"Nay, Ambrose must be older: I cannot remember him but as an old man."

"He himself," the smith's wife put in, "says that Death has overlooked him."

"No, Dame Crossbones never overlooks anyone; but she leaves him to the last, that he may repent. For he is greatly hardened."

Bylitsa continued, after a long silence: "I remember the time when there were no more than fifteen peasants' farms in Lipka." He moved his hand hesitatingly towards Roch's snuff-box, which the latter offered him at once, saying:

"And now there are a couple of score."

"So the land must be divided again and again. Whether the harvest be rich or poor, the folk must always grow poorer. Ye cannot make the land to stretch. Yet a few more years, and there will be too little for us to live upon."

"In truth, we are straitened enough as it is now," the smith's wife observed.

"Yes; and when our lads marry, there will be no more than one acre apiece for their children."

"Therefore," Roch said, "they will have to go abroad."

"And what will they do there? Shall they clutch at the winds, and grasp them in their bare hands?"

"But," he somewhat ruefully observed, "there are some German settlers who have purchased land of the Squire of Slupia, and are working it now: seventy acres to each settlement."

"Of that I have heard. But the Germans are wealthy, and know much: they do business with the Jews, and profit by the sufferings of others. Were that same land to be taken up by empty-handed peasants like us, they would not sow it thrice! For us, there is scant room in Lipka. While that man—why, he has no end of broad acres that lie fallow close by!" And with a sweep of his arm he pointed to the Manor lands beyond the mill, shelving up towards the forest, and black with heaps of lupines.

"All that land," he went on to say, "is close to our own, and might be parcelled out into thirty small holdings.—But the Squire would never sell it: such a rich man cares naught for money."

"Rich? He?" the smith's wife broke in. "He needs money as a mudfish needs mud. Why, he is driven to borrow from the very peasants. The Jews are dunning him now for what they advanced him upon the forest he cannot sell them. He is in arrears with the taxes, does not pay his own people—they have not yet received what is due them in kind for the New Year. He is in debt to everyone; and now that the government has forbidden him to cut down any timber till the peasants' consent is obtained, how is he to get money to pay? He will not be master of Vola very long, not he!—They say he is seeking a purchaser."
Here she broke short as unexpectedly as she had begun, and all Roch's efforts to draw her out a little more were useless;

she put him off with a few commonplace remarks, and presently withdrew with her little ones.

"Her goodman," old Bylitsa thought, "must have told her many things, but she fears to speak of them. . . . True, the lands close to Lipka are fertile, and the meadows give an aftermath. Even so . . ." And he went on pondering, with his eyes fixed upon the fields adjoining the forest, and on the Manor farm-buildings.—Roch had meanwhile perceived Kozlova near the pond with other women, and gone over to her in haste.

Meanwhile Bylitsa thought: "We now have beaten the Squire. Now is the time for us peasants to make the most of our advantage.—Surely.—We might found another village: there would be lands enough, and hands enough willing to till it. . . ." But the babies had got out into the road, and this put an end to his musings.

The bells had sounded for Evensong.

The sun was rolling down towards the forest; and over the roadway and mill-pond the shadows were growing longer. All was so quiet that, far away in the distance, a cart was heard to clatter, or a bird to cry out in the copses.

Some women had come back from town, and everyone was running to hear the news they had brought.

His Reverence had driven over to Volka, directly after Vespers: to a party at the Manor, Ambrose said. The organist had gone with all his people to visit the miller, and his son Yanek, in splendid attire, had accompanied his mother, saluting on his way the lasses behind their garden-palings, who peered out at him.

As the evening drew on slowly, the afterglow filled half the sky with sheets of blood-red fire, scattered about like brightly burning embers; and the waters turned crimson, and the window-panes gleamed ruddily, as more wagons came back from town, and in front of the cabins the noise grew louder.

Though Hanka was not yet home, there was plenty of life and din in front of her hut too. A number of little girls of Yuzka's age had come to see her, and were all

warbling and twittering around her like a bevy of finches,
and laughing at Yasyek Topsy-turvy: while Yuzka was
treating them to such dainties as the cabin afforded on
that day.

Nastka, much older than any of the others, was their
leader. She was making fun of Yasyek, because, blockhead
though he was, he tried to give himself rollicking airs.
He stood just then before them all, wearing a brand-new
spencer and a hat cocked at a considerable angle, and
saying with a smiling look and arms akimbo:

"All of you must respect me—me, the only man in the
village!"

"Not so: others as good as you are tending the kine!"
said one.

"Or wiping babies' noses!" cried another.

Yasyek, in no wise taken aback, answered them loftily:

"Such chits as ye are—mere goose-girls as yet—are not
to my taste!"

"Why, the fellow kept kine last year, and he would play
the man now!"

"Yet he runs away from a bull so fast that his breeches
come down!"

"Go, marry Magda, the servant of the Jew: she's the girl
for you."

"Nurse to the Jew's brats, she'll wipe your nose likewise!"

"Or," someone said still more sarcastically, "take old
Agata to wife, and go on pilgrimages with her."

"Oh," he retorted, "if I would but send my proposers to
any one of you, she'd fast on dry bread every Friday of her
life to thank God for her luck!"

"But," Nastka cried, "whom would your mother let you
marry? You're needed to wash the platters at home."

"Provoke me not, you! else I go and marry Mary
Balcerek!"

"Aye, do: go to her; she'll receive you with a broom-
stick—or worse!"

"Go—but take heed not to lose aught on the way!"
Nastka said, with a laugh and a slight pull at his breeches,

that were indeed, like the rest of his clothing, much too
large for him.

"They were his grandsire's once!"

Jests and gibes fell round him, thick as hail: he laughed
as heartily as anyone, and slipped his arm round Nastka's
waist. But a girl put her foot out: down he sprawled upon
the floor, and could not get up, for they pushed him down
again.

"Girls, let him be! How can you?" said Yuzka, coming
to the rescue, and helping him up. Though a zany, he
was a farmer's son, and her kinsman through her mother.

They then played at blind man's buff with him, who of
course was blindfolded, and did not succeed, much as he
tried, in catching any of the girls. These flew about him,
nimble as swallows, and the noise and laughter and uproar
grew louder and louder.

Twilight was falling, and the game was at its height,
when the sudden cry of many fowls was heard in the yard.
Yuzka, who ran there at once, found Vitek in the outhouse,
holding something behind his back, and young Gulbas,
whose flaxen head of hair was seen peeping over a plough.

"'Tis naught, Yuzka," Vitek said in confusion, "'tis
naught!"

"Ye have been killing a hen: I can see the feathers about!"

"Nay, nay! I only took a few from a cock's tail, which
I needed for my own bird.—But, Yuzka, it was no cock of
ours! Oh, no! This boy Gulbas brought it here to me."

"Show!" she commanded sternly.

He laid at her feet a bird quite plucked of all its feathers,
and in a pitiable state.

"No doubt it is not one of ours," she said, though she
could not make sure.

"Now show your marvellous toy!"

Vitek then unveiled an artificial cock, that he had just
finished; it was made of wood, plastered over with dough,
into which the feathers had been stuck, and it looked as if
alive, with a real head and beak mounted on a stick.

It had been fixed upon a board painted red, and very

cleverly attached to a small cart; and when Vitek began
to pull at the shaft, the bird would at once dance and flap
its wings, Gulbas crowing the while till the hens cackled
in reply.

Yuzka squatted down to admire this miracle of art.

"Lord! why, never in my life have I seen aught so
wonderful!"

"'Tis good, hey, Yuzka?—I have hit it off well, hey?"
he whispered, full of pride.

"And ye have made the thing all out of your own head?"
She was overwhelmed with amazement.

"Aye, all by myself, Yuzka! Yendrek here only brought
me this live cock.—Aye, all by myself!"

"Dear, dear! how life-like it moves! And yet 'tis but
wood.—Show it to the girls, Vitek! How they all will
marvel!—Show it to them, Vitek!"

"Ah, no. We shall go round to-morrow for the *Dyngus*,[1]
and then they shall see it. I must still put up a railing all
round to protect it."

"Then come round to our big room and work at it, as
soon as you have seen to the kine. There will be more
light there."

"So I will, but I have something else to do first in the
village."

She returned, but the company had finished the game and
was now breaking up. For it was dark; lights gleamed in
the huts and twinkled in the sky, and the evening chill
was rising from the fields.

By now, everybody save Hanka was back from town.

Yuzka prepared a glorious supper: *barszcz* with shredded
sausage, and potatoes seasoned with much fried bacon. She
set it on the table, where Roch was waiting already; the
little ones were whimpering, and Yagna had been looking in
more than once. At that moment Vitek glided in noiselessly,

---

[1] *Dyngus,* called also *Smigus;* a popular festival, with a great
deal of horseplay, drenchings and even dousings, on Easter Monday;
believed to be a custom surviving from the time when the Poles
(in the tenth century) embraced Christianity and were baptized *en
masse.—Translator's Note.*

and sat down at once before the smoking dishes. His face was red as fire and he ate but little; his teeth were chattering, his hands trembling; and before supper was ended, he had slunk away.

Yuzka, wondering what was the matter, met him afterwards outside the sty, taking some draff out of the trough, and questioned him sharply.

For some time he tried to hold back the truth, and put her off with fibs; but all came out at last.

"Well, I have got my stork back again from his Reverence!"

"Gracious Lord! and no one saw you?"

"No one. His Reverence was away from home, the dogs were at their meal, and there stood my stork in the porch. Maciek had seen it, and came to let me know. I wrapped it close in Pete's capote lest it should peck at me, carried it off, and hid it . . . somewhere!—But do not, my Yuzka, my golden girl!—do not breathe one word of this. In a few weeks I will bring it round to our cabin, and you'll see it strutting about in front of the porch; and none will know it for the same. Only betray me not!"

"Betray you? have I ever done that? . . . But I am amazed at your daring.—Good heavens!"

" 'Twas but my own property I have taken back again. I said I would never give it him: and behold, I have it once more. A likely thing indeed, that I should tame it all for the delight of others! Yea, surely!"—And he ran off, whistling.

Returning presently, he came in and sat down by the fireside with the little ones, intent on finishing his creation.

The cabin became a drowsy tedious place. Yagna had gone over to her side of the hut, and Roch was sitting outside with Bylitsa, who felt very sleepy.

"Get home," Roch said to him; "there, Mr. Yacek is waiting to talk with you."

"Mr. Yacek . . . waiting?" he stammered, astounded and

thoroughly waked up.—"To talk with me? Well, well!"
And away he hurried.

Roch stayed where he was, murmuring prayers, and
looking out into the impenetrable depths of the nocturnal
sky, vibrant with twinkling stars, wherein the moon was
rising—a sharp bright semicircle that cut deep into the
darkness.

In the cabins, the lights had gone out one by one, like
sleepy eyes that close fast: stillness reigned, disturbed only
by the quiet rustling of leaves, mingling with the bubbling
of the distant stream. At the miller's alone did the windows
all shine brilliantly, and the folk enjoyed themselves late
into the night.

At Boryna's all was still; everyone had gone to rest and
the lights were out, except for the dying embers about the
pots on the hearth, where the crickets chirped unseen; but
Roch stayed up, waiting outside for Hanka. It was near
midnight, when hoofs were heard beating upon the bridge
by the mill, and the britzka came rolling in.

Hanka was extremely depressed and taciturn; and it was
only when, supper over, Pete had gone to the stable, that
Roch made bold to ask if she had seen her husband.

"All the afternoon. He is in good health and spirits,
and asked me to send you a greeting. . . . I saw the other
lads also.—They are to be set free, but none will tell when.
Also I saw the lawyer who is to defend Antek. . . ."

She was, however, keeping back something that lay like
a stone at her heart, and went on talking of other and indifferent matters: till suddenly she broke down, bursting into
tears, and covering her face, while the drops came pouring
through her fingers.

"I shall come to-morrow morning," he said. "Ye need
rest. You have been much shaken, and it might do you
harm."

"Oh!" she burst out; "if I could but die and have done
with this agony!"

He bent his head and withdrew, saying nothing.

Hanka went at once to lie down by her children; but, tired though she was, she could not sleep. Ah! Antek had treated her as though she had been some importunate dog. He had eaten the Hallow-fare with a good appetite, taken a few roubles without asking whence she had got them, and not so much as said he was sorry the journey had tired her!

She had told him all her doings at the farm: he had listened with not a word of praise, but more than one of sharp censure. Then he had asked about all the village—and forgotten his own little ones! She had come out to him with what a faithful loving heart, with what intense yearning for his caresses! Was she not his own wife, the mother of his children? And yet he had not fondled her, nor kissed her, nor even inquired after her health. He had behaved like a stranger, and looked on her as one. At last, when she could speak no longer for the pain that strangled her, and her tears flowed forth, he had shouted: "Have you come all this way to whine and blubber at me?"—O God! the anguish of that moment! . . . And that was her reward for all the hard work she had done for him, all that toil so far beyond her strength, all her bitterness of woe!— Nothing; not one word of endearment, of comfort even!

"O Christ! look down on me in Thy mercy, for I can bear no more!" she moaned, her face pressed hard down upon the pillow, not to wake the children, as she lay there, weeping, sorrowing, full of deep humiliation and the sense of cruel wrong.

Neither in his presence, nor before anyone else afterwards, had she been able to pour forth her soul: only now did she at last give vent to the despair of her heart, and to those tears, more bitter than any bitterness on earth.

.   .   .   .

The next morning—Easter Monday—the weather was still more beautiful, the country-side more abundantly bathed in dew, in azure mist-wreaths, in sunshine and in joy. The birds' songs were more sonorous; the warm gales, rushing through the trees, made them murmur, as it were, a quiet prayer. The folk rose earlier, too, that day, opening doors

and windows wide, and going outside to gaze upon God's
world—on the verdurous orchards; on the vast landscape,
garlanded with spring greenery, sparkling all over with
diamonds, bathed in the light of the sun; on the autumn-
ploughed fields, with young tawny blades waving in the
wind, and rippling up to the cabins like sheets of water
teased by the zephyrs.

The boys ran about with squirts, drenching each other to
the cry of *Smigus!*—or else, hiding behind the trees round
the pond, they would deluge with water, not only the passers-by, but anyone who peeped out of doors; so that many
a cabin-wall dripped with wet, and puddles glistened all
around them.

Along all the ways and about the enclosures, the lads ran,
chasing their victims with uproarious laughter, and dead
set against the lasses, who enjoyed the pastime as much as
they did, emptying pails on their heads and dodging them
through the orchards; and as there were plenty of grown-up
girls among them, these soon got the upper hand, driving the
boys back with indomitable energy. Even Yasyek Topsy-
turvy, who had attacked Nastka with a fire-hose, was himself tackled by the Balcerek girls, drenched from head to
foot, and then flung into the pond to crown their victory.

But he, being nettled, and loath to brook such shame,
that girls should get the better of a man, called to his aid
Pete, Boryna's servant: who with him laid an ambush
cunningly for Nastka, got her fast in their clutches, dragged
her to the well, and flooded her until she screamed aloud.
. . . Then, taking Vitek to help them, and young Gulbas,
with some bigger lads, they pounced upon Mary, daughter
of Balcerek, whom they deluged so, that, stick in hand, her
mother was obliged to run and rescue her! Yagna too they
caught and drenched thoroughly, nor did they spare even
Yuzka, though she begged them hard, and ran in tears to
Hanka to complain.

"Complain she may!" they cried; "but yet she likes it:
see, her eyes sparkle with glee!"

"Pestilent fellows! they have wetted me all over!" Yagustynka growled, though pleased, and entered the cabin.

"Whom will those rascals spare!" Yuzka grumbled, as she changed to dry clothes. Yet she could not for all that forbear coming out into the porch to witness the scene: all the roads alive with noise and tumult, and the whole place thrilling with the hubbub. The lads, frantic with delight, ran about in large bands, driving all who came nigh within range of the great hose, till at last the Soltys, seeing that no one could leave his hut for them, had to put an end to this merry-making, and disperse them.

"Are ye no worse for yesterday's drive?" Yagustynka queried, as she dried herself by Hanka's fire.

"I am. It moves within me with continual leaps; I feel nigh swooning!"

"Prithee, lie down, and drink a hot infusion of wild thyme.—Ye were too much shaken yesterday."

She was greatly concerned; but, scenting the reek of fried blood-pudding, sat down to breakfast with the others.

"And you too, mistress, eat ye a morsel: hunger can do no good."

"I have a loathing for meat now: I'll make myself some tea."

"That's good to cleanse the bowels; but ye'll be sooner well if ye take hot vodka, boiled with lard and spices."

"No doubt: such medicine might even raise one from the dead," Pete laughed. He had ensconced himself close to Yagna, following her eyes, offering her courteously anything she happened to look upon, and trying to enter into conversation. But she took little notice of him; and so he presently came to ask Yagustynka about the prisoners she had seen.

"I have seen them all," she said. "They are not in cells apart, but in large rooms, as in a Manor, with plenty of light and good floors. Only, at all the windows there is a sort of cobweb of iron, lest they should take a fancy to walk out of doors. As for their food, it is none of the worst. . . . I tried the pease-porridge they get at noonday. It seemed to have been boiled in an old boot, and seasoned with axle-

grease! . . . There was fried millet, too.—As to that, our
dog Lapa would not have touched it, no, nor smelt at it
either, but done something else, belike! . . . They have to
live at their own expense; and if anyone lacks money, let
him pray over his food to improve it," she wound up in her
usual sour fashion.

"Some, they say, are to come back next Sunday," she
added, lowering her voice with a glance at Hanka. At this,
Yagna started up and left the room; and Yagustynka set to
talking about Kozlova's expedition.

"They came home late, having quite failed; but they be-
held sausages on every side, and had a good look round at
the Manor. They inform us, it smells otherwise than do
our cabins!—But the Squire said he could in no wise help
them; that was the affair of the Commissioner and the
Government. Even were he able, for no man of Lipka would
he do aught: he was the greatest sufferer of all, and because
of them!—Look you, he has been forbidden to sell the
forest, and the merchants are now bringing actions against
him on that account.—He swore brimstone oaths, and cried
out that, if he had to be a beggar because of the peasants,
he hoped the plague might destroy them all!—All the morning, Kozlova has been carrying this news from hut to hut,
and threatening revenge."

"The more fool she. What harm can threats do?"

"My dear, we all know that the very weakest can find a
place where to strike home!"—Here she broke off abruptly,
and ran to support Hanka, who was leaning helpless against
the wall.

"Good God!" she murmured in dismay; "is a miscarriage
coming on?" And she put her to bed. Hanka had fainted,
her face was covered with drops of perspiration, and flecked
with yellowish spots; she lay scarce breathing, while the old
woman dabbed her temples with vinegar. Then she put
some horse-radish to her nostrils and Hanka opened her
eyes and came to.

The others went to fulfil their several duties. Vitek alone
remained, and when a convenient opportunity offered itself,

begged his mistress to let him take his automaton into the village.

"Well, you may; but take heed to behave yourself, and not soil your garments. Tie up the dogs, lest they run after you everywhere.—When will you start?"

"After Vespers."

Yagustynka then put her head in at the window, and said:

"Where are the dogs, Vitek? I was taking food to them, but neither of them comes to eat."

"Aye, and I have not seen Lapa in the byre this morning. Hither, Burek! come hither!" he cried, running to and fro; but no bark answered his calls.

"They must," he said, "have wandered out some distance."

No one could think where the dogs had gone. After some time, however, Yuzka heard a faint whining sound, that seemed to be somewhere in the yard. Finding nothing there, she went into the orchard, fancying that Vitek was punishing some dog that had strayed on to the premises. To her surprise, no one was in sight; the place was now silent, the whining had ceased. But, going back, she stumbled over Burek's body. It lay dead close to the cabin, its head beaten in!

Her cries at once brought the whole household to the place.

"Burek has been killed—by thieves, I doubt not!"

"Surely and indeed, 'tis so!" Yagustynka screamed, seeing a lot of earth dug out, and a large pit yawning beneath the foundations.

"They have dug through, even to Father's store-room!"

"Why, a horse might have been dragged through so large a hole!"

"And the pit is sprinkled all about with grains of corn!"

"O Lord! peradventure the robbers are still in there!" Yuzka cried.

They rushed into Boryna's dwelling. Yagna had gone out; the old man lay like a log; but in the store-room that was usually dark, there now was light from the hole which had been dug, and everything within was plainly visible, strewn about in the greatest disorder. The corn had been poured out over the floor pell-mell with articles of clothing torn down from the poles they had been stretched on; and among these, pieces of wool, unspun or spun into many a yarn and hank, lay twisted and torn and tangled.—But what had been stolen? No one could tell as yet.

Hanka nevertheless was sure this was the blacksmith's doing, and reflected with a hot flush that, had she waited but one day more, he would have found and taken the money. She bent forward over the pit to hide from all present her feelings of satisfaction.

"Is naught missing in the byre?" she asked, feigning uneasiness.

By good luck, all was right there.

"The door," Pete observed, "has been properly locked"; and, striding over to the potato-pit, he pulled out a big bundle of straw that closed the entrance, and dragged thence Lapa, alive and whining.

"The knaves thrust it in there, 'tis clear; but how could Lapa let them do it? So fierce a dog!"

"And how was it no bark was heard last night?"

They sent to inform the Soltys, and the news flew over all the village. People thronged into the orchard, the pit was as much besieged as a church confessional: everyone peeped in, looked Burek over, and gave his opinion.

Roch also came. He calmed Yuzka, who, voluble, excited, and tearful, was telling them what had occurred; then, going in to Hanka, who had lain down again, he said:

"I feared lest ye might take this too much to heart."

"Wherefore? Glory be to God, he has stolen nothing." She added, in a low voice: "For he came too late."

"Have ye any guess who it is?"

"The blacksmith! I'd lay my life on't!"

"Then—was he searching for aught in particular?"

"He was: but failed.—I name him only to you."

"Certainly.—Unless he had been taken in the very act, or ye had witnesses.—Well, well! Money makes a man dare awful things!"

"Good friend," she entreated, "not even Antek is to know of this!"

"I am not one to talk at random, as you are aware. Moreover, 'tis easier to slay than to beget.—I knew the fellow for a knave, yet would never have suspected him of that."

"Oh, he sticks at naught: well do I know him."

The Voyt, arriving with the Soltys, then set to make a thorough search, questioning Yuzka carefully.

"Were Koziol not in jail," he muttered, "I should think it to be his deed."

"Hush, Peter," the Soltys interrupted, nudging him; "there is his wife, just coming up."

"They must have been frightened away; nothing has been taken."

"We must notify the gendarmes, of course. . . . More work! Satan will not let a man rest, even in this holy time."

The Soltys bent down and picked up a bloodstained rod of iron.

"It was with this Burek was done to death."

The thing passed from hand to hand.

"It is one of those rods out of which they make tines."

"Perhaps stolen out of Michael's forge."

"The forge has been closed ever since Good Friday!"

"They may have stolen it and brought it hither: I, the Voyt, tell you so. The blacksmith is not at home: what's to be done? This is no one's business but mine—and the Soltys'!" He raised his voice and shouted at them to go home and not waste time to no purpose.

Little as they cared for his blustering, it was now time for church; so the crowd melted away quickly, for parishioners from other villages were dropping in already, and the bridge was rumbling with carts.

When all had gone, Bylitsa went out to the orchard, to look at his dog, talk to it softly, and try to coax it back to life.

Hanka remained lying alone in bed, when everybody had

gone to church, and the hut was empty. For a time she
prayed and thought of Antek; then, the old man having
taken the little ones out into the road, and all being very
quiet, she fell fast asleep.

Time slipped away, and she was still sleeping when, near
noon, the sound of the organ playing and the people singing
in unison came wafted on the breeze, and the bells tolling
for the Elevation made the windows vibrate. What woke
her at length was the noisy clatter of the wagons driven home
at full speed along the road, past holes and ruts; for on
Easter Monday it is the custom to try who will be first
home after High Mass. It was a confused torrent of horses,
carts and people, of whips rising and falling all the way,
twinkling athwart the orchard-trees. They raced so furiously that she felt the cabin tremble, as the wind bore the
clatter and the din of laughter to her ears.

She had a mind to get up and take a look outside; but
her people were home now, and Yagustynka set about getting
dinner ready. She meanwhile related how the church had
been so crammed that half the people had to stand outside;
how all the Manor folk had been there; and how his Reverence had, after Mass, called all the farmers to the sacristy
to confer with them. Yuzka prattled about the way the
young Manor ladies were dressed.

"Know ye that the damsels of Vola wear humps on their
hinder parts, and look like turkey-cocks when they put up
their tails?"

"They pad themselves with hay or rags," the old woman
explained.

"But their waists! They are drawn in like wasps. One
might cut them in two with a whip. And where they stow
away their bellies, none can say! Oh, I was close to them,
and saw them well!"

"Their bellies? Why, they cram them in under their
stays. A Manor servant, who had once been chambermaid
at Modlitsa, told me that some of those damsels starve themselves, and gird their waists tight while they sleep, lest they
should grow stout! At the Manors 'tis fashionable for girls

to be thin as laths, with only the back parts swelled out!"

"Not so with us; lads laugh raw-boned girls to scorn!"

"They are right. Our lasses should be even as ovens, all rounded out and full of such heat flowing from them that men feel warm when they come near," said Pete, his eyes feasting on Yagna, who then was removing the pots from the fire-place.

"Why, I declare!" thundered Yagustynka; "that fright! He has just had a spell of rest and a morsel of meat; and lo, he is at once hankering for something else!"

"When such a one is at work, it is a marvel her bodice does not split at every motion!" he went on; and would have served them some further specimens of his eloquence, when Dominikova, coming in to tend Hanka, drove him from the room.

They took dinner outside in the porch, where it was bright and warm. The early verdure quivered and glittered on the boughs, fluttering like butterflies; and the warbling of birds came to them from the orchard-trees.

Dominikova forbade Hanka to leave her bed. Veronka came in with her children immediately after dinner. A bench was placed close to the bed, and Yuzka brought in some portions of the Hallow-fare, and a flask of vodka sweetened with honey. Hanka, though not without difficulty, offered these (according to the dignified custom among peasants on such occasions) to her sister and to the neighbours who had dropped in to visit and sympathize, taste the vodka, nibble slowly at the sweet cakes, and talk of various topics—especially the hole dug to rob the store-room.

Outside, too, folk had come to chat with the household, and walk to and fro in the orchard, much exercised in mind at the sight of the hole, which the Voyt had not allowed to be filled up till the arrival of the scrivener and gendarmes.

Yagustynka had repeated the whole story for about the hundredth time, when the lads entered the yard with the automaton cock. Bravely attired, even to wearing boots and Boryna's cap (much on one side), Vitek led the band. After him came the others: Maciek, Klebus, Gulbas, Yendrek, Kuba, and the son of Gregory the Wry-mouthed. These had sticks in their hands and scrips on their backs; but under his arm Vitek bore Pete's fiddle.

They strutted out in procession, first of all to his Reverence, as the young men had done in past years, entered the garden boldly and formed up in line in front of the house, with the cock trundling before them, Vitek scraping his fiddle the while. Gulbas then, having wound up the machine, began to crow, and they all, stamping and striking the ground with their sticks, began singing in a shrill tone certain doggerel lines, winding up with an appeal for a present.

They sang for a long time, and ever louder, till his Reverence came forth, admired the cock, gave each of them a five-kopek piece, and sent them away delighted.

Vitek was sweating with fear, lest his Reverence should say something about the stork. But he seemed to have passed him over amongst his companions, and after he had retired, sent the housemaid to them with some pieces of sweet cake. Loud they raised their song of thanks, and then went on, first to the organist's, then all through the rest of the village, where they had much ado to protect their machine from rough handling and the pokes of inquisitive sticks.

Vitek, their leader, had an attentive eye to everything, stamping for them to commence singing, and signalling with his bow when to raise and when to drop their voices. In short, the whole *Dyngus* was performed with such life and spirit that their strains filled the place, and people wondered to see such mere urchins already playing so well the part of grown-ups.

It was near sunset when the big dame Ploshkova, having first gone in to see Boryna, came also to call upon Hanka.

"As ever, as ever! O Lord!—I spoke to him: no word in reply. The sun is shining on his bed, and his fingers catch at the beams, as if to play with them: just like a little baby. Ah, I could have wept to see what such a man as he has come to!" So she said, seated by Hanka's bedside; but she drank the vodka and reached out for the cake as willingly as any.

"Does he eat anything now? He seems to have put on flesh."

"Yes, he can take a little: maybe he is getting better."

Yuzka rushed in, screaming: "They have taken the cock over to Vola!" but, seeing Ploshkova there, turned and ran out to Yagna.

Hanka called after her: "Yuzka, you must see to the kine: it is time now!"

"Yes, yes," said Ploshkova. "'A holiday is a holiday, but the belly must have its dues alway!'—The lads came to me likewise. A clever fellow that Vitek of yours, and a keen-sighted one too!"

"But ever first to play and last to work!"

"My dear, servants are never good for much. The miller's wife told me she could not keep a single girl for six months."

"They get too much new bread there—and go wrong in consequence."

"That's as it may be; but they have the journeyman to help them that way, or the son—him at school—who looks in at times; aye, and the miller himself will let none of them alone, they say. . . . 'Tis true that our servants grow bolder daily. My own herdsman, now the goodman is away, treats me shamefully and insists on milk in the afternoon! Who ever heard of such a thing?"

"Oh, I know their humours, I have a man myself. But I must agree to all he wants, else he would leave me when work is heaviest; and on such a large holding, what could I do without him?"

"Have a care they do not take him from you!" she said, lowering her voice warningly.

"Do ye know of anything intended?" Hanka exclaimed, greatly alarmed.

"Something I heard of—a rumour, peradventure a lie: I cannot say.—But I talk and talk, and forget what I have come for. Several have promised to come to my cabin for

a chat. Do you come too. All the best folk will be there:
young Boryna's wife must not be away."

This was flattering; but Hanka had to excuse herself,
for she felt too unwell. Ploshkova, much annoyed, went
to invite Yagna. She too pretexted a previous engagement
with her mother.

From outside the hut, Yagustynka's mocking voice was
heard:

"Ye would fain have gone, Yagna, but ye are hankering after the lads, and there's no one at Ploshkova's but old
fogies like Ambrose. No matter: they wear hose just the
same as young men!"

"You! every word you say is a stab—as usual!"

"For I," she jeered, "being merry, would that all might
have their desires!"

Trembling with rage, Yagna left the house, staring vacantly in front of her, and scarce able to choke down her
tears. *It was true;* the longing she felt was intolerable.

What though the very air told of the feast-day, and folk
swarmed to and fro, and the village resounded with shouts
of laughter, and echoed to the songs of women seen far
away, crimson against the grey sown fields? She laboured
none the less under a deep oppression, an unbearable sadness of craving, which she had been suffering ever since the
morning. To drive it off, she had gone round to her acquaintances, taken long walks along the roads and meadows,
even changed her clothes twice or thrice: all would not do.
Still, and yet more intensely, did she pine to go somewhere,
do something, seek . . . she knew not what!

And now she wandered out upon the poplar road, gazing
at the huge red disk, slowly descending and throwing streaks
of light and shadow athwart the highway.

The cool of twilight soon began to envelop her, though
the still warm breath of the plain filled her with a thrilling
rhythmical sense of pleasure. The noises of the village came
faintly to her ears, and the fiddle, wailing mournfully, smote
upon her heart-strings.

On she went: whither and urged by what, she could not say.

She sometimes moaned heavily, sometimes motioned with her hands as she roved, sometimes stopped short, helpless, darting fiery glances round her. And then she walked on farther, weaving thoughts as subtle and impalpable as gossamer, or those threads of light upon the water which disappear at the touch of the hand. She looked sunwards, and saw—nothing: the rows of poplars before her seemed blurred, and as if seen in memory only. But she was mightily conscious of her own Self, and of something possessing that Self, making it smart and cry out and shed tears; of something that was carrying her away, making her wish she could take the wings of the birds she saw flying westward, and sail with them whithersoever they went. She felt in the grip of a Power instinct with burning tenderness, that forced tears from her as well as flames. . . . And on her way she plucked at the poplar-shoots, to cool her parched lips and her eyes that shot fire!

Now and again she would sink down beneath some tree, rest her chin upon her hands, and fall into a day-dream. . . .

All this was the spring, singing, as it were, its glowing hymn within her, pervading all her being, working in it as it does in the fruitful fields, in the trees swelling with young sap that burst into a song of life as soon as the sunbeams warm them.

She tottered along, her eyes tingling, her fainting limbs barely able to support her any more. And a new desire came over her: to weep aloud, to dance, to roll amongst those soft fleeces of growing corn, cool with pearly dews; and then again she craved to leap in among the brambles, dash through the thorny copses, and feel the sweet wild tearing pain of wrestling and of strife!

Suddenly she turned back, and, hearing the sound of a violin, went in that direction. Ha! how everything was seething wildly within her, and brimming over with such abnormal excitement that she had a mind to leap about, to revel in some close-crowded tavern, even to drink herself to death—what did she care?

Upon the way from the churchyard to the poplar road, now quite drowned in the ruddy rays of sundown, someone was coming along, book in hand, and had stopped beneath a clump of silver birches.

It was Yanek, the organist's son.

She tried to get a glimpse at him through the trees, but he caught sight of her.

She was minded to run, but her feet seemed rooted to the ground, and her eyes were fixed on him as one fascinated. He came forward smiling, and showing white teeth between rosy lips: a tall stripling, slender, and of milk-white complexion.

"Did ye not know me, Yagna?"

His voice struck a chord that resounded somewhere within her.

"How could I fail to? . . . But yet ye are somehow different, Yanek, not quite the same."

"Why, of course, as we grow, we surely must change.— Have you been to see someone at Budy?"

"Nay, only wandering about: ye know, Eastertide does not end till to-morrow."—Touching his book with her hand, "Religious, is it?" she asked him.

"Not in the least. 'Tis of far-off lands and the seas that surround them."

"Heavens! of the seas? What, then are not the pictures ye have there images of the saints?"

"See!" He opened the book before her, showing the illustrations. With heads bent down, touching almost, they stood there, shoulder to shoulder, hip to hip, inadvertent. Now and then he explained some picture; and she was enraptured, raising her eyes to admire him, not daring to breathe for emotion. Now they pressed closer still, for the sun was under the forest, and it was hard to make out the pictures.

All of a sudden, a shudder went through him; he shrank

back a little, murmuring: "Twilight has fallen; 'tis time to go home."

"Let us go, then."

So they went on in silence, and almost unseen in the shadows. Now the after-glow had faded, and dusk was trailing its bluish haze over all the fields. That day no gorgeous sunset blazed in the western sky, but through the tall poplars the daylight was seen to die away in a bright expanse of gold.

"Is it true, what they print there?" Yagna inquired of him, stopping awhile.

" 'Tis true: every word true!"

"Lord! such vast waters, such wonderful countries! 'tis hard to believe it."

"Nevertheless, 'tis the truth, Yagna," he whispered, and looked kindly into her eyes, and so close that she held her breath, and a shiver passed through her frame. She bent forward with a gesture as of one who yields all, expecting him to embrace her, pressed to the bole of a tree hard by, and was opening her arms to him, when he suddenly started back, saying: "I must be off: it is late. Farewell, Yagna!" and vanished.

Many minutes elapsed before Yagna could move from the spot.

"What! has the boy cast a spell on me? What is this that I feel now?" she wondered, as she dragged along slowly, with her brain in a whirl, and strange tremors running all through her.

Passing the tavern, she caught the muffled sounds of the music and conversations. She looked in at the window. Mr. Yacek, standing in the middle of the room, was sawing away at his violin. Ambrose, reeling close to the bar, was talking loud to the *Komorniki* and from time to time reaching out his hand for a glass.

Someone caught her by the waist unexpectedly: she screamed and tried to wrench herself loose.

"I have you now, nor will I let you go.—Come for a drink with me!" It was the voice of the Voyt, who held her firm in his grasp; and they both went by a side-door into the tavern parlour.

No one had seen them, for few were out in the road, and it was very dark.

Now the village was quiet: all the outside sounds were hushed and the crofts were empty and silent. Everybody was at home. Eastertide, that dear time of rest, was nearly over; and the toilsome morrow was lurking outside on the threshold, already baring its sharp fangs for them.

Lipka therefore was rather melancholy and subdued that evening: only at Ploshka's was there a numerous party. Her neighbours had come together and were conversing with dignified mien. The Voyt's wife sat in the place of honour: by her side Balcerek's wife, stout and loud-mouthed, was maintaining her opinion: close to her sat Sikora's dame, raw-boned as heretofore; Boryna's cousin, much given to babbling; and the blacksmith's wife, her babe at her breast; and the Soltysova, talking in low devout tones: and, in short, all the foremost women in the village.

As they sat there solemnly, stiff and formal of mien, one was somehow reminded of a lot of brooding hens with ruffled plumage. They wore their best holiday attire: kerchiefs let half-way down the back (Lipka-fashion), and great frills standing higher than their ears, with all their possessions in the way of coral beads hung over them. They enjoyed themselves, however, after their slow fashion, and their good humour increased little by little, as their cheeks grew flushed. And presently, tucking up their petticoats carefully, lest they should crumple them, they edged nearer and nearer to one another, and soon were engaged in more than one wordy tussle.

But after the smith, who said he was but just back from town, had joined them, they waxed merrier still. The fellow was a rare talker; and being rather tipsy, he began to humbug them with such comical mystification that he made them hold their sides with laughter. The whole room was in a roar, and he himself laughed so loud that they could hear him at Boryna's.

The party lasted a long while, and Ploshka had to send three times to the tavern for vodka.

At Boryna's they sat in the court-yard. Hanka had risen and joined them, with a sheepskin coat over her shoulders to protect her from the chill night air.

So long as there was light enough, Roch read to them; but when darkness had fallen over the land, he went on to tell them many a thing of wonder that they were most curious to hear. The dusk soon became so deep that the party were barely outlined on the white cabin-walls. It was cool outside, and no stars shone; a dull stillness, broken only by the bubbling waters and barking dogs, pervaded the place.

They all were together in one group—Nastka and Yuzka, Veronka and her babes, Klembova and Pete, seated almost at Roch's feet: Hanka was sitting on a stone, a little apart.

He told them much about the history of Poland, and also many a holy legend, and tales of the wonderful things in the world, of which he related so many a marvel that no one could remember all he said.

They listened motionless and hushed, drinking in those honey-sweet words of his, as the parched earth drinks in the warm raindrops.

And he, barely seen in the gloom, spoke in a low solemn voice words such as these:

"To all who await spring in prayer and toil and readiness, it surely cometh at the end of winter. . . .

"In the end, the oppressed ever triumph: therefore have ye trust. . . .

"Man's happiness is a field to be sown with blood and sacrifice and labour: whoso has sown it thus shall see the crop grow and shall reap the harvest. . . .

"But he that careth only for daily bread shall not sit at the table of our Lord. . . .

"Who only complaineth of evil, and doth no good, he maketh the evil worse."

He spoke long, but in words of wisdom hard to bear in mind; in a voice ever lower and more loving he spoke, until

the darkness quite swallowed him up. Then it seemed as
though some holy being were speaking from beneath the
ground: as though the dead ancestors of the Borynas,
graciously permitted to revisit the earth at this sacred
Eastertide, were now uttering words of solemn warning to
their descendants, out of those crumbling walls, those bent
gnarled trees, that thick dense gloom around.

Over all these utterances their minds pondered deeply;
like a bell in the depth of their hearts they resounded,
arousing within them dim emotions—strange, eerie, unac-
countable desires.

They did not so much as remark that all the dogs in the
village had set to barking, nor that the feet of many people
were running fast.

"Fire! Podlesie is burning!" a voice cried to them from
beyond the orchard.

It was true. The farm buildings of the Manor domain of
Podlesie were on fire, and crimson-red bushes of flame were
growing in the night.

"Heaven save the mark!" Yagustynka ejaculated, as the
memory of Kozlova's threats flashed through her brain.

"A judgment of God upon him!"

"For the wrong he has done us!" many voices cried in
the dark.

Doors slammed; the folk, half clad, ran out, and crowded
more and more numerous on the bridge by the mill, from
where the conflagration could best be seen In a few minutes the whole village was there.

The farm stood on a hill-side close to the forest, a few
versts away from Lipka, whence the increase of the fire was
plainly visible. On the black background of the wood, the
fiery tongues now multiplied, and dark-red rolling volumes
of smoke burst forth. There was no wind, and the conflagration leaped straight up, higher and higher: the buildings burned like bundles of resinous fire-wood; and a ruddy
flickering blaze swept up into the shadows of the night, with
pillars of dark, towering smoke.

The air was soon rent by the sound of agonized bellowing.

"Their cattle-shed is on fire: they can save but few, for there is but one door!"

"Ah, the cornstacks are burning now!"

Others cried out, in consternation: "So are the barns!"

The priest, the smith, the Soltys, and the Voyt (though in his cups, and barely able to stand) came on the scene, crying out to the people to rush to the rescue.

No one hastened to move. A savage growl ran through the multitude:

"Let our lads be freed, and they will save the farm!"

Imprecations, threats, and even the priest's tearful entreaties, were all of no avail. They stood gazing stolidly on the fire with sombre looks, and remained immovable.

Kobusova even shook her fist at the Manor servants she could see. "Those sons of dogs!" she shrieked.

Only the Voyt, the Soltys, and the smith drove over to the fire at last; and that without any appliances, the peasants refusing to let them take so much as a bucket with them.

"The dirty scoundrel who touches one of them shall be cudgelled to death!" they all shouted in chorus.

The whole village was there in a close-packed crowd, down to the youngest, busily soothing the cries of infants in arms. Few spoke. All looked on, greedily feasting their eyes and hearts, enjoying the thought that the Lord had punished the Squire for the wrong done them.

It burned on far into the night, but no one went home. They waited patiently till all was over, till the whole farm was one sea of fire, and the burning thatches and shingles flew up and came down in a red rain, and the vermilion reflections from the great sheets of fire waving in the dark, tinged the tree-tops and the mill-roof, and threw a faint glimmer on the pond, strewn as it were with dull glistening embers.

Rolling carts, men's shouts, the din of bellowing, and fearful threats of destruction, echoed through the village:

and still there the people stood like a living wall, feeding their eyes and souls with vengeance.

But there arose from outside the tavern old Ambrose's husky drunken voice, continually singing the same unvarying song!

CHAPTER VI

IT was a strange piece of news that Hanka heard the next morning; one that made her start up in bed. But Yagustynka luckily caught hold of her in time, and pressed her down on the pillow.

"Hold ye still! Is the cabin afire?"

"But he says such things!—He must be mad!"

"Nay," Bylitsa replied, stooping to sneeze after an abundant pinch of snuff; "nay, I am in my right mind, and what I say I know. Since yesterday, Mr. Yacek is my lodger!"

"Hear ye? He has quite lost his wits! . . . Pray look whether they are not coming home yet: it must be starved, my new-born!"

The old woman went on tidying and sanding the room.

Hanka's father sneezed so violently that he was thrown back on to a bench.

"Ye're loud as the trumpet that tells the time in the market-place."

"Ah, because it is strong snuff: Mr. Yacek gave me a whole packet!"

It was early. The sun, bright and warm, looked into the cabin; the orchard trees waved; through the half-open door appeared the straight necks of geese, with coral beaks at the end; and a whole family of muddied and noisy goslings tried to scramble over the high threshold. Thereupon a dog growled: the geese screamed, and brooding hens in the passage cackled in alarm, and began to flutter out of their nests.

"Please drive them to the orchard; they will have grass to pluck, at any rate."

"I will, Hanka, I will, and see that no hawk come nigh them."

"What are the farm-lads about?" she asked, after some time.

"Oh, Pete is ploughing the potato-fields close to the hillock, and Vitek harrowing our field of flax."

"Is that land still wet!"

"It is: clogs stick fast; but it will dry speedily, when harrowed."

"I may perchance leave my bed, ere the land can be sown."

"Oh, have a care for yourself just now. Do not fear lest anyone steal your work!"

"Have the kine been milked?"

"By me! Yagna had set the pails outside the byre, and gone away."

"She runs about Lipka continually, like a dog: a useless woman on whom there is no counting.—Tell Kobusova I will let her have the cabbage-patches. Pete will take her manure, and plough it in; but she must work four days a week for every field. Half to be done when we plant the potatoes, and the other half in harvest-time."

"Kozlova would gladly take the flax-fields on the same terms."

"She would not do: too lazy.—Let her seek elsewhere: last year she wagged her tongue against Father all through the village, saying he had treated her unfairly."

"Please yourself: yours is the land, do as ye will with it. —Ah! Filipka came for potatoes yesterday, while you were lying in."

"To be paid for in cash?"

"No, in work. In that hut there is no money: they are starving."

"Let her have a bushel now. If she wants more, she must wait till we have done planting them. I cannot say how much we shall have to spare. Yuzka will go and measure out a bushel for her.—Though Filipka is but a poor worker."

"Whence should she get the strength? Too little food, too little sleep, and every year a baby!"

"Hard times! Harvest over the hills and far away, and dearth at our thresholds!"

"Thresholds, say ye? Nay, within doors, and choking the life out of us!"

"Have you let the sow loose?"

"She is lying by the wall.—A splendid farrow, and each one as round as a roll."

Here Bylitsa appeared in the doorway.

"I have left the geese among the gooseberry-bushes," he said.—"Well, who should come to me at Easter but Mr. Yacek, saying: 'I will live with you, Bylitsa, be your lodger, and pay you well'? I thought he was flouting me, as the gentry are wont to flout the peasant folk; so I replied: 'Oh, I don't mind getting a little money, and I have a room to spare.'—He laughed, gave me a packet of snuff (prime Petersburg quality), looked round my place and said: 'If you can abide here, so can I; and I'll fix up your hut so that it will soon look like one of our houses'!"

"Well, I declare!" said the old woman in amazement. "Such a great man—own brother to the Squire!"

"So he made himself a bed of straw beside mine—and there you are! When I went out, he was on the door-step, smoking a cigarette, and throwing some corn to sparrows."

"But what will he have to eat?"

"He has some pots with him, and is continually making and drinking tea."

"There must be something underneath all this. One so high-placed would not do this without some reason."

"The reason is that he has lost his reason! All men seek and strive to better themselves: why should one such as he strive to be worse off? Only because his wits are gone," said Hanka, raising her head, for voices were heard within the enclosure.

They were coming back from the christening. Yuzka opened the march, with the baby, swaddled in a pillow, and covered with a shawl; then came Dominikova escorting

it, then the Voyt and Ploshkova, the godfather and godmother; and, last of all, Ambrose limping along after
them.

But before entering, Dominikova took up the child, and,
crossing herself, carried it all round the cabin, stopping at
each corner according to some old prehistoric rite, and saying:

"From the East cometh Wind.

"From the North cometh Cold.

"From the West cometh Night.

"From the South cometh Heat.

"And on every side, O human soul, beware of evil, and
put thy trust in God alone."

"H'm!" laughed the Voyt; "that Dominikova seems such
a pious one, but she's a famous warlock all the same!"

"Truly," Ploshkova replied, "prayers do good; but all
know that a few charms thrown in do no hurt."

They entered all together. Dominikova undid the child,
and put it, stark naked and red as a crayfish, into its mother's
arms.

"O Mother, we bring you a real Christian, who in holy
baptism has received the name of Roch. May he live and
thrive and be your consolation!"

"And may he beget a dozen young Rochs! A roaring
fellow he is! No need was there to pinch him at christening; and how he spat the salt out!"

The little one was wailing and kicking out its legs upon
the feather-bed. Dominikova wiped its eyes and mouth
and forehead with some drops of vodka; and only then
did she allow Hanka to take it to her breast. To this it at
once turned, clung ravenously, and was hushed.

Hanka then thanked the godfather and godmother very
heartily, kissing them and the others present, and excusing
herself that the christening was not such as befitted the son
of a Boryna.

"Then have another one next year," said the Voyt, merrily,
wiping his moustache, for the vodka glass was coming his
way; "and that one will make up for this."

Here Ambrose blurted out thoughtlessly: "A christening without the father is like a sin without absolution!"

This opened the floodgates of Hanka's grief, until the women presently drank to comfort her, and gathered her into their arms with great compassion. Presently she was soothed, begged their pardons, and asked them to take something to eat. And, indeed, a great dish of scrambled eggs and minced sausage was spreading its fragrance through the air.

It was Yagustynka who served the visitors, for Yuzka was crooning to the new-born child, rocking it to sleep in the large kneading-trough, for the old cradle had lost its rockers.

Long did spoon after spoon go tinkling into the dish, nobody speaking the while.

Children were crowding outside in the passage, and more and more little heads came peeping into the room; so the Voyt flung a handful of caramels out into the yard to them, for which they had many a scramble and fight.

"Why, even Ambrose has lost his tongue," Yagustynka said, being the first to speak.

"Ah, he is thinking of a farm for our man-child to run . . . and a girl for him to court!"

"To find the land is the father's business: to find the girl be ours," said the godfather.

"Of them there is no lack at all. They are thrown at your heads, with a dowry besides for the one ye may choose!"

"I fancy the Voyt's wife is thinking of another child: I saw her the other day airing her dead babe's clothes on the hedgerow."

"Belike the Voyt has promised her a christening in autumn."

"And, being such an able official, has surely not forgotten the needful for its fulfilment."

"Oh, yes," he answered gravely; "to be cheerful, a cabin must have a racket of children!"

"They do indeed give much trouble, but are pledges of hope and comfort."

"Very fine!" growled Yagustynka.—"But even gold may be bought too dear!"

"True, some children are evil, and set their parents at naught. But 'tis a hard law: 'As the dam is, so the lamb is'; and 'one reaps what one has sown,'" Dominikova replied.

Yagustynka, feeling the application of the words to herself, was infuriated.

"Ye may well jeer at others, having such gentle boys, who spin and milk and wash the pots as well as the best-trained wench."

"Because they have been bred up in the right way—the way of obedience."

"And they are as like their father as any picture—even to offering their cheeks to the smiter! Aye, 'as the dam is, so the lamb is': ye have spoken truly. And I remember your deeds with the lads in your young days: small wonder, then, that Yagna goes your way, and imitates you so well. If," she hissed in her ear, "a wooden post—topped with a man's hat, set on it jauntily—should ask her, she were too good-natured to say No!" Dominikova turned deadly pale and bowed her head down as the words were spat forth.

Just then Yagna was going through the passage. Hanka called her in to take a drink. She complied, but, without even glancing at anyone, went out and into her own rooms.

The Voyt awaited her return, but in vain, and was visibly disappointed.

He had little more to say to the others; and when she came out again and went into the court-yard, his eyes wandered stealthily after her.

The talk began to flag. The two older ones sat glowering and glaring at each other, while Ploshkova whispered something in Hanka's ear. Ambrose alone was faithful to the bottle, and though no one took any notice of him, talked on and told of things incredible.

The Voyt shortly took his leave, making as if to go home; but he whipped round through the orchard into the yard, where Yagna was sitting on the byre-step, giving a mottled calf her finger to suck.

He peered cautiously round, and putting some caramels into her bosom:

"Take these, Yagna," he said; "and come to the private bar this evening; you shall have something still better."

And without awaiting her reply he hurried back to the cabin.

"Aha!" he cried; "ye have there a goodly bull-calf, I see: 'twill fetch a high price."

"No, we keep it for breeding: it comes of good Manor stock."

"And a splendid profit ye'll have of it: the miller's bull is good for nothing now. How pleased Antek will be to see the money flow in!"

"Ah me! when will he see that? when?"

"In no long time. It is I who tell you so: trust me."

"We all are waiting wearily from day to day!"

"And any day they may be back—all of them; and I know something of these matters, I fancy."

"But the fields will not wait: that is the worst of it."

"And ah! when I look forward to autumn . . ."

A cart rattled by. Yuzka peeped out and announced that it was the priest, along with Roch, bound for somewhere.

"To purchase wine for the Mass," Ambrose explained.

"And why," Yagustynka asked with a sneer, "has he rather chosen Roch to try it with him than Dominikova?"

The latter had no time to retort: just then, in came the smith, and the Voyt raised his glass.

"Michael, you are late; come and make up for lost time!"

"I shall soon catch you up: here they come to take you from us!"

Even as he spoke, the Soltys rushed in breathless.

"Away, Peter; the scrivener and the gendarmes need you."

"Mother of a dog! what, not an instant of rest? . . . Well, duty first!"

"Get rid of them quick and rejoin us."

"Can it be done? There's the Podlesie fire business, and they come, too, about the hole dug here."

He went out with the Soltys. Then Hanka, fixing her eyes on the smith:

"They will come," she said, "to take informations. Tell them *all*, Michael."

He scratched his moustache, and eyed the child with much apparent attention.

"What can I say? Just as much as Yuzka could."

"I shall not send the girl to an official: 'twould be unseemly. But say to them, you, that, so far as we can tell, naught has been stolen from the store-room. Whether this be so or not, no one knows but God . . . and . . ."—She broke off, stroking the feather-bed with a nervous cough, disguising the mockery she felt visible on her face. He replied only with a shrug, and went out.

"Oh, the dishonest knave!" she said to herself, smiling softly.

"Because the christening was a poor one, they have broken it up quite," Ambrose grumbled, taking up his cap to go.

"Yuzka, cut a piece of sausage: he can celebrate the christening at home."

"Am I a man to eat dry sausage?"

"Then moisten your inwards with vodka now, and stop grumbling."

"They were wise who said: 'Count the grains of barley put in the pot, but look not at your fingers when they work, nor count the glasses drunk at any festival'!"

They continued talking and drinking for a time, till the Soltys came round to all the cabins, ordering the people to meet the scrivener and gendarmes at the Voyt's.

This put Ploshkova in a passion. Setting her arms akimbo, she began to storm.

"Not one jot do I care for the Voyt's commands! Is it any business of ours? Have we invited them to come? Have we time for gendarme-parties, say? We do not come to heel to the first that whistles: no dogs are we! If they want to know aught, let them come and inquire. . . . 'Tis the only thing to do. . . . No, we do not go!" And with

that she ran out into the road, shouting to a group of terrified women who had come together by the mill-pond:

"To your work, neighbours; to the fields! whoso has to
do with any goodwife should know where to seek her!—Let
us not wait upon them, as if we were going to give all up at
their command, and sit like dogs at their doors! The rascals!"—So she screamed, being mightily ruffled in spirit.

Now as she was, after Borynova, the foremost goodwife in
Lipka, the women obeyed her, and dispersed in all directions
like frightened hens; and as the most part had already been
in the fields since dawn, the village now seemed empty,
except for the little ones playing about the pond, and the
old people basking in the sun.

Of course the scrivener was furious, and loaded the Soltys
with a profusion of insults; but he had to go to the fields all
the same. There he plodded to and fro for a long time,
asking each whether they knew anything about the fire in
Podlesie. They told him just as much as he himself already knew; for what he wants to keep to himself, who
would let a gendarme know?

The whole time till noon was lost in floundering about
most villainous roads, and at times getting dirtied up to the
waist with mire; for the fields were still very muddy here
and there.

Their exasperation was therefore at its height when the
scrivener arrived at Boryna's hut to draw up a statement
of facts concerning the pit dug there. He was swearing like
a trooper; and, chancing to meet Bylitsa in the porch, he
rushed at him, shaking his fists and shrieking:

"You hound's face, you! Wherefore do you not watch,
when robbers dig under your hut, eh?" And he proceeded
to mention Bylitsa's mother, with the foulest outrage.

"Mind the business you have to do: I am no servant of
yours! D'ye hear!" the old man, grievously offended,
broke in.

At this the scrivener roared: "Hold your tongue when
you speak to an official, or I'll jail you for contempt!"

But the old man's blood was boiling. He drew himself up, and cried in a hoarse voice, and with blazing eyes:

"And who are you? A servant of the public, paid by the public! Then do what the Voyt commands you, and let us free peasants alone!—Look at him! That scribbling fellow there! He has grown fat on our bread, and now would fain ride roughshod over folk!—But you have your superiors to account to, and they can punish you!"

Here the Voyt and Soltys came forward to pacify him, for he had worked himself up so, that his fingers were twitching for some weapon at hand.

"You! set down a fine for me: I'll pay it, and toss you a coin for vodka besides, if I am so minded," he called out.

But the clerk paid no more heed to him, and was taking notes of everything, and inquiring into every detail of the occurrence: while the old man rambled about the place, muttering, peeping into corners, and quite unable to come to himself. He even gave a kick to the dog!

When all was over, they would willingly have taken a morsel; but Hanka sent them word that she was just then short of bread and milk: only a few potatoes remained from breakfast.

They accordingly repaired to the tavern, loading Lipka with all imaginable maledictions.

"Ye did well, Hanka," the old man said; "and they can do nothing to you.—Why, the old Squire, though I was his serf then, and he had the right, would never, never have insulted me so!"

In the early afternoon, news came that they were still in the tavern, and the Soltys had given orders to bring Kozlova to him.

"He may as well run after the wind in the plain!" Yagustynka said, scornfully.

"No doubt she is in the forest, seeking dry fire-wood."

"No; she has been in Warsaw since yesterday. She went to get children from the hospital, and is to bring over a couple. Foundlings, I suppose."

"Yes, and let them die of starvation, as she did those she had two years ago," said Hanka.

"Poor things! Perhaps it is better so; they will not have to drag out a long life of misery."

"Aye, but even a bastard is of human blood, and 'tis no light thing to answer for their lives to God, as she must."

"But," Yagustynka pleaded, "she does not starve them of set purpose: oft she has not enough for herself; whence can she get food for them?"

"She has not taken them out of charity; she has been paid for their keep!" replied Hanka, sternly.

"Fifty *złoty* a head per year is no great sum."

"It is nothing. She drinks it all at once, and the little ones starve!"

"Not all of them.—Your Vitek, for instance, and another lad now in a hut in Modlitsa."

"Oh, but Father took Vitek from her when he could hardly toddle; and the other was in like case."

"Am I defending Kozlova? Nay, but only telling you things as I see them. Something the poor creature must earn, since she has naught to eat."

"Surely: her goodman is away, and so can steal naught for her."

"And then she made but a sorry business with Agata. That old thing, instead of dropping off—what does she do but get quite well again and leave her? And now she grumbles all over the village that every day Kozlova upbraided her for living on, to her loss!"

"She will no doubt return to the Klembas: where else should she take shelter?"

"She is offended with them. Klembova would have kept her because of her bedding and ready money. But she would not stay, had her locker taken over to the Soltys', and is now looking for a hut to die in peacefully."

"She'll not die yet. There's work for her everywhere, if only geese to tend.—Now, where in the world has Yagna gone?"

"She's at the organist's, belike, embroidering a frill for the daughter."

"As if there was too little to do here!"

"Ever since Easter," said Yuzka in a tone of complaint, "she has been there continually."

"I'll give her a lesson she will remember.—Let me look at baby."

She took it to bed with her, and as soon as dinner was done, sent everyone off to work. Soon she was alone in the room, listening to the children playing outside under Bylitsa's eye, and thinking how old Boryna lay gazing at the sunbeams that streaked the counterpane, trying to catch at them with his fingers, and babbling vague incoherent words, like an infant.

The village was deserted, for—the weather being first-rate—all who could had gone out to work.

Since Easter, it had been warmer and brighter every day.

And the days were lengthening out: misty at dawn, hot though cloudy at noon, and gorgeous with burning sunsets: true spring days.

Some, cool, bright, clear, passed by in quiet beauty, with a sprinkling of yellow dandelions, white daisies, and green buds coming out all over the willows.

And some were downright hot—burning hot; moist, soaked in sunlight, smelling of all fresh scents, and pregnant with such mighty power that when at evening the birds were still and the villagers asleep, one almost felt the upward thrust of life in the roots and growing corn, the hushed rustling of the opening buds, and the motions of all the creatures now coming forth into God's world.

But there were other days, too, totally unlike these.

Sunless, foggy, of a livid grey, with bellying clouds low down in an air so dense that it turned the head like strong drink; and the trees tossed and rocked, and all things swelled with indistinct cravings towards they knew not what: men only longed to shout, to yawn, to roll about the wet meadows of lush grass, like the silly dogs around them!

Then there were days of rain, that commenced with

dawn, with a hempen funeral pall over everything, making the roads invisible, as were the cabins too, buried in their drenched orchards. And steadily it fell, in regular tremulous grey threads that seemed unwound from an unseen spindle between sky and earth; while everything bent patiently beneath the streaming downpour, and hearkened to the many-voiced bubbling of the rills, white with foam, that ran down the dark-hued fields.

But this was a customary thing, to which no one paid heed, all going forth to work at peep of day, and coming home late in the dusk, having had scarce time enough to swallow a morsel and breathe awhile.

For whole days, then, Lipka stood abandoned, with only a few old people to guard it. Sometimes a *Dziad* would drag his aged limbs along the way, or a cart jog on to the mill; then all was deserted once more, and Lipka stood plunged in the ever-thickening greenery of its orchards.

So the days crawled by, full of hard toil, not always warm, sometimes even snowy. Small wonder if there was no noise or quarrelling in the place: they had no time for that, and every neck was bent beneath the heavy yoke of labour.

As soon, then, as morning opened its heavy eyes, and the first lark piped up, the whole village sprang to its feet with noise and din and cries of children and screams of driven geese; horses were brought out and harnessed to the plough, potatoes carted away to the fields in sacks—and lo! all was silent anew! Even Holy Mass had but a scanty attendance, and often the organ, played in an empty church, was heard only by those in the neighbouring fields, and men knelt down there to say their morning prayers when the tinkling bell announced the beginning of the service.

All worked hard: yet the land seemed as untouched as when they were not there. Only a close observer could have descried here and there a plough, with horses straining forwards along the furrows—a cart moving on the field-paths—or women, like red caterpillars, digging away in the vast plain under the bright vault of sky.

Around them, in all the hamlets visible above the orchard-tops—white walls on a blue-grey background—the air vibrated with roars and shouts and songs of toilers. To the very hills at the sky-line, the eye could see hosts of peasants, sowing or guiding the plough, and folk busy planting potatoes, and pillars of dust rising up on sandy soil wherever the harrow passed.

The Lipka lands alone, smitten as it were with the scourge of barrenness, made a mournful exception. There they lay, alas! all but fallow; for ten women, were they to strive and sweat from daybreak till night, could not do so much as one single man.

By themselves, for what were they fit? Only for delving or hoeing, to plant potatoes or flax. Over the rest of the lands the partridges piped undisturbed, ever bolder and bolder; or a hare would be seen running, but so deliberately that you could count the white flashes of its scut; or flocks of crows would fly flapping over slope and hummock.

What though the days were marvellously fine, rising like golden monstrances dipped in silver light? What though, luxuriant in verdure, they brimmed over with warm fragrance, and were made melodious by the voices of many birds, where every ditch was all full of the gold of the dandelions; where every field-path was transformed into a green ribbon embroidered with daisies, and the vast plain sprinkled all over as with a rosy dust of flowers? What though each tree was oozing and dripping with the most lovely verdure, and the whole world simmered, bubbling over with the great seething of the spring!

For round Lipka the lands lay untilled, unsown, unmanured, like lusty young swains basking lazy in the sunshine: and on their rich fruitful surface, instead of corn, wild marjorams began to peep forth, thistles grew apace, rusty sorrel plants rose up; the charlock spread amongst the autumn-ploughed fields, and mulleins and burdocks swarmed in the stubble. All those parasites of the farmers' crops, taking courage, were now creeping on far and wide, and where they had hitherto skulked about in fear and trembling, they came up boldly and grew fast, invading and conquering the ground, furrow by furrow.

It was depressing to look upon, that waste and lonely land!

It seemed as though the forests, bending down from the hills they crowned; and the brooklets that wound timidly through those deserted plots and patches; and the black-thorn thickets already swelling with their white flower-buds; and the wild pear-trees, scattered along the field-paths; and the birds of passage; and the solitary wanderer from foreign parts; and even the crosses and statues of saints that watched by the roadsides—as though they were all looking on astounded, and inquiring of the sunny days and the plots running to waste:

"Whither have the peasants gone? Those songs, those bursts of merriment, where are they? What has come over Lipka?"

The women's wailing alone told them all.

So things went on, with no change for the better, rather for the worse; because the women, unable to get even with the home-work, came more rarely to the fields.

At Boryna's, indeed, things went on as usual, though more slowly than before and not so well, since Pete had never been accustomed to that sort of work; but they went on somehow, and there were hands enough to labour.

From her bed, Hanka directed all, and with such shrewd-ness and energy that even Yagna was obliged to bear a hand along with the others. And Hanka took thought for every-thing—for the live stock—for the sick man—for the time to plough, for the seeds and where to sow them—and for the little ones, whom Bylitsa, having fallen ill, had not been able to care for since the christening. She lay alone all day long, seeing no one but her people at dinner-time and in the evening, and Dominikova who looked in once a day. None of the neighbours, not even Magda, gave sign of life, and Roch was no longer heard of: since his departure with the priest, he had not come back. She was utterly weary of lying in bed; and, in order to recover more quickly, she no longer grudged herself fat victuals, eggs, and meat. She even had a fowl killed to make broth! True, it was far too old to lay eggs: but would have brought a couple of *złoty* in the market, all the same.

In consequence, she got well so speedily that she was on her legs by Low Sunday, and resolved (in spite of all dissuasions) to have her "churching." So she went to church with Ploshkova at once after High Mass.

She was still very shaky on her legs, though, and had to lean on her companion's arm.

"It smells of spring so, my head is whirling."

"That will pass off in a day or two."

"Why, a month's change has come about in a week!"

"Spring rides a swift horse; there is no overtaking it."

"How green all round is, O Lord! how green!"

Yes: over every orchard there floated a cloud of verdure, and nothing was seen of the huts except the white tops of the chimneys. Deep in the thickets, the birds were twittering with all their might; and genial breezes came up from the fields beneath, made the weeds in the hedges wave, and the mill-pond ripple and eddy.

"The buds are big on the cherry-trees: soon we shall see the blossoms."

"We shall have plenty of fruit, unless a sharp frost nips them."

"There is an old saying: 'When the harvest is rare, there'll be fruit and to spare.' "

"I fear it looks like that for Lipka," she sighed; and the tears dimmed her eyes as she glanced at the unsown fields.

The "churching" was soon over; for the baby roared amain, and Hanka was presently so tired that she had to lie down at once on her return. But she had not lain a breathing-space, when Vitek rushed in, crying:

"Mistress, the Tsiganes! the Tsiganes are coming!"

"Evil news, in truth! Have we not enough to plague us? —Call Pete; let him lock all the doors, lest they make off with anything." And she went out in great alarm.

In a short time, the whole gang was all over the place: black-avised, in rags and tatters, with infants carried on their backs, these beggars, importunate beyond all measure, were running about everywhere, offering to tell fortunes, and even trying to make their way into the huts by force. There were but ten of them, but they made as much noise as a whole village.

"Yuzka! drive the geese and hens into the yard, and take the children within doors; they might be stolen!"

Down she sat in the porch to watch; and, perceiving a Tsigane woman trying to enter the enclosure, set the dog on her.

Lapa attacked her with savage pertinacity, and would not be driven off, though the hag lifted her staff at him and muttered sundry words and curses of magic might.

"Your curses, they are less than naught to me, you thief!"

"There would be no spells cast on us at all if ye let her come in," said Yagna, who looked annoyed.

"No, but our things would be stolen! There is no safety against such a creature, even should your eyes follow her hands all the time!—and if ye want your fortune told, why, go ye after her."

She had shrewdly guessed at the unspoken desire of Yagna, who ran out into the village, and followed the Tsiganes about all the afternoon. Unable either to free herself of a vague dread, or to overcome her curiosity to know the future, she returned to the cabin many a time, and went out again as often; and it was only when twilight fell, and the Tsiganes were going off to the forest, that she saw one of them enter the tavern, followed her in, and, in extreme terror, crossing herself again and again, had her fortune told, heedless of the bystanders.

At Boryna's cabin in the evening, Pete told them about the Tsiganes: how they had a king, who went about covered with silver bosses, and was so perfectly obeyed that, should he even in jest command one of them to hang himself, he would do so at once!

"A king of thieves!" whispered Vitek; "a mighty man whom they set the dogs at!"

"Accursed heathens!" the old woman chimed in; and, drawing nearer, related how the Tsiganes were wont to kidnap children all about the villages.

"And, to make them black, they put them in a bath of alder-bark, so that their own mother would not know them; and then they take a brick and rub away the flesh—even to the bone—where the holy, oil of baptism had been set: they simply make little fiends of them."

"And 'tis said," a girl's voice piped shrilly, "that they know charms and incantations awful even to name!"

"Aye, indeed; one would have but to breathe on you, and moustache would sprout out to a cubit's length at once!"

"We are told that a man of the parish of Slupia once set his dog on a Tsigane hag: she only waved a mirror before his eyes, and he was struck stone-blind!"

"Belike, they can change a man into anything they may choose—into a beast even!"

"Ha! whosoever drinks overmuch does truly change himself into a swine!"

"But what of that farmer in Modlitsa, who barked and ran on all fours?"

"He was possessed of an evil spirit that his Reverence cast out of him."

"Gracious Lord! can such things be? It makes my flesh creep to think of them."

"Yea, for the Wicked One prowleth on every side as a wolf round the fold!"

Terror clutched at their hearts; they gathered closer together, while Vitek, all of a flutter with dread, faltered out:

"But this place too is haunted!"

Yagustynka was down upon him at once: "Don't be a fool; don't talk nonsense."

"I do not. For I know that Something walks the stable at night, and shakes out the provender, while the horses neigh. . . . And then it passes out beyond the haystack;

for Lapa follows it, first growling, then fawning and wagging
its tail: and yet there is no one to be seen. . . . It must be
Kuba's ghost," he added in a low voice, looking round him
with dread.

"Kuba's ghost!" echoed Yuzka, and crossed herself several times.

All were greatly impressed, and cold to the very backbone.
The door opened, creaking: they all started and cried out.
It was only Hanka standing on the threshold.

"Pete, where do the Tsiganes lie to-night?"

"They said in the forest, beyond Boryna's cross."

"This night ye must watch, lest they make off with aught
of our things."

"So near their camp, they would scarcely steal from us."

"That's as it may be. Two years since, they lay in that
very place, and went off with a sow of Soha's," said Hanka,
as a warning. At bedtime, she saw to it that the byre and
stable were well locked; and, returning, she looked in at her
father-in-law's door.

"Yuzka! run and fetch Yagna: tell her to come at once:
this night I'll not leave the door unlocked for her!"

Yuzka was soon back. No lights were in Dominikova's
window, and almost all Lipka was asleep.

"The gadabout!—Well, I'll not let her in. She may spend
the night out of doors," Hanka said, as she shot the bolts.

It must have been very late when, awaked by someone
pushing at the door, and going to open it, she shrank back
with disgust: it was Yagna, positively reeking of vodka.
Her state was clear by her fumbling at the door-latch; and
then she was heard stumbling over the furniture and falling like a log on to her bed.

"Had it been a fair-day, she could not have quaffed
deeper!—Ah, well!"

The night was fated to bring trouble. Just before daybreak, such a lamentable cry thrilled through Lipka that
all those who still were sleeping donned their clothes and
ran out, thinking the village was on fire.

Balcerkova and her daughters were running about, with

shrieks and screams. They had just found their horse stolen!

The whole population was instantly outside her cabin, where, in the utmost disorder of attire, and with many a sob and wailing ejaculation, they were telling how Mary had gone out before dawn to put provender in the rack . . . to find the door open and the stable empty!

"O Lord, have mercy!—Good people, help me, do something!" the old woman shrieked, clutching at her own hair, and dashing herself against the fence.

The Soltys came and sent for the Voyt, who arrived directly, but so drunk that he scarcely could stand. Utterly incapable, he only stammered unintelligibly, and ordered the people away, till at last the Soltys was obliged to remove him.

The calamity, however, was so grievous that few paid any attention to his state. Everyone was in consternation, going from the road to the stable and back again, talking one to another, hesitating as to what course to pursue, and completely dismayed. But suddenly someone shouted:

"This is the Tsiganes' work!"

"So it is: they are still in the forest, and came round to us but yesterday."

"Let us," cried Gulbasova, "go to them quickly, take the horse back, and thrash them soundly!"

When the wild uproar that arose at her words broke out, it was just sunrise. They set to pulling stakes out of fences, and running about with clenched fists to excite each other, and were ready to set out, when a fresh development took place.

Up came the Soltys' wife, all in tears, crying that their cart had been stolen from them!

The news was like a thunderbolt, and for a time they stood breathless, staring at each other with panic-stricken looks.

A horse and cart stolen together! such a thing had never been heard of.

"There's a curse upon Lipka!"

"And it is heavier every week!"

"Of old, fewer mishaps took place in a year than now in one month."

"What, oh, what will be the end of it all!" they whispered, stricken with awe.

They all immediately hastened to Balcerkova's orchard, wherein the footprints of a horse were distinctly seen on the dewy grass and the damp earth; these they followed to the Soltys' granary. It was there that the horse had been harnessed and driven round about the path near the miller's, into the road that ran towards Vola.

Half the village followed the traces in that direction; but these at last disappeared near the burnt cornstacks in Podlesie so completely that no further clue could be found.

This robbery had dispirited them all so that, in spite of the magnificent weather, few were in a state to work. They went about dejectedly, wringing their hands, condoling with Balcerkova, and each of them most anxious for the safety of her own property.

As to the old dame, she stood beside the stable-door as by a catafalque, weeping bitterly, and pouring out by fits and starts words interspersed with sighs:

"O my chestnut horse, my only one, my beloved, you the best of all my servants!—Ah me! he was but in his tenth year; I had bred him from his foaling! Even as one of my own children he was. . . . Foaled the very year my Staho was born!—What shall we do without you now, alas!"

Her complaints were all the more sincere and hearty, because just then, no men being on her farm, it was as bad to lose both her hands (she said) as lose her horse.

Of course her neighbours surrounded her with quaint attempts at consolation, and general praises of her horse's good points.

"A first-rate beast, still in its prime, and gentle as a child!"

"It kicked my boy, neighbour; but all the same, 'twas a splendid animal."

"And though it had a spavin on one leg, it was worth forty roubles any day."

"As playful as a kitten, it was! How it used to pull down the bedding from the fences!"

"We shall not look upon its like soon," they all agreed, speaking as of a dead Christian!—And whenever Balcerkova cast a glance at the manger, her sorrow welled forth afresh, and the empty stable, like a freshly-dug grave, evoked the remembrance of her loss, and the cruel injury done to her; and she was only soothed a little when she learned that the Soltys had taken Pete from Boryna's, Valek from the priest's, and, together with the miller's man, had started off after the Tsiganes.

"Ye may as well pursue the wind in the plain. 'They that steal, can conceal,' " said one.

And indeed they returned very late, announcing that every trace of them had disappeared like a stone in the water.

The Voyt showed himself at last, and, dark though it was, took the Soltys with him to report to the police; while Balcerkova and Mary went to explore the neighbouring hamlets.

They came back with no news, save that thefts had been numerous in other villages as well. So thus there now came another weighty affliction to torment the people: anxiety for the safety of their possessions. The Voyt therefore organized a "Vigilance Band"; and, for lack of young men, told out two girls nightly to make the round of the village and watch, together with all the bigger boys: besides which, the lasses were to sleep in the byres and stables.

All this was of no avail. The very first night, certain thieves went to Filipka's hut (over the water), and made off with her sow, just about to farrow!

The woman's grief could not have been more violent if her own child had been stolen. For this was all she depended on to pull through till harvest-time; and her howls of despair, as she banged her head against the walls, were frightful to hear. She went with her tale of woe to his Reverence, who gave her a rouble, kindly promising her a young pig of the farrow he himself expected at harvest-time.

They were at their wit's end how to put a stop to these robberies: everyone was filled with dreary forebodings, and went about in fear of what the coming night might bring forth.

Luckily Roch appeared in the evening with news simply too good for belief. On Thursday—the day after next—a whole troop of neighbours was coming round to help Lipka in tilling the lands!

No, they could not believe it; but when his Reverence came to confirm the news solemnly, at last their joy burst forth. The same day, when it had ceased from raining, and the steaming pools glowed scarlet in the sundown, all the roads swarmed with people. The huts seethed with the excitement of it; neighbours ran out to talk the news over with neighbours, and wonder; the robberies were quite forgotten, and the unexpected assistance rejoiced them so much that but few troubled to watch that night.

Early the next day, preparations were made to receive their visitors: the huts were cleaned, loaves baked, carts made ready, potatoes cut up for planting; and the manure that lay in heaps on the fields was scattered about over them. In every cabin, too, much trouble was taken to get food and drink for these unforeseen guests; for it was well understood that they must be treated well, and as behoved farmers. Many a fowl and goose which they had meant to sell was now put in the pot; many a loan, too, was taken from the innkeeper and the miller. In short, Lipka was, as it were, on the eve of some great festival.

No one was more enraptured and transported than Roch himself. The whole day he trudged about, hastening the preparations where needful, and so bright and chatty that, when he came round to the Borynas', Hanka, who was unwell and had taken to bed again, could not help remarking:

"Your eyes gleam as if ye were sick with a fever!"

" 'Tis with joy they gleam! for I never yet felt so happy. Oh, think of it: so many peasants coming over to Lipka for two whole days to do all the most urgent work! How can I help rejoicing?"

"But I cannot make out how this aid is to be—gratis, paid only with a 'God reward you!'"

"Aye, for those three words they will come to our help, like true Poles and true Christians. Aye, this has never yet been seen, and therefore has evil flourished in the country. . . . Things will grow better still: ye shall see!—Our folk will gain understanding, and know that we should look only to ourselves; that none will assist us, unless we ourselves do so, each helping the other in time of need.—Ye shall see: the time will come!" he cried, radiant, stretching forth his arms as though to embrace the whole people and unite it in the strong bonds of love.

But when they asked him who had worked the miracle, he slipped away and wandered amongst the huts, where the girls were getting ready the morrow's dresses—almost holiday attire—in the hope that some unmarried man might be coming over.

The first rays of morning had but just shone upon the roofs, when the whole place was in readiness: chimneys sent up their smoke, girls darted from hut to hut, and little boys climbed up to the ridge-pole to look out along the roads. All was in solemn silence. The day was not sunny; sombre rather; but warm, with a touch of melancholy in the air. Birds chirruped loud in the orchards, but the people's voices were subdued and in keeping with the mild dank weather.

They waited a good while, and it was only just before Mass that the dull beat of the hoofs on the highways was heard, and a procession of carts appeared coming out of the distant bluish haze.

"Here they come, from Vola!—From Rzepki!—From Debitsa!—From Przylek!"

With these shouts, they ran towards the church, in front of which the first carts had stopped. Presently the whole space was thronged with horses in harness, and with men. Gaily dressed peasants leaped out of the carts, saluting the women who came crowding in on every side: while the little ones, as usual, bawled a noisy welcome to the strangers.

The service was beginning; so in they went to hear Mass first of all.

As soon as it was over, the villagers grouped themselves round about the belfry, the goodwives foremost, and the girls on either side of them, a little behind; while the *Komorniki* stood apart in a heap, unwilling to appear too bold in the presence of his Reverence, who soon appeared, gave all a hearty greeting, and, in concert with Roch, settled who should work on each farm, taking care that the wealthiest peasants should work on the best farms.

Half an hour had not elapsed before all were distributed; there only remained in front of the church a few *Komorniki* in tears, who had vainly hoped that some worker might fall to their share. And now every homestead was in motion, benches set out in front of the huts, and breakfast laid on the tables; while nips of vodka were tossed off "to their better acquaintance." The lasses served with alacrity, for most of the visitors were unmarried men, and clad almost as though they had come rather to a betrothal than to a long spell of toil.

There was no time for conversation. Nor did they linger much over breakfast; for, as they politely remarked, "they had not yet deserved hospitality."

So they speedily made for the fields, under the goodwives' guidance.

And now arose a day of high solemnity along that countryside. Waste and, as it were, palsied erewhile, it took up a new life now. Wagons rolled out of every farm-yard, ploughs moved forth on every road; all the field-paths were alive with people, hailing each other with merry cries across orchards and enclosures; horses neighed, dogs gave tongue, running wildly after the colts; a strong lusty joy of life, filling all hearts, went brimming over into the very fields! And on potato-patch and barley-plot, free space and weedy fallow, there arose a din full of gladness and excitement and racket, as in a ball-room just before the dance.

And then came silence, broken by swishing whips, and tinkling harnesses; the horses pulled amain; the ploughs,

still rusty, cut deep into the soil, turning up their first
black glossy furrows. And the people, drawing a long
breath, crossed themselves, cast their eyes over the fields, and
stooped down with a will to labour and to toil.

It was like a huge church in which the service had just
begun. With what piety did they bend over the glebe!
with what profound devotion and trust in Mother Earth did
they cast forth the sacred seed, that was to bring forth
much fruit on the morrow!

Like a swarm of bees, they beset the odoriferous soil—a
multitudinous, laborious, silent crowd: while the lark sang
overhead, poised upon unseen wings, and the wind, blowing
by, rocked the trees, tumbled the women's garments, stroked
down the rye-blades, and then fled away with a laugh to
the forest.

For many long hours they worked on at a stretch, only
from time to time straightening their bent shoulders just
for a breathing-spell. Even at noonday, they did not quit
the scene, but sat down in the field-paths to rest awhile and
eat the food brought in pots from the cabins. But no
sooner had the horses done their meal than the men returned
to the ploughs again without a moment's lingering. Only
the falling twilight at last put an end to their labour.

And now the village shone bright, and every cabin blazed
through open door or window: within they were all busy
getting supper ready. Louder grew the noise and uproar:
children clamoured, horses whinnied, gates swung rasping
rustily, calves bleated, geese gaggled, driven home from
their pastures: all Lipka effervesced with commotion and uproar.

With the evening meal there came a hush. The visitors
were invited to table, and offered the first places, as honoured
guests: they were pressed to eat of all that was best: meat
was plentiful, and vodka flowed freely.

Through the open doors and windows, the circle of heads
round the tables could be seen, spoons were heard scraping
the platters, and far into the roads came the savoury scent
of fried bacon.

Roch passed from hut to hut, sowing the seed of good words, as a thrifty farmer, full of care for his lands—yet at the same time not less happy, perhaps happier, than anyone else in the village.

At Hanka's, too, the day of joy was felt. Though they needed no assistance, yet they had, in order to be of service, invited to supper two men from Rzepki, who had been working at Veronka's and at Golab's.

These she had chosen because the Rzepki community claimed to be of noble blood.

In Lipka, indeed, people laughed that claim to scorn; but no sooner had they come in than Hanka was aware of a subtle distinction that stamped all they did.

They were undersized, thin, wore black well-fitting capotes like townsmen; their moustaches, of the colour of hemp, stood out stiffly; their looks were dignified, their manners courteous, and they spoke after the fashion of gentlemen. Very well-behaved folk they were, praising all they saw with courteous grace, and so pleasing of speech that the women felt mightily flattered.

Hanka paid such attention and had such an eye to all their needs that, during the plentiful supper she had had prepared and laid out over a clean white cloth on the table, her folk were continually dancing attendance on them. As to Yagna, who had made a first-class toilet for the occasion, she was in the seventh heaven, her eyes simply glued on the younger of the two men.

But when Yagustynka whispered: "He has only his own ladies to think of; a barefoot lass is of no account to him!" she turned very red, and hurried out to her own room.

It was then that Roch came in to take a look at the table.

"How amazed our men will be," he said, "to learn that the Rzepki folk have come to help them!"

"If we fought you in the wood, it was no private concern of ours: therefore do we bear no grudge," the elder of the two replied.

"Whenever two men come to blows, a third is sure to gain thereby!"

"Roch, ye say true. And if these twain make friends, may not that third have to smart for it?"

"He may. Sir, you speak most wisely."

"What Lipka must bear to-day, may be Rzepki's burden to-morrow."

"Every village must be a prey to the foe, my good sir, if they wrangle amongst themselves, instead of uniting. Wise friendly neighbours are as sure a defence as walls and palings: no swine can pass to root in their fields."

"We, Roch, know that; but our young men do not as yet, and there's the pity of it."

"Ah, but the time is coming, honoured sir: they become wiser!"

And thereupon they went out into the porch, where Pete was playing on his fiddle for the girls who had gathered to hear him.

The night was quiet, with but little wind; white mists were hovering over the lands, the lapwing piped in the morass, and the cluttering of the mill-wheels went on as ever. But Lipka was noisy for a long while, with laughter and merry whispers, and walks and talks by the mill-pond, men and girls together; while their elders, sitting in front of their cabins, chatted with the older guests, and enjoyed the rest and the cool air.

Everybody was afoot the next day, almost ere the sky had begun to redden in the East.

The day was clear, and, as the night had been frosty, made the landscape gleam like silver out of the cold shadows of the chilly morning. Birds were screaming, trees murmuring, waters gurgling; and the gale that shook the thickets carried away with it rattling, bawling, roaring sounds, and the songs of the lasses as they went to work.

For some time, the fields lay frosted under the dawn, lost in sound sleep, pregnant with swelling life; but the workers soon pressed in on every side upon those slumberous strips of land, now drowned in sun-soaked dust-clouds, and silently attacked every patch. And now, from the soil, and the trees, and the grey-blue distances; from the glitter-

ing reaches of the brooks, and the red-hot disk in the skyey
vault—from all these spring was pouring itself forth with
such intoxicating might that one held one's breath for
very joy, and a blessed feeling came and made the tears
to start, the knees to bend, the bosom to heave, in the
presence of that holy miracle of Life, visible in the meanest
blade that tossed in the spring breeze.

Therefore did the people gaze around with long looks of
awe, and cross themselves, and, having said their morning
prayers, set to work in silence, so that the Mass-bell had
not yet rung when everyone was at his post.

The mists soon dissolved, and all the fields shone in sunlight. As far as the eye could reach over the village lands,
divided by long green strips of autumn-sown corn, they were
swarming with red skirts, flashing with ploughs, broken up
with harrows (pulled by farm-girls), and hoed by ranks
of potato-planting women. Often, too, along the narrow
stretches of dark soil there would pass a peasant, with a
great piece of canvas round his loins; who, slightly bending
forward, would with a reverent motion of his opening hand
fling the corn down upon the expectant soil.

All toiled zealously, scarcely noticing his Reverence, who
appeared directly after Mass beside his farm-servant,
ploughing close to the road; and their amazement was extreme when they saw him coming round to the corn-plots,
hailing his parishioners jovially, offering them snuff, and,
after some friendly words, patting the children's heads,
joking with the younger women, seizing a bough to drive
a flight of sparrows from the barley, blessing the first handful of seed to be sown, or even sowing a handful himself:
all the while urging the work on so energetically that no
overseer could have done better!

He visited them again, too, immediately after dinner; for
though (as he told the women) it was St. Mark's day, the
procession was not to take place till the octave, on the 3rd
of May.

"We must not interrupt our work, for our helpers will no
longer be here to-morrow."

He stayed on in the open till the very end, with cassock tucked up, and leaning on a stick, as he was a corpulent man; yet going about unweariedly, and only now and then sitting down to wipe the perspiration from his bald forehead.

They were most pleased to see him; and somehow the work seemed to go on faster and easier under his eye: moreover, the peasants felt vastly pleased at his Reverence's kindness in coming to superintend the work.

The red sun was rolling forestwards, and they were already finishing the more urgent work in haste, because they were anxious to be home ere dusk.

Several of them would not even stay to sup, but departed after swallowing a mouthful of food; others quickly stowed away the contents of the dishes offered them; for their horses were harnessed and waited in front of the cabins.

The priest went round again with Roch, thanking every man, and especially those of Rzepki, for their friendly assistance.

"What you give to the needy you give to Jesus Himself. Aye, and though ye are not liberal in your offerings for Masses, and forget the wants of the church, and though I have for a whole year pointed out to you that your pastor's roof lets in the rain—still I shall always remember you in prayers for your generosity towards Lipka." So he spoke, moved even to tears, and kissing each man's head as it bent before him.

They were then close to the blacksmith's, and on their way to the farther end of the village, when they were stopped by a crowd of weeping *Komorniki*, headed by Kozlova.

"Excuse us, your Reverence; we have come to ask whether these people are not going to help us too," she said boldly, in a loud tone of voice.

"We were waiting for our turn to come."

The others chimed in here: "Are we poor wretches to remain without any help?"

The priest, much embarrassed, grew exceedingly red in the face.

"What am I to do?" he said; "there were not enough workers for all. . . . As it is, they have kindly given us their toil for two whole days . . . and . . . and . . ." he stammered, looking from one to another.

"Yes," sobbed Filipka, "they have helped—but whom? Why, the landowners . . . the wealthy men only!"

"For us, pestilent creatures, no one has cared or thought at all!"

"No, not even for a furrow or two, driven through our potato-plots!" they muttered gloomily.

"But, good women, they are leaving now . . . and . . . yes, something will be done for you. Truly, I know it is hard . . . your husbands are in jail with the others. . . . Yes, I assure you, something shall be done!"

"And for that something," cried Gulbasova, "how long are we to wait? If we cannot plant our potato-patches, we may as well seek a rope at once!"

"But something shall be done, I tell you! Ye shall have my horses—aye, even for one whole day . . . but pray do not tire the poor beasts. . . . And I will be the miller too: and the Borynas may also give help perhaps . . ."

"Perhaps!" roared Kozlova. "While the grass grows, the steed starves!—Come away, women!—Everything is for the farm-owners, and we, miserable starvelings, may eat stones and drink our tears!—This shepherd only cares for the sheep he can shear: we have no wool for him!"—But here the priest stopped his ears and took to flight.

They stood huddled together, sore and angry. Roch did all he could to pacify them, promising sincerely he would procure assistance, and succeeded in getting them away from the road, along which the friendly helpers were now going home in their noisy carts, with cries of gratitude from every threshold.

"May our Lord be your reward!"

"Health and happiness!"

"We'll be quits some day!"

"Remember and see us every Sunday: we're kinsfolk now!"

"Greet your parents! Bring your wives when you come!"

"Should you ever need aught, count on us!"

"God prosper you, dear ones!"

So they cried, caps and hands waving.

The lasses and all the children escorted them out of the village.

It was evening now, and the after-glow was still red upon the waters here and there; silence came down with the mists of night, but the frogs fell a-croaking in concert.

They went with them as far as the cross-ways, and parted from them with shouts and laughter, one of the girls striking up a song as they drove off.

> "Yasio, will you wed me now?
> Father's wagon comes, I trow,
>   Rattling on the way—
>   Da dana!
>   Rattling on the way!"

To which the lads answered, turning round in the carts:

> "Now, 'tis cold and we should freeze;
> Whom can frosty kisses please?
>   Let us wed in May!
>   Da dana!
>   Let us wed in May!"

And the fresh young voices echoed over the dewy grass and rolled on and afar.

CHAPTER VII

"**O**UR boys are returning!"
The news came like a flash of lightning, and spread through Lipka like wildfire.

Were they, truly? And if so, when?

No one knew.

Only one thing was sure: the constable of the commune had been at the Voyt's with a certain paper, and told it to Klembova, who was just driving her geese to the mill-pond. She had instantly rushed round to her neighbours; the Balcerek girls had cried the news out to the nearest huts: and in the space of an "Ave Maria," the whole place was quivering with glad emotion, and all the cabins were in tumult.

It was an early May morning, rather dull and rainy, drizzling and dripping over the blossoming fruit-trees.

"The men are coming back!"—All the cabins rang with a merry peal of joy; a flame was in every heart, and a cry in every throat.

The excitement grew more and more: doors banging, children rushing about, women dressing in front of their huts, and looking wistfully out into the rain through the blossoming trees which concealed the distant roads.

"All are coming back—farmers, servants, young men: every one of them!—They are here!—Out of the woods!— Upon the poplar road!" they cried, one voice after another; and those more ardent sallied forth, almost beside themselves.

Clogs clattered and splashed through the mud, and they hurried on, past the church to the poplar road. But on all the length of that long wet highway, there was nothing to be seen but deep ruts and pools of dirty water: not a single living being along the whole interminable arcade of rain-beaten poplars.

Bitterly disappointed, they hastened away to the opposite end of the village, for the men might also be coming in that direction.

That other road was empty too. Across its width, full of hollows, the rain beat, forming a mobile veil; its ditches brimmed with clayey water that overflowed the adjacent furrows and swept down quantities of drifting foam; and on the blossomy brambles which bordered the green fields, the flowers seemed shrinking in the chilly air.

They went on a little, till someone, coming out of the charred ruins of Podlesie, appeared on the road and drew nigh them.

He was a blind old *Dziad*, known to all of them. The dog he held back by a string barked furiously, straining to break loose and attack them. The man listened awhile, his staff in readiness; but soon, hearing their voices, he hushed the dog, greeted them in God's name, and said gaily:

"Ye are Lipka folk, are ye not? And a good many of you, I think."

The girls came thronging round him, talking all at once.

"A flock of screeching magpies has beset me, i' faith!" he grumbled, but listened the more attentively as they pressed closer.

So they all returned together to the village, the *Dziad* in their midst, swinging along on his crutches, his distorted legs dangling below, and his large sightless face stretched forward above: a somewhat tubby man, with red puffed cheeks, eyes sheathed with a white film, grey bushy brows, and a huge red nose.

He listened patiently till he had learned what they were out for, and then said:

"It was these very tidings I was hastening hither to bring you! A certain unbaptized one had told me in secret that your men were coming back to-day; and I hoped to be

first here with the good news. Besides, Lipka is a fine
village to visit. Now, who are these around me?"

They told him their several names.

"Why, the very flower of Lipka, I declare!—Oho! ye were
out after your young men . . . and found a blind old
beggar instead, did you?"

"Nay!" they roared; "each of us was after her father!"

"Dear, dear! Blind I am, but not deaf!"

"We were told they were coming, and went forth to meet
them."

"Far too early. If the goodmen are home by noon, it will
be well; the young fellows may not be here even at nightfall."

"If set free together, they surely will come home likewise."

"Oh, but the town and its pleasures! Are the girls there
few? What in the world should draw them hither? Ha,
ha?" he said teasingly.

"Let them enjoy themselves! We shall not fret, not we!"

"Right," said Nastka, sulkily. "There are plenty of
wet-nurses in town, and of Jews' servants too: for those
that like such, 'tis just what they want."

"If they prefer the slums and dens of towns, they are not
the men for us!"

"Have you been long away from Lipka, Father?" one of
them asked.

"Very long: in fact, since last autumn. I spent the winter
with kindly people, and lived at the Manor all the time."

"What! at Vola? with our Squire?"

"With the same. I am always welcome there, both to the
masters and to the masters' dogs: all know me, and treat
me well. I had a warm corner, close to a stove; and all the
time I plaited straw-bands and praised the Lord. . . . I
have put on flesh, and so has my dog.—Ho, ho! the Squire
is a wise man. He's a friend to the *Dziads,* for well he
knows they will share all they have with him. Ha! ha!"
He shook with laughter, and blinked his blind eyelids as he
added:

"But when God sent the springtime back again to us, it

irked me to dwell in their chambers. . . . I longed for the peasants' huts and the wide world.—Ah, this drizzling rain! it is a shower of gold, warm, abundant, fertilizing; making the young grass smell sweet throughout the land.—But whither are ye running, girls?"

He heard their footsteps as they scampered off, leaving him close to the mill, and called them once more, but to no purpose. They had seen women going by to the Voyt's, and flown that way.

About half the village was there by this time, eager for some positive news.

The Voyt, who it seemed had just risen, was sitting in shirt and nether garments on his door-step, calling to his wife for his boots, and wrapping his feet in foot-clouts, used instead of socks.

All rushed at him, breathless, greedy, and impatient to the last degree.

He let them talk, put on his grease-anointed boots, washed his face in the passage, and then, while he combed his thick fell of hair at the open window, answered them flippantly:

"Want the boys so much, do ye?—Have no fear: they will be home to-day most certainly.—Mother, hand me the paper the constable brought in; it is behind the picture."

He turned it about, and tapped it with his fingers, saying:

"Here it is, as plain as noonday.—'The Christian in-habitants of Lipka, commune of Tymov, county of . . .'— Here, read it yourselves! Your Voyt tells you they are returning, and return they will."

The paper he flung them passed from hand to hand, and though no one could make out a single letter, they knew it to be official, and, staring at it with joy mingled with dread, passed it from hand to hand till it got to Hanka, who took it in her apron and returned it.

"Good friend," she asked the Voyt timidly, "are they all to be freed—all?"

"So it is written, and so must it be!"

"My dear," said the Voyt's wife, "come in here out of the rain, you will be wet through"; but Hanka had no mind to stay, and, throwing her apron over her head, was the first to withdraw.

She walked slowly, however, being rent with conflicting joy and terror.

"Antek—Antek will be here!" she said to herself, and a strange faintness came over her, and she was fain to hold to a fence not to fall. She struggled for breath a long while, and felt weak even to swooning.—"Antek is coming— coming back!" and she would have cried aloud with delight, but for a sense of dread, of disquietude, of blind uncanny fear that surged up within her heart!

Slowly she plodded on, holding to the fences. The whole road was full of women, flushed with exhilaration, and uttering roars of laughter, and screams and exultant shouts. Some, heedless of the drizzle, had gathered to talk outside the huts; some stood by the pond: all were greatly excited.

Yagustynka met her.

"So, ye know at last?—Well, this is good news. We have been waiting for it so long that, now it has come, I feel stunned.—Have you seen the Voyt?"

"Aye; he says it is true; has even shown us the paper."

"Then—then all must be right!—Glory to Thee, O Lord! the poor men will come back . . . our farmers will return to us!" she said fervently, clasping her hands.

From the dim eyes there dropped tear after tear: which made Hanka wonder not a little.

"Why, I expected ye would be angry about this, as about everything else: and behold, ye are weeping. Oh, wonderful!"

"What would ye? Can anyone be wroth at such a time? True, now and again, out of sheer bitterness, I let my tongue wag; but there is something else at the bottom of my heart that makes me, willy-nilly, rejoice or grieve with other folk. Nay, one cannot live quite separated from all. . . ."

Now they were nearing the smithy, where hammers were clinking in cadence, flames of a peach-red hue flying out of the forge, and the blacksmith, trundling a red-hot tire, made it shrink in cooling upon a wheel that lay close to the

wall. At the sight of Hanka, the smith stopped, drew
himself up, and fixed his eyes on her face.

"Well, has Lipka cause for rejoicing at last? I hear that
some are returning."

"Some? nay, but all!" Yagustynka corrected him. "Did
not the Voyt read it so?"

"All? but he never meant felons. No: crimes must be
punished."

Hanka's brain whirled at those cruel words. She crawled
on, struck to the heart, but said as she passed:

"May your wicked tongue cleave to the roof of your
mouth!"

His laugh tore her like the fangs of a wolf, and she
hurried forward to escape from the sound.

She only felt quite recovered at the door of her cabin.

" 'Tis wet to-day," said Yagustynka; "we shall find the
ground difficult to plough."

She made light of it.

" 'Wet morning weather, and an old dame's dance, last not
long'!"

"Meanwhile we must be planting our seed-potatoes with
the hoe."

"I am expecting the women.—These tidings have delayed
them, but they will come. I sent round to them last night,
and they all promised they would not forget."

In the cabin the hearth blazed; it was warmer and brighter
than out of doors. Yuzka was peeling potatoes, and the
baby screaming for food: Hanka, kneeling down by the
cradle, gave it suck.

"Now, Yuzka, Pete has to cart the dung from Florka's
shed to the field we have, by Paches' rye-plots. He can get
several cartloads there before the rain is over."

"Ye are no friend of the slothful here!"

"Nor am I a sluggard myself!" she returned, as she covered her breast.

"Oh, I had quite forgotten. It is a holf-holiday: St.
Mark's procession, that was postponed till the octave!"

"Why, the processions are to be only on Rogation Days!"

"He announced one for to-day: we shall go as far as the roadside 'figures,' and bless the village boundaries without any Rogation procession."

"Ha!" cried Yuzka to Vitek, who entered just then; "and you boys will be thrashed at the boundaries to make you remember them." [1]

"Here are the women; run ye, and see to them. I stay inside, to make order and get breakfast ready, while Yuzka and Vitek take the potatoes to the fields."

So Hanka gave her orders, looking out at the *Komorniki* who in their smocks and aprons, with baskets and hoes in hand, ranged themselves along the cabin-wall, beating their clogs against it to clean them.

Presently they were at work in the fields, two and two, two couples to each strip, each turned towards her companion, digging hollows in the ground, throwing in a potato, and covering it with earth again; and so on across the patch.

Old Yagustynka acted as overseer to prevent idling.

The work went slowly, all the same. Their hands were stiff with cold, their clogs full of water from the soaked ground; and though the drizzle was not cold, still it was continuous and drenched them.

Soon, however, the weather changed; the sky became dappled and mottled with blue; swallows, pioneers of sunshine, began to dart about; and the crows, leaving the house-tops, came flapping low over the land.

The women, bent down and stooping, delved on, looking for all the world like heaps of sodden tatters. They did their work leisurely, with long rests, and talking among themselves. After a time, Yagustynka, who was sowing haricot beans between the rows of potatoes, called out, as she gazed around:

"To-day there are but few goodwives to be seen out of doors!"

[1] In England and Scotland there was once a similar custom, now become a mere "perambulation." See "Chambers' Encyclopædia," art. "Beating the Bounds."—*Translator's Note.*

"Ah, no! their men are coming; 'tis not work they are thinking of!"

"No, indeed: only cooking fat dishes and warming feather-beds!"

"Oh, ye laugh!" said Kozlova; "yet ye are yourselves all of a twitter because of them!"

"Lipka, without the boys, is no place to live in: that's sure.—Old as I am, I tell you plainly—rascals and be-trayers and bullies though they are—let but the ugliest lout amongst them all show himself, the world at once grows merrier and lighter to bear. And whoso says No to this, is a liar!"

"Yes," one of them sighed, "we women have been pining for our men, as the kite is pining for a rainy day!"

"Ah, more than one will pay dear for her pining; and the lasses most of all!"

"Before next spring, the priest will have no end of christenings!"

"Old woman, ye are talking nonsense. What did our Lord create women for? Is it a sin to bear a child?" Thus spoke the wife of Gregory the Wrymouth, who always contradicted.

"Ever the same, you! What? standing up for bastards!"

"Surely, and till my dying day I'll tell anyone this to his face: bastards or no bastards, the little ones are of our own blood, and have as much right to live as any. And the Lord Jesus will judge them all justly and only according to the good or the evil they do!"

They shouted her down, and jeered at her; but she only smote her hands together, and nodded her head.

"God speed your work!" Hanka cried to them from the stile. "How goes it?"

"Thanks: well, but somewhat damp."

"Are the potatoes sufficient?" She seated herself on the cross-bar of the stile.

"Quite; but cut into too few parts, I think."

"Nay, they are halved; and at the miller's, all the smaller

potatoes are planted whole. Roch tells me that this gives twice as good crops."

"That must be a German fashion," Gulbasova cried peevishly. "Ever since Lipka has been Lipka, we have always made as many bits as there were eyes."

"My good woman, folk are not more stupid now than they were of old."

"No, indeed! the egg would fain teach the hens, and rule the poultry-yard."

"Ye say true. But 'tis also a truth that years do not bring wisdom to some," Hanka said, as she left the stile.

Kozlova looked askance after her, and growled:

"Cocksure, as if she were really mistress at Boryna's!"

"Say no word against her!" cried Yagustynka. "She's no everyday woman, but a heart of pure gold. I do not know anyone better and brighter than her. I am with Hanka night and day; I have eyes to see, and am no fool. Oh, what that woman has had to endure!"

"Aye, and she will have to endure still more. . . . Is not Yagna in the same cabin with her? Trouble and distress will begin once more, when Antek comes back."

"I heard," Filipka bleated, "of Yagna having taken up with the Voyt: is that true?" But they laughed at her asking what the very sparrows twittered among themselves.

"Let not your tongues wag!" said Yagustynka reprovingly; "the wind may hear your words and carry them where it should not."

They set again to work, with hoes flashing, and at times clinking on a stone; but they talked on as they worked, sparing no one in the village.

As she walked away to take a look at the farm-yard, Hanka stooped, passing under the cherry-trees; for the wet boughs, laden with buds and white blossoms and sprouting leaves, were catching at her head and sprinkling it with dew.

She had scarce been out at all since Easter, having suffered a relapse after her "churching." To-day's tidings had brought her out of bed, and set her on her legs; and though she still felt very shaky, she peered everywhere, and with growing vexation.

The cows had been ill cared for, and their flanks were clotted with dung; the sucking-pigs were in poor condition; even the geese seemed unnaturally silent, as if they had been badly fed.

"Why," she cried out angrily to Pete, who was driving off to cart the manure, "why have you not rubbed down the horse?" But he only went past, muttering something between his teeth.

A fresh motive for exasperation. In the granary, Yagna's pig was devouring the seed-potatoes heaped on the threshing-floor, while the fowls were pecking at a quantity of inferior corn that ought long since to have been taken up to the loft. For this she rated Yuzka soundly, and pulled Vitek's curly hair till the boy wriggled himself loose and made off, while Yuzka slunk away, weeping and querulous.

"I am always at work, yet ye scold me continually: Yagna never does aught, and you let her be!"

"Now, now, be still, silly one! You see but too well all that goes on here!"

"But how am I to do everything? How can I?"

"Be still, I say.—Now carry them the potatoes, or they will have to stop work."

It was no use scolding, she saw. "True, the girl cannot suffice for all; and as to the hirelings—mercy on us! even ere noon, they are looking forward to sunset! As well engage a wolf to tend sheep, as think to get profit out of a hireling. They have no conscience!"

Revolving these bitter thoughts in her mind, she discharged her fury on the pig, that ran off squealing, with Lapa savagely hanging on to its ear.

Looking into the stable, she saw, with yet greater annoyance, that the mare was biting at the empty manger, and the colt, in a most filthy state, eating straw out of its litter.

"To see this would have broken Kuba's heart!" she said, putting hay in the racks for both, and patting their soft warm nostrils.

But here she broke down. A sense of depression took hold of her, and she felt she must cry; so, sitting down by Pete's truckle-bed, she gave way, and wept aloud. . . . She knew not why.

All her energy had collapsed, her heart felt heavy as a stone. Her fate was too much for her, and not to be struggled against. Completely alone in the world and forsaken, her life was as a tree growing in a windy place, exposed to every evil blast! No one even to complain to; and no end of her ill fortune in sight: only eternal mortification and sorrow; only endless trouble, and looking forward to worse things still!

The colt licked her face; and letting her head drop upon its neck, she burst out crying afresh.

Successful farming—respect paid her by all—what did it signify, if she had not one instant of internal happiness?

She went back to the hut. The baby was once more screaming for her breast. Having satisfied it, she looked out vacantly through the window, dingy with a sweat of trickling drops.

But the baby still whimpered and wailed uneasily.

"Hush you, little one!—Father's coming, my boy, and will bring you a toy, and you'll ride on his knee, because he's set free, and how happy we'll be!" She walked to and fro in the room, singing and rocking him in her arms.

"Perhaps he is really coming!" she repeated to herself, and stopped on a sudden.

She flushed, straightened her stooping shoulders, and thought to go to the store-room and cut him a piece of ham, and then to the tavern for vodka. . . . But the smith's words echoed within her bleeding heart, and swooped down, tearing it as with the sharp talons of a hawk. She stopped dead, looking round her as for help: unable to tell what to do, what to think even!

"O Lord! what if he should never come back?" she moaned, raising her hands to her head.

As the children were noisy and quarrelsome, she put them

out and prepared breakfast, about which Yuzka, popping
her head in more than once, had been greedily expectant.

Tears and grief had to be thrust back again; the yoke
of daily labour, pressing heavily on her soul, reminded her
that her work could not be put off.

She did her best, though her legs shook under her; only
from time to time she dropped a tear, and looked wistfully
out into a dimly seen world.

"Is that Yagna going to help in potato-planting?" Yuzka
cried through the window.

Hanka left the pot of beet-root soup on the hob, and
hurried over to the other side of the hut.

The old man lay on his side, seemingly contemplating
Yagna, who was combing her long bright hair before a
looking-glass, set upon a locker.

"Ye are not at work; is it, then, a saint's day?"

"I am not going unkempt."

"Since dawn ye could ten times over have done your
hair."

"I could, but have not."

"Yagna, I will not be trifled with: beware!"

"Of what?" she snarled back fiercely. "Of being turned
out, dismissed from service, eh? I am not here at your good
pleasure, nor in your house!"

"And in whose then, pray?"

"In my own, and I'd have you remember it!"

"Should Father die, we'd soon see what right ye have
here!"

"But while he lives, I can show you the door."

"What? What did you say?"

"Ye are beyond bearing! I never say one idle word to
you, and ye always quarrelling with me."

"Thank God, you, that I do no worse!" she said, slouching
forward with a threatening mien.

"Try your utmost! I am alone, with none to help me;
but we'd see who would have the upper hand."

She threw her hair back: their eyes, full of rage, struck

at each other like knives. And Hanka utterly lost control of herself, and shook her fists and stormed with all her might.

"What! Do you threaten me? . . . Set to, then, O innocent thing, O most injured one!—Aye, aye, all the parish knows of your doings.—More than once they have seen you in the tavern with the Voyt!—And when the other night I opened the door to you, home from your dirty pleasures, you were drunk—drunk as a pig!—Of a truth, who lives noisily will be whispered about.—Ah! but your power is ending, and neither Voyt nor smith will protect you then—you!—you!"

She spat the words at her with a shriek.

"What I do, I do: let folk leave me alone . . . or beware!" Yagna vociferated, suddenly throwing back her beautiful flaxen hair over her shoulders.

Exasperated to the utmost, and burning for a fight, she waved her hands nervously about her hips, with a glare of hatred that made Hanka quail; without another word she left the room, slamming the door.

The brawl had overtaxed her strength. She had to sit down by the window with the child, and let Yuzka serve out the breakfast to the workers.

It was only when they had gone that she felt a little stronger, and thought to put her work off, and go to see her father, who had been ailing for some days past. But this also was too much for her, and half-way there she had to return.

After some time, however, a little strength came back to her, and she was able to do some manual work mechanically, while her thoughts were with Antek and far away.

As the weather was improving, they expected the sun to come out about noon; for the swallows now flew high in air, and flocks of gold-fringed clouds were sailing by; and in the orchards, snowy with blossoms, the birds were singing loud.

Lipka began to hum like a hive; its chimneys bore each a plume of smoke: savoury dishes were preparing within

doors. Gaiety spread from hut to hut with the babble of
women; the girls adorned themselves with ribbons plaited
in their tresses. Some hurried away to get vodka; for the
Jew, much pleased that the peasants were to come back, was
willing now to give anything on trust to whoever asked him.
And from time to time, someone went up on the roof with a
ladder to inspect all the roads that led from the town.

Few went afield, so busy were they with preparations.
They even forgot to drive the geese out, letting them gaggle
and scream in the yards; and the children, left to their own
devices, went about playing very naughty pranks. The
bigger boys, armed with poles, climbed the poplars, and
knocked down the crows' nests; while the parent birds,
looking like great smuts in the sky, wheeled about, croaking
distressfully. The other youngsters found a mischievous
pleasure in chasing the priest's blind old horse, which had
been harnessed to a water-tub on runners, and which they
tried to drive into the pond. It managed to resist its tor-
mentors for a while, but at last, taking fright at the smell
of fire in its nostrils, bolted into Boryna's enclosure, knock-
ing down the gate and getting entangled in the bars: of
which they took advantage to come to close quarters and
beat it.

It might have broken a leg in its plunges to escape; but
luckily Yagna came up, drove the urchins away and extricated the poor animal; then, seeing they were still lying
in wait for it, she led it back to the priest's.

This took her down a lane between his garden and the
Klembas', just as the organist's britzka came up. Yanek
was bidding his family good-bye on the door-step, and his
mother had taken her seat already.

"I am bringing back the priest's horse," she said de-
murely; "a lot of urchins were ill-treating it."

"Father, call Valek to take it," cried the organist's wife;
then, as Valek appeared, "You lout you! to let that horse go
alone! It might have broken its leg!" she added.

Yanek, seeing Yagna, glanced at his parents, and held out
his hand to her.

"Yagna! God be with you!"

"Going back to school?"

His mother answered with pride: "I am taking him to begin studying for a priest."

"A priest!"

She raised her eyes and looked at him in admiration. He sat down on the foremost seat, but with his back to the horses.

"By this means, I shall see Lipka awhile longer!" he exclaimed, casting a fond glance on the lichen-covered roof of his house, and on the orchards around, all bathed in dew and overladen with blossoms.

The horses trotted off.

Yagna went after the britzka, Yanek once more bidding farewell to his sisters in tears in front of the house, but gazing only on those moist azure eyes, wonderful as the sky on a May day, which looked into his; on that fair head, crowned with braided locks that went three times round and ended in curves about her ears; and on that face, so white, so dainty, so . . . just like a wild rose!

She walked along, fascinated by the look in his bright eyes. Her lips were quivering so, that she could not close her mouth. And how her heart was beating! and how humbly she followed him with her eyes, almost swooning for the marvellous sweetness that flooded her! A strange drowsy feeling came over her, and a soporific fragrance seemed to be blunting her senses. . . .

It was only after the britzka had turned off to the poplar road, and their eyes could no longer meet, that she awoke with a shock to the dreary emptiness of all around her, and ceased to follow him. Yanek had waved a last farewell with his cap, and they had disappeared in the shades of the poplars.

She rubbed her eyes, waking as it were from a dream.

"Lord, Lord!" she ejaculated; "such eyes might draw one down to hell!

"An organist's son! . . . And looks like a young Squire!

. . . A priest, a priest! . . . Perchance he will be sent to Lipka!"

Again she looked round; but the britzka, though not yet unheard, was no longer in sight.

"Such a mere stripling! Almost a boy! . . . And yet, when he looks at me, I feel it like an embrace, and grow dizzy."

She shivered slightly, licked her scarlet lips, and stretched herself stiff, with voluptuous zest.

Suddenly she shuddered. Her head and feet were bare: she noted it only now. And she was almost undressed— only in her smock, with a tattered shawl on her shoulders!

She blushed for shame, and started for home by the most unfrequented paths.

"Know ye that the lads are coming?" girls and women and children called out to her from within their enclosures. They were all breathless with the gladness of the tidings.

"Coming or not, what is the difference?—The fools!" she murmured, annoyed at the mad joy they all felt at their husbands' return.

She looked in at her mother's. Only Andrew was at home. That day he had left his bed for the first time, and his broken leg was still in bandages. He was sitting on the door-step, weaving a basket, and whistling to the magpies that hopped about.

"Yagna, do you know? Our folk are coming home!"

"All day long naught else have I heard!"

"And Nastka is simply crazy over Simon's return!"

"Why?" Her eyes flashed sternly; they had her mother's steely glance.

"Oh, for no reason! . . . My leg is hurting me again," he faltered, frightened to have betrayed a secret. "Be quiet, plaguy ones!" he vociferated, throwing a stick at a number of cackling hens.

Then he pretended to rub his leg, and looked with anxiety into her strangely louring face.

"Where is Mother?"

"Gone to the priest's.—Yagna! About Nastka . . . I
. . . I said . . . what I should not . . ."

"You ass! To think none knows of that!—They'll marry,
and there's the end of it."

"But—will Mother let them? Nastka has but one acre."

"If he asks, she will refuse. But he is old enough to
know what to do, and how to do it."

"He is, Yagna. And if he fall out with Mother and be
disobedient and marry in despite of her, then he will take
his share of the land, and settle down on it."

"Talk ye and gabble as much as you like; but take heed
lest Mother hear you."

She felt out of temper. What! that Nastka! she too, to
have a sweetheart and rejoice with the others! Each one
was returning to his own darling to-day: she raged at the
thought.

"Yes, yes, they all are coming back!"

But then a sudden thrill of excitement filled her mind!—
Leaving Andrew, who remained in great awe of her, she
went straight back to her cabin, to smarten herself up like
the others for the home-coming, and like them, too, to await
the freed prisoners with feverish anxiety.

She made her toilet with great care, singing the while
for joy and longing, and running out at times to look down
the road towards which they all were turned.

"And whom are your eyes seeking?" was the unexpected
question put to her by someone.

Her arms dropped to her sides, as a bird's broken wings,
and a cruel agitation fluttered her heart.

Truly, whom had her eyes to seek? No one was hastening
back to her.—"Only Antek, peradventure!" she murmured
low, and heaved a sigh, while remembrances rose up in her
mind, as of a wonderful dream, but dreamt, ah! so long ago!

"Yet the smith told me only yesterday that he would not
be set free with the others, but lie in prison for many a
year."

"But if perchance he is freed—what then?" She said the
words again, as if her soul were bent on expecting him.

Nevertheless, it was not with joy or exultation: rather with a lurking sense of distaste.

"What though he comes?" she said, pettishly; "he is nothing to me now!"

At that moment old Boryna gabbled inarticulately. It was, she knew, his way of asking for food, but she turned her back on him with aversion.

"Die and have done with it!" she said with a sudden burst of spite, and went out into the porch not to see the man.

Down at the pond, there were batlets beating the linen, and washermaidens showing crimson through the green boughs. A dry breeze just moved the willows. Now and again the sun peeped from behind a veil of white cloud, making the little pools glitter, and golden rimples dance about the pond. The rain-mists had gone; and above the low grey stone walls rose the orchard-trees, with their blossoming tops, like immense nosegays, wafting fragrant odours and twittering notes through the air.

"And perhaps, too, I may see him!" she thought dreamily, turning her face towards the wind and the dews which fell dripping from the drying blooms and leaves.

"Yagna!" shouted Yuzka from the yard; "are ye going to help in the potato-field or not?"

Yes; she did not mind. She even willingly obeyed an order that took her away from herself and her incertitude: though she was still under the influence of a melancholy which brought tears to her eyes. But she set to work with such goodwill that she had presently distanced all the hired workers; and so she kept on, paying no heed to Yagustynka's taunts and gibes, nor to the eyes of the other women, that followed her every movement with the air of surly dogs ready to bite.

At times, indeed, she would straighten herself for a moment, as does a pear-tree after bending to the blast, showering its scented blossoms on every side, and (perhaps) remembering the past storms of winter.

She thought of Antek sometimes, but more often of

Yanek's glowing eyes, and of Yanek's cherry lips; and the sound of Yanek's voice echoed in her ears. And she clung with all the force of her will to those yearnings of her memories: they made such sunshine in her heart! For her nature was that of the wild hop, that for its growth and blossoming and life, must needs twine round some other plant; else, left without support, it falls and perishes.

The *Komorniki*, having flung whispers about to their hearts' content, were now taking kerchiefs and aprons off their heads, because it had grown warm; they talked louder among themselves, and stretched their limbs, yawning and longing for the noonday rest.

"Kozlova, ye are highest: pray look whether no one is coming along the poplar road."

She stood on tiptoe, but answered: "No one in sight!"

"They cannot so soon be here; the way is long: they will come at dusk."

"Besides," Yagustynka added, after her bitter fashion, "there are five taverns by the way!"

"Poor things! what do they care for taverns?"

"They have had so much to bear all this time!"

"Oh, indeed! they have had to bear warm beds and plenty to eat!"

"Of fare no better than nettles and chaff!"

"Also, freedom with a potato is better than the very best jail!" Gregory's wife said.

"A strange thing," Yagustynka mused, "is that same freedom, that we relish so: freedom to starve without paying a fine, nor being taken by the gendarmes."

"Very true, my dear; but captivity is captivity all the same."

"And a dish of pease and bacon is not a broth made of aspen pegs!" Yagustynka replied, mimicking her voice so that they all burst out laughing.

She followed up her success by abusing the miller, who "lent rotten flour to borrowers and gave short weight when paid in cash"; and then, in concert with Kozlova, set to running down everybody in Lipka, his Reverence not excepted.

Gregory's wife tried to stand up for some: which made Kozlova cry:

"Ye would fain defend even church-robbers!"

"For we all have much need of being defended," she answered gently.

"Especially Gregory, when ye lift your hand-mangle against him!"

"Right and wrong have naught to do with you, you wife of Bartek Koziol!" she returned in a hard voice, drawing herself up to her full height.

All were fluttered, and expected the two would come to blows at once; but they went no further than a defiant glare. And then Vitek came to ask them to dinner, and to take their baskets, the afternoon being a half-holiday.

At dinner, which Hanka served out to them outside the cabin, they talked but little. The sun was shining bright, and everything looked beautiful, with snowy blossoms scattered all about.

The day continued fine, and the breeze moved the tree-tops as gently as the hand of a mother caressing her little one's cheeks.

No more field-work, then, was done that day. Even the cattle were driven home: only a few of the poorest villagers led the hungry cow (their food-giver) by a rope to graze along the field-paths, or about the ditches.

When the sun had begun to throw somewhat longer shadows, the people gathered in front of the church, conversing in tones as low as the chirping of the birds within the lofty maples and lime-trees that spread their branches, scarce covered as yet with leaves, above the church-roof.

As usual when it has rained in the morning, the sun was hot. The women, in holiday garments, stood together in groups, some of them looking eagerly over the wall towards the poplar road; and the blind *Dʒiad* sat with his dog at the lich-gate, droning hymns in a singsong whine, listening attentively to every sound he heard, and holding out a platter to the passers-by.

In a little, his Reverence came out, clad in surplice and stole, but with uncovered head, his bald crown glistening in the sun.

Pete carried the cross, for the way was too far for Ambrose; the Voyt, the Soltys, and some of the strongest girls bore the banners, which waved and flapped and gleamed resplendent with many a hue. Michael, the organist's pupil, swung the holy-water stoup and brandished the sprinkler; Ambrose distributed the tapers; and the organist, book in hand, took his place by the side of his Reverence. So they started off in silence, through the blossom-sprinkled village; and as they went along the pond, its still waters reflected the whole pageant.

On the way, many more women and children joined them; and finally the miller and the smith pressed in by the priest's side. Last of all, lagging far behind, came Agata shaken with her churchyard cough, and the blind old *Dziad*, swinging along on his crutches; but the latter turned off at the bridge, and made for the tavern.

They lit the tapers only on passing the mill: the priest donned his biretta, made the sign of the cross, and intoned Psalm XCI: "He that dwelleth . . ."

The whole procession took it up with fervour, and on they went by the riverside, through the meadows where there was still many a pool, and they had more than once to go ankle-deep in mud. Shading the tapers with their hands, they wound on by the narrow footpath, the women's skirts forming a long red line like the beads of a rosary.

Shimmering in the sunbeams, the river purled and meandered through the verdurous meadows, spangled with white and yellow flowers.

Overhead the banners waved, as birds flapping wings of red and gold. In front, the cross lumbered along, and through the still transparent air rose the slow voices of the singers.

On the river-banks, thickly studded with marsh-marigolds,

the waters splashed on as a gentle echo of the psalms, rolling towards the distant sky-line on which every eye was fixed, and towards the hamlets seen on the far-off heights, now scarcely visible through the bluish haze, amid the whitely blooming orchards in which they nestled.

Walking with his assistants immediately behind the cross, the priest sang with the others.

"What a multitude of wild ducks!" he whispered, glancing to his right.

"They are widgeons," the miller answered, looking down to the riverside, overgrown with last year's withered reeds and alders, out of which flocks of wild ducks flew out at times on heavy wings.

"There are also more storks than last year."

"They find plenty to eat in my meadows: so they come here from all parts."

"Ah! mine is gone: it left me about Eastertide."

"Gone off, belike, with a flock of others flying by."

"What have you there, on those muddy stretches?"

"I have had an acre of land sown with maize: the soil is rather damp, but they say the summer will be dry; so I may make something by it."

"May it not be like my last year's maize! the crop was not worth gathering."

"Except by the partridges. It fed many a covey," said the miller, with a chuckle.

"Aye, the partridges were for the Squire's table, and my poor beasts had nothing to eat."

"If mine succeeds, I'll send your Reverence a cart-load."

"Many thanks; my last year's clover was but a poor crop, and, should we have a drought, things will go ill for me!" He sighed, and continued the psalm.

They had just come to the first landmark, a mound so overgrown with flowering blackthorns that it rose up clad in beauty, arrayed in white blossoms and sonorous with swarms of bees.

They surrounded it with a circle of flickering lights; the cross towered aloft; the banners dipped and unfurled themselves; the people knelt around, as before an altar whereon the hallowed majesty of spring stood revealed amid flowers and the hum of bees.

The priest then read a prayer that no hail might fall, and sprinkled holy water to the four cardinal points, over the trees, the earth, the water, and the heads of the humble worshippers.

The people then struck up another chant, and went forward.

This time, turning somewhat to the left, they crossed the meadows up a gentle slope. But the children stayed behind a little; and the sons of Gulbas, aided by Vitek, and according to the immemorial custom, here thrashed several boys so soundly that there was a great uproar, and the priest was obliged to intervene and quiet them.

Farther on, they came to a wide place of pasturage at the parish boundaries, dotted over with little thickets of juniper, growing at the border. This pasture land wound hither and thither, like a green river, with waves of grass, and so full of flowers that even the old cart-ruts abounded in daisies and dandelions. In places, too, there were large trees, so fenced about with brambles that there was no approaching them; and then came wild pear-trees, all in bloom, sung to by myriads of bees, and towering aloft, most beautiful and godlike of shape; one felt ready to fall down and kiss the ground which had brought them forth!

And then, the birch-trees! How they arched their lovely trunks, attired in silvery bark, quite over-canopied with green braids and tresses, and reminding you of a young maiden, intensely quivering with pure emotion, who goes to her first Communion!

Little by little, they trended uphill, circling Lipka from the north, and along the miller's fields, lush with rye: first the cross, then the priest, afterwards the girls and younger women, then the old folk straggling by twos and threes abreast, and, last of all, Agata, hobbling and coughing.

When they were out on the plain, the hush deepened. The wind had fallen; the banners hung limply down, and the procession lengthened out to the extent of a furlong, the women's bright dresses set off by the surrounding greenery, and the taper-flames trembling and fluttering like golden butterflies.

And, high above, the sky was quite blue, except for a few woolly clouds, white sheep on the immensity of those azure fields, through which the huge hot sun rolled on, bathing the world in heat and splendour.

The chants now grew louder, resounding from full throats and hearts with such deafening clamour that the birds flew frightened out of the trees that stood near; and sometimes a partridge rose in alarm from under their very feet, or a leveret went bounding away.

"The autumn-sown lands are getting on well," the priest whispered.

"I have seen corn already in the ear there," said the miller.

"Whose is that field, so badly tilled? The furrows are half full of dung!"

"Some poor *Komornik's* potato-patch: it looks as if ploughed with a cow!"

"Probably his Reverence's farm-hand has ploughed it, then," the blacksmith put in with quiet malice.

His Reverence turned angrily upon him, but said no word, and set once more to singing along with the people; now and then casting his eyes over the vast expanse of fields, swelling out here and there like the breasts of a mother giving suck, and seeming to heave gently, as if she would gather together and feed all who came to her bosom.

Sunset was gilding the corn, and the trees in bloom were throwing lengthier shadows; the mill-pond shone dazzlingly in its lovely frame of orchards, snowy with fallen blossoms. The village lay beneath them as at the bottom of an enormous dish, and so compassed about with trees that the grey barns were but seldom visible. The church alone lifted its white walls up above all the huts, its golden cross gleaming bright in the sky.

"How still it is! I hope it will not rain to-night," said the priest.

"It will not; the sky has emptied itself out, and there's a cool breeze."

"In the forenoon it was raining; and now, not a trace of water!"

"In spring the water vanishes quick," the blacksmith chimed in.

Now they had come to the next mound, that formed a landmark of the commune. It was very large: they said that men lay under it who had been slain in "The War." It was topped by a small cross of shaky timber, adorned with last year's images and garlands, and draped with many a scarf. Close by stood a willow with forked and rotten trunk, that hid the fissures of old age under the new shoots that it bore. The place was drearily waste and sinister: no birds made their nest near it. Fruitful lands extended on every side; but among these the mound lifted up its barren flanks, with yellow streaks of sand, and abounding only in houseleeks that spread here and there in patches like a foul tetter, along with the dried stalks of last year's mullein and nightshade.

They recited the prayers against the plague, and, quickening their pace, turned on again to the left, beyond the poplar road, following a narrow and deeply rutted cartway.

But Agata stayed behind a little to tear off some bits of scarf from the cross. These, as she once more went after the procession, she buried one by one in the field-paths, for some superstitious purpose of hers.

The organist now began the litany, which, however, was taken up but feebly, only a few of the people responding.

Meanwhile, the priest, now much exhausted, was wiping his bald head, looking round on the neighbouring lands, and conversing with the Voyt.

"I see the pease have come out finely here."

"An early crop, no doubt, and well-prepared soil."

"I sowed some before Holy Week, and yet mine are only just peeping out!"

"Because your Reverence's land lies low and is exposed to the north."

"Why, the barley here sprouts up as regular as if sown with a drill!"

"The Modlitsa folk are good husbandmen, and till their lands like the Manor people."

"Ah, but how wretchedly our fields have been tilled, God forgive us!" the priest ejaculated mournfully.

The blacksmith laughed sneeringly. "Tilled by charity! One must not look a gift-horse in the mouth!"

"You little rascals! If you don't leave off, I'll pull your ears!" the priest cried out to some urchins who were shying stones at partridges.

The conversation ceased, for the organist began to chant, the smith accompanying him, and the women's voices rising up in a dolorous chorus; and the litany floated across the land like a bevy of birds that, tired by a long flight, sink slowly down towards the ground.

On they pushed through the green plots, and the men of Modlitsa, and even those farther away, stopped work to take off their caps or even kneel down in the fields, while the cattle raised their horned heads and lowed.

They were about a furlong away from the third mound and the poplar road, when someone gave a loud shout:

"There are peasants, coming out of the wood!"

"Our own people, perchance!"

"Our own! our own!" they cried, and there was a rush forward.

"Stay!" the priest commanded severely. "God's service first!"

They obeyed indeed, but stamped on the ground with impatience. All now crowded together behind the priest, who, though he kept them back, hurried his steps himself.

A breeze had sprung up, putting the tapers out, waving the banners, and making the rye, the brushwood, and the trees in bloom to bow before the procession as it passed. The people sang more loudly, and were almost breaking into a run, peeping the while between the roadside trees to make out the peasants' white capotes.

"They will not run away from you!" the priest said, reprovingly, for they were pressing close, treading on his
heels.

Hanka, who walked in the ranks of the goodwives, cried
out aloud on perceiving the white capotes. And though
without hope to behold Antek with the others, the sight filled
her with the most intense delight.

Yagna too, who was walking by her mother's side, felt
impelled to run forward. A fever of desire had taken hold
of her, and her teeth chattered so that she could not clench
them. Nor were the other women less eager to meet their
loved ones. More than one of the lasses and lads could not
hold back any more, and, though called back, ran on by a
short cut to the road, their legs twinkling as they ran.

The procession was soon at Boryna's cross, just in front
of the mound which formed the boundary between the Lipka
territory and the Manor lands.

And there, under the birches that overshadowed the cross
—there they stood all—their goodmen—their sweethearts!
On seeing the procession, they had uncovered their heads,
and all the women could see the long-desired faces of their
husbands and fathers and brothers and sons: emaciated and
haggard, but shining with joy!

"The Ploshkas!" — "The Sikoras!" — "Matthew!" —
"Klemba!"—"Poor dear ones!"—"Our best-beloved!"—"O
Lord Jesus!"—"O Holy Mother!"—Invocations, cries, whispers of love filled the air: every eye blazed with gladness,
every hand was stretched forth, every mouth uttered shouts
of exultation. But the priest silenced them all with a word,
and, advancing towards the cross, he calmly read the
prayer: "From fire . . ." But he could not read fast; he
was unable to help looking very frequently aside to cast com-
passionate eyes on those poor worn faces.

And when he had done, he sprinkled holy water over their
bowed heads, and cried with all his might:

"Praised be Jesus Christ!—O my dear people, how is it
with you all?"

They answered him in chorus, pressing round him as sheep round their shepherd, some kissing his hands, some embracing his knees. He strained each of them to his heart, stroked their thin cheeks, and asked about their health with the kindest attention. At last, quite wearied out, he sat down under the cross, wiping sweat from his brow and tears of fatherly love from his eyes.

Around him, his people gave way to all the impetuosity of passionate tenderness.

Then arose a tumult of laughter and of kissing, of happy tears, childlike prattle, words of fire, ardent whispers, and cries that burst out like songs from their rejoicing hearts. Women took their husbands apart, men stood swaying about in a ring of women and children, and speech and weeping rose in blissful confusion. All this lasted many minutes, and would have lasted longer, but that the priest saw it was getting late, and gave the signal to depart.

So they went on to the last mound on the road by the forest, skirted with young junipers and pine-saplings.

The priest intoned: "O most beloved Mother! . . ." which all took up as one man with a great cry, their hearts brimming over with bliss; and the hymn, like a spring tempest, burst forth and smote on the forest with darts of fiery jubilation.

And the forest bent its head over the road, looking down on them, waving its tree-tops in the evening sun, but within its depths so hushed and calm that the very tappings of the woodpeckers were clearly heard, and the cuckoo's call, and the twittering of the field-birds.

In places, their way led them along upon the verge of the tilled lands; and the peasants, silently passing in serried ranks by the road-ditches, stooped down to cast their eyes over the green expanse; to gaze on the blossoming trees, all on fire in the sundown, and the long strips of cornland lying prostrate before them, and those fields, covered with long waves of winter-corn, that seemed rolling up to their feet with a jubilant murmur. And how their eyes gloated over that land, their true foster-mother! Some even saluted it with doffed caps; all knelt down in spirit, mutely and fervently worshipping Her, the Hallowed, Her, the Much-desired!

After these first salutations came more noisy chat and freer rejoicings of heart. Many a one, too, would fain have run into the wood and shouted himself hoarse, or lain down to shed tears of pure happiness in the fields.

Hanka alone felt herself cut off from them all. Around her everywhere and before her, the men went about, loud in talk, and women and little ones crowded about them, enraptured and, as it were, pressing together under their wings. She alone had no one there who cared for her. All were boisterous with uncontrollable delight, and she, though in their midst, drooped and pined—as she had seen trees surrounded with lush underwood, but dying away, wherein even the crow would not build its nest, and whereon not a bird would alight! Few troubled to greet her. Of course; each was hastening to his own people.—And so many of them had been sent home! even that Koziol, after whose return they would again need to watch the store-rooms and lock the sties! The ringleaders too were back: Gregory, the Voyt's brother, and Matthew. Only Antek stayed in jail: perhaps never again to be seen by her!

Those thoughts were fast becoming unbearable: they were oppressing her so that she could hardly walk. And yet walk she did, with head erect, and apparently as brave and high-spirited as ever. When they sang, she joined in with a firm voice: when the priest offered up prayers, she was first—though with pallid lips—to repeat them after him. It was only in the intervals of silence, hearing round her whispers of ardent love, that she had to fix her eyes upon the glittering cross, and march on, careful lest her tears—those traitors making their way beneath her reddened eyelids—should let them know what she felt. She refrained even from asking after Antek, fearing to break down and show what she suffered. No—no! she had borne so much, and she could go through yet more, and suffer all patiently.

One other suffered also with her. Yagna was no better
off than Hanka. She walked along, moving amongst them
shyly, like some startled animal of the woods. She had at
first been so transported with joy that she had run first
of them all to greet the men; but no one had come forward,
nor gathered her into his arms, nor kissed her! She had
seen from afar Matthew, towering above the others, and
her flashing eyes had glanced towards him, instinct with
sudden long-forgotten desires; and she had pushed through
the throng. But he had, it seemed, failed to recognize her;
and before she got there, his mother had her arms about his
neck, his sister Nastka and the other children were embracing and hugging him on every side; while Teresa (the
soldier's wife), bathed in tears and careless who might see
her, was grasping his hand!

Her fire was quenched at once, as with a stream of icy
water. How intense had been her wish to feel herself one
of that crowd, part and portion of the crush; to join in that
thrilling tumult of salutes, and enjoy herself like the others!
For indeed, like them all, her heart had glowed with enthusiasm, and been ready for every transport of tenderness:
and now she found herself isolated, out of it all: just like
a mangy dog, she thought!

It was very, very bitter for her, and she barely refrained
from tearful complaints, as she moved on, louring as a
dark cloud that may at any time pour down a torrent of
rain.

More than once she had thought to slip away home, but
could not: it was too hard to leave the procession! So
she remained with the others, but as bewildered as Lapa
seeking his master in a crowd. She felt no inclination to
go either with her mother or with her brother Simon, who
had purposely slipped away with Nastka among the juniper-
bushes on the road.—All these things had finally made her so
furious that she would have liked to stone all the lot of them,
with their silly grinning faces!

She was somewhat relieved that they had now left the
forest on one side.

The last mound stood by the crossways, one of which ran straight down to the mill.

The sun had set, and a chilly wind blew from the lower levels. The priest, for whom Valek was waiting with a britzka, now hastened the service. They still went on singing, but with tired voices; the men asked in whispers about the farm which had been burnt at Eastertide, and whose blackened ruins they saw quite near; and they also gazed with curiosity at the Manor lands close at hand.

There the Squire was to be seen, riding about the fields on his sorrel horse; also some men who appeared to be measuring the ground with long rods. Close to the cross, just where the roads forked, and over against the burnt cornstacks, a large yellow britzka was to be seen.

"What may this mean?" someone asked.

"They are measuring the land, but do not look like surveyors."

"Tradespeople, I dare say: they have not the air of farmers."

"Of Germans, rather."

"Aye, aye: dark-blue capotes, pipes in their mouths, and long trousers."

They stared and whispered with great curiosity, not unmixed with a vague sense of uneasiness; and they were so taken up that they did not notice the blacksmith who quietly slunk away, crawling by the ditches until he got to the Squire.

"Are they buying the Podlesie farm, by any chance?"

"I certainly heard them say at Easter that the Squire was looking out for purchasers."

"But Heaven protect us from such neighbours as the Germans!"

The procession was now over. The priest got into his britzka and drove off with the organist; while the people broke up into small parties, trudging slowly home, some by the road, some along various pathways and in Indian file, each taking the nearest way to his dwelling.

The dusk was gathering over the land and the carmine

of the sunset sky passing higher up into a pallid green.
From beyond the mill white vapours came rolling up in
flocculent masses. Through the stillness now descending
over the country-side, the *klek-klek-klek* of the stork resounded loud and sharp.

No human voices were heard there any longer, for the
procession had quite melted away in the fields.

But soon the village became filled with sounds: on every
side, they were coming noisily in. Every man made the
sign of the holy cross on the threshold that he had quitted
so long since; many a one fell prostrate before the holy
images, sobbing for very fullness of heart.

And now there were fresh greetings, and the chattering
of women and the prattle of infants, and many a narrative
begun, interrupted by hot kisses and bursts of laughter.
The women, flushed and blowzed, set the dishes before the
poor sufferers, offered them food in plenty and pressed it on
them with the utmost eagerness.

And so happy were they to be back again and with their
families, that this made them forget all their past injuries,
and the long months of their separation, and they again and
again hugged their dear ones to their bosoms, asking them
questions without end.

Then, after supper, they went out to look at the farm-
yard; and though it was growing dark, still they managed
to go about the orchards and outhouses, patting their live
stock, or stroking the heavy blossom-laden boughs, as though
they were the heads of beloved children.

But it is quite impossible to describe the raptures of
Lipka that evening.

With the exception, indeed—and a great one—of Boryna's
cabin.

The place was well-nigh deserted. Yagustynka had gone
home to her people; Yuzka and Vitek had found some other
hut where there was more company and greater merriment.
Hanka remained apart in the dark dwelling, nursing her
wailing child, and yielding at last to her anguish with bitter
burning tears.

She was not, however, quite by herself. In the next room sat Yagna, in prey to the very same tortures, and like a bird beating its wings against the bars of its cage.

A strange fate it was that had fallen on both alike!

Yagna had arrived sooner than the rest, and, though sombre and black of looks as night, had set to work at once; had milked the cows, watered the calf, even fed the swine; and Hanka wondered, and could hardly believe her own eyes. But Yagna, indifferent to everyone, worked away with a sort of fury, as if to drown her misery in fatigue.

It would not do. Her arms dropped with lassitude, and she thought her back would break, but the tears welled up all the same, and trickled down her cheeks, and her distress and desolation only grew more and more.

Her eyes were so dim, she noted no one around her, not even Pete, who had been at her heels ever since she came home, eager to help, following her everywhere with his eyes, and often approaching so close that she unconsciously moved aside. And at last, when they were both in the granary heaping cut straw into a basket, he caught her by the waist, pushed her close against a partition wall, and sought her lips with a muttered ejaculation.

Engrossed as she was, and unsuspicious of anything more than the rough horse-play of a farm-hand, perhaps rather pleased, too, at finding herself not so absolutely neglected, she suddenly saw his intent when he threw her down on the straw, and pressed his moist hot lips to hers. With the fury of a whirlwind she started up, and cast him from her like a truss of hay; and he measured his length on the threshing-floor!

"You foul eyesore!" she gasped, catching hold of a rake. "You plague-spotted beast! you swineherd, you! Only dare to lay a finger on me again, and I'll break every bone in your body! I'll teach you to make love, and a bloody lesson it will be!"

In a few minutes, however, she thought no more of him, got all her work done, and went into the cabin.

On the threshold she met Hanka. Out of eyes glazed

over with weeping and sorrow, the two exchanged glances—
and then passed each other by in a moment.

But the doors of both rooms stood open, and the lamps
had been lit, so that they happened every now and then to
look at each other.

Later, too, when getting supper ready together, they came
closer perforce; though neither breathed a single word.
Each well knew what the other had to endure, and they
often flung mutual glances of deep rancour, and their dumb
set mouths said with silent malice:

"It serves you right—right—right!"

Yet at certain other instants they felt a sort of compassion one for the other, and might have conversed kindly if
either of the two had chosen to begin. They even lingered
near each other with side-glances of expectation: their hates
seemed lulled, and their common hard fate and loneliness
were drawing them nearer. But it went no further. Something held them back—now a wail from the little one, now
a sense of abasement, now the sharp memory of wrong suffered. And after a time they fell apart again, their resentment awake once more, and their souls sweltering spite
afresh.

"It serves you right!—right!—right!" each of them hissed
in thought, with flaming eyes, ready for a quarrel, aye,
and even for a fight, whereby they might discharge their
mutual detestation.

Luckily, it did not go so far; for Yagna went out to her
mother's directly after supper.

A warm dark night. In the sombre depths of the sky a
few stars twinkled. Upon the marshes lay a thin white film
of haze; and there the frogs set up their croaking, and the
stray piping of affrighted lapwings sounded now and then.
The slumbering trees stood out against the sky, the orchards
loomed grey, as though lime-sprinkled, and wafted fragrance as from censers: cherry-blossoms, half-open lilac-buds,
water, dew-drenched soil—all breathed perfumes; each particular flower gave out its own sweet scent, all mingling in
a deliciously intoxicating aroma.

There were still a few sounds of talk within the village, on the door-steps, about the dwellings now plunged in shade; and people swarmed in the roadways, overshadowed by the trees, and only traversed in places by streaks of light from the windows.

Yagna's intention had been to call on her mother, but she turned aside towards the mill-pond, stopping very frequently; for at every step she met couples, arm about waist, conversing eagerly and in subdued tones.

There were her brother and Nastka, embraced and kissing passionately.

She also came unintentionally upon Mary Balcerek and Vavrek, standing close to a hedgerow, kissing tenderly and forgetful of everything in the world.

There were others whom she knew by their voices. From every shadow about the pond or the fences came whispers, words softly breathed, burning sighs, and sounds of rustling and struggling. The whole village seemed boiling over with tender passion; and even flappers and mere boys were playing at love-making down in the lanes.

A sudden feeling of disgust came over her, together with the resolve to go on at once to her mother's. On the way she met Matthew face to face, but he took no more notice of her than of a tree-stump. He was walking with Teresa, in rapt conversation, both clinging close together; they passed her by, and she still heard their voices and smothered laughter.

Turning back brusquely, she took to her heels as if pursued by a whole pack of dogs, and ran for her cabin.

The evening meanwhile flowed on tranquilly, redolent of spring, instinct with the gladness of all these meetings and all the unearthly serenity of immense happiness.

Far away in the night, either among the sweet-smelling orchards or out in the fields, a flute was twittering a love-tune—the accompaniment, as it were, to all those murmurs and kisses and raptures.

And in the marshes the frogs had set up a grand croaking concert, interrupted at times, while others replied to them

from the mist-covered pond with long slumberous snoring
croaks, fainter by degrees; and the youngsters who played
about the lanes caught up their song, vying with them with
doggerel mimicry.

> "The stork's bad, bad, bad:
> May he choke, choke, choke!
> He shall croak, croak, croak,
> And be glad, glad, glad!"

CHAPTER VIII

IT was a delightful day, warm, yet bracing: a day on which the peasant, after a hearty sleep, jumps up as he wakes, and—his prayers first said—sets to work with scarce the shadow of a yawn.

A huge red globe was slowly ascending the sky, on whose immeasurable expanse, amongst a few thin filaments of haze, there floated cluster on cluster of woolly clouds.

The breeze bustled about, with the air of a farmer calling his household up at dawn; rousing the limp corn, blowing away and dispersing the mists, tossing about the overhanging branches, rushing round the orchards and dashing in and scattering the last cherry-blossoms like snow upon the ground.

Lipka too was waking and getting up swiftly. Many a dishevelled head peeped out upon the world with drowsy eyes: some were washing; not a few half-dressed women carried water to their houses. Here a man was splitting logs; there carts were being wheeled out into the roadway. Smoke rose in festoons from the chimneys, and lie-abeds were rated by shrill tongues.

Early it was. The eastern sun was not more than a man's height in the sky, and shooting its ruddy rays aslant through the orchard-trees; yet everybody was already in lively motion.

The wind had fled away somewhere; they enjoyed a pleasant calm, a fresh balmy morning: the sun played upon the waters, from every roof the dew dripped in pearly drops, swallows swept through the clear air, storks seeking a regale flapped away from their nests. Chanticleer beat his wings and crowed lustily on the hedges, and cackling geese led their fledgelings down to the rose-red pond. In the cow-

216

sheds the cattle lowed: around them and about the yards, cows were being hurriedly milked. From every enclosure they were driving oxen into the roads, and they lumbered along, bellowing lazily, and rubbing themselves against trees and fences; while sheep that went by, lifting their heads and bleating, flocked to the middle of the ways amid clouds of dust. All these were hurried to the open space in front of the church, where elderly peasants on horseback, cracking whips and swearing to the top of their bent, assembled the scattering droves and flocks, and urged the laggards forward.

Somewhat after these came the gooseherds, driving their snowy gaggling bands, or one leading a cow, or taking out a hobbled horse to feed in the fallows.

All these, however, had soon passed out, and the rest of the villagers were making ready to go to the fair; this was about a week after the men's return from prison. Everything in Lipka had little by little returned more or less to its usual state.

Not that all was yet as it should be. They were still rather indolent, often lying too long abed. Some paid too frequent visits to the tavern—to be abreast of the news, they said; and not a few would squander half a day going about and gossiping: others would scamp their most pressing work. To get into gear again, when once out, was no easy matter, after such a spell of forced inactivity. But things were improving daily: the tavern had fewer and fewer guests on work-days, for want had caught men by the throats, and was forcing them to labour in the sweat of their brows.

All the same, as that day there was a fair in Tymov, they preferred to go there and put the work off.

Besides, the days of dearth before harvest-time had begun early and with such severity that a bitter cry now arose in most huts. Whatever, then, they still had to sell, they took in all haste to the fair. And others also went, but only to chat with their neighbours and have a look round, and perhaps drink a nip of vodka.

"I cannot read any farther: 'tis useless. But Matthew would manage, no doubt."

She flushed a deep purple, and returned in a faint voice: "O Nastka! I do entreat you, tell him naught of this letter!"

"Were it but in print! I can read any book, I know the letters perfectly.—But I can make nothing of these strokes and crooks and curls. . . . Just like a fly dipped into ink, and crawling over the paper."

"But, Nastka, you'll not tell him?"

"Only yesterday I said to you that I could not be mixed up in this.—But, if your man is coming home, all will have to come out!" she added, rising to her feet.

Teresa could not answer a word; the tears she was trying to keep back choked her.

Nastka withdrew, rather out of humour, calling her fowls as she went; and Teresa, making up five ducks' eggs in a bundle, went to the organist's.

She was a good while getting there, stopping as she did every while, and slinking about in the shade, and staring at the incomprehensible symbols before her.

"Perchance he is returning." . . .

She writhed in the grip of dread, her knees shook, her heart throbbed wildly; with misty eyes she staggered on, as one in sore need of succour; more than once she had to lean against the trees not to fall.

"And perhaps he is only writing about money!" . . .

Her steps began to flag; the letter had become a burden, a torment to her; she was always shifting it from hands to bosom and back again.

Nobody seemed at home at the organist's. All the doors were open, all the rooms empty. One window had a petti-coat hung up in lieu of curtain, and a sound of snoring pro-ceeded thence. She advanced timidly towards the passage, looking round her at the yard. A servant-girl was sitting at the kitchen-door, churning butter and driving flies away with a bough.

"Where's your mistress?"

"In the garden; ye'll hear her soon!"

Teresa remained standing there, crushing the letter in her hand, and drawing her kerchief forward over her head, for the sun was now shining directly from above the sheds.

Fowls cackled noisily from the priest's yard, separated only by a hedge from the other: ducks were riotous in pools, little turkeys plaintively clamorous near the hedge; big gobbling turkey-cocks, with drooping wings, made furious onsets at sucking-pigs wallowing in the mire; and pigeons circled in air, slowly settling—a snow-white cloud—on the red roof.

Teresa's eyes were wet. She averted her face to ask:

"Is the organist within?"

"Where else? His Reverence is away, so he has lain down to sleep again."

"The priest has gone to the fair, no doubt?"

"Ah, yes; to purchase a bull."

"What, has he not possessions enough?"

"Whoso has much wants more," the servant grunted.

Teresa was silent awhile. It was hard that she should have so little, and others so much!

"Mistress is coming!" the servant announced, working the dasher up and down in the churn so violently that the cream spurted out.

" 'Tis all your doing, lazy boy! you let the horse into the clover on purpose because ye had no mind to go as far as the fallows!" she was heard to scream. "Two rods of clover eaten! But I'll tell your uncle at once, you good-for-nothing, and you'll get such a beating!"

"But I drove it to the fallows myself, I did, and tethered it to the ring!"

"No lies! Your uncle will have a talk with you!"

"But I tell you, Aunt, I did not drive any horse there."

"Who did, then? His Reverence, eh?" she asked sarcastically.

"Ye have guessed, Aunt. Aye, the priest has grazed his horses there," the lad replied, raising his voice.

"Are you mad? Hold your tongue, lest someone hear."

"I will not! To his face I'll say it!—I went at daybreak

to fetch the horses in; the bay one was lying down, the mare feeding: both just where I had left them last night. I loosed them and mounted the bay one, when I saw horses grazing in our clover. It was grey dawn.—I rode on aslant, nigh the priest's garden, to head them off; so I passed along Klemba's pathway. And then I saw the priest saying his breviary, and looking round, and whipping his horses further and further into the clover!"

"Hush, Michael! . . . What an unheard-of thing! . . . The priest himself! . . . I always said that last year's hay . . . But silence; here comes a woman."

She waddled in hurriedly, and the organist called for Michael from under his bed-clothes.

Teresa handed over her eggs, embraced the goodwife's knees, and begged to know the contents of her husband's letter.

"Just wait a little."

Some time later, they called her into the room. The organist, scantily attired—in shirt and drawers only—was taking his morning coffee. He began to read to her.

Her heart died within her as she listened. Yes, he—her husband—was coming back at harvest-time, along with Kuba Yarchyk of Vola, and Gregory, Boryna's son! The letter was affectionate: he longed to see her, asked about everyone at home, sent messages to his acquaintances, and felt brimming over with gladness at the thought of returning. Gregory added a few words, asking her to tell his father he was coming. Poor fellow! he little knew what had taken place.

Those kind words smote Teresa like a whip and cut her to the heart. She did her best to bear up against this dreadful news, but her eyes were soon wet and streamed with telltale drops.

"How pleased she is that her goodman is coming!" the organist's wife said, with derisive emphasis.

At the words, she wept yet more abundantly, and took to flight that they should not see her break down yet more. For a long time she went crouching about the hedges.

"What shall I do? Oh, what shall I do?" she cried
helplessly, in bitter pain.

Her goodman was coming . . . and would learn everything! Terror, like a destroying blast, swept over her at
the thought. Her Yasyek was a good-natured fellow, but
very impetuous, like all the Ploshkas. Never would he
forgive the wrong done; he would kill him. "O Lord,
have mercy!" she cried, but without one thought for herself.
Full of tears and rent within her soul, she found her way
after a time to Boryna's cabin. Hanka was out; she had
left long since; Yagna was working at her mother's. Only
Yagustynka and Yuzka were at home, spreading out linen
to bleach in the orchard.

She told them about Gregory, wishing to get away at once.
But the old woman took her aside, and said in a low and
unusually kind tone:

"Teresa, control yourself; be reasonable. Evil mouths
cannot be prevented from speaking. . . . Your Yasyek will
return, and will know all in any case. Think of it: a lover is
but for a month, a husband for life. 'Tis good advice I
give."

"What do ye mean?" she stammered, feigning not to
understand.

"Do not pretend: we all know all about you both. Send
Matthew about his business while it is yet time. If ye do,
Yasyek will not believe what they say. He has been yearning for you; easily will you make him believe anything!
Matthew has had a liking for your bed, but is not bound to
it: get rid of him while you can. . . . A love! it passes by in
a moment, as yesterday has passed: were you to lay down
your life for it, it would not stay. A love—'tis but a
Sunday dainty: who feeds on it daily will care not for it
at all.—Folk say: 'Love of heart makes us smart: when
we wed, then we're dead!'—It may be; but death with a
goodman and children is better than wild outlawed freedom.
—Do not whimper, but save yourself while it still is time.
What if your man should cease to love you, because of this
your deed, and chase you from his home? Whither should

you go? To your ruin: to be the laughing-stock of every-one! Fool! Every man has breeches: Matthew and Kuba, both alike: everyone swears the same oaths, and is sweet as honey so long as his fondness endures.—Now think well, and take to heart what I say; for I, your aunt, wish you well."

But Teresa would hear no more. She fled away into the fields, and sat down in the rye to give a free course to her grief.

But it was in vain that she attempted to think over Yagustynka's advice. Her passion for Matthew was such that the very idea of giving him up made her writhe on the ground like a wounded beast.

Some time elapsed before the sounds of a quarrel close at hand made her start to her feet.

Just in front of the Voyt's cottage a fierce brawl was in progress.

The Voyt's wife and Kozlova were loading each other with the fiercest invectives.

Opposite to one another they stood, with the road and their respective enclosures between them, clad only in their smocks and petticoats, each panting with fury, reviling the other with all her might, and shaking her fists at her.

The Voyt was loading his cart, and now and then glancing at a peasant from Modlitsa, who, sitting in the porch, en-joyed the scene with keen relish, and set the women on.

The cries were heard afar; and soon many a head peeped from behind the neighbouring hedges and hut-corners.

And, Lord! how they both stormed! The Voyt's wife, usually so quiet and mild-tempered, was terribly on the rampage to-day, and her rage waxed higher every minute; and Kozlova, as of set purpose, taunted and mocked her, omitting nothing to increase her fury.

"Talk, talk, talk, my lady Voyt!" she called out; "talk away! There's no dog can outbark your ladyship!"

"Not a week goes by, but something is missing from my premises! Laying hens—chickens—even an old goose— have disappeared. Aye, in my garden, in my orchard, I

have untold losses to put up with! Ah, may the wrong
done to me poison you! May it choke you to death!"

"Very good!—Screech, old crow! Screech, my lady Voyt!
'Twill soothe you!"

"Why, this very day," she said, addressing Teresa, who
stood in the road, "I had taken five pieces of linen out into
the orchard to bleach. . . . After breakfast, behold, I come
out to sprinkle them—one is missing! . . . I seek it!—
Swallowed by the earth, as it were!—And lo, I had weighted
it with stones; and of wind there was none at all! . . . Good
linen, fine linen! Ye could get none better at any shop . . .
and behold, it is gone!"

"Your eyelids are so puffed out with fat, you could not
see it!"

"I could not, for you, thief, have stolen it!" she vociferated.

"I, a thief!—Say, oh, say that once more!"

"You thief! you thief! Thereto, and before all men,
will I bear witness! And that you'll confess when I take
you to jail in irons!"

"She—she has called me a thief!—People, have ye heard?
As there's a God, I'll bring an action for that.—Ye all have
heard her. What, have I robbed you, you blockhead?
where are your witnesses?"

At that, the Voyt's wife snatched up a stake, and dashed
out into the road with the rush of an infuriated dog, shrieking: "I'll witness it on you with my stick! I'll prove it!
I'll . . ."

"Come on, my lady Voyt! Yah! only touch me, you pig!
Only touch me, you scarecrow of a bitch!" she cried,
running forward likewise.

She pushed aside her goodman, who would have kept her
back, and with legs wide apart and arms akimbo, called out
jeering:

"Strike me, strike me, my lady Voyt, and you'll lie in
jail for it!"

"Hold your peace, woman!" the Voyt interposed, "or I'll
send you off to jail first!"

"Lock up your own mad dog, 'tis your duty; tie up your wife with a rope, lest she bite!" Kozlova screamed, exasperated.

"Woman!" he shouted, threatening her. "When I speak, do respect my office!"

"I spit on your office"—but the words used were bolder far—"do you understand me? He threaten, he?—Look at him! He may just as well have stolen the stuff himself to get his light-o'-love a smock! Why, the money of the community is all gone that way; you have drunk it all, you toss-pot!—Oh, we know about your doings, never fear!—Aye, you too, my lord the Voyt, will lie in jail!"

This was the last straw: both of them flew at her like wolves. The Voyt's wife hit her first with her stick across the face, and then, with a savage cry, went at her with her nails, while the Voyt belaboured her wherever he could find a place.

Bartek flew instantly to the rescue of his wife.

They all three closed together like fighting dogs; no one could tell whose fists, whose heads, were seen whirling through the air, nor whose voices were bellowing. From fence to road, from road to fence, they went staggering and tossing like sheaves blown along in a great wind, till in their fury of fighting they fell to the ground on a sand-heap.

Plunging in a cloud of dust, they were audible still with their imprecations and invectives; but presently they got out into the road, fighting and shrieking at the top of their voices.

At times one or other of them fell apart, and now and then they were all upon their feet; then, clutching one another by the hair, or the throat, or the nape of the neck, they began the battle again.

But all the village was soon aroused by the noise; women came hovering helplessly around the battle-field; and at last men arrived and separated the combatants.

But the curses and imprecations and wailings and threats went on, and were beyond all description. The neighbours made off at once, fearing they might be called in to bear witness: but throughout the village the whisper went that the Voyt and his wife had given the Koziols a fearful thrashing.

A few minutes later, the Voyt, with a swollen face, drove off accompanied by his wife, also much battered and scratched, to depose against their enemies.

About an hour afterwards, the Koziols started likewise: old Ploshka having very kindly offered to take them to town gratis—to pay out the Voyt for siding with the Squire.

They went to make their complaint, just as they were at the end of the fight, and without doing anything to make themselves more presentable.

They drove slowly through the village, telling everybody, as they went, about their ill-treatment, and showing the wounds received.

Koziol's head was cut open to the bone, so that his face, neck, and breast, visible through a rent in his shirt, were all covered with blood. The hurt was in reality not great; but at every moment he would press his side and moan:

"My God! I can bear no more! He has broken every one of my ribs!—Help, good people, help! or I die!"

His wife then took up the lament.

"He took a club to beat him with!—Ah, poor man! be easy; you have had much to suffer, but there's justice to punish ruffians, there is! . . . Yes, he meant to slay my man, and folk had hard work to prevent him from doing it: as they will all testify in court." These explanations she would frequently interrupt with dreadful howls. Indeed, she was disfigured almost past recognition: bare-headed, with tufts of hair torn out scalp and all, her ears torn and bleeding, her eyes running blood, and her whole face clawed, scratched, harrowed like a field. And though all knew well what a "daisy" the woman was, the sight roused pity in many a heart.

"Dear, dear! 'twas too bad to treat them so horribly!"

"A sin and a shame it is! They have been well-nigh killed."

"Aye, they have been frightfully beaten. But is aught forbidden to my lord the Voyt?—Such an official, such a great man?" Ploshka put in maliciously, addressing the people.

They were completely bewildered, and remained astounded and upset long after the Koziols had passed out of sight.

Teresa, who had taken cover during the fray, did not show her face till both parties had gone.

She looked in at the Koziols', Bartek being distantly related to her. No one was in; but the three little children that Kozlova had just brought with her from Warsaw, sat outside the cabin, huddled together, greedily devouring some half-boiled potatoes, defending their food from the pigs with their spoons, and crying out at them. They were so wretched, so miserably neglected, so filthily dirty, that her heart pitied them, and she took them into the passage, and shut them in from their foes; then she ran off to tell the news.

At the Golabs', there was no one but Nastka.

Matthew had, before breakfast, gone over to Staho (Bylitsa's son-in-law) to look over the ruined hut and see if anything could be done with it. The old man, too, was with him, now and then stammering a word or two. Mr. Yacek, sitting as usual at the threshold, smoked a cigarette and whistled to the doves that circled about over the cherry-trees.

Noontide was not far off.

The heated air was quivering over the fields like rippling water; the fields and orchard-grounds basked delightedly in the sunbeams; now and again, a blossom fell from Bylitsa's cherry-trees, flickering down like a white little butterfly.

It was well past noon when Matthew had finished his examination. While still poking the timbers here and there, he gave sentence:

" 'Tis all rotten wood, crumbling to dust: ye can build nothing with it. Quite useless."

"Perchance," Staho said anxiously, "I might buy some new timber, and then . . ."

"Ye'd require timber for a whole cabin. Not one beam here is fit for aught."

"Gracious heavens!"

"But the lower beams may hold yet," old Bylitsa faltered; "we should only have to get new upper timbers, and clamp the woodwork together and prop it up."

"Then do so, if ye be so clever! I do not build with touchwood!" he retorted, putting on his coat.

Here Veronka, lamenting bitterly, and holding a child in her arms, came on the scene.

"What, alas! what shall we do now?"

"A new hut," said Staho in sore distress, "would cost about two thousand roubles.—Yet we might get some timber from our forest; and I could manage for the rest. . . . An application to the Government Board . . ."

"But the forest is now in the hands of the law court: what timber would they give us just now? Why, we are even forbidden to gather wood there for fuel! Wait till a sentence is given, and then build!" was Matthew's advice.

"Indeed! Very fine!—And where shall we dwell this winter, I ask?" said Veronka, with a fresh burst of tears.

No more was said. Matthew put his tools together, while Staho scratched his head, and Bylitsa blew his nose round the corner.

In that moment, Mr. Yacek stood up, and raising his voice:

"Weep not, Veronka," he said; "the timber for your cabin shall be found!"

All stood open-mouthed, lost in amazement; till Matthew, recovering himself first, burst out with a loud guffaw.

"Clever men promise, fools believe them!—He has not where to lay his head, yet talks of giving cabins to others!" he cried roughly, staring at him under his bent brows; but Mr. Yacek sat down again, went on smoking and playing with his beard, his eyes fixed on the sky-line.

"In a little, he will promise you a whole farm!" Matthew said, with a laugh and a shrug, as he left them.

He at once turned to the left along the path that led to the outhouses.

Few were at work in the gardens that day: there was but the red glint of a stray petticoat, or the sight of a man here and there mending a roof, or pottering about the granary gates, open to the fields.

Matthew was in no hurry; he loitered about willingly, chatting with the neighbours on the topic of the Voyt's battle, grinning and talking merrily with lasses, or making such strong-flavoured jokes with the elder women in the gardens that they could not help laughing; many a one sighed and cast fond looks after him, as he passed out of sight.

And a handsome fellow indeed he was: built like an oak, and the king, as it were, of all the young men in Lipka; first in strength (after Antek Boryna); and as a dancer, not inferior to Staho Ploshka. And withal, a man of much ability in every field of work; able to construct a cart, to set up a chimney, to repair a cabin; and he played the flute beautifully too. So, though he had next to no land at all, and was so open-handed with everybody that he never put anything by, many a mother would have gladly drunk with him the price of a calf, could she but have disposed him favourably thereby towards marriage with her daughter; more than one girl, too, had allowed him much intimacy, hoping to get the banns sooner published.

All would not do. He drank with the mothers, made love to the daughters, but on the question of marriage was slippery as an eel.

" 'Tis hard to choose.—Each one has her good points; and others are growing up, worth more than any.—I'll wait," he would say, when match-makers beset him.

Then, the preceding winter, he had that entanglement with Teresa, and lived almost openly with her, disregarding both gossip and cautions.

"When Yasyek comes, I'll give her back to him, and he'll stand me treat into the bargain for having taken good care of her," he once said laughingly, shortly after his return. He was tired of her, and slowly drifting apart.

And now, as he went in to dinner, he chose a longer way round, merely to joke with the girls, and have some horse-play with those who would let him.

And thus, quite unexpectedly, he came face to face with Yagna, weeding her mother's garden.

"Ah! Yagna!" he cried out, joyfully.

She suddenly shot up to her full height, tall and graceful as a hollyhock.

"So you've noticed me? Oh, how very soon! Not more than a week since your home-coming!"

"Why, you look lovelier than ever before!" he said in low tones of wonder.

Her dress was tucked up to the knees; and beneath her red kerchief, knotted under her chin, those great sweet turquoise eyes of hers looked out, her white teeth gleamed between cherry lips, all her face glowed apple-red—and so fair, it seemed asking to be kissed.

She boldly set her arms akimbo, and shot such irresistibly bright glances at him as thrilled him through and through. Looking round carefully, he drew nearer.

"For a whole week I have been seeking you—in vain!"

"Tell a dog lies: it may believe you.—Ha! the man goes grinning about the gardens every evening; every evening he flatters another girl: and now he'll dare tell me 'tis not true?"

"Why, Yagna, is this your greeting to me?"

"Better fall on my knees and thank you for remembering I exist, eh?"

"Last year I had another welcome!"

"But this is not last year!" She turned away from him and hid her face. He at once stepped forward, clasping her with eager arms.

She tore herself in anger from his grasp.

"Let me alone; Teresa would tear my eyes out because of you!"

"Yagna!" he sighed.

"Get back; make love to her, the soldier's wife; render her every service till he come back to her.—You were in prison, and she fed you well: now must you make her some return!"

Each word of hers was like a blow, and uttered with such scorn that Matthew, taken aback, could find no answer.

Shame took hold of him; he turned a dusky red, hung his head and took to flight at once.

Though Yagna had but told him what she felt and had been feeling all the week, she now regretted her words. Never had she expected he would have been so offended as to leave her.

"Foolish one! I spoke but out of spite!" she thought, gazing sorrowfully after him. "To be so angry all at once with me!—Matthew!"

Rushing away through the orchard as if running for his life, he did not hear her call.

"That wasp! that vixen!" he growled, making straight for home now, anger and astonishment alternately uppermost in his mind. Before, she had always been so sweet, so mild! And now she had treated him like dirt. He felt the shame so keenly that he looked round to make sure no one had heard.

"And she reminded me of Teresa! Silly thing!—Teresa is naught to me—naught but a toy!—How her eyes blazed! In what a posture she set her arms!—Ah, it were no shame to be stung by such a one . . . if only the honey were forthcoming afterwards." He was now close to his hut, and slackened his pace.

"She was angry that I alluded to the past.—But was I in the wrong? . . . As to Teresa"—here he made a wry face, as one who has gulped down vinegar—"I have enough of that cry-baby. I have taken no oath to remain with her, have I? . . . The tail sticks to the cow, but I am no cow's tail! . . . And then she has a goodman of her own; and I might get a public rebuke from the pulpit on her account. . . . Such a woman is the ruin of a man.—To the devil with women!" he concluded, in a most cantankerous mood.

Dinner was not ready at home. He scolded his sister

for dawdling, and went in to Teresa, who was milking in the orchard, and raised to him very sad tearful eyes.

"Whimpering again? And wherefore?"

She excused herself, looking on him fondly.

"Pay more attention: the udder squirts milk upon your petticoat."

Why was he so unkind, so hard to her to-day? she wondered. What had come over him? She was as gentle as could possibly be; yet he snapped her up fiercely at every word she said.

He seemed looking about the orchard for something, but ever and anon flung a furtive glance at her, and wondered more and more.

"Where had I mine eyes? . . . Such a paltry flabby thing! . . . Neither beauty nor savour! . . . Raw-boned and sour-tasting! . . . Black as a gipsy, too; and of carriage, none whatever!"

True, her eyes, and they alone, were beautiful; perhaps as much so as Yagna's: large, bright as a blue sky, and peering under black brows. But as often as he met them, he turned aside and swore softly to himself.

"She rolls her eyes like a calf!"

Those looks of hers made him impatient and angry.

"I will not see them, I will not!—Yes, yes, ogle as much as you like, ye will not catch me."

They had dinner together, but he never spoke once to her, nor so much as glanced in her direction. To Nastka he spoke, indeed, but no pleasant words.

"A dog would not touch these groats: they are disgustingly burnt!"

"Only a little: just enough to have a taste."

"Do not cross me!—And ye have put more flies than bacon-scratchings in them!"

"What, do you object to flies now? Don't be so very dainty! They will not poison you."

The cabbage dish, he then complained, had been cooked with rancid lard.

"Ye might as well have seasoned it with axle-grease!"

"You don't know how that would taste? I do not, nor will I try," she returned sharply.

But he continued to seek every occasion to grumble. Teresa was dumb all the time; so he set at her directly after dinner, seeing her cow rubbing herself at the corner of the hut.

"She's filthy with dung, crusted all over: can ye not rub her down?"

"Our byre is wet, and she gets dirty there."

"Wet, indeed!" he vociferated. "There are pine-boughs enough in the forest for dry fodder: but ye must wait for someone to collect them and bring them here to you. And the beasts might rot their flanks off with the dung meanwhile.—So many women in the hut, yet not a stiver's worth of cleanliness!"

But Teresa never answered back; she durst not defend herself, and only begged his mercy with her eyes.

She was quiet and obedient, and as hard-working as an ant: she felt even glad to see him so masterful and high-handed with her! Which was precisely what angered him yet more. Those loving timorous eyes enraged him; so did her quiet footsteps, her humble mien, her way of following him about. He was on the point of crying out: "Away from my sight!"

"Blood of a dog!—Plague take it all!" he exclaimed at last; and, taking up his tools, without any after-dinner rest, he passed over to the Klembas', where he had something to do about the hut.

They were all out in the yard, and at dinner still.

He sat down by the wall for a smoke.

The Klembas were talking of Gregory Boryna's return from the army.

"What? home so soon?" he asked.

"Why, know ye not?" said old Klemba. "Together with Yasyek, Teresa's goodman, and Yarchyk from Vola."

"They are to be here in harvest-time. This morning, Teresa went to get the letter read by the organist, who told me about it.—That's news for you, that Yasyek is returning!" he blurted out.

A silence followed. All eyes were fixed on vacancy, and the women, stifling their desire to laugh, turned very red. He gave no heed, and seemed pleased at the news, remarking tranquilly:

"'Tis well that he returns: now they will peradventure cease from slandering Teresa."

Their spoons stopped, suspended in air over the dish, so confounded were they all. He looked round him, unabashed, and then added:

"Ye are well aware how little they spare her. She is naught to me but a distant relative on my father's side. But if any dirty sneak should hint at anything else, I'd stop his mouth so that he'd never forget it! But women are the worst of all; they never spare another woman. Be she white as snow, they would find means to foul her!"

"Quite so, quite so," they replied, with their eyes upon the dish.

"Have ye been at Boryna's yet?" he inquired, anxiously.

"I have long been about to go; but something always prevented me."

"He suffers for us all, and we—we forget him!"

"And you—have you looked in there?"

"I?—Should I go in by myself, folk would say I was after Yagna!"

"As particular as a girl after she has tripped!" muttered old Agata, who sat by the hedge, with a small bowl on her knees.

"Well, but I have enough of all this yelping."

Klemba laughed. "The wolf," he said, "changes his life when his teeth are gone."

"Or," Matthew added, "when he thinks of settling down."

"Ho, ho! we shall soon have you sending messengers to some lass?" young Klemba cried in high glee.

"Aye, I am weighing the matter seriously."

"Make your choice quickly, Matthew, and ask me to be your bridesmaid!" piped Kate, the eldest daughter.

"Ah, but there's the rub. All are equally excellent, and every one's better than the other. Magda's the richest, but she's toothless and blear-eyed; Ulisia's a flower, but has one hip too big, and no dowry but a barrel of sour-crout; Franka has a baby; Mary is too friendly to all the boys; Eva has a hundred *złoty*, all in coppers; but she's a sluggard, always lying abed. All would fain eat fat things, drink sweet things, and do nothing. Oh, they are pure gold, these girls! And others there are besides, nice, but not yet grown up."

They all laughed till the pigeons flew off the roof.

"I say true. Till she is grown up, I care naught for a girl, be she ever so comely."

Here Dame Klemba rebuked him for talking of such things.

"Oh, I am only joking. And girls like these jokes, they say, as well as any."

At this the lasses were offended, and grew red as turkeys in angry protest.

"A fine fellow he is: not one of us is good enough for him!"

"If there are none in Lipka you can like, then take one from elsewhere!" they cried.

"But there are, there are! 'Tis easier to find an old maid here than a silver *złoty*. Ah, how many there are! They every Saturday beautify themselves at daybreak very thoroughly, and braid their hair, and chase chickens through the orchard to barter with the Jew for vodka, and are all the afternoon on the watch for messengers bringing a proposal. Why, have I not seen them on the roofs, waving their kerchiefs at me, and shouting: 'Come to me, Matthew, come!'?—And the mothers, too, taking up the cry: 'To Kate first, Matthew, to Kate! I'll add to her portion —a cheese and eight eggs: Matthew, come to Kate!'"

The men were near splitting their sides with laughter, he

amused them so; but the girls, indignant, made such an uproar that old Klemba interposed:

"Hush, girls! ye're as noisy as magpies before rain."

The din went on nevertheless. So, to end the squabble, he inquired:

"Were you present, Matthew, at the Voyt's affray?"

"Not I. But the Koziols were very soundly swinged, they say."

"Aye, swinged with a vengeance! They were awful to behold.—Well, well, the Voyt has had his fling, i' faith."

"He has waxed fat on the Commune's bread, and now he plays pranks!"

"Aye, indeed, he fears none. Who would stand up to him? Any other should pay dear for such sport—he'll not lose a hair thereby. He knows men in office, and can do as he pleases here."

"Because ye are but sheep to let him. He puts you down, and sets himself above you all!"

"Having chosen him ourselves, we must respect his rule."

"But they that set him up can put him down again."

"Hush, Matthew, not so loud: folk may hear your words."

"——And tell him. Then he'll know what I have said.— Let him fall foul of me, though, if he dare!"

"Matthias, who alone could have held against him, is at death's door. No one else would put himself forward: each has troubles enough of his own," the old man concluded, rising from his seat.

All rose with him, and went, some to rest awhile, some to stretch their legs and loosen their girdles; others—the lasses —to wash the dishes in the pond, and take a little recreation. But Matthew went directly to set up props and stays for the cabin, while Klemba lit his pipe and sat on the door-step.

As he puffed, his mind reverted to the late talk. "Who stands up for others, shall have many bothers!" he growled.

The sun was high above the cabin, the afternoon hot. The orchards stood motionless, the sunlight trembled

through their rustling leaves, and many a petal floated
down upon the grass. Bees buzzed among the apple-tree
boughs; athwart the greenery, the mill-pond shimmered, and
the birds were all hushed. A pleasant afternoon drowsi-
ness pervaded the place.

Klemba, who wanted to keep awake, sauntered over to
his potato-pit.

A little later he returned, puffing hard at his extinguished
pipe, and spluttering, and throwing back the long hair that
had fallen over his brow.

"Have you seen?" his wife asked him, peeping out at the
door.

"I have. Our potatoes will only last us till harvest, if
we cook them but once a day!"

"Once a day only!"

"What's to be done? We are so many!—Ten hungry
mouths, the ravenous maws beneath them!—We must think
of something."

"Not of the heifer, at any rate. I tell you, I will not
have her sold. Do what ye will, the cattle must not
go!"

He waved his hands, as if to drive away an importunate
wasp; when she had gone, he lit his pipe again.

"A pig-headed old thing! . . . If needs must . . . A
heifer's no holy thing to die for!"

The sun now shone in his eyes; he only turned his back,
and puffed more slowly. Loosening his girdle (the meal
of potatoes lay heavy upon him), he began to nod. The
doves cooed on the thatch, and the leaves were quivering
with slumberous murmurs.

"Thomas!"

It was Agata's voice. He opened his eyes. She was sitting beside him, with an anxious look.

"These months before harvest are hard times for you,"
she said. "If ye are willing, I have a little money: ye
could take it. I was keeping it for my burial; but if ye
are so hard pressed, I'll lend it. Why sell the heifer? I
stood by when she was dropped; she's of a good race of

milkers. Perchance I may, God willing, live on till harvest . . . and then ye will give the money back. 'Tis no
shame, even for a farmer, to take from his own folk, when
in need. So here!" And she pressed into his hand three
roubles, all in silver *złoty*.

"Nay, take it back: I shall manage."

"Here, I can add half a rouble more. Take it," she
begged him in a whisper.

"Nay. But thanks notwithstanding. It is exceeding kind
of you."

"There, then: here are thirty *złoty* all told: pray take
them!" She looked into her money-bag, counting out five-
kopek bits and keeping down her tears. It was a hard
sacrifice for her; every coin she told out gave her a sharp
pang.

The money glittered very temptingly in the sun. His
eyes shone with desire as he gloated over them; they were
all new bright pieces. But, heaving a deep sigh, he mastered
himself with a great effort, and said to her:

"Hide all that carefully, or folk may see it, and peradventure rob you."

She still went on imploring him in a low voice; but he
said no more, and she slowly put her treasures back again.

"Wherefore will ye not dwell with us?" he asked her,
after a while.

"How can I? I am good for nothing, not even to follow
the geese—I am very weak, expecting my end day by day.
It would truly be more pleasant to die amongst one's own
kinsfolk: much more. Yea, even in the stall where the
heifer has been.—And I have forty *złoty* ready for my
burial: perhaps 'twould also suffice for a Mass . . . as befits
a farmer's kinswoman! . . . I should leave my feather-bed
to you. . . . Fear ye not: I should fall asleep quietly
amongst you, and sooner than ye expect; very soon . . ."
she faltered anxiously, waiting with a throbbing heart for
him to say: "Stay with us!"

He did not, but made as if he had not followed the drift
of her rambling talk; and stretched himself, and yawned,

and walked uneasily about before the hut, the barn, the hayrick. . . .

She sobbed and moaned plaintively. "How could he, indeed? He, a husbandman of such repute—and I, a wretched beggar-woman!"

And thereupon she started on her daily search for some place in the village where she could die in good odour, as a respectable peasant-woman.

On and on she crawled to find some such nook, and ever drifting about like gossamer in the gale, to stick fast no one knows where.

People joked about her, and enjoyed saying that she ought to stay with her family, and telling the Klembas, with mock friendship:

"Why, she is of your family, and she has money for her funeral besides, and then she will not trouble you very long. Where else should she be but with you?"

Dame Klemba thought of those words, when her goodman told her at night of what Agata had said that day. They were in bed at the time, their children had begun to snore, and she whispered to persuade him:

"There will be room for her . . . She may lie in the hay . . . Or we shall drive the geese out into the shed.— For her food, she wants next to naught . . . And she cannot drag on very long . . . Moreover, she will be buried at her own cost. So people will not speak against us . . . And then, the feather-bed would be ours: we could not easily get such another one." This she pointed out to him very eagerly.

In answer, Klemba merely snored at the time; but in the morning he said:

"If Agata were quite destitute, I should take her in; it were then God's will, and I could not do otherwise. But, as things stand, they will say we have taken her in for the sake of what she leaves us. As it is, they blame us for having let her go and beg.—Nay, it cannot be."

Klembova obeyed her husband in all things, but she

sighed bitterly over the feather-bed lost to them, and got
up to hurry the girls out to their work; for that day they
had to plant the cabbages.

It was then May weather at its best. The breeze blew,
stirring the corn in rippling waves. The orchards whispered
as they waved, and shook down their blossoming petals; and
heavy clusters of lilac and bird-cherry blossoms filled the
air with perfume. From the fields, songs came borne on
the wind; and in the smithy, the hammer rang on the
anvil. Since morning, the roads had been full of people
and racket, and the women wended their way to the cabbage
patches, bearing young plants with them in sieves and
baskets.

Before the morning dew was quite dry, the black fields,
cut into many a furrow full of water sparkling in the sunshine, were dappled all over with red aprons and skirts.

Dame Klemba went with her daughters, the while her
goodman with his sons were helping Matthew to repair their
cabin.

Old Klemba, however, presently finding the sun too hot,
called Balcerek and went over to see Boryna.

"A fine day, friend," he said, taking a pinch from Balcerek's snuff-box.

"Splendid. But let's hope this great heat will not last."

"Rain is falling on all sides: our turn must come soon."

"Yet it looks like drought: the trees are covered with insects."

"And the vegetables, how late they have come up! A
drought would destroy them. But, by God's grace, it may
not come to that."

"Well, and what of the fair? Any news of your horse?"

"I gave the police officer three roubles, and he gave me
promises."

"We have naught in safety! We live in constant alarm,
as hares do, and there's no help for it."

"Our Voyt is a mere figure-head," suggested Balcerek, in
low cautious tones.

"We ought," Klemba rapped out, "to seek another."

Balcerek gave him a warning look; but he went on, excitedly:

"He brings the village to shame.—Have ye heard what he did yesterday?"

"Oh, his brawl? that's naught.—But there's more, and we may have to pay dear for his spell in office."

"But there are checks on him: the cashier, the scrivener, the rest of the council."

"Like dogs set to watch over meat! Aye, they'll watch so well that we peasants will have in the end to pay for their negligence."

"What's to be done?—Any other news?"

Balcerek spat and tossed up his hand; he cared little to talk, being a cross-grained man, and henpecked besides, which made him still more taciturn.

They arrived at Boryna's. In the porch, Yuzka was peeling potatoes.

"Ye may go in; Father is lying there alone. Hanka is out planting cabbages, and Yagna working at her mother's."

The room looked very empty. A lilac-bough now and then peeped in at the window, and the sunlight filtered in through the verdure outside.

The old man lay as usual, but much emaciated, with his grey beard bristling all over his discoloured cheeks. His head was still bandaged, and his ashen lips were moving as if to speak.

They greeted him. No answer, no movement in reply.

"Do ye not know us?" said Klemba, taking his hand.

He seemed totally unconscious, or lost in rapt listening to the twittering swallows, building their nests under his thatch, or the brustling of the leaves against the wall outside.

"Matthias!" Klemba said, shaking him slightly.

The sick man started, his eyelids quivered, he looked round at them.

"Do ye hear?—This is Klemba, this Balcerek, your companions: surely ye know us!"

They waited a little, gazing into his eyes.

"Boys!" he cried suddenly, in a thundering voice. "See me here alone! To the rescue! Smite them, those sons of dogs! smite them!" He raised his arms as to ward off a blow, and fell back on his bed.

At the cry, Yuzka rushed in, and put fresh moist bandages on his head. And now, once more, he lay quite motionless: in his wide-open eyes there gleamed an expression of intense fear.

They went away, distressed and disheartened.

"Why," said Klemba, "he is no longer a living man . . . he's a corpse!"

Vitek's stork was stalking about the orchard; the wind now and then swept the branches into the open windows to shade them.

Back they went, plunged in sad silent thought, as if they had been to visit a grave.

"We must all come to this!" Klemba said at last.

"Truly," sighed the other. "He has perished, and others gain thereby."

" 'A goat dies once, and then—never again!' "

"We too shall follow him shortly."

And they looked with hardening eyes at the world around; at the waving corn; at the forest, clear-cut and plain in the distance; at the green-growing fields, and at the bright warm day of springtide: and their spirits settled down in a stony resignation to the will of God.

"No; man cannot shun what is to be."

And so they parted.

Others, too, both on that day and afterwards, came to visit the dying man: but he recognized no one, and at last they came no longer.

The priest had said: "All he needs is prayers for a speedy departure."

And as everyone was full of his own cares and troubles, they naturally forgot him, or spoke of him as of one dead.

Who was there, indeed, to take thought of him?

There were even days when he remained without a drop of water, and might have died of starvation, but for the kind heart of Vitek, who would snatch up anything he could get and take it to "Master"; and he would sometimes milk the cows in secret, and bring him to drink. He was indeed filled with attention and respect for the sufferer, and with disquietude also: which made him at last question Pete:

"Is't true that whosoever dies without confession must go to hell?"

"Most true. Why, the priest tells us so in church ever so often."

"Then . . . Master shall also go to hell?" And he crossed himself in dismay.

"He's a man like any other!"

"What? Master a man like any other?"

"You are as senseless as a cabbage-head!" said Pete, growing angry; for he saw that Vitek did not believe him. . . .

And thus did the days go by at Boryna's cabin.

The village meanwhile, on account of the Voyt's battle, was in a state of great animation, each party eagerly looking for witnesses in its favour.

It was of no great importance in itself: yet the Voyt exerted himself with might and main; and his influence in Lipka proved so considerable that more than half the inhabitants were on his side. They knew him to be no saint; but he was their Voyt all the same, and able to make things hot for opponents. So, by dint of insistence, flattery, and vodka, he got together as many witnesses as he required.

Koziol was very ill in bed, and the priest had been to him with the last sacraments. As to that illness, opinions differed: some went so far as to whisper low that it was only a feint to give the Voyt more trouble.—But who knew really what to think of it?

In the meantime Kozlova was going about all day, telling the people that she had sold her sow and farrow to purchase medicines for her goodman; and well-nigh daily she stationed herself outside the Voyt's house, loading him with invectives, shrieking that her Bartek was about to die, and calling God and all honest people to witness in her favour and take sides with her.

Only the riff-raff of the community, however, and a few tender-hearted women, were with her; Kobus also, a third-rate farmer and a most litigious and quarrelsome man. The others would not listen to her. Some paid no notice to what she said; others, in her own interest, advised her to make friends with the Voyt.

Many broils arose thence; for Kobus had an ungovernable tongue, and was very ready with his fists; while the women, on their side, used extremely violent language. Their anger and acrimony were most intense: for how could they hope to get the better of the farmers and the Voyt together?

In the end, the Jew himself treated the Koziols with contempt, and refused them credit.

Within a week after the battle, everyone had enough of the affair, and the complaints and lamentations connected therewith, and would not listen any longer.

But at that juncture, new helpers came, and the village was again in an uproar.

Ploshka, joining forces with the miller, now stood up openly and strongly for the Koziols.

Not that they cared for their cause in the least: each had his own aims and sought his own advantage.

Ploshka, an underhanded and much-aspiring man, put unbounded trust in his own wealth and cleverness: and as to the miller, he would have risked his life for money.

And thus the struggle between the two parties began, fierce, yet courteous: they treated each other to shows of friendship, and conversed as before, and even went sometimes arm in arm to the tavern together.

The shrewder Lipka folk were soon aware that this coalition aimed at something more than the mere redress of Koziol's grievance—possibly at the Voyt's office itself.

And the elders nodded their heads, saying:

"One man has made a good thing by the office: others may do so too!"

And as the days passed by, the village dissensions increased.

Once, about that time, there came round to every hut the news that there were Germans stopping at the tavern.

As someone guessed, they were no doubt bound for Podlesie.

The people were taken with a fit of uneasy curiosity. The news flew from orchard to orchard, it was discussed over the fences, and many a one hurried to the tavern to see.

It was true. Five large tilted wagons, each painted yellow and blue, and fitted with iron axle-trees, stood outside the inn. They were laden with articles of furniture, and women were sitting inside. In the tavern bar, ten Germans were drinking.

They were tall, stout, bearded fellows, clad in dark-blue capotes, with silver chains that dangled from their bulging waists, and faces that literally shone with good feeding.

The peasants stood grouped together at a distance from them, calling for vodka, looking on and listening to their talk, but unable to make anything out. Matthew, who could speak Yiddish, tried speech with them by that means, and so fluently that the tavern-keeper looked at him in amazement. The Germans eyed him, but answered nothing. Gregory, the Voyt's brother, then said a few German words to them: at which, grunting among themselves as swine do over a trough, they turned their backs on the peasants.

Matthew took fire at this. "Let's punch their snouts for them!" he cried.

"Aye; or tickle their sides with a cudgel to make them speak."

And Adam Klemba, a fiery young fellow, exclaimed:

"I'll hit this nearest one in the stomach; and if he strikes back, ye all come in for fair play."

But they restrained him; and the Germans, probably guessing some harm was intended them, took with them a barrel of beer, and left the place.

"Hey, ye Long Trousers, do not hurry so: they might fall down by the way!"

And as they drove off, the peasants shouted after them:
"Breed of swine!"

No sooner had they left than the Jew informed the peasants that the Germans had almost completed the purchase of Podlesie: fifteen families were to settle on that farm.

"And then we shall be hemmed in and squeezed to death on our poor strips of land, while they stretch and multiply over those broad acres!"

"Then let us bid higher and keep them out!" said Staho Ploshka to Gregory, who had spoken last. "Use your wits, since ye think yourself clever!"

"Blood of a dog!" Matthew shouted, thumping the bar with his fist; "'tis a ruinous business, this! If they settle down in Podlesie, 'twill be a hard thing for us to keep our homesteads in Lipka." Of this he was sure: he had been about the world, and knew what Germans were.

His hearers were at first incredulous. All the same, it troubled them, and they fell a-thinking: how could evil come to them in Lipka from neighbours in Podlesie?

Every day, herdsmen and wayfarers came to tell how the lands of Podlesie were being measured, and landmarks laid down, and wells dug. Of this, too, so many as wandered out of curiosity in the direction of Vola had ocular demonstration.

But what was the true situation of affairs? That as yet they had not ascertained.

They urged the smith to find out, for he had made friends with the Germans and shod their horses; but he fought shy, and either learned or told them nothing.

It was Gregory who at last sought information and got at the truth.

The fact was that the Squire owed a certain German fifteen thousand roubles, which he could not pay. The latter proposed taking Podlesie for the debt, and paying the difference in ready money. The Squire seemed inclined to agree to this, but secretly looked out for some other purchaser, the German offering only sixty roubles an acre.

"He will have to agree," Gregory declared. "The Manor

is swarming with Jews, all crying out for their money. And the forester told me the Manor cows had been attached for the taxes. How, then, can he pay them? Everything is sold! And he may not cut down the forest, so long as his lawsuit with us is not ended.—No, he must sell Podlesie at any price."

"Why, such land is worth a hundred roubles an acre!"

"Then buy it at that price, and he will be only too glad to sell!"

"Alas, money is short! Whence is it to come?"

"So then, the Germans must get all, and we nothing!"

They talked on, with sad forebodings. How hard it was that such land should be lost to them—so near, so fruitful, so suitable for their sons and sons-in-law! They could have founded another village there, with fertile meadows and water in abundance. . . . But there, all was of no avail! The Germans were there, they would get the upper hand and crush the life out of the poor peasants.

"And whither shall all these go?" the old men murmured sadly, looking on while their children played about the roads in the evening—so numerous that the huts could scarce contain them. "But how is it possible to purchase any land, since we get barely enough to live on out of ours?"

They cudgelled their brains not a little; they even went to the priest for advice. But he could give them none. "Out of an empty pot, nothing is ever got!"

"Ah! 'money makes the mare go'; but, 'wherever the poor man goes, the wind against him blows!'"

Useless complaints, useless lamentations!

To make matters worse, the weather grew excessively hot: July weather in May. The sun rose in the very East, a vast fire in the azure: on every height, in all sandy soil, the vegetables drooped and faded. The grass was sear and burnt upon the fallows; and the potato-plants, which had at first sprouted well, hardly covered the ground with their poor puny shoots. The autumn-sown lands were alone to suffer little; being already in the ear, they grew splendidly

and very high: the low cottages they surrounded seemed to
have shrunk yet lower, crouching earthwards with only their
roofs well above the forest of waving corn.

The nights being so hot and sultry that it was painful to
lie in the huts, people slept in the orchards.

As a consequence of the great heats, of those troubles
which beset them in troops, and also of the hard times preceding the harvest (harder than usual that year), it came to
pass that the people of Lipka quarrelled and fought among
themselves more than ever. Everyone seemed to enjoy
thwarting his neighbour, and life there became a real torment. From the peep of day, the village rang with bickerings and angry words, some new contest taking place every
day. Now it was Kobus and his wife, who had such a
set-to that the priest had to go and rebuke and reconcile
them; now Balcerek's wife, who came to blows with Gulbas
over a pig that had strayed into her carrot-patch; now
Ploshkova, who had a row with the Soltys, on account of
their goslings' getting mixed: besides countless wrangles
about the children, or unneighbourly behaviour, or anything
that could serve for a squabble and outcries and noisy invectives. There seemed to be a curse on the village, bringing no end of altercations, breaches of the peace, and law-
suits.

Ambrose even made fun of this waspish disposition before
strangers.

"This year times are not so very hard for me before harvest, by the goodness of Providence! No one dies, no one
is born, no one is married; but they daily offer me vodka,
and flatter me, and beg me to bear witness for them! Let
them but wrangle so a few years more, and I shall have
drunk myself to death!"

Lipka was in a bad way indeed; but things went worst of
all at Dominikova's.

Simon had returned with the others, Andrew's leg was
well now; they were not in sore straits as others were, and
things ought to have gone on as of old. Far from it!

Her sons would no longer obey her. They were grown rebellious, always at loggerheads with her, objected to being beaten, and refused to do woman's work!

"Ye must hire a maidservant," they said tartly, "or do the work yourself."

Now Dominikova had ruled them with a rod of iron, and tyrannized over them for many a year; so she was very much shocked to see her own children rise up against her now.

"Grant me patience!" she would scream on such occasions, flying in a rage, and taking up her stick; but they made stout resistance, and were as stubborn as she. Every day there were fearful quarrels, hunts all over the premises, and so on, till the neighbours would rush in to smooth matters over.

The priest himself called her sons to him, and exhorted them to live in concord and obedience. They heard him out with patient respect, kissed his hand and humbly embraced his knees as in duty bound; but they behaved as before.

"We are no children; we know what to do, and Mother must yield. Why, the whole village was making laughing-stocks of us!"

Choler and exasperation had made the old dame yellow as a quince. Do what she might, she could not get the better of them; and now, instead of attending church services or gossiping as she had been accustomed, she had to work at home! She was always calling on Yagna to assist her; but from her too she got shame and sorrow in plenty.

The Voyt would look in frequently, to take her advice, he said: in reality, to get Yagna out with him, and play pranks with her in the garden.

Nothing can be hidden in a village: all knew perfectly well what was going on. And their guilty love becoming more and more openly scandalous, certain good people spoke several times to the old woman on the subject.

What was she to do? Yagna, notwithstanding prayers

and supplications, flaunted her wantonness as though to spite
her mother. The most grievous sin, the most shameful
obloquy, was preferable in her eyes to staying by that husband whom she loathed.

Hanka too did nothing to oppose this state of things, and
said so openly.

"So long as there is no one to prevent the Voyt from
wasting the community's money, she may do as she pleases.
He grudges her naught, fetches her all he can from town,
and would, if he could, put her in a frame of gold. Let them
have their sport . . . and see the end of it!—I have naught
in common with them!"

And truly, she had troubles enough of her own. She had
given the lawyer whatever he asked, but could as yet not tell
when Antek was to be tried, nor what destiny awaited him.
And meanwhile he was pining away in prison, hoping God
would have mercy on him.—In the cabin, besides, things
went ill.

Pete had grown insolent of late—no doubt the smith had
tampered with him; he did no more work than he chose.
Once she had been in town: he had spent the whole day out
of doors; and as she threatened to call him to account before Antek on his return:

"On his return?" was the jeering reply. "Bandits are
never set free in such wise!"

The impertinent words made her blood boil, and she would
have longed to strike him on the mouth; but what good
would that have done? She had to pocket her affronts, till
the right time should come. Otherwise, the man would
leave, and all would be thrown on her hands. She could
hardly manage to pull through as it was, and her health was
breaking down under the strain. "Steel is devoured by rust,
and rocks last but for a season"; how, then, could a feeble
woman hold out for ever?

One day—May was then drawing to an end—the priest
had driven off with the organist to a local festival. Ambrose had been drinking so deep with the Germans (who now

looked frequently in at the tavern) that he was not there to
toll the evening Angelus, nor to open the church-door for
the May service!

It was therefore decided to have the service in the burying-
ground, where, close to the lich-gate, there stood a little
shrine containing a statue of the Mother of God. Every
May, the girls adorned it with paper ribbons and a gilt
crown, and cast wild flowers all around, doing likewise all
they could to preserve it from complete ruin. It was of
great antiquity, and so cracked and crumbling and dilapi-
dated that the birds no longer made their nests in it; and
if a shepherd-boy ever took shelter there, it was only during
the autumn rains. To some extent it was screened from
the winter storms by the churchyard trees, the old lindens,
some slender birches, and a few crosses which stood near,
leaning out of the perpendicular.

A good many people had assembled, and quickly decked
the shrine with flowers and verdure; and, having placed a
taper and some small lamps at the feet of the statue, they
knelt down piously.

The blacksmith bent in front before the threshold,
sprinkled with tulips and eglantine blossoms; and he struck
up a hymn.

It was then much after sunset, and growing dark; but the
sky was still burning and golden in the West, with pale
emerald higher up. All was very still; the long locks of the
birches streamed down in cascades, and the corn stooped
down, as though listening to the shrill quavering of the
crickets.

The herds were wending their way home; and from field
and village and pathways now unseen, there floated the
graziers' noisy songs, mingled with long melancholy lowings.
And the people looked into their Mother's face, and lifted
up their voices, while she stretched her hands out in benediction over the world.

> "Good night, O Lily white!
> Good night!"

The scent of the young birch-trees filled the air, and the nightingales began to try their notes, first in broken bursts, then gathering force, and finally breaking out into foaming streams of golden euphony—wonderful trills of long-drawn music, of melody dropping like pearls; while at no great distance resounded the violin of Mr. Yacek, which accompanied the human singers so sweetly, so gently, and so powerfully at once, it seemed that it came from the rye-stalks rustling against each other, or that the soil itself were breathing that chant of May.

All then sang together in ecstasies: the people, the birds, the violin; and when they paused to take breath awhile, an innumerable choir of frogs raised their husky voices all in tune and whirringly, as if hurrying them on to begin again.

So the chant went on—now these singers, now those.

The service lasted very long, and in the end the smith called out more than once to those behind him:

"Pray, do not drag the words so!" For many of them were lengthening out the notes beyond measure.

His remark to Matthias Klemba went even farther: "Don't bellow so; you're not following the oxen!" And at last they sang together all in harmony, and their voices were like a flock of doves soaring up in the dusky sky.

> "Good night, O Lily white!
>   Good night!
> Mary, our hearts' delight,
>   Good night!"

It was now black overhead, warm, and very quiet; but a few stars began to appear and sparkle and twinkle like dew-drops.

The girls in couples, arms about waists, sang together as they went home.

Hanka was returning alone, carrying her baby and absorbed in thought, when the smith approached and walked by her side.

She held her peace until close to her home; then, seeing him still beside her, she said:

"Are ye coming in, Michael?"

"Only into the porch," he answered in a low tone; "I have to speak with you."

She felt somewhat agitated. Had he any fresh misery in store for her?

"You have probably been to see Antek," he said.

"Yes, but was not let in."

" 'Tis what I feared!"

"Say, then, what ye know!" She was shaking with apprehension.

"What I know? Only so much as I could get out of the police inspector."

"And what is that?" She pressed her little one closer.

"That Antek is not to be released until after the trial."

"How is that?" she stammered hoarsely. "The lawyer told me the contrary."

" 'Tis because he would take to flight. In such cases, a prisoner is never set at liberty. Bear in mind that I come to you as a friend to-day.—Bygones are bygones. . . . Though you will see one day that I was right. . . . But hear what I have to say now: I am speaking the truth as in the confessional.—Antek is in a very sorry plight, and sure to be cruelly punished: perchance for ten years! You hear?"

"I do, and believe not one word," she said, with sudden self-control.

"Seeing is believing; and I have told you the truth."

"After your fashion," she replied, smiling ironically.

He seemed offended, and assured her warmly that he had come for no other purpose but to give her friendly advice. She listened as he talked, looking round impatiently; the cows lowed unmilked in their byres, the geese were still out of doors, the colt and Lapa sporting in the enclosure, and the little ones playing in the barn: while of all he was telling her she believed nothing. "But I'll let him talk on," she thought, "till I find out what he's aiming at"; and she held herself on the alert.

"What is to be done?" she asked mechanically.

"There is something," he whispered.

She faced him suddenly.

"Pay down enough money, and he will be released even before the trial. And then he can escape. Even to 'Hamerica'! They will not catch him there."

"Lord! to 'Hamerica'!" she cried, appalled.

"Hush! I tell you in great secrecy. 'Tis what the Squire said to me. 'Let him get away,' he said; 'ten years of Siberia will ruin any man's life.' . . . That he told me but yesterday."

"What! and flee from our village . . . our children . . . our lands?" It was the only misfortune that appealed to her.

"Pay the sum wanted, and Antek will do all the rest.— Give it to them."

"But where—where am I to get it? . . . O my God! . . . Away to the very back of the world. . . . So far from everyone!"

"They ask for five hundred roubles. Why, ye have father-in-law's money: take it and pay; we shall reckon together later—only save Antek!"

She saw the trap, and started to her feet.

"Obstinate dog! Always on the same trail!" she said, about to leave him.

"This is foolishness!" he exclaimed, losing patience. "'Twas but a word that escaped me. Must ye take offence at a word, when your man is rotting in jail?—Oh, he shall know how much ye do to set him free!"

She sat down again, quite bewildered.

He talked to her for some time about "Hamerica," and folk he knew that had gone there, who wrote letters home, and even sent their families money. Antek might get away at once; Michael knew a Jew who had wafted many a one over the frontier. Multitudes got away thus. Hanka, too, might follow later, without attracting attention. Gregory would return from the army, and repay all from the inheritance; or if he could not, a purchaser would readily be found.

"Take ye counsel of the priest," he concluded; "he will

approve my plan, as ye will see. I have only urged you to do right, and for no profit of my own.—But breathe not a word of this to anyone else, or the gendarmes will know of it. And then he would not get out of prison at all, and be perchance put in irons into the bargain," he concluded grimly.

"But where is the money to come from that will set him free?" she said, with a groan.

"I know a man in Modlitsa who would lend it—at high interest. Oh, the money can be found! I'll lay my life I could manage that!"

For a long while he went on counselling her, and at last slipped away abruptly. She, lost in thought, took no note of his going.

Everybody else had gone to bed, except Vitek, who seemed to be waiting for his mistress. The moon went up through the heavens, a silver reaping-hook moving athwart the deep expanse. Over the meadows crept white sheets of mist; above the rye was hanging the dust of its saffron pollen; moveless as an ice-field, the mill-pond glittered amongst the trees. Broken by the nightingales' rills of bubbling music, the silence made the ears ring and tingle.

"Heavens! To flee one's village, and one's land—and all!" she thought, the same idea ever returning; and her dread grew more intense, and she felt her trembling heart shrink in the clutch of pain.

Lapa then howled aloud; the birds sang no more, and the gales whistled and moaned among the dark shadows of the branches.

"Lapa now sees Kuba's ghost!" Vitek muttered, and crossed himself with awe.

"Foolish one! go to bed!" said Hanka.

"But indeed he does come, and looks after the horses, and brings them their fodder. Aye, and not once only!"

She took no notice of his words. All was now plunged in deep stillness; and there she sat, repeating, as one paralysed with appalling anguish: "To flee a whole world away!— And for ever, merciful Jesus!—For ever!"

CHAPTER IX

THE green Whitsuntide boughs, decorating the cabin-doors, had not yet quite withered, when one morning Roch dropped most unexpectedly into the village.

It was only after hearing Mass, however, and having a long talk with the priest, that he went round to the village. There were but few people about, most of them being occupied tumping their potato-plants; but when, with its usual speed, the news had gone about, a good many hastened to bid him welcome after his long absence.

He came, according to his wont, slowly, leaning on his staff, but with head erect, and wearing the same grey capote and the same rosary about his neck. The wind blew his grey hair loose, but his thin features were gleaming with kindness and geniality.

He gazed around him, smiling gladly upon all he saw, with a special greeting for everybody; patting the little ones' heads, and accosting the women with great pleasure to find everything in its former state.

When they inquired curiously of him where he had been so long, "In Chenstohova, to gain the indulgences," he replied.

Glad to see him back, they at once set to telling him all the village news: asking advice, complaining of their neighbours, and all wishful to explain their troubles to him in private.

He was extremely tired, he told them; they must wait: he would be staying in Lipka a day or two.

At that they all begged him to stay with them. But he said he was engaged for the beginning by his promise to Hanka; after, if anyone would take him, he might stay longer. And so he made for Boryna's.

Hanka of course was overjoyed to receive him. No

sooner had he laid down his staff and wallet than he went over to the old man.

"Ye will find him lying in the orchard: it is too hot in the room.—Meanwhile we are boiling some milk for you . . . and eggs too, if you care."

Roch was at once in the orchard, bending under the drooping branches, as he made his way to the patient, who lay in a basketwork contrivance, covered over with a sheep-skin coat. Lapa, curled up at his feet, watched over him; and Vitek's stork was strutting bravely about amongst the trees, as if on guard.

In this old leafy orchard, the well-grown trees kept the sun out so completely that only a few spots of light, like golden spinners, moved about on the grass beneath.

Matthias lay upon his back. The boughs waved their dark mantle over his head, murmuring softly, and only now and then, when tossed by the winds, letting a patch of blue sky peep through, and a sunbeam fall on his face.

Roch sat down by his side. The patient at once turned to him.

"Ah! Matthias, don't you know me? don't you know me?"

A slight smile passed over Boryna's face, his eyelids fluttered, and his ashen lips moved; but no sound came from them.

"If it be our Lord's will, ye may yet recover."

This he must have understood, for he shook his head, and —unconsciously, it seemed—turned his face away, to look at the tossing boughs, and the bright rays that from time to time shone into his eyes.

Roch sighed, made the sign of the cross over him, and went back.

"Well," Hanka inquired, "is not Father better now?"

He pondered some time; then replied, in low grave tones:

"A lamp always flickers more brightly just before going out. Belike Matthias is passing away. For my part, I wonder he has held out so long."

"He eats naught: often will he not even take milk."

"Ye should be ready for the end any day."

"We should indeed.—Ambrose told me so only the other day, and advised me not to delay having a coffin made."

"Ye may," he answered mournfully; " 'twill not be empty very long.—The soul that is panting to leave this world nothing can keep back, not even our tears. Else some should remain with us for centuries." And, supping the milk she had prepared for him, he asked her about things in the village.

What she told him he had learned on his way to her; but she afterwards dilated at length and eagerly on her own troubles.

"Where is Yuzka?"

"In the fields, tumping our potatoes along with the *Komorniki* and Yagustynka. Pete is off to the forest, fetching Staho timber for a new hut."

"What, is he building one?"

"Aye. Mr. Yacek has given him ten trunks of pinewood."

"Given him? I heard something of that sort, but could not believe it."

"For it is incredible! No one would credit the thing at first. The man had promised; but that anyone can do. 'Promises are toys made to give fools joys,' as the saying is. —Well, Mr. Yacek gave Staho a letter he was to carry to the Squire. Even Veronka said no to that: why should he wear his boots out for nothing, and be laughed at into the bargain for believing a Squire? But he would have his own way. And when he had given in the letter (he told us) the Squire called him into his room, offered him vodka, and said: 'Bring ye wagons, and the forester shall mark out ten logs for you.' Klemba and the Soltys gave him wagons, and I gave him Pete besides. The Squire was actually in the clearing, waiting for him, and himself chose ten of the straightest and longest of all, that had been hewn down in winter for the Jews! And now Staho is setting up a beautiful cabin.—No need to say how or with what excuses he thanked Mr. Yacek; whom indeed we all held for a pauper and a lackbrain, forasmuch as no one can tell what his

means are, and he plays the fiddle under the holy figures or
in the corn, and sometimes talks in rambling wise, and as
one not in his right wits.—Yet is he such a big man that the
very Squire does his bidding. Who could have believed
such a thing?"

"Look not upon the man, but on his deeds."

"But to give such a quantity of timber, worth (Matthew
says) a thousand *złoty* at least, and all just for a Thank-you-
kindly! Why, it is unheard of!"

"They say he intends to take over the old cabin, to live
in for the rest of his life."

"Absurd! it has the worth of a split wooden clog: no more.
—Folk were so suspicious of something underhanded that
Veronka went to ask his Reverence about the whole busi-
ness; who scolded her, and called her a silly woman."

"So she was.—Take what is given you, thanking God for
His goodness."

"Aye, but to get aught for naught is so monstrous a
thing: and out of a Squire besides! So unheard of! Did
anyone ever give a peasant anything at all for love? When
we want the simplest advice, they look to see what our
hands offer. Just accost an official empty-handed: how
surely he'll tell you: 'To-morrow,' or 'Come next Sunday'!
Oh, Antek's business has taught me how things are done,
and I have spent not a little that way already."

" 'Tis well ye put me in mind of Antek.—I have been in
town."

"And seen him?"

"No time for that."

"I too went not long ago, but did not see him. God
knows when I shall."

He smiled. "Sooner perchance than ye think."

"Good Lord! what is it ye say?"

"The truth. I have been told at head-quarters that Antek
may be released before the trial. But someone must stand
bail for him to the amount of five hundred roubles."

"The very sum the smith spoke of!" And she told him
Michael's advice, word for word.

"There is something in it; but, coming from him, 'tis unsafe! He surely has only his own gain in view.—Be not hasty to sell: 'A man rides away from his lands on a stallion, but on foot he comes back—a tatterdemallion.'— Would anybody stand bail? We must seek someone.—If the money were but at hand!"

"Perhaps it is," she said timidly. "I—I have a little cash in hand, but cannot count it aright."

"Show it me; we shall do the sum together."

She disappeared, and soon returned, shot the bolt, and laid a parcel on his knees.

It contained notes, some silver and some gold pieces, besides six strings of corals.

"These belonged to his dead wife. He gave them to Yagna, and (I suppose) took them back again later," she whispered, squatted down by the settle on which Roch was counting.

"Four hundred and thirty-two roubles, five *zloty*.—From Matthias, hey?"

"Yes—yes!" she faltered, turning red. "He gave them to me after Eastertide."

"It will not suffice entirely, but you might dispose of some of the animals."

"It might be done. Our sow could go . . . and the barren cow likewise. The Jew asked to buy her; she might still be worth some bushels of corn to us."

"Then we shall bail Antek without aid.—Is it known to anyone that ye have this money?"

"Father gave it to me to set Antek free, forbidding me to say one word of it to any creature. You are the first to know.—If Michael . . . !"

"Be easy; your secret is safe. When I hear the time has come, we shall go together and free Antek. The clouds will roll by and the weather clear up, my dear child!" he said, and kissed the top of her head, as she fell at his feet to thank him.

She wept tears of joy. "My own father could not have been fonder," she sobbed.

"Your man will return to you, thank God!—Where is Yagna?"

"She started for town this morning in company with her mother and the Voyt. They say Dominikova is going to the notary, intending to make all her land over to Yagna."

"All to Yagna?—And her sons?"

"They want her to divide the land, and she would spite them. Hell is in their cabin now, and the Voyt is on Dominikova's side: at the father's death, he was named the orphans' guardian."

"Is it so? About the Voyt I had heard another tale."

"Ye have heard true. He does indeed care for Yagna, but in such wise as I shame to speak of. He is past his prime, but still vigorous; and she, a wanton. I do not repeat hearsay; myself I saw them in the orchard."

"I would lay me down somewhere: may I?"

She wanted him to sleep on Yuzka's bed, but he preferred going to the stable.

"Keep your money safe!" he said on leaving her.

He was not seen until dinner-time. After the meal, he was making for the village, when Hanka hesitatingly proffered a request.

"Roch, would you help us to adorn our altar?"

"Ah! yes: to-morrow is Corpus Christi Day.—Where are you to erect it?"

"Where we do every year: outside our porch. I am sending Peter instantly to the forest for young fir-trees and pine-bough decorations, whilst Yagustynka is to hurry off with Yuzka and get flowers for garlands."

"And have ye the tapers and candlesticks yet?"

"Only this morning, Ambrose promised to bring me some from the church."

"And on whose premises are altars to be set up besides?"

"At the Voyt's, on this side of the pond; on the other, at the miller's and at Ploshka's."

"I shall help: but first I must see Mr. Yacek. Ere dusk, I am here again."

"Then pray tell Veronka to come over by daybreak to-morrow, and make herself useful."

He nodded, and walked away towards the ruins of Staho's hovel.

Mr. Yacek was, as usual, on the threshold, smoking, stroking his beard, and looking far away to where the birds fluttered above the undulating corn.

In front of the hut, close to the cherry-trees, lay several enormous trunks; ancient Bylitsa went pottering among them, now dealing a blow at them with an ax, now smoothing away some protruding knag with a hatchet, and talking to them all the time aloud:

"Aha! So you have come into our yard. Many thanks! Matthew will soon cut you asunder into shapely beams that shall do you no little honour. Aye, you shall dwell here secure from moisture: fear not."

"He talks to it as though it were a living thing!" Roch observed in some surprise.

"Sit ye down: he is mad with joy to-day.—Hark to him!"

"And you too, poor sufferer, lived in the forest; now will you rest, and none shall come to trouble you any more!" continued the old man, patting the resin-stained bark with loving hands.

Then, stepping over to the largest trunk, that had been flung down by the roadside, and crouching close to the flat sawn resin-sweltering surface with yellow rings that he gloated fondly upon, he muttered:

"So great a one? yet overcome all the same, hey? The Jews would fain have carried you to town, but through our Lord's grace you remain here with your own, your husbandmen: they will hang sacred images upon you, and the priest will bless you with holy water. Aye, Aye!"

At this, Mr. Yacek smiled faintly, and, having spoken a few words with Roch, took up his violin, and made for the forest by the field-paths.

Roch stayed listening to Veronka as she talked, and evening slowly came on.

The morrow being a festival, the day's work was sooner ended than usual. Women began to weave festoons outside the cabins, children came in, bringing armfuls of green flags and rushes. In front of Ploshka's and the miller's houses, birch and fir-boughs were piled in heaps, to be planted wherever an altar was raised; and the girls decked the walls behind them with greenery. They also filled up many hollow places in the roads with gravel and sand.

Roch, who had left Veronka, was just emerging on the poplar road, when someone on horseback appeared, galloping at breakneck speed in a cloud of dust. The carts that carried Staho's timber impeded him and he tried to pass round them by the field.

"If ye haste so, you will founder your horse," they cried in vain. He went by them, and galloped on, till the horse was panting and blown.

"Adam!" Roch exclaimed; "wait a minute!"

Young Klemba just stopped long enough to roar:

"Know that two people lie murdered in the forest. O Lord! how frightened I am! I had been just by, tending the horses, and was coming home with the lad Gulbas, when—just at Boryna's cross—my horse shied. I looked and saw two people lying in the juniper-bushes. I called out to them; but they made no more answer than if dead."

"O fool, what fable are you telling us now?" his hearers cried.

"Then go look yourselves: there they lie! Gulbas saw them as well, but he ran away to the *Komorniki.*"

"Good God!—Then make haste to the Voyt and tell him."

"He is not yet back from town," someone said.

"Then to the Soltys! He is near the blacksmith's, mending the road with other workmen," they called after him as he clattered away.

The news of the murder had flashed round the village, and people were crossing themselves with fear. Someone informed his Reverence, who came out to ask about it; and all most impatiently awaited the return of the Soltys, who at once had gone in a cart, with Klemba and some labourers.

They waited for ever so long. It was growing dusk when he came back, and—to everybody's amazement—along with the Voyt's horse and britzka; in a very ferocious humour too, cursing, slashing at his poor jade, and doing his best to pass through the crowd. But someone seized the bridle; and, forced to stop, he cried:

"Those mischievous boys! they have been trying a practical joke. There was no one slain: only some people asleep in the bushes. Oh, let me but catch that young Klemba, he shall pay for the fright given—and that soundly!—So I met the Voyt and brought him home with me . . . and that's all!—Vee—o! Little One!"

"But," one man remarked, looking into the open cart, "what ails the Voyt? He is sprawling there like a sick man!"

"He's asleep, that's all!" And the Soltys whipped the horses into a trot.

"What mischievous rascals! To make up such a story!"

"It's all young Gulbas' doing: he is always the first in such games!"

"Rub them both down with an oaken towel! Teach them to scare folk for nothing!"

Very indignant over the whole affair, they were going home, when on their way they met the *Komorniki*, with heavy faggots on their backs, and Kozlova marching at their head, though nearly bent double with her load. Seeing them, she leant back, and remained propped up by her burden.

"He has duped you finely, has the Soltys!" she sneered, almost speechless with fatigue. "Ha! No dead men indeed were in the forest, but worse perchance."

A large group was soon attracted by her words; and then she burst forth with her tale.

"I was going back to the cross by the forest-path, when Gulbas, scared to death, came running to me, telling of dead folk that lay in the juniper-bushes hard by. I thought it were well to look at them, at any rate. We went, and I saw from afar two people lying as dead. Filipka pulled my sleeve to drag me away, and Gregory's wife was pattering her prayers, and I too felt creepy all over. . . . But I crossed myself, went up to them, and looked—and what do I see? My lord the Voyt, lying, with his coat off, and beside him Yagna Borynova: both sleeping very deep. . . . And how they reeked of vodka! . . . And she, unclad in such guise that I shame to say. . . . It was as bad as Sodom! I am old, but such a scandal I never yet heard of.—So the Soltys came up, and Yagna ran off; but his Lordship the Voyt was hard to get into the cart.—Drunk as a pig!"

A voice was heard: "Merciful Lord! this is a new thing in Lipka!"

"If it had been only a farm-hand with a wench!—But a husbandman, a father, and our Voyt!"

"Boryna lies close to death, with no one to give him to drink; and she! . . ."

"I would escort her with tapers out of the place, the harlot! Nay, I'd beat her with rods before the church!" Kozlova shouted once more.

"And where is Dominikova?"

"They left her in town; she was in their way."

"Oh, the sin, the scandal of it! And the shame extends to us all."

"That Yagna—so careless of honour—ready to do the same again to-morrow!"

In their huts, they went on complaining, full of horror and indignation, some of the kinder-hearted women also weeping, in fear of God's judgment upon all of them; and all the village was full of talk and lamentation.

Some young fellows took Gulbas aside to question him about particulars.

"A famous fellow with women, that Voyt of ours," said Adam Vahnik.

"He'll have to pay for this: his wife will tear his hair out!"

"And hold aloof from him for six months."

"Oh, he will not care so much for that now!"

"Yes, one might do any folly for such a lass as Yagna!"

"Surely. Among the Manor damsels, none more fair than she, and when she but looks at any man, she sends a thrill through him!"

"So honey-sweet!—No wonder if Antek Boryna . . ."

"Hold your tongues, men! Gulbas is a liar; so is Kozlova: all this they say out of spite, and we do not know the truth as yet," Matthew interfered, in tones of great concern; but he was interrupted by Gregory the Voyt's brother's arrival.

"Well? Is Peter still asleep?" they asked him. He answered:

"That man was my own brother; but after what he has done, he's no more to me than a dog!—But," he added with a burst of fury, "that carrion is the cause of all!"

" 'Tis a lie!" vociferated Pete, the farm-servant at Boryna's, pushing forward towards Gregory; "and he that utters it is a yelping cur!"

They all were amazed at this unexpected explosion; and he went on, with clenched trembling fists:

"No one is guilty but the Voyt. Was it she gave him corals? or enticed him to the tavern? or lurked for him in the orchard all night long? How he tempted her, how he forced her on! Oh, I know too well! He may even have drugged her: do I know?"

"You plague-spotted protector of hers, be still, or your girdle may come off!"

"But she'll know how you've stood up for her . . . and reward you well!"

"Peradventure with a pair of breeches Matthias wears no more!"

They jeered and laughed till they nearly burst their sides.

"Since her goodman cannot speak for her, I who can will. Aye, I will, blood of a dog! . . . Let me but hear another word against her! O you loud-mouthed curs, how silent you'd have been had she been your sister or your wife!"

"Now then, hold your peace, you stable-boy!" Staho Ploshka thundered. "What right have you to meddle here? Meddle with your horses' tails!"

"And beware," Vahnik added, "lest you get more than this rebuke!"

"And leave farmers alone, you filthy matted-pate!" was the shout they sent up as they withdrew.

"O you scurvy bumpkins!—A stable-boy I am, yes; but never at least did I take a measure of corn in secret to the Jew! Ye know me not!" he called after the retiring group; and they, feeling somehow small and mean, answered nothing, but went home.

The weather was strange that evening: windy, but very bright. Long after sundown there yawned huge gulfs of blood-red fire far up in the depths of the sky. There prevailed a feeling of unrest; the gale howled aloud, but so high above that it only tore at the lofty tree-tops. Geese, no one knew why, would fall a-clamouring in the enclosures all together; dogs ran about nervously, even beyond their homes. No one remained in the house or sat on the door-steps; all gathered at some distance from the dwelling, and talked with their neighbours in low voices.

Hanka had with her a few friends, who had come to condole, and learn something more about Yagna. But when they came to the subject, she answered them scornfully:

" 'Tis a shame and a sin, but an affliction too!"

"Certainly; and the whole parish will know all to-morrow!"

"And will say we are the worst village of all."

"And the shame will fall upon all the Lipka women."

"Because they all are so good that, driven like Yagna, they all would do the same!" Yagustynka said, mocking.

"Be silent! 'tis not the time for jeering now!" snapped Hanka, with such stern rebuke that she uttered not another word.

Hanka was still half choked with shame; but the anger which at first surged up within her had now passed away. And when her friends had gone home, she looked in at the other side, ostensibly to see to Matthias. Perceiving Yagna lying asleep in her clothes, she bolted the door and undressed her carefully in the dark.

"May God have pity on such a fate as hers!" was the thought which came to her a little after, flooding her with immense compassion.

Yagustynka must have noted this change of attitude; for she said, though reluctantly:

"Yagna is not guiltless, but the Voyt is still more to blame."

"True; and it is he—he!—that ought to be punished for everything," Hanka returned, in such energetic agreement that Pete cast a look of gratitude towards her.

They had gauged the common feeling. Till late in the night Ploshka and the Koziols were going about the village, stirring people up against the Voyt. The former would enter the huts and say, as in jest:

"Well, well, we have got a splendid Voyt: the most strapping fellow in all the district!"

And, finding them slow to follow his drift, he would take them with him to the tavern, where some of the smaller farmers were gathered already; plied them assiduously with vodka, and returned to the attack when he saw them flushed.

"Our Voyt is great for doing things, hey?"

"And not for the first time either," Kobus replied, cautiously.

"I know about him . . . I know . . . I know . . . what I'll not tell," growled Sikora, who was tipsy, and leaned heavily against the bar.

"And about you too, I know . . . I know . . . what I'll not tell," he went on growling.

"The only thing," said Ploshka, ordering glasses round again, "is to depose him. Whom we have made Voyt, we can unmake. What he has just done shames all the village; but he has done worse. He has always held with the Squire, to the hurt of our community. He would have had a school opened in Lipka; [1] and 'twas he no doubt who recommended the Voyt to sell Podlesie to the Germans. He revels and drinks continually; he has built a barn and purchased a horse; weekly he eats flesh-meat; and he drinks

[1] A Russian Government school, that is.—*Translator's Note.*

tea!—At whose expense, pray? Not at his own, belike!"

"I know," Sikora growled, interrupting, "that the Voyt is a swine, but also that in this trough you would fain put your snout too!"

"The man's drunk and talking nonsense!"

"And likewise do I know that you shall never be Voyt!"

Thereupon they went apart from him, and took counsel far into the night.

On the morrow the Voyt's adventure was talked about yet more loudly, for the priest had forbidden the altar which had been in former years erected before his cabin. Early in the morning, he had sent for Dominikova, who had not come home till midnight the day before; and he was so angry that he even chid the organist, and gave Ambrose a beating with his long pipe-stem!

Corpus Christi, like the former days, rose serene and splendid, but remarkably sultry and still. Ever since dawn, the sun had been blazing pitilessly; the air was so parched that all the leaves drooped; the corn bowed earthward, faint and limp; the sand burned the bare feet like hot embers, and great drops of resin came trickling out of the walls.

This heat was really a visitation, but the people troubled little about it, plunged as they were in their preparations for the service. The girls appointed to bear the feretories and shrines and pictures in the procession ran like mad from cabin to cabin to try on their robes and comb their hair, while their elders were adorning the altars as fast as they could—at the miller's, outside the priest's (instead of at the Voyt's), and before Boryna's cabin, where Hanka with her household had been working hard ever since the peep of day.

They were also the first to have done the work, and so artistically that everyone admired it even more than the miller's altar.

It was indeed finer. In front of the porch there stood a sort of little chapel, made of interwoven birch-boughs, covered with pieces of woollen cloth, striped in many a hue; whilst inside, on a platform, rose an altar with white napery and fine linen, embellished with tapers and flowers in pots, to which Yuzka had stuck various patterns in gilt paper to adorn them.

There hung above the altar a large-sized painting of our Lady, and several smaller ones on either side. To enhance the effect of the whole, they had suspended over the altar a cage containing a blackbird that Nastka had brought.

From the very gate a lane had been made of fir-branches, alternating with birch-boughs, planted and neatly tumped with yellow sand; and the sanded path had been sprinkled over with sedges.

Yuzka had brought whole armfuls of cornflowers, lark-spurs and field vetches, with which she wreathed images, candlesticks, and whatever else could be wreathed, even strewing flowers all over the ground before the altar. The cabin too came in for its share: walls and windows were drowned in verdure, and waving sedges stuck all along the top of the roof.

Everybody was hard at work, except Yagna alone, who early in the morning had slipped out of the hut, and was not seen any more that day.

So they were the first to be ready, but not before the sun shone well over the village, and the clatter of the carts coming in from the other hamlets began to increase.

Very hurriedly they made ready for church.

Vitek alone was to remain in the enclosure; for swarms of children came pressing in to admire the altar and whistle to the blackbird. He tried to keep them at a distance with a bough, but it would not do. So he loosed his stork, that came on stealthily, prodding and thrusting at their bare legs with its sharp beak, and made them disperse with screams.

They started all together, just as the Mass-bell began to tinkle. Yuzka went in front, dressed all in white, book in hand, and with bows of bright red to her shoes.

"What do you think of this, Vitek?" she had asked, spinning on her heel before him.

"You're as fair to see as the whitest goose!" he answered in admiration.

"Your boot knows as much about it as you do! But Hanka says no one in all the village is clad so well," she said, stamping and pulling down her short skirt.

"Your red knees can be seen through the skirt, as the flesh of a goose through the feathers!"

"Silly lad!—But," she added, in a warning whisper, "hide your stork away! The priest will come with the procession, and might see and know it again."

"Oh, but how fine the mistress looks! For all the world like a turkey-cock!" he murmured in ecstasy, gazing after them down the road; and then, mindful of Yuzka's warning, he shut the stork up in the potato-pit, and let out Lapa to watch before the altar: after which he betook himself to Matthias, lying as usual in the orchard.

The village was deserted. In the church, the service had commenced. The priest came out for Mass, the organ pealed; and, the sermon ended, all the bells were set ringing till they frightened the doves off the roofs. Then the people poured out, streaming through the great door, with banners dipping forward, tapers flaming, holy pictures borne by white-clad maidens, and, at last, the red canopy over the priest, who bore the golden Monstrance.

They formed in procession, with a long lane, edged with flickering lights, cut through the dense throng; and his Reverence intoned:

"Lo, at Thy gate I stand, O Lord!"

to which all the multitude answered, thundering in unison— one great Heaven-reaching voice!—

"My soul hath waited on Thy word."

Singing, they moved forward, with a great crush about the narrow lich-gate; for the concourse was immense, consisting of the whole parish. All the folk of all the Manors were present: several Squires supported the priest on either side, or walked close by, taper in hand. The canopy was borne aloft by husbandmen of the parish: only (perhaps on account of the recent disgrace) none of them men of Lipka.

From the churchyard shadows to the open space beyond, white, dazzling, broiling hot, where the burning sun made the eyes to blink with its living fires, on they walked to the sound of the whole tolling belfry. The chants rose up, the incense-smoke soared forth along with clouds of dust; lights scintillated, and bright showers of flowery petals fell continually, scattered at the feet of his Reverence.

The crowd surged along, heavy-footed, chanting mightily, like to a noisy many-coloured stream; and in its midst— a boat in the rapid current, as it were—floated the crimson canopy. And the holy banners waved and tossed beside the pictures and statues of saints, veiled in gauze and gay with flowers.

Onwards they moved, dense, serried, squeezed, heads close to heads, and each one singing for all he was worth—each as if the whole world sang with him the glory of the Lord —as if those tall lime-trees, those dark alders, those waters sparkling in light, those tapering birches, those lowly or- chards and green fields and vague distances beyond human ken—all and everything—were adding to the hymn their hearty and joyful accompaniment; and the notes rolled and flew through the heat-laden air, up to the radiant sky, up to the sun!

That choral song stirred the very leaves upon the trees, and brought the last blossom-petals floating down!

The priest read the first Gospel at Boryna's altar, and, after a short rest, went forward to the miller's.

It was now still hotter than before, and fast growing un- bearably hot. Every throat was dry as dust; a whitish haze had come over the sun; athwart the bright sky long filmy streaks were floating; the overheated air made the outlines of things quiver and wave as though seen through boiling water.—A storm was at hand.

The procession had lasted a full hour; the priest was drenched with perspiration and as red as a beetroot: yet he continued to officiate with grave dignity, going from altar to altar, listening to the various Gospels sung and intoning the various hymns.

There were moments when the people ceased from chanting; and then the larks took up the song, and the continual cry, Cuckoo, Cuckoo! rang out. Meanwhile, and never-endingly, the great bells boomed.

And though the chants recommenced, and the peasants roared with stentorian throats, and the women's thin shrill voices joined in with the pipings of the children, and the rippling music of the tiny jingling bells carried in the procession, and the loud footsteps upon the trampled earth: still the voice of that grand tolling was loud all the time—pure, high—with deep golden notes that reached to Heaven, full of joy and gladness and sonorous beauty: as if hammers, beating on the sounding disk of the sun, were striking out of it those mighty notes, making the whole country-side toss and ring again!

Then came the return to the church, and a long service within doors: organ pealing loud, voices lifted up!

At last the congregation dispersed: when on a sudden the sky grew dark, the rolling of thunder resounded afar, a dry blasting wind came in whirling gusts, the trees lashed each other, and volumes of dust filled the air.

The people from the neighbouring villages drove away at once and at the top of their speed. A drizzling rain fell, making the air still more close and sultry, while the sun went on pouring down its pitiless heat. The frogs' croaking grew fainter and more drowsy to the ear. The gloom came nearer, and the far-off landscape was now already shrouded; the thunder growled again, and from the livid East brief pallid lightnings flashed forth.

It was from the East that the storm came, extending crescent-wise its ponderous masses of slate-blue clouds, pregnant with rain—possibly with hail. It whistled in the tree-tops, it tore along the corn, while the birds flew with noisy cries to the shelter of the eaves, and even the dogs sought the cabins. The cattle, too, were coming back from the fields; whirls and pillars of dust were dancing along the roads, and closer and closer still came the sound of the thunder.

Presently the sun was submerged in a mass of rusty-hued vapour, through which it shone as through a pane of semi-transparent glass. The thunder growled close to the village, and such gusts came now and then as might have torn the trees up by the roots. The first thunderbolts struck somewhere far away in the woods; the whole sky quickly became of a dark livid tint; the sun vanished. Gusts flew raging by; bolts fell in quick succession; the earth shook with thunder, and the black sky shone brilliantly with flashes whose sudden glint plucked the eyes out.

The very dwellings quivered to the sounds, and all creation quailed and shrank with fear.

Luckily, however, the storm passed over on one side. The lightning struck somewhere far away, the wind went down, having done no harm, the sky brightened up again, after a plentiful rain had fallen a little before Vespers, bringing with it such a flood of water that all the corn was laid instantly, the mill-stream ran in spate, and every ditch, field-path and furrow was flowing with foaming water.

It was only at evening that all was as before, the rain having given over, and the sun shining forth behind the western clouds—a huge bright-red ball.

Then did Lipka breathe once more, its inhabitants looked out upon the world again, gratefully inhaling the cool air and the scents of the land after the rain, especially those of the young birches and the mint-plants in the gardens. The pools all along the roads burned in the sunset, the leaves and grasses sparkled, and the frothy waters seemed liquid fire, as they bubbled with joy, streaming down to the mill-pond.

A slight breeze rustled the laid corn; a bracing cool now breathed from the woods and fields. The children, shout-

ing merrily, went out to paddle in the brooks and ditches;
birds chirruped in the boughs, dogs scampered about; the
metallic notes of the priest's guinea-hens sounded from
the hedge: in all the roads and all about the huts there was
a din of talk and merry calls. Soon, too, not far from the
mill, rose the sounds of the love-ditty:

> "Long, long waiting, I am drenched with dew:
> Loved one, loved one, take me in to you!"

And from the fields, together with the bellowing of the
cattle driven homewards, there floated a song bawled by
some herdsman:

> "Sweetheart, your rye once reaped, you said
> That me without delay you'd wed:
> Rye, wheat and oats are reaped; and yet
> My marriage lines I cannot get!
> Oy dana, da dana!"

Now the carts of those who had stayed out the storm
began to drive off; but a good many farmers from the
neighbouring places remained as the guests of the Lipka
folk—those, that is, who had so kindly come to help the
women not long since. They were received in the homes of
the wealthier farmers with plenty to eat and drink; but
the poorer took their kind friends to treat them at the
tavern, so as to enjoy the pleasure of company: the more,
the merrier.

Some musicians came too; and, immediately after Vespers,
there was heard inside the tavern the thin melody of the
violin, the rumbling of the bass-viol, and the deep-toned
boom of the drum.

People crowded all the more eagerly to enjoy themselves,
because since Easter there had been no occasion for merry-
making.

So many had gathered together that there was not room for
all, and quite a crowd had to be satisfied with the logs
that lay outside the tavern; but as the weather was now
fine, with a grand display of gold in the sky, they sat down
there in numbers, and called for drink.

The tavern itself was brimful of young people, and they at once set to dancing the *Oberek*, making walls and floors groan with their impact and tread as they whirled along. And who led the dance with Nastka?—who but Simon, son of Dominikova? In vain did his brother Andrew dissuade him, plucking him by the sleeve; he was in a gay unruly mood, and drank vodka, and pressed it on Nastka and his boon companions, and flung five-kopek pieces to the band, that they might play with more spirit. And he took Nastka round the waist, vociferating with might and main: "Come, boys, be lively! Stamp and tramp as Poles do!"

And he galloped about the room like a runaway colt, shouting and striking the floor with great violence.

"He has no straw in his boots, that young blade!" Ambrose muttered, his throat twitching greedily, as he looked on at the drinkers. "As a flail, so wields he his limbs! . . . I hope they may not come off!" he added louder, and coming near.

"Take care lest one of yours come off!" Matthew retorted grimly, alluding to the other's wooden leg.

"Oh, I wish so much to drink friendship with you!" he answered, with a propitiatory smile.

"Here, drunkard! and have a care to leave the glass unswallowed!" Matthew replied, pouring out a full glass, and turning his back. Gregory, the Voyt's brother, was holding forth to his group in low tones; they listened, crowded up against the bar, and with such attention that they neither noted the dancers around nor the vodka that stood before them. They were six, all of the best families in the place, and very keen on the matter under discussion; but as the noise and the crowd increased, they presently passed into the Jew's private parlours, which he occupied along with his guests.

It was a small place indeed, so crammed with the beds of the Jewish brats that it was hard to find room at the table. A single tallow candle, stuck in a brass chandelier that hung from the rafters, burned with a smoky flame.

Gregory passed the bottle twice, and they drank, but no one referred to the talk they had broken off, till Matthew cried tartly:

"Now, Gregory, let's hear you: we all sit here like crows expecting rain!"

But before the latter could begin, the blacksmith entered, greeted them, and looked around for a seat.

"Pah! Here comes Sooty-Face, always springing up where he has not been sown!" Matthew blurted out; but, stifling his annoyance, he at once added: "Michael, here's to you!"

The smith tossed the liquor off and, trying to put a good face on the matter, remarked as if in jest: "I care not to learn the secrets of other folk, and perhaps I am not wanted here?"

"As you say!" Ploshka returned. "Being so friendly with the Germans—eating bacon on Friday and drinking coffee with them—would you not rather be still with them on a holiday like this?"

"You speak as one of the drunkards speaks!"

"I say but what all men know: you are ever in converse with them."

"I work for them that give me work: I do not pick and choose."

"Work!" hinted Vahnik; "there's more than work between them and you!"

"Of such work," Prychek added significantly, "as you did with the Squire and our forest."

"Oho! It seems I have met my judges here!—Much ye all know of the affair!"

"Let him be," said Gregory, staring sternly into the smith's shifty eyes. "He is free to do his business by himself . . . as we too to do ours by ourselves."

"Should a gendarme look through the window here," said the smith with a poor attempt at mockery, while his lips were twitching with rage, "he would take you for conspirators."

"And perchance we are, but not against you, Michael: you're not worth it."

At that he pulled his cap on, and made his exit, slamming the door.

"He scented something in the wind, and came here to find out all about it."

"He might even play the eavesdropper outside."

"Let him: he will hear something about himself that he will not like!"

"Now hark to me, boys!" Gregory said, gravely. "As I told you, the Germans have not purchased Podlesie yet, but the deed of sale may be signed any day. They talk of next Thursday."

"That we know: the question is, what's to be done!" Matthew cried impatiently.

"Advise us, Gregory, you who can, who are book-learned and read the papers."

"You see, if the Germans buy it and settle next to us, it will be like Gorka over again: we shall not have room to breathe in Lipka."

"Our fathers sigh, and scratch their heads, and cannot make out what to do."

"Yet they will not give up their farms to us!" several voices exclaimed at once.

"The Germans, what are they?" cried another. "Some settled in Lishka, and our peasants bought them out to the last acre.—True, in Gorka it was the other way round, but by our own fault: we drank, we went to law continually, and we all went a-begging in the end."

"Why, then, we too may buy Podlesie later!" said Yendrek Boryna, Antek's cousin.

"'Tis easy to talk. At present, we cannot manage to pay so much as sixty roubles an acre: how shall we ever pay a hundred and fifty?"

"If our fathers would but give each man his proper portion, we should mend matters more easily."

"That's sure. I should know what to do directly."

Here Gregory interfered. "O ye fools, ye fools! With all their land entire, our elders can scarce make both ends meet; and ye think to lay by from a part thereof?"

They were struck dumb—stunned by the evidence of the truth he uttered.

"No," he went on to say; "the evil is not that our fathers will not give up their holdings, but that Lipka has too little land and too many people. A plot that gave food for three in our grandfathers' time must now be shared by ten."

"How true you speak!—Aye, it is the truth," they all agreed, much abashed.

"Then," someone proposed, "let's buy Podlesie, and share it amongst ourselves."

"Ye may buy a whole village; but whence shall the money come?" Matthew grunted.

"Wait a little: peradventure we may find a means."

"Wait, do as ye please; I have enough of waiting, and am disgusted.—I'll leave the country and go to the town!"

"Please yourself. But we—the others—must stay and take some step or other."

"The devil take it all! We are so close that I wonder the walls do not fall apart, so many we are in each hut, with misery clamorous therein: while hard by, there are broad lands, asking but to be taken up. No, were we starving, there's not the wherewithal to purchase it; nor can we borrow aught from anyone. To the devil with it!"

Then Gregory told them how things went on in other countries, and they listened mournfully, until Matthew interrupted him:

"Others are well off: what is that to us? Show a hungry man a dish and put it by: shall he fill his belly with the sight thereof? Elsewhere folk are protected; not so here, where every man grows like a wild tree upon waste land, and whether he succeeds or fails—provided only that he pay the taxes, serve in the army, and obey the officials—who cares?"

Gregory heard him out in silence, and started afresh.

"There is but one way to get Podlesie into our hands."

Here they pressed closer to him, for a sudden hubbub had filled the great room: the panes were shaking with it, and the music had ceased. Someone went out and returned to tell them with a laugh what had taken place. Dominikova had come in with a stick for her sons, and caused a dreadful disturbance. She would have beaten and driven them home; but they had stood up to her, and made her leave the tavern; and now Simon was drinking to his heart's content, and Andrew, completely muddled, was howling up the chimney.

They cared to hear no more, for now Gregory set to expound his plan. It was for the village to be reconciled with the Squire and then barter each acre of the forest for four acres of the Podlesie land!

The possibility of such a solution equally surprised and delighted them; and Gregory went on to tell them how a similar agreement had been made with a village near Plotsk, of which he had read in the papers.

"Good for us peasants!—Jew, more vodka!" Ploshka called out through the door.

"Aye, for every three acres of forest, exactly twelve of cornland!"

"And for ten, a big holding!"

"But he ought to let us have some faggots besides for firing!"

"And an acre of meadow-land each by the wood-skirts into the bargain!"

"And some timber for building also!"

Everyone had a fresh condition to add.

"And a horse apiece too," Matthew sneered, "with a cart and a cow!"

"Be quiet!" cried Gregory.—"And now the farmers must meet, then see the Squire, and say what they wish to have. It may be that he will come to terms."

Here Matthew cut in.

"That he will not, unless the knife be at his throat. He needs money now: the Germans will give it him any day. Whereas, ere our people have scratched their heads and agreed on one single point, and ere their wives too have given their advice, a month will pass by, and the Squire will by then have sold the land and turned his back on us, having money to await the result of the lawsuit.

Gregory's plan is good; but, to my mind, it needs setting upside-down to work well."

"Say on then, Matthew, and advise us."

"Not to talk—not to take counsel—but to act! . . . as we did for the forest!"

"To act is possible sometimes, and sometimes not," Gregory muttered.

"I tell you it is possible . . . not by the same means, but to the same end.—Let us go tell the Germans not to venture on purchasing Podlesie!"

"Are they such fools—to fear us and obey?"

"If they refuse, we tell them they shall not either sow or build . . . nor move one step beyond their fields. Will they have no fear, think ye? Why, they would be like a fox that we smoke out of its earth."

But here Gregory burst out: "As there's a God in heaven, such threats will get us put in prison once more!"

"We should not lie in jail for ever; and when we got out, 'twould be all the worse for them! . . . They are no fools, and will first take good thought whether they have aught to gain by fighting us.—And when we have driven his buyers away, the Squire will take another tone.—Or if not . . ."

Gregory could keep silence no longer. Starting up, he did all he possibly could to dissuade them from such a reckless plan of campaign. He pointed out what actions at law must come of it, what fresh calamities to all of them, and the possibility of their being clapped in prison as rebels, and for several years! He showed, too, how everything might be arranged peaceably with the Squire alone. He went on talking to them till he was crimson, kissed them all, begged and implored them to give up that idea. All would not do, his words were in vain, and at last Matthew said:

"Ye are preaching! Ye talk like a book; but 'tis not what we want!"

At this they all set to banging their fists on the table, speaking at the same time, and shouting enthusiastically:

"Hurrah! Hurrah!—Down with the Germans! Away with the Long-Trousers! Matthew is right, we'll do as he says, and whoso fears, let him hide his face!"

They were so excited, there was no reasoning with them.

At this juncture the Jew came in, bringing a bottle: he listened, as he wiped the vodka spilt upon the table; then he said diffidently:

" 'Tis good advice that Matthew is giving you."

"What! is Yankel against the Germans now? Can this thing be?" they cried in amazement.

"Because I prefer to hold with those of my own land. We live here—wretchedly, but by God's help we live. . . . But when the Germans have come, then not only a poor Jew, but even a dog, will have no food to eat. . . . Oh, may they all drop down dead! May the pestilence sweep them away!"

"What, a Jew to side with our folk! Who ever heard of such a thing!" They were astounded, stupefied.

"Yea, I am a Jew, but not a wild man of the woods: born here as you were, as my father and grandfather were too! . . . Am I not, then, one of you? . . . What is better for you will be better for me: the bigger farmers you will be, the more business I shall do with you.—And this wise plan of yours against the Germans I am ready to back thus, offering a whole bottle of rum! . . . To your healths, O farmers of Podlesie!" he exclaimed, drinking to Gregory.

They then drank very copiously, and became so joyful that they scarcely refrained from kissing the Jew's long beard: they set him in their midst, and went over the whole matter again, consulting him on every point. Even Gregory began after a time to feel less gloomy.

But now the meeting came to an end, for Matthew sprang to his feet. "To the big room, boys! let's stretch our legs!" he cried. "We've done enough for to-day." And they went in together.

Matthew immediately took Teresa out of another man's arms into his own. Following his example, the others brought the girls out of the corners, called to the musicians and began to dance.

These suddenly set to playing up with great liveliness, being well aware how quick Matthew was both with kopeks and with blows.

In the tavern they were now at last dancing in earnest, with hot and steaming brows; and the din, and the stamping and music and boisterous cries, poured out of doors, as out of a boiling pot, by every aperture; and those outside, too, were enjoying themselves well, clinking glasses, drinking one another's health, and chatting ever louder and more excitedly.

It was night; the stars' rays shone keen and vivid, the trees rustled and murmured; from the marshes came the frogs' hoarse glee, and now and then a beetle passed by with a buzz. Nightingales sang in the orchards, and all was warm and fragrant. The people, too, longed to enjoy the cool night air, and now and again a couple, arms round waists, would leave the tavern to vanish into the shadows; while outside the conversation became so loud, everyone besides speaking quick and all together, that they were nearly unintelligible.

". . . And hardly had I let the hog go, ere it had even time to put its snout among her potatoes, behold! she was upon me, bellowing!"

". . . Drive her out of the village! Away with her!"

". . . I remember that they did the same to one such in my young days. She was scourged even to blood in front of the church, and then driven outside our boundary marks; and we had peace."

". . . Jew, a whole measure, and quickly!"

". . . We must elect a new one: so say all."

". . . Weed the evil out, ere its roots strike too deep!"

". . . Now drink you to me, and I'll tell you what!"

". . . Take the bull by the horns, nor loose it till 'tis down!"

". . . Two acres and one are three: three and one are four!"

". . . Drink, brother, dear as if you were my own!"

Thus scraps of sentences spurted out of the darkness, it being doubtful who spoke and who was spoken to: except when Ambrose, much the worse for liquor, was heard to pass from group to group, with his everlasting and whining request for a dram, though he staggered so heavily that he could hardly walk.

"You, Voytek, I baptized; I rang your wedding-bell until my arms were stiff: O brother, but one glass!—Or will you stand me a full dram? I'll ring her 'Everlasting Rest' and bring a second wife to you—a young one, firm of flesh as any turnip is!—Brother, a full dram, pray!"

And the young people danced on unweariedly; and the whole room was full of the rustling of waving skirts and capotes. Songs too were sung to the tunes of the music; the revels grew so wildly uproarious that even old women joined in leaping and capering with shrill screams; while Yagustynka, pushing forward to the middle, set her arms akimbo, and stamped on the floor to the lilt of the doggerel stave:

> "I'd never fear wolves, were they more
>   Than a score;
>   Nor foes, were I fighting with men
>   Ten times ten!"

CHAPTER X

THE days between Corpus Christi and the next Sunday passed slowly for Matthew, Gregory, and their friends. Matthew had to suspend his work on Staho's cabin, and the others too gave up their occupations, all their days and evenings being devoted to stirring up the people against the German settlers, and urging upon them the necessity of driving the latter out of Podlesie.

On his side, the tavern-keeper was lavish of persuasions and—with opponents—of free drinks, and even loans. Nevertheless, it was very uphill work. The elders would scratch their heads and heave a deep sigh, but go no farther without consulting their women, who unanimously condemned any such enterprise against the Germans.

"What folly is this?" they cried. "Have we not suffered enough on account of the forest? One affliction is not yet past, and they would bring down another upon us?" And the wife of the Soltys, usually a quiet woman, was near taking a besom to Gregory!

"If you'd egg us on to another rising, I'll give you up to the gendarmes! The lazy rogues!—they won't work, and only want to lounge about!" she bawled at him outside her hut.

Balcerkova, too, stormed at Matthew as fiercely:

"Ye pack of idlers! I'll set the dogs at you! . . . Aye, and have boiling water ready besides!"

So they stood up stubbornly and unanimously against all persuasions, deaf both to arguments and to prayers, and would not hear reason. They clamoured against the men uriously, and often added tears to their clamours.

"I'll not let my goodman go! I will hang to the skirts

of his capote, and hold fast, aye, should they break my arms!
We have had woes enough!"

Matthew cursed with rage. "May a brimstone thunderbolt blast you all!—Like magpies before rain: always
shrieking, shrieking!—You'll sooner teach human speech to
a calf than words of wisdom to a woman," he declared,
bitterly disappointed.

"Let them alone, Gregory; you'll never get at their understanding," he complained. "Were the woman your wife,
perchance she might listen then. Otherwise, the only argu-
ment for her is—a stick!"

"Nay, force is useless here," Gregory said; "we must
employ some other means with them. We must not con-
tradict them at first, we even must approve . . . so as to
bring them round little by little."

He was unwilling to give all up for lost. Though he had
at first opposed the plan, he had, when convinced it was
the only thing to do, gone in for it afterwards with heart
and soul. A bold stubborn fellow, determined to succeed
in whatever he undertook, he allowed nothing to discourage
him. They shut the door in his face; he talked to them
through the window. They used threats; he, without loss of
temper, flattered them freely, speaking to them of their
children, praising their tidy ways, and little by little coming
to the point; and if unsuccessful with one, he would go on
to another. For two whole days, the village was full of
him: in the cabins, in the gardens, even about the fields,
talking of one thing, then of another, and at last coming to
his subject. For such as found it hard to follow, he would
draw a map in the dust of the domain of Podlesie and its
divisions, so as to show forth the advantages of the plan of
campaign to everyone. Yet in spite of these artifices his
trouble would have been lost had it not been for Roch's
assistance. On Saturday afternoon, seeing they could not
carry the village with them, they asked Roch to come behind Boryna's granary; and there they opened their hearts
to him, though much fearing lest he would oppose their
scheme.

But after thinking a short time, he replied:

"A lawless proceeding it is; but we have no time to proceed otherwise.—I'll help you willingly."

At once he went to the parish priest, who was sitting in his garden, while his servant mowed the clover hard by. The servant told them later that his Reverence was at first angry with Roch, would not listen, and stopped his ears, but that they afterwards sat together talking for a long time. Roch had no doubt convinced him; for when the people came back at dusk from the fields, the priest went out as if to take the air, and, passing from cabin to cabin, he (talking first of indifferent matters) came at last to confer with the women chiefly, and dropped words to the following effect in the ears of each:

"The lads mean well. While there's yet time, haste must be made. Take your determination: I shall go to the Squire and advise him to agree." So, when he had overcome the women's opposition, the husbandmen began to perceive that a plan approved by the priest was worth following.

They still spent the evening in debate, but early on Sunday morning they had decided to go after Vespers with Roch at their head, who would talk matters over with the German settlers.

This he had promised them to do; and when they had gone home, shouting loud cuckoo-calls of delight, he remained seated in Boryna's porch, telling his beads and pondering deeply.

It was as yet early; they had but just cleared away after breakfast, Pete having lingered over his: a warm though yet not too hot day, with the swallows cutting the air swift as bullets. The sun had risen over the cabin, the grass glittered with dew in the shade; a fresh corn-scented breeze blew from the fields.

The hut, as usual on Sundays, was silent: the women busied with tidying the place, and the children out of doors, eating together at their porringer, and keeping Lapa off with spoons and cries. The sow grunted at the wall in the sunshine, the little ones nuzzling against her belly for milk;

the stork was driving the hens off and running about after
the colt that frisked in the court-yard. The orchard trees
whispered, their branches waved; from the fields outside,
the humming of bees on the wing resounded, and the lark's
song rang through the air.

This Sunday quiet was so deep that only the quacking of
ducks about the pond was heard, or the laughter of the
lads as they washed themselves there.

The roads lay deserted and bright in the sun, with very
few wayfarers. Girls combed their locks on the door-step;
and the notes of a shepherd's pipe bubbled forth.

Roch, as he said his rosary, heard all these sounds, but
was mostly thinking of Yagna, whom he could hear bustling
about within, sometimes coming close behind him, sometimes going out into the yard, and, as she returned, dropping
her eyes before his, and flushing a deep red. He felt sorry
for her.

"Yagna!" he whispered kindly, raising his eyes.

She stopped short with an intake of the breath, expecting he would say more. But he, as though doubtful of what
he ought to say, only murmured a few inarticulate words
and was silent.

She went her way again and sat down at the open window,
where, leaning on the sill, she looked out mournfully upon
the sunny scene and on the white clouds, wandering like
wild geese through the bright fields of heaven. A heavy
sigh burst from her bosom, and tears dropped more than
once from her reddened eyelids, rolling slowly down her
cheeks, now somewhat worn and thin. For ah! how much
she had gone through in those last days! The women
turned their backs upon her when she passed, and some
spat after her. Her friends looked another way; the
youngsters laughed contemptuously, and the youngest of
the Gulbas family had once flung mud at her, calling out:

"The Voyt's leman, you!"

The words had stabbed her like a knife; and she felt
suffocated with the shame of it.

But, in God's name, was she to blame in all this? He had

made her drunk—so drunk that God's world had vanished from her eyes!—And now they all accused her; the whole village fled from her as from one tainted, polluted: no one stood up in her defence.

And whither should she go now? They would slam the doors in her face—nay, set their dogs upon her. To flee to her mother's availed nothing: she, in spite of entreaties and wailings, had all but driven her away. . . . And, had it not been for Hanka, she would have done herself a mischief. . . . Aye, it was she—the wife of Antek—who alone had held out a helping hand to her and protected her from her enemies! . . . No, no, no! she was not guilty, the Voyt was! guilty of tempting her, of forcing her to sin . . . But the most guilty of all was . . . he! . . . that old monster! (She meant her husband!) "He has fettered my whole life . . . Had I been a free woman, would any have dared to injure me so? Nay, none. . . . And what have I enjoyed with him? Neither life nor freedom!"

As she went on brooding, her grief turned to passion, and she set to pacing the room under its sway. "In truth, he is the fountain-head of all I suffer . . . Without him, I should have lived in quiet still, as all the others do . . . The devil set him in my way, tempting my mother with that land . . . And now I must endure . . . endure!—Oh, may the worm devour you speedily!"

At this height of fury, she looked through the window, and perceived the litter with her husband in it under the trees. She ran out and, bending over him, hissed cruelly:

"Die, old dog! die! And the sooner, the better!"

He rolled his eyes at her and mumbled something; but she had gone. The outburst relieved her: she had someone on whom to revenge her grievances!

When she returned, the smith was standing in the porch, but feigned not to see her, and continued talking to Roch, raising his voice:

"Matthew is telling everyone in the village that ye are to go at their head and encounter the Germans."

"As they have begged me, I intend to go with them and

meet our new neighbours," he replied, with a stress on the last word.

"The Lipka people are forging fresh fetters for themselves—that's all. The affair with the Squire has turned their heads, and they fancy that a mob with sticks and shouts can deter the Germans from buying."

He was so angry that he could scarce control himself.

"Perhaps they may prefer not to buy: who knows?"

"Oh, indeed! The lots are measured out; the families have arrived. They are digging wells and laying cornerstones!"

"This much I know: the deed is not yet signed before the notary."

"It is as good as signed: so they have sworn to me."

"I speak of my own certain knowledge; and, should the Squire find better purchasers . . ."

"Not in Lipka, at any rate: no one smells very strong of money here."

"Gregory has made a few calculations, and, as I take it . . ."

"Oh, Gregory!" he interrupted rudely. "He is a meddler who misleads folk, and will only bring evil on them!"

"Well, we shall see how it turns out; we shall see!" Roch returned with a quiet smile, noting how the smith in his exasperation was tearing out his moustache.

"Here comes Paul of the police station!" he exclaimed, seeing the messenger enter the enclosure.

"An official paper for Anna Boryna," Paul said, taking an envelope out of his pouch.

Hanka turned it about uneasily, uncertain what to do with it.

"I'll read it for you," Roch said.

But as the smith came behind, to read it over his shoulder, Roch folded the paper immediately, saying without interest:

"A permission for you to visit Antek twice a week in future."

Roch waited till the smith had gone, and then followed Hanka into the cabin.

"The letter was not what I told you: I did not think the smith ought to know of it. Ye are advised that, either on your giving a sufficient guaranty or paying five hundred roubles into court, Antek will be set free directly.—What ails you?"

No reply. Her voice had failed her; she stood motionless, her face suffused with crimson first, then pale as death, her eyes blinded with tears. She stretched out her arms and, drawing a deep breath, fell on her face before the holy images.

Roch went out and, sitting down in the porch, read the document over again, smiling with joy. It was some time before he looked in again.

Hanka was on her knees, glowing with gratitude, her heart almost bursting with gladness. Short broken sighs and whispered ejaculations seemed to be filling the room with flashes and pillars of flame, fed with the fire of her life-blood, and rising up to the feet of Our Lady of Chenstohova. The bliss of it was almost too much for her to bear: her tears flowed in torrents, washing away the memory of all her past sorrows and sufferings.

At length she rose, and, wiping her tears away, said to Roch:

"And now I am ready for anything in the future. The worst that may hap will be less evil than what has been."

He looked with astonishment at the change that had taken place in her. Her eyes sparkled; her cheeks were no longer pale, but full of colour; she stooped no more, and looked ten years younger.

"Sell the things, quick," he said; "get the sum together, and we shall go to fetch Antek to-morrow or on Tuesday."

Dazed, she again and again repeated the words: "Antek is coming back—coming back!"

"Not a word about it! When he comes, why, folk will know of it anyway. Ah! and we must let it be supposed that he was set free unconditionally, or the smith would want to know where the money came from."

All this he told her in a low voice, and she promised to

obey, excepting Yuzka, however, whom she had to tell, and trust with the joyful secret; Hanka could hardly have borne alone such an awful weight of gladness. She went to and fro like one flushed with strong drink, kissed all the children twenty times over, talked to the colt, talked to the pig, and frisked with the stork; and as Lapa followed her about, looking wistfully into her eyes as if he understood something of the matter, she said in his ear:

"Tell no one, silly one! The goodman is coming home!"

Then she laughed and cried by turns, and spoke to Matthias, telling him all about it, till he rolled his eyes as if in fear, and made an indistinct murmur. And she so forgot the whole world that Yuzka had to remind her she must get ready for church.

She was so happy that she even wanted Yagna to come with them; but Yagna refused.

Her no one had told the news, but she easily guessed at it, from words dropped here and there, and from Hanka's extraordinary gaiety. The news elated her likewise, and touched her with a sort of silent hope; and, heedless of meeting people, she ran over to her mother.

She dropped in just when a terrific quarrel was at its height.

Directly after breakfast, Simon had sat down by the window, smoking a cigarette, and spitting about the room, while he considered and reflected for a long time, casting many a look at his brother. At last he said:

"Now, Mother, give me some money, for I have to put up the banns. The priest told me to come after Vespers for the examination in Religion."

"And whom would you wed?" she asked, with a bitter sneer.

"Nastka Golab."

She said no more, but busied herself about the pots on the fire-place. Andrew put some more wood on, and though the fire drew very well, he blew upon it out of sheer trepidation. Simon paused for a reply, and, getting none, spoke once more: this time in a more decided tone.

"I shall need a five-rouble note, for there is to be the betrothal ceremony besides."

"Oh!—And have ye sent her the proposers yet?"

"Klemba and Ploshka went to her."

"And the answer was Aye, no doubt?" Her chin wagged with chuckling.

"Most surely."

"She's the 'blind hen that happened on a grain,' hey? —The idea of a Nay from her, the beggarly thing!"

Simon knitted his brows, but waited to hear her say more.

"You, fetch me water from the pond; and you, Andrew, let the pig out: it is squealing."

They both obeyed mechanically. But when Simon returned to his place, and his younger brother was again pottering about the fire-place, the old dame commanded sternly:

"Simon, give the heifer to drink!"

"Do that yourself: I am not your maidservant!" he returned boldly, sprawling on the settle.

"Have you heard?—Drive me not to punish you on the Lord's Day!"

"Have ye heard me asking for money?"

Then she exploded: "Neither money nor leave to marry will I give!"

"Leave I can do without!"

"Simon, keep your temper. Make me not angry!"

On a sudden he bent down before her, humbly clasping her feet.

"See, Mother, I beg, I implore you; I am crouching at your feet like a dog!"

His voice was choked with sobs.

Andrew too fell prostrate at her feet, and kissed her hands, beseeching her and moaning pitifully.

She repulsed them both with fury, shaking her fist.

"Dare but to oppose my will," she cried out, "and I'll sweep you to the four winds of heaven!"

But Simon's hesitation was over now. Her words had roused him, and his blood boiled. The inborn stubbornness

of the Pacheses had laid hold on him: he stood up erect,
and, striding forward:

"Give me the money!" he roared. "I shall wait no longer,
nor beg for it any more!"

"Never!" she cried stormily, and looked about her for
some weapon of offence.

"Then will I seek it!"

With a wildcat's leap, he bounded to the great chest,
wrenched the lid open, and began to empty the clothing
it contained on to the floor. She shrieked and darted at
him, at first endeavouring to force him back; but she could
not move him an inch. Then she caught hold of his thick
fell of hair with one hand, battering his face with the other,
while kicking his body and screaming all the time. He
shook her off, and went on searching for the money; but,
having received a terrible kick in the groin, pushed her away
with such strength that she fell down flat upon the floor.
She was up again, however, in an instant, and, seizing the
poker, rushed at him. Unwilling to fight with his mother,
he only tried to defend himself, attempting to wrest the
poker from her hand. The din made the room ring again;
and Andrew, in floods of tears, was hovering round them,
weeping aloud and crying out:

"O Mother! for God's sake! O Mother!"

Yagna, coming in then, ran forward to stop the struggle.
In vain. Dominikova stuck to him like a leech, and battered him with insane fury, though he tried to give way and
leap aside: she assailed him all the more fiercely, raining
down blows on him, till, maddened by pain, he struck back
again.

So they flew at each other like quarrelling dogs, staggering
backward and forward about the room, and hitting the walls
and furniture with extreme violence.

The neighbours were now coming in, and striving to
force them apart, but to no purpose. The fight went on, the
mother belabouring the son, the son seeking to keep the
mother at bay. But, at last losing patience, he put forth
all his strength, grappled her round the waist and flung her

from him. She stumbled and fell like a log on to the blazing fire-place amongst the pots of boiling water; and the
whole range came down on her with a crash!

They extricated her at once from among the fallen
brickwork. She was fearfully scalded: yet, recking nothing of the pain nor of her burning petticoats, she wanted to
fly at him still!

"Unnatural child! Accursed one! Away, away with
you!" she bellowed with insane frenzy; and they had to use
force to hold her back and quench the flames. They put
wet compresses on to her scalds, and she yet was ready to
rush at him again.

"Quit my sight! let me behold you nevermore!"

As for Simon, breathless, beaten all over, unable to utter
a word, and streaming with blood, he stood staring at his
mother in the utmost bewilderment and dismay.

The uproar had scarce begun to subside, when she tore
herself free from the women round her, darted to the
pole behind the fire-place on which Simon's things were
hanging, pulled them all down and threw them out of the
window.

"Go! may mine eyes not see you any more! Naught is
yours here, all is mine! . . . You shall not have one strip of
land, not one spoonful of food, were you dying of hunger!"
she vociferated with the rest of her failing strength; and,
overcome at last by the intensity of her pains, she then fell
to groaning and screaming most horribly.

So she was carried to her bed.

So many people had pressed in that the cabin was chock-
full, and the passage as well; even the open windows were
blocked up with heads.

Yagna, at a loss what to do, was completely disconcerted.
The old woman was now howling in frightful agony. No
wonder: all her face and neck were scalded fearfully, her
arms were burnt, her hair was singed off, and her eyes were
all but sightless.

Simon had gone out and was sitting in their little orchard
close to the cabin-wall, his chin resting on his fists, stiff as

a corpse, bruised all over, with clots of blood upon his face: he was listening to his mother's groans.

After a while, Matthew came up to him, saying, as he took him by the hand:

"Come over to our hut. You have naught to do here now."

"Go I will not! . . . The land is mine, the land of my forefathers, my own: here will I remain!" he growled with sombre obstinacy.

Neither arguments nor entreaties could prevail against him; he sat still, and spoke no more.

Uncertain what to do, Matthew seated himself near him; but Andrew made a bundle of the clothing just thrown out and, placing it before his brother, said timidly:

"With you, Simon! I'll go away with you!"

"O mothers of dogs!" cried the other, beating on the wall so hard that Andrew winced to hear him; "once for all I have said that I will not budge; and budge I will not!"

Now they were again silent; dreadful shrieks were heard within. Ambrose had come to bandage the old woman. He put fresh unsalted butter on the scalds and burns, covering them with the leaves of certain herbs, over which again he put a layer of curdled milk, and bound up the whole with moist bandages. Having directed Yagna to pour some cold water on the clouts every now and then, he hurried away to church, hearing that the Mass-bell was already beginning to tinkle.

It was Mass-time indeed; the roads were swarming with people, carts were rattling by, and so many acquaintances sought to call on the patient that Yagna was at length compelled to close her door on her prying neighbours, and only Sikora's wife remained with her.

And now there was again quiet in the hut. Dominikova was mute. The still murmurous drone of the organ was just audible; and the voices of the singers, with their plaintive, soothing, quavering melody, were wafted along through the orchards.

Both the young men were still sitting outside the hut. Matthew was talking on in a low voice; Simon nodding in reply; while Andrew, lying on the grass, gazed on the smoke of his brother's cigarette, rising in tangled threads above the thatch, like bluish gossamer.

Matthew rose at last, promising to come again in the afternoon. He intended to go to church, but at the sight of Yagna sitting at the water's brink, he drew near her.

Her pail stood full by her side; she was bathing her feet in the mill-pond.

"Yagna!" he whispered very low, approaching beneath the alders.

Instantly she let her skirt down over her knees, and bent a look on him—a look so tearful, so full of pain and sorrow, that he felt cut to the heart.

"What is it, Yagna? are you ailing?"

The trees waved very silently, pouring down their rain of lights and shadows upon her bright head, like a shower of green and gold.

"No, but things go not well with me. Not well." And she looked away from him.

"If I could but aid . . . or advise you . . ." he went on kindly.

"What? did you not lately turn away from me in my garden . . . and never come near me since?"

"For you had spurned me! . . . How could I dare? O Yagna!" His tone was gentle and full of sympathy.

"Aye, but I called after you, and you—you would not hearken!"

"Did you call me back, Yagna? Truly?"

"Truly.—I might have died and no one have come near me. I am a poor forlorn creature, that everyone is free to humble and ill-use!"

Her face was burning; she turned it away in confusion, splashing the water with her feet.—Matthew was reflecting.

All through the silence which ensued, the symphony of the organ went on trickling in a soothing gentle stream—a

streak of mellow sound.   The mill-pond shimmered, rolling
sinuous ripples from Yagna's feet, like iridescent serpents:
while between her and him there passed warm glances,
wreathed and twined together.

Matthew was growing more and more fascinated; he
longed to take her in his arms and fondle her like a little
child, pressing her to his breast and comforting her with
the tenderest caresses.

"And I thought you unfriendly!" she whispered.

"Never was I that; and you know it."

"Never last year, peradventure," she said, but added un-
thinkingly: "All the same, ye have gone with the others
now!"

All at once he remembered, with anger and jealousy gnaw-
ing at his heart.

"Because . . . because ye have . . . ye are . . ."

He could not utter the hateful words that choked him, and,
checking himself, said harshly:

"Fare ye well!"

And he turned to leave her, lest he should reproach her
with the Voyt.

"So once again you go!—But why? what harm have I
done you?"

She felt startled and pained.

"None—none. . . . But—" and he spoke hurriedly, looking into her deep-blue eyes, and feeling sorrow, anger and
tenderness rise up within him by turns—"but—Yagna! do
put away from you that abominable creature!   Put him
away!" he repeated most earnestly.

"Ha! did I ever speak him fair? am I now doing aught
to keep him?" she cried out angrily.

Matthew stood perplexed and hesitating.

A tempest of weeping shook her, and the tears poured
down her glowing cheeks.

"Oh, the cruel wrong he did me!—To take my senses
away! . . . And yet no one came forward on my behalf to
accuse him! . . . No one has any mercy; ye all cry: Down,
down with her!" she lamented bitterly.

"The villain! I will pay him out for it!" Matthew exclaimed, clenching his fist.

"Aye, pay him, Matthew! pay him! And ye shall have . . . !" Her eager appeal died away on her lips.

Without another word he hastened to the church.—She sat for a long time by the pond, wondering whether he would indeed take her part, and suffer no more wrong to be done to her.

"Antek, perchance!" the thought flashed through her brain.

She returned home, her mind agitated by secret but not unpleasant anticipations.

The bells were pealing as the people came out of church, and the air rang with their laughter; but those who passed by Dominikova's cabin went silently, with gloomy looks and meaning glances at one another.

None of the merry sounds that echoed through all the rest of the village during the noonday meal was heard in her hut. Nor was anyone eager to visit her, as she lay there moaning and feverish. Yagna, to whom a long stay by her side was unbearable, went out at times to the porch, now and then walking as far as the gate; or she would sit by the window, looking out with weary desire for change. Simon sat motionless outside. Andrew alone remembered that the dinner had to be cooked, and set about cooking it.

Some time after dinner, Hanka came to look in. She was in an odd state of excitement, asking questions without number, deeply interested in the sufferer, but at times casting a stealthy troubled glance in the direction of Yagna, and sighing deeply.

After a time, Matthew dropped in to see Simon.

"Will you go forth with us to the Germans?"

"This place will I not quit: 'tis my father's land and mine; from it I will not budge," he answered, full of one thought only.

"A great ass you are!—Sit ye here till to-morrow, if you will." Matthew was annoyed at this foolery; and as Yagna was then seeing Hanka to the gate on her departure, he went out with her, without bestowing so much as a look on the other.

They went along by the mill-pond road.

"Has Roch left the church yet?" he asked.

"Aye, and a good many peasants are waiting for him."

He glanced back, and saw Yagna gazing after them. Quickly turning his head round, and with eyes cast down, he inquired of Hanka:

"Is it true that the priest has denounced anyone from the pulpit?"

"Why ask?—Ye have heard."

"I came too late for the sermon.—They told me something, but I thought they were lying."

"He denounced . . . more than one.—Oh, how he clenched his fists!—To be stern with sinners, to throw stones at them —anyone can do that.—But there is no one can prevent the evil thing!" She felt deeply mortified at the slur on her own family, and her mood was very angry.—"But," she added, dropping her voice, "he made no allusion whatever to the Voyt."

Matthew cursed savagely. He would have put one other question, but hesitated; and they moved on in silence, Hanka much vexed at the whole business. Yes, Yagna had sinned, she said to herself. Yes, she deserved punishment. . . . But to be rebuked from the pulpit, and almost by her name—it was too much! . . . She was the wife of Boryna, and not a common drab!—He had said naught against Magda or the girls in the mill: yet all knew of their doings!—And the lady of the Manor of Gluhov: did not all know of her fondness for peasant lovers? Had he said one word of her? Her dignity as a Borynova was hurt.

"Did he . . . did he mention Teresa?" The question was put at last, so low that she scarcely heard it.

"Aye. He mentioned both. And everyone guessed of whom he was speaking. Someone must have set him against her."

He was near exploding with rage.

"They say it is either Dominikova's work or Balcerkova's. The former is avenging herself on you for Simon and

Nastka; the other would fain have you for her own girl Mary."

"Aha! Sits the wind in that quarter? I should not have dreamed it."

"Men only see what is under their noses."

"Well, Balcerkova has lost her trouble; and she may well be trounced for it yet by Teresa. Besides, to spite Dominikova, Simon shall marry Nastka: I'll see to that myself. —Those miserable hags!"

"They work out their schemes, and honest folk have to suffer for them," she said with sorrow.

"Each one tries to hurt everyone else: 'tis hard to bear life here."

"So long as Matthias was with us, they had someone to keep them in bounds, someone to listen to."

"Very true. Our Voyt is a fool who knows naught, and who plays such pranks that the folk can abide him no longer. Oh, if Antek were but to come back!"

"He will—he will! And shortly! But"—and her eyes sparkled—"would he be obeyed?"

"Yes. 'Tis settled between me and Gregory and the others. And when he returns, we shall set the village in order, with him at our head. Ye shall see."

"It is high time. Things here are getting loose, as a wheel when the linchpin has dropped off."

They were now at the hut, where several people had already gathered in the porch—somewhat under a score of farmers ready to start, along with the best of the farmhands. Yet (as previously, and for the forest expedition) all the villagers had declared that they would go . . . to a man!

"Our Voyt ought to come with us," someone observed, stripping the bark off a stick.

"The Head Official," another answered, "has summoned him to the District Office; and the scrivener says he will be ordered to call a meeting and get a school voted by Lipka and Modlitsa."

"He may call a meeting, but we'll vote no school!" laughed Klemba.

"We should have at once so much more per acre to pay in taxes. Just as in Vola."

"Surely," the Soltys admitted; "but when the Head Official gives an order, we have to obey."

"What orders have we to take from him? Let him order his gendarmes not to join with the thieves to rob us!"

"Gregory, you are growing saucy," said the Soltys severely. "Men's tongues have ere now taken them farther away than they wished to go!"

"Ye shall not put me down. I know our rights, and fear no Head Official. Only you poor ignorant sheep shake from head to foot before every Jack in office."

He spoke so loud that they were shocked at his rashness, and more than one felt his flesh creep. Klemba went on to say:

"But truly, such a school is of no use to us! For two years my boy Adam went to the school in Vola. The teacher got three bushels of potatoes a year from me, and eggs and butter from my wife besides at Yuletide and Easter. And what has come of it all? He can neither read a Polish prayer-book nor say his ABC in Russian! Whereas my younger ones, whom Roch taught last winter, can both make out writing, and read the books our gentry read."

"Then," said Gregory, "let us engage Roch to teach our children."

Here the Soltys stepped a little aside from the group, and said, lowering his voice:

"Roch would be the best, I know, and he has taught my boys; but it cannot be. The police have found out something, and they are on his trail. The Superintendent saw me in the office, and inquired diligently about him—said he was sure that Roch taught the children, and distributed Polish books and newspapers to the folk.—We must tell him to take good heed."

"That's a bad business," said old Ploshka. "He's a good

religious man; but the whole village may come to great harm through him. . . . Yes, measures must be taken—and quickly."

"What, man!" said Gregory in an indignant whisper; "are ye such a coward as to think of betraying him?"

"Should he stir up the people against the Government to the destruction of us all, we ought all to do so. You are young; but I recollect well what took place in the war of the gentry, and how we peasants were cudgelled formerly for the least thing we did. With them we have naught in common."

"Ah, ye would fain become Voyt! And ye are no more good than a boot with a hole in it!"

They said no more, for Roch then came out of the cabin, looked round at the people, crossed himself, and cried:

"It is time!—On, in the name of the Lord!"

He stepped forward, and behind him surged the mass of peasants in the middle of the road, with a few women and children after them.

The heat of the day was over, the bells were just pealing for Vespers, and the sun was rolling forestward. It was fine bright weather, and the sky-line showed so clear that the remotest villages were made out distinctly.

To keep up their spirits, some of the men were striking the ground with their oaken cudgels; some spat in their palms, and put on an indomitable mien as they marched along.

The women went no farther than the mill, while the men went on slowly up the slope, their feet raising puffs of dust.

They trudged on in silence, with proud hard faces and eyes glittering defiantly.

Their ranks moved as solemnly as in a procession, and if anyone began talking, the stern looks of the others silenced him soon. It was no time for conversation then: each man withdrew within himself to find courage and strength there for what was coming.

At the cross and the village landmarks they stopped awhile to rest. But they were still silent, gazing out upon the land-

scape: on the huts of Lipka, scarce visible amongst their
orchards; on the gilt cupola of the village church; on the
vast expanse of green, green fields. And, as they listened
to the shepherds' pipes playing far away and drank in the
sweet peace and joy of springtime all around, many of them
felt a dull sinking of heart, and looked out towards Podlesie
with painful misgivings.

"Come!" Roch cried to stir them up; "we are not here to
trifle the time away!" For he saw in his men clear signs
of weakening resolve.

They turned and made straight for the farm-buildings.
Their way led them through lands overgrown with weeds,
miserable rye-fields, blue with corn-flowers, patches of late-
sown oats, all yellow with flowers of gold, land where the
thin wheat crop was quite scarlet with wild poppies, and
plots where the potatoes were hardly above ground yet.
Gross carelessness and neglect were seen at every step.

"A Jew could not have tilled the land worse! It is an
eyesore!" growled one of the men.

"The worst farm-hand would have done better work."

"This one, though a great owner, has had no respect for
the sacred land which is his!"

"No, he treats it as one that only milks and never feeds
his cow: small wonder if it gives him naught!"

They had now reached the fallows. At a slight distance
rose the dingy ruins of the burnt buildings; the orchard
was black with charred trunks. Around stood the mes-
suages, some of the roofs fallen in, and the chimney-stacks
standing up stark and black. Near the houses a group of
persons was to be seen: they were the Germans. A cask of
beer stood upon the paving-stones; a man on a door-step
played the flute; the others, either lolling on benches or upon
the grass, were taking their ease, in shirt-sleeves, with pipes
in their mouths, and drinking beer out of earthenware jugs.
Some children frisked outside the house, and lusty cows and
horses grazed hard by.

They saw the men coming; for they started up, looking
in the direction of the new-comers, shading their eyes, and

bawling out in their own speech. But one of them, an old man, said a few words, and they sat down quietly to drink again. The flute-player played his sweetest strain; high above their heads the larks sang; while from the corn, the rapid and incessant shrilling of the crickets dinned yet louder in the ear, and the piping of the quails was heard from time to time.

The ground, baked by the sun, sounded hard beneath the peasants' feet, and the stones rang under their hobnailed boots as they drew near: the Germans remained motionless, as though they had not heard anything, but sat enjoying their beer and the fragrance of the evening air.

The men, coming in with slow ponderous tread, were close to them now, grasping their sticks tight and striving to breathe easily; but their hearts were throbbing, a hot thrill ran down their backs, and their throats went very dry. Nevertheless, they drew themselves up, and glared boldly at the Germans.

"Praised be . . . ," said Roch in German, coming to a halt, while the whole company drew up in a crescent behind him.

The Germans replied in chorus, but without moving from their places. The grey-bearded old man alone rose and gazed around him, turning somewhat paler.

"We," Roch began to say, "have come to see you on a certain matter."

"Then sit ye down. I see that ye are husbandmen of Lipka: let us talk together in neighbourly wise.—Johann! Fritz! bring settles for our neighbours."

"Many thanks, but our business will be soon over: we may as well stand."

"Soon over?" he cried in Polish. "Can that be, when the whole village has come?"

"That is but because the matter interests all equally."

"Also," Gregory added meaningly, "we have left thrice as many at home."

"Well, we are glad to see you.—And, since ye have been the first to pay a visit, perchance ye will taste some beer with us."

"How generous!" cried several voices. " 'Twas not for beer we came!"

Roch hushed them with a glance. The old German said dryly:

"We are listening."

A stillness ensued, in which quick short breathing was heard. The men of Lipka drew closer together, trembling with excitement; the Germans rose like one man and faced them in serried array, exchanging fierce looks with the peasants, and muttering low, and twirling the strands of their beards.

The women looked on, terrified; the children ran to hide in the passages; close at the wall, a few tan-coloured dogs began to snarl: while, for the space of one "Hail Mary" at least, the men stood facing one another in profound silence, like a troop of rams, with fiery eyes rolling, backs tense, heads lowered, and ready at any moment to charge one at the other. Then Roch broke the silence, thus speaking in Polish, in clear ringing tones:

"We come in the name of the whole village to request you—and in friendly wise—not to complete the purchase of Podlesie."

"Right! Quite right! We come for that!" they all agreed, striking on the ground with their sticks.

For the Germans, this was a thunderclap.

"What says he? What would he have? We understand naught," they stammered, thinking they had not heard aright.

Roch therefore repeated his request, this time in German; and when he had done, Matthew burst out with the words: "And to take yourselves away—you and your long trousers —to all the devils!"

At this, they jumped as though doused with boiling water. The quarrel then began and waxed furious, all the more embroiled by their fierce-sounding unintelligible jargon, as they stamped their feet and waved their arms; some of them, with lifted fists, making as if to rush at the peasants, who stood firm and immovable as a wall, eyeing them with bold looks and clenched teeth, while their hands twitched nervously upon their cudgels.

"What, are ye all mad?" exclaimed the old man, with uplifted hands. "Would ye forbid us to purchase land? Wherefore? and by what right?"

Roch calmly explained the whole situation in all its details; but the German, reddening with anger, cried out:

"The land belongs to him that pays for it!"

"We," Roch replied gravely, "think otherwise: we think the land should belong to him that hath need of it."

"Belong? And how? Without payment, by robbery peradventure?" he cried with a sneer.

"Our hands can give exceeding good payment," Roch answered in the same tone.

"Why shall we waste time bandying jests? We have bought Podlesie; it is ours, and ours it shall remain. And whoso likes not this, let him go his way, and not come near us!—Well, wherefore do ye wait?"

"Wherefore?" Gregory exploded. "To tell you: 'Hands off the land that's ours!'"

"Take yourselves off it, you!"

Here someone called out: "Mark this: ours has been a neighbourly request . . . so far!"

"Ye threaten us? Then we'll go to law! Oh, there are means to master you. Your term of jail for the forest brawl is not yet done: you will get some more, and do both terms together!" The old man attempted to laugh, but was too much upset, and his companions were exasperated.

"Ye lousy devils!"

"Thievish, stinking hounds!" they shouted in German, writhing about like snakes disturbed in their nest.

"Dogs' blood! be silent when men speak to you!" Matthew thundered at them; but they cared nothing for him, and began to come on in a body.

Roch, fearing there would be violence, got his men together and urged them to be calm; but they were out of hand, each vociferating louder than the other.

"A slap in the face to the first who comes near us!"

"They want to have a little blood let!"

"What, boys! shall we let them flout all our people thus?"

"No, no! we must not—we must not!" cried the rest, pressing threateningly forward, till Matthew, setting Roch aside, pushed on to the Germans, showing his teeth like an angry wolf.

"Hear me, ye Germans!" he roared, clenching his fists. "We have spoken to you words of kindness, with honest intent; and you not only menace us with prison, but insult us as well! Good; but we play another game with you henceforth. Ye refuse to agree: therefore here we swear to you, before God and man, that you shall never settle down in Podlesie. We came to offer peace: you chose war. Very well: war let it be! Ye have the courts for you, the officials for you, the power of money for you; and we—nothing but our bare hands. And who will get the better—we shall see!—Let me say, besides, that ye may remember it after: Fire can burn, not straw only, but even brick-built houses, even unripe corn; and cattle may come to fall down in the pasture-lands; and men may be unable to escape deadly misadventure. Remember this that I have told you: war by day, war by night, war in every place."

"War! War!—So help us God!" they all cried together.

The Germans sprang to their long staffs, standing by the wall; some ran for their guns or took up stones, while the women shrieked aloud.

"Let but one man shoot at us: all the villages will be here anon!"

"Kill one man, Long-Trousers! and ye'll be beaten to death, as men beat a mad dog!"

"O Swabians! tackle not us peasants, or ye'll be tackled yourselves."

"And so well that the hungriest dog would not touch your carcasses!"

"Dare but to touch us, Long-Trousers!" they cried in loud defiance.

And now both parties were about to close, each glaring at the other, stamping, beating on the ground with their sticks, flinging menaces and insults broadcast, and boiling over with eagerness to clapperclaw the enemy. But Roch at last succeeded in drawing his party somewhat to the rear; and his men, wheeling round, carefully protected their flanks as they withdrew, followed by the derisive shouts of the Germans.

"Away from our country, abominable swine!"

"Or stay till the Red Cock wake you up at night!"

"We shall look in again to dance with your maidens!"

Their language at last grew so strong that Roch was obliged to silence them.

And now twilight had come; a cool wind swept the corn, the dew lay silver-grey on the damp grass, and evening, quiet and fragrant, reigned over the land.

The men were coming home, their white capotes flapping behind them. They talked and sang till the woods rang again, stopping from time to time, whistling and gloating over the Podlesie fields.

"They are easy to portion out, these lands," said old Klemba.

"Aye, we can divide them into complete farms—each with its own meadow and bit of pasture."

"Provided the Germans give in!" said the Soltys, with a sigh.

"No fear: we know they will," Matthew said reassuringly.

"I should like the piece near the road, just at the end," said Adam Prychek.

"And I," said another, "the one in the middle, near the cross."

"And I," said a third, "want the patch close to Vola."

"Oh," sighed a fourth, "could I but get the garden-plot in the farm itself!"

"No fool you! You would snap up the best lot of all!"

"Come, come; there's enough for us all," Gregory said to pacify them, for they were near quarrelling over it!

"If the Squire agrees and gives up Podlesie to you," observed Roch, "you will all have a great deal of work to do."

"We shall manage to get through with it, though!" they cried in great glee.

"Work on one's own land is never hard toil!"

On such terms, who would not willingly take all the lands of the Squire?"

"Let him but give it you—you would see!"

"Why, we should take root in the soil, like trees; let him pluck us thence who can!"

And so they talked on, as they neared home; faster now, for they saw the women running out to meet them.

CHAPTER XI

IT was early dawn, and all the country was covered over with a deep azure bloom of haze like a ripe plum, when Hanka drove up to the cabin, whose inmates were all asleep as yet. But with the sharp clatter of the wheels, Lapa fell to barking for joy, and leaping up in front of the horses.

"Why, where is Antek?" Yuzka exclaimed on the doorstep, putting on her skirt over her head.

"He is to be released in three days only," was the tranquil reply, as Hanka kissed the little ones, and distributed pastry among them.

Vitek now came running out of the stable, and after him trotted the colt, whinnying and going straight to the mare, still in harness, while Pete was taking the parcels out of the cart.

"Have they begun to mow yet?" she asked, sitting down at once on the threshold to give suck to her baby.

"Yes, they began at noon yesterday: five of them. Philip, Raphael and Kobus to work out their debts to us; Adam Klemba and Matthew for hire."

"What?—Matthew Golab?"

"I too thought it strange; but he would have it so. Said his carpentry work made him stoop too much, and he wanted to get straight again, scythe in hand."

Yagna then opened her window and looked out.

"Is Father sleeping still?" she was asked.

"Aye, in the orchard. We left him out at night, so hot it is within doors."

"And your mother, what of her?"

"As usual; perhaps somewhat better. Ambrose, who tends her, came yesterday with the shepherd of Vola, who fumigated her, rubbed her with ointment, and said that, provided

she stays at home till the ninth Sunday from now, she will
by then be healed."

" 'Tis the best remedy for a scald!" she said, and, passing
her baby to the other breast, listened attentively to what
had occurred in her absence. But not for long: it was now
broad daylight, the sky flushing red with bright streaks
athwart the air. Dewdrops fell from the trees; birds were
garrulous in their nests; bleating and lowing resounded all
through the village, and hammers, hammering scythe-blades,
whose thin keen tinkling made a piercing din.

No sooner had Hanka undressed after her journey than she
ran to Boryna, who was lying asleep under a bed of down,
in a great basket beneath the trees.

"Hark!" she said, pulling him by the arm; "Antek will
be home in three days. He had been taken to the Government prison. Roch followed him with money that must
be paid. Both will come home together."

On a sudden the old man sat up, rubbed his eyes, and
seemed to listen; but he sank back at once, pulled the down
covering over his head and fell asleep again.

There was no more talking with him; besides, the mowers
were just then coming into the yard.

"Yesterday," Philip told Hanka, "we mowed the meadow
adjoining the cabbage-plot."

"To-day ye will go beyond the river, by the boundary-
market; Yuzka will show you where."

" 'Tis in Duck's Hollow; a big piece of land."

"And the grass comes up to the waist, lush and rank:
very different from yesterday's meadow."

"Was the grass so poor there?"

"Aye, all but dried up: it felt like cutting a brush."

"Then it may be tossed this very day, since the dew will
soon be quite dry."

They started at once: Matthew, smoking a cigarette in
Yagna's room, was the last, and cast a rueful look behind
him as he went, like a cat balked of its bowl of milk.

The rest of the village, too, soon poured forth its troops
of mowers.

Scarcely had the sun risen, huge and ruddy, when the weather grew warm, and presently very hot indeed.

On the mowers marched, in Indian file, preceded by Yuzka, dragging a pole after her.

They passed the mill. The meadows were veiled in a low creeping haze, through which tufts of alders peered out like puffs of dark smoke; here and there the river peeped from under its greyish screen, glittering brightly; the dew-drenched grasses drooped their heads in the meadows, and the piping of lapwings came on the eastern breeze, scented with the bland fragrance of many blossoms.

Yuzka, having taken them as far as the landmarks, measured the extent of her father's meadow-land, stuck the pole up at the border, and scampered away home.

Pulling off their spencers and tucking their breeches up, they formed into line, and thrust the scythe-handles into the ground, to sharpen the blades with their whetstones.

"The grass is as thick as the wool of a fleece; some of us will sweat soundly," said Matthew, who stood first, testing the sweep of his scythe.

"Thick it is—and tall!" said his neighbour. "Well, there'll be plenty of hay."

"Yes, if the weather be fine," said a third, glancing up at the sky.

"When you're mowing a meadow, rain always is ready," remarked the fourth, with a grin.

"The saying's not true this year!—Come, begin, Matthew!"

They all crossed themselves. Matthew tightened his girdle, straddled forward, spat on his palms, took a deep breath, and launched his scythe far into the grass, plying it with swift strokes; the others following him one after another, in a slanting line, for fear of accidents. So they cut their way into the mist-covered meadow with a steady rhythmical advance, their cold blades glistening, with a swish at every stroke, and forming long swaths heavy with dewdrops.

The breeze rustled in the grass; overhead, the lapwings

screamed more and more plaintively: and they, rocking their bodies from right to left, mowed on unweariedly, conquering the meadow foot by foot. Only now and again did one or another of them halt to whet his scythe or straighten his back, and then once more he mowed away with a will, leaving behind him ever more and more numerous swaths.

Before the sun had risen above the village, all the meadows echoed beneath the strokes of the mowers: the blue steel of the scythe-blades flashed everywhere; everywhere could be heard the stridulous clang of the whetstones; everywhere the strong perfume of mown grass was inhaled.

It was perfect weather for haymaking. An ancient adage says, indeed: "Begin to make hay: rain will fall the same day"; but this year it was quite the other way round. Instead of rainy weather, there was drought.

The days began, moist with dew, and yet parched, like a man in a fever; they ended in nights baked with heat. Some wells and rills had been dried up; the corn was turning yellow, the plants withered away. Countless insects assailed the trees, which began to cast their yet unripe fruit. Cows, returning hungry from the sere grass of the pastures, had ceased to give milk; and the Squire allowed none to graze their beasts on his clearings but those who paid him five roubles a head.

Very many had not so much cash to pay him.

But, setting aside these particular inflictions, the hard times usual before harvest were this year harder than ever.

They had reckoned on rain falling surely in June, and the field crops benefiting thereby: nay, money had even been offered for Masses to that intention. And now, some had really nothing to put in the pot!

But the worst of all was that not even the oldest inhabitant could remember a time when there had been so many law troubles: the great forest action not yet settled, and the Voyt's affair still setting people by the ears, and Dominikova's quarrel with her son, and the Germans, and many another matter of dispute between neighbours: so many, in fact, that what with such incessant brawls and wranglings, they almost forgot their more material afflictions.

Of course then, as soon as ever haymaking time had come round, all the people began to breathe more freely, the poorer among them hurrying off to seek work at the Manor farms, and the wealthier peasants, deaf to all other matters, setting at once to mow their grass.

They did not, however, quite forget the Germans, but got someone or other to go daily and see what they were about.

They still were there, but had given up digging wells and fetching stones to build; and, as the blacksmith announced one day, they had laid a complaint against the Squire for money matters, and against the men of Lipka for "threats and conspiracy."

At this the peasants laughed very heartily.

It was just this topic which was discussed that day in the meadow at dinner-time.

An intensely hot noontide, with the sun overhead, the sky hanging above with a whitish glow, a blasting heat around as from an oven; no breath of wind; leaves shrivelling up; birds silent; short thin shadows that scarcely shaded at all; the strong aroma of the heated grasses; corn and orchards and huts standing as if wrapped in white flame; all things, as it were, melting away in the air that trembled like water simmering on the fire. Even the river ran more slowly, its stream shining like fused glass, so transparent that beneath the surface-currents every gudgeon, every stone at the sandy bottom, every crayfish scuffling about in the luminous shadows of the banks, showed forth clear and distinct. A deep calm, spinning its slumberous web, crept over the sunlit earth; and nothing was noisy save the buzzing flies.

The mowers sat down on the river-bank, beneath a clump of tall alders, eating their dinner out of the porringers brought, for Matthew by his sister Nastka, for the others by Hanka and Yagustynka. These seated themselves on the grass in the sun's full glare, and, with their kerchiefs drawn over their heads, listened attentively to the talk.

"I," said Matthew, scraping his emptied porringer, "have always held that the Germans would take themselves off one of these days."

"The priest held so too," Hanka remarked.

"And so they will, if the Squire wills it," growled Kobus, always ready to argue, stretching himself out under a tree.

"What?" Yagustynka asked, sneeringly as usual; "did they not fear the noise ye made, and run?"

Her jeer was unnoticed, and someone observed:

"The smith said yesterday that the Squire would come to terms with us."

"Strange that Michael is on our side now!"

"He has," the old woman hissed, "found he would get more thereby."

"The miller too, they say, has pleaded at the Manor-house for the village."

"Those good souls! They are all on our side now!" said Matthew. "Why?—I'll tell you. The Squire promised the smith a goodly reward for the reconciliation. The miller fears the Germans may set up a windmill on the high ground in Podlesie. And the tavern-keeper befriends the people out of fear for himself: he knows well that where a German settles, no Jew can get his bread."

"The Squire wishes to be reconciled: does he fear us peasants, then?"

"Ye have hit the mark, Mother; of all of them, he is the most afraid."

Here Matthew broke off; Vitek was coming from the village at full speed.

"Mistress, come at once!" he bawled from a distance.

"What, is the house on fire?" she faltered, terrified.

" 'Tis Master, and he is crying out for something."

She ran off instantly.

The fact was that, ever since morning, Matthias had been strange, plucking at his coverlet and seeming to look for something. Before setting out for the meadow, Hanka had charged Yuzka to take special care of him, and the latter had many a time gone to look; but he had lain quiet till about dinner-time, when he suddenly fell a-shouting very loud.

On Hanka's arrival, he sat up, and called out:

"My boots—where are they? Give them to me, and quickly too!"

"I'll get them from the store-room in an instant!" she said, to pacify him; for he seemed quite sensible, and looked keenly about him.

"Mother of dogs! how I have overslept myself!" and he yawned wide and deep.

"It is broad day, and ye are sleeping, all of you!—Let Kuba get the harrow ready," he commanded; "we shall go out and sow."

They stood before him, hesitating, when he suddenly collapsed, falling helpless to the ground.

"Fear not, Hanka, I had a fit of dizziness. Is Antek afield, hey?—Afield?" he repeated, when they had replaced him on the bed.

"Aye," she stammered. "Ever since daybreak." For she feared to cross him.

He looked about him brightly and talked much; but one word out of ten was sense, and the rest drivel. He again wanted to get up and go out, called for his boots—and then put his hands to his head and moaned pitifully. Hanka knew that the end was at hand; so she ordered him to be borne within doors, and sent for the priest in the afternoon.

He came presently with the Holy Sacrament, but could only give him Extreme Unction.

"His state needs nothing more," the priest said; "in a few hours he will be with his fathers."

In the evening, many people visited the cabin, for he seemed on the point of death; and Hanka put the lighted taper of the dying in his hand. But presently he fell into a quiet sleep.

The next day there was no change. He recognized people, and spoke sensibly, but lay for hours together as still as a corpse.

The smith's wife was at his bedside continually; also
Yagustynka, who wanted to fumigate him!

"Let alone; ye may set the place on fire," he burst out
unexpectedly.

And at noon, when the smith came and looked into his
half-closed eyes, he smiled strangely, and uttered these
words:

"Do not trouble, Michael; I shall drop off soon enough—
soon enough!"

So saying, he turned his face to the wall, and spoke no
more. He was evidently going rapidly downhill, so they
now watched him with care; especially Yagna, over whom
an extraordinary change had come.

"I alone shall tend him! It is my right," she had told
Hanka and Magda so peremptorily that they had not opposed her.

She no longer left the cabin at all: a vague terror oppressed her.

All the village was out in the meadows: the haymaking
had been going on since dawn; ever since the very first
faint flush in the sky, they had started for the meadows.
Rows of peasants in shirt-sleeves, looking like grey storks,
were now all over the lands, whetting their flashing scythes,
and mowing amain all day long; all day the hammers rang
upon the scythes, and the girls sang their merry impromptus
as they raked up the cut grass.

All those verdurous glossy flats were swarming with
people, noise and clamour; loud ditties and peals of
laughter resounded to the accompaniment of the tinkling
blades, and the work went on everywhere with energy and
goodwill. Every day, too, when the blood-red sun was
descending towards the woods, and the air full of the twittering of the birds, and grass and corn alike seemed quivering
to the crickets' merry notes, while the frogs in the marshes
struck up their croaking serenade, and perfumes rose from
the incense-breathing earth—then all along the roads were
crawling great heavy wagons filled with hay; the mowers

went home with songs, and on the meadows, now yellow and trampled, stood close crowds of haycocks and ricks, like so many fat gossiping dames, squatting down to have a quiet talk together. Amongst these the storks strutted, above them the lapwings wheeled, with their sad piping cry; and on towards them the white mists came driving up from the marshes.

Through Boryna's window there came these voices of men and of the land—the glad sounds of life and toil, and the aromatic scents of corn and meadow and sunlight; but Yagna was deaf to them all.

The undergrowth round the cabin protected it from the glare and spread within it a greenish slumberous twilight. Flies buzzed; and now and then Lapa, watchful beside his master, would yawn, and then go and fawn upon Yagna, who sat for hours without motion or thought—as still as a statue.

Matthias spoke no longer, moaned no longer. He just lay still; but his eyes rolled unceasingly—those bright eyes of his, as shiny as glass globes, following her with cold persistency, piercing her through and through like knife-blades.

She turned her back on him, endeavouring to forget. It was in vain—in vain! They peered out at her from every sombre nook, floated in the air, glowing with fearful brilliancy, and a fascination so irresistible that she had to obey their call and stare back into them as into some unfathomable abyss.

At times, as though waking from a horrible dream, she would beseech his mercy: "Prithee, look not thus: ye are tearing my soul out of me: look not thus!"

No doubt he heard her: a quiver passed over him, his face twitched dumbly, as if to cry out, his eyes stared yet more gloomily, and big tear-drops rolled down his livid cheeks.

Then, driven by sheer terror, she would rush from the hut.

Hidden in the shade of the trees, she would peep out at the meadows full of people and of tumultuous joy.

And the sight made her cry bitterly.

Then she fled to her mother's. But hardly had she looked in and seen the darkened room and scented the rank pungency of the medicines, when she would hasten away once more.

And again she would weep.

Then she wandered abroad, and looked out upon the country-side with longing eyes. But thence sprung yet more bitter and dreary and agonizing tears; and she mourned grievously over her own sad lot, like a bird with broken wings, deserted by its mates.

Thus one day after another went by without any change. Hanka, along with the rest of the village, was absorbed in haymaking, and it was only on the third day that she stayed at home since morning.

"'Tis Saturday: Antek is sure to come!" she thought joyfully, setting the cabin in order to receive him.

Noon came and went, and he was not there yet. Hanka ran beyond the church to look up the poplar road.

They were carting the hay, hurrying it home, for the weather was about to change. The air was stiflingly sultry, cocks were crowing, hailstorm clouds hanging about in the sky, winds wheeling and whirling.

All expected a storm with a great downpour, but there only came down a short though plentiful rain, at once swallowed up by the thirsty soil, and only cooling the air a little.

The evening, somewhat less sultry, was redolent of hay and of the sprinkled earth. Mists rolled along the ways; the moon had not risen yet; the dark sky was but scantily studded with stars. Through the orchards, the light of the cabins glimmered like glow-worms, reflected in the pond and multiplied to myriads. Everywhere the people took their supper out of doors. Hard by, the air trembled with the ripplings of a pipe; from the fields came floating the crickets' feeble ditty, along with the voices of the land-rail and the quail.

At Boryna's, too, they were all outside the hut: the hay

being brought home, Hanka had invited them to a first-
class supper; and the great dish clinked with the tapping
of the spoons in a lively measure. Yagustynka's rasping
tones were often heard, accompanied with shouts of laughter.
Every now and then, Hanka would fill the dish again from
the pots, while anxiously watching all the time for any
least sound on the road; and she frequently slipped out
into the enclosure, looking for Antek.

There was not the least trace of him; and only once
did the shape of Teresa, leaning against the hedge, no doubt
waiting for somebody, meet her eyes.

Matthew, unable that day to get speech of Yagna, who
was then sullen and unpleasant of mood, was beginning to
wrangle with Pete out of sheer ill humour, when Andrew
came to call his sister, whom her mother wanted to see.

The party broke up thereupon; but Matthew lagged behind for some time.

Hanka also went out a little after for another vain look
into the darkness, when she heard his voice, gruff and cross,
wafted from the mill-pond bank.

"Why dog me so? I shall not flee you. . . . Are we not
enough on the lips of folk already?"—He added still more
cruel words, to which there came in answer a storm of sobs
and a flood of tears.

But there was nothing in that to interest Hanka, who
was awaiting her husband: she cared little then for other
folks' doings. Yagustynka did the evening household work
for her, whilst she herself dandled in her arms the baby,
that was rather troublesome; carrying it out with her and
rocking it, she went to see the patient.

"Antek may be here at any moment!" she cried from the
door-step.

Boryna was lying with eyes fixed on a lamp that smoked
above the fire-place.

She whispered in Boryna's ear: "He has been released
to-day, Roch is awaiting him," and her beaming eyes
watched him to see if he had understood. It seemed not:
he neither moved nor looked at her.

"He may be in the village by now. Belike it is so," she thought, as she ran out every now and then to see.—So sure was she of his return, so agitated with her long wait, that she spoke to herself, walking unsteadily as one drunk. To the darkness she talked about her hopes, and confided in the cattle as she milked them, informing them all that their master was coming back.

She waited on.—But every minute was wearing out her strength and her patience.

Night was there, the village abed. Back from her mother's, Yagna had gone to rest at once. All in the house were sleeping presently. Hanka still watched outside the hut, and far into the night; but at last, exhausted with weariness and crying, she too put out the light and lay down.

The whole land was now plunged in the deep stillness of repose.

The village lights had gone out one by one, like eyes that close in slumber.

The moon rolled up the soaring black-blue sky, sown with a twinkling dust of stars, and rose higher and higher, as a bird that wings its way athwart the void on silver pinions. The scattered clouds slept, huddled up into balls of soft white down; whilst on the earth all creatures lay quiet, wearied out and lost in sleep. Only a bird sang sweet exuberant lays from time to time; only the waters whispered drowsily; and the trees the moonlight bathed stirred now and again, as if they dreamed of day. Sometimes a dog growled, or the night-jar flapped its wings as it passed by; and low earth-clinging vapours now began to wrap the fields, but slowly, as a tired-out mother wraps her child.

The sounds of quiet breathing rose from the almost invisible orchards and buildings, about which the people lay in the open air, trusting to the mildness of the night.

In Boryna's room as well, sleep and tranquillity prevailed, except for the *cree-cree-cree* of the cricket on the hearth, and Yagna's breaths, fluttering like a butterfly's wings.

It must have been at some time in the small hours (the

first cock was crowing already) that Boryna began to move,
the moon at the same time shining through the window-
panes, and pouring on to his face its cold though seething
torrents of silvery splendour.

Sitting up in bed, and clearing his throat, he attempted
to call out, but could utter no other sound than a gurgle.

Thus he sat for a time, looking round with a vacant
stare, and fumbling with his fingers in the light of his coverlet, as though he thought to grasp that luminous stream of
moonbeams that struck his eyes.

"Day has come. . . . It is time," he mumbled at last,
standing erect upon the floor.

He looked out of the window, and, like a man awaking
from a deep sleep, thought that it was day, that he had
slept overmuch, and that some pressing work was awaiting
him.

"I must get up, it is time," he repeated, crossing himself again and again, and beginning his morning prayers.
Then he glanced round for his clothes. Not finding them,
he forgot them quite, and, passing his hands over himself,
made a feeble attempt at dressing. His prayer broke off
in the saying, and he could only mutter a few incoherent
fragments in a soundless voice.

His brain was vexed with vague thoughts of things to do,
remembrances of things done, and, as it were, the echoes
of what had gone on around him when he was lying ill.
In evanescent flashes there came to his mind dim recollec-
tions, activities that had been indistinct as the furrows on
reaped land, and now started up clear and sharp; they took
shape in his brain, struggling to come forth, and every instant formed some fresh phantasm which vanished away
ere he could grasp it, like rotten tissues that crumbled into
dust; so that his mind was as restless as a wandering flame
that finds nothing to feed upon, and strays perforce.

And thus, whatever he now did, he did out of mere habit,
like a horse that has for years walked round, turning the
beam of a threshing-machine, and when set at liberty still
goes round.

He opened the window and looked out; he gazed into the
store-room, poked the fire-place after much pondering—and
then, just as he was, barefoot and in his shirt, walked out.

The door was ajar, the passage flooded with the rays of
the moon. Curled up on the threshold, Lapa was sleeping.
At the sound of a tread, he woke, growled, and, recognizing
his master, followed him out.

Matthias halted outside the hut, scratched his ear, and
strove hard to remember what that urgent piece of work
that awaited him could be.

The dog was leaping up joyfully at his master, who
patted him as of old, whilst staring bewilderedly about him.

It was bright, like day. The moon had now risen above
the cabin, casting deep blue shadows on the white walls, and
making the mill-pond waters shine like a mirror. Lipka
was still as death, but a few birds were noisily fluttering in
the thickets.

Something came to his mind on a sudden: he hurried to
the yard. All the doors were wide open, and the men
snoring in the shadow of the barn. He looked into the
stables, patted the horses; they whinnied at his touch.
Then he peered into the byre: the cows lay in a row, and
only their rumps were visible in the light of the moon.

He then tried to drag a cart out of the shed; but a glittering plough hard by the sties drew off his attention, and he
moved towards it . . . and ceased to think of it before he
got there.

In the middle of the yard he stopped short and looked
round on every side, for he thought someone had called
him.

The well-sweep stood high in front of him, throwing a
long shadow.

"What is it?" he asked, and paused for a reply.

The orchard, slashed with moonbeams, seemed to block
his way; its silvered leaves were whispering to him.

"Who calls?" he asked, stumbling against a tree.

Lapa, following at his heels, uttered a whine. At the
sound he stopped and drew a deep breath; then he said,

gaily: "Quite right, good dog! Aye, it is seed-time!"

And this idea too passed from his mind in an instant: everything slipped out of his memory, as dry sand creeps through the fingers.

Continually fresh thoughts kept him moving, puzzled, bewildered, and like a spindle that is turned round by the thread that runs out, though it turns in the same place.

"Aye, aye, it is seed-time," he repeated, and moved quickly to the part of the premises which adjoined the fields. There he saw before him that hayrick of bitter memory, burnt down last winter, and but just set up again.

He meant to pass by it, but started back on a sudden. In a flash he saw the past, which memory made present. He tore a stake from the fence; brandishing it in both hands like a pitchfork, he dashed forward with rage in his eyes, ready to smite and slay; but before his blow could be struck, the stake fell from his grasp, now weak and slack.

Beyond the rick, along the road that skirted the potato-field, there stretched a long strip of ploughed land. Here he stopped, and cast troubled glances round him.

The moon had gone through half her course, bathing the earth in misty beams; it lay covered with pearls of dew, and, as it were, silent in rapt attention.

Impenetrable depths of silence came down from the upper fields, and from where earth and sky met in the hazy distance; from the meadows rose up white vapours, crawling over the corn, enveloping it in its warm damp folds, as it rose.

The tall yellow-green rye-borders bent over the field-pathways, drooping under the weight of the ears, that hung down like the saffron-hued beaks of unfledged birds in their nests; the wheat stood upright boldly, as straight as so many pillars, lifting their glossy and dusky heads; the oats and barley, as yet in the blade, lay green as meadows, but silvered by the moonlight and blurred with dark veils of mist.

It was about the second cock-crow now, and the night far spent. The fields rested, lost in profound sleep, sometimes rustling quietly as it were with an echo of the day's toil and troubles, and sighing as a mother may sigh when she lays herself down to rest with her little ones.

Boryna knelt down immediately, and set to gathering earth in a fold of his shirt, like seed-corn in a sower's bag, and in such quantity that he could scarce rise. He made the sign of the cross, swept his arm round to try his reach, and began to sow.

Bent down beneath the burden, he went slowly, step by step, sowing the field with that semicircular sweep of his arm, like a priest's benediction.

Lapa followed him; and when some frightened bird rose from before his feet, he would run after it awhile, and then go back to his master.

In this charmed world of night and spring, Boryna, gazing straight before him, walked on through the patches of corn, like a spirit blessing every clod of earth, every ear of corn; sowing on, sowing ever.

At the furrows he stumbled; at the hollows he staggered, sometimes even fell. But of this he was unconscious— aware of nothing but the dull irresistible craving to sow the land.

Thus he walked on to the end of the field. When there was no earth remaining for him to throw, he took up more and sowed on. When his way was barred by trees and brambles, he would turn back.

He had walked a good distance. The birds' twitterings were no longer to be heard; the whole village had disappeared in the misty darkness, and the billowy sea of tawny cornfields surged all about him. There he stood, forlorn and lonely and lost—as a soul that is wandering away from this world.—And then, once more he came back towards the village, towards the ring within which the twittering of birds was again audible, and towards the circle of human activity, now stilled for a time: he, a waif thrown back to the shores of life and existence by those waves of the surging sea of corn!

So the time passed, and so he went on sowing indefatigably, stopping at times to rest his limbs a little. Then he would again take up his bootless toil and vain exertions.

Later, and near the close of the night, he worked more slowly, stopped oftener, forgot to gather the earth for his seed, and sowed empty-handed: as though he were now sowing his very being in those fields of his fathers—all the days he had lived, all that life he had received, and was now giving back (a sacred harvest) to the Everlasting Lord!

And in those last moments of his life there came to pass a very wonderful thing. The sky turned grey, like a shroud; the moon set; all light went out; the whole land was plunged in murky inextricable depths of sudden and utter darkness. And then a Something beyond all thought seemed to arise from . . . none knew where—and to walk in those shadows with footsteps so ponderous that they made the very earth to rock.

Then a long blast blew from the woods, with an ominous murmur.

The trees in the fields were shaking; the corn, the grass, waved shudderingly; from the trembling plots of land there came a low moan of dread:

"O Master! Master!"

The green ears of barley quivered convulsively, as if weeping, and bent to kiss his weary feet.

"O Master!" the rye-patches trilled, stopping his way, and shaking down a shower of dewy tears. Birds gave forth a melancholy cry. The wind sobbed over his head. The mist enveloped him in her dank dripping folds. And the voices sounded ever louder, ever more sadly, and always repeating:

"O Master! Master!"

At last he paid heed to them, and said, under his breath: "Lo, here I am: what will ye, say?"

No answer came; but when he would have moved on farther, sowing with that tired empty hand, the earth cried out to him, in a mighty voice:

"Remain with us! Remain with us! Remain!"

And he stood in astonishment. All things seemed pressing forward against him. The grasses came crawling, the corn billowing towards him; the fields beset him round; the whole country-side rose up and fell upon him. Dismayed, he would have cried aloud; but his fast-closed throat let no voice pass. He tried to flee; his strength failed him quite. The ground caught his feet, the corn entangled them, the furrows tripped him up, the stubborn glebe balked his steps, the trees shook their boughs at him to stop his way. He was pricked by thistles, hurt by stones, chased by the angry wind, and led astray by the night and the many voices crying out from everywhere:

"Stay with us! Oh, stay!"

On a sudden he became motionless, and all things with him. His eyes, now growing dark in death, saw clear with a lightning flash. Heaven opened out before him—and there, seated on a throne of wheat-sheaves, the Everlasting Father stretched out His hands, and said to him mildly:

"Come unto Me, O human soul; O weary toiler, come thou unto Me!"

Boryna reeled at the words, and, stretching forth his hands (as at the Elevation):

"O Lord God, I thank Thee!" he cried, and fell prostrate on his face before that most holy Majesty.

So he fell, and so he died, in the hour of God's loving-kindness.

.   .   .   .

Dawn was rising; and over him Lapa howled long and mournfully.

END OF PART III

A NOTE ON THE TYPE IN
WHICH THIS BOOK IS SET

This book is set (on the Linotype) in Elzevir No. 3, a French Old Style. For the modern revival of this excellent face we are indebted to Gustave Mayeur of Paris, who reproduced it in 1878, basing his designs, he says, on types used in a book which was printed by the Elzevirs at Leyden in 1634. The Elzevir family held a distinguished position as printers and publishers for more than a century, their best work appearing between about 1590 and 1680. Although the Elzevirs were not themselves type founders, they utilized the services of the best type designers of their time, notably Van Dijk, Garamond, and Sanlecque. They developed a type face which is open and readable but relatively narrow in body, permitting a large amount of copy to be set in limited space without impairing legibility.

SET UP, ELECTROTYPED AND PRINTED
BY THE VAIL-BALLOU PRESS, INC.,
BINGHAMTON, N. Y. · ESPARTO
PAPER MANUFACTURED IN
SCOTLAND AND FURNISHED
BY W. F. ETHERINGTON &
CO., NEW YORK · BOUND
BY THE H. WOLFF ES-
TATE, NEW YORK